⚕

Geirolf dropped his loincloth.

Merry-Death's green eyes just about popped out of her head. She made a low strangling sound in her throat.

He chuckled with satisfaction. 'Twas the reaction of most women on first viewing his man parts. The gods had been generous with him in that regard.

"You . . . you—" she sputtered as he swaggered past her and through the open door.

He kept his pace deliberately slow, shoulders thrown back, so she could get a good look. Mayhap now she would appreciate the honor he bestowed in taking her as bedmate.

"Come back here," she shrieked like a banshee. "And put your clothes back on!"

SANDRA HILL

The Last Viking

AVON

An Imprint of HarperCollinsPublishers

AVON BOOKS
An Imprint of HarperCollins*Publishers*
10 East 53rd Street
New York, New York 10022-5299

Copyright © 1998, 2011 by Sandra Hill
ISBN 978-0-06-201905-9
www.avonromance.com

First Avon Books mass market printing: August 2011

Avon Trademark Reg. U.S. Pat. Off. and in Other Countries, Marca Registrada, Hecho en U.S.A.
HarperCollins® is a registered trademark of HarperCollins Publishers.

Printed in the U.S.A.

10 9 8 7 6 5 4 3

This book is for my cousin Peggy Follmer, who was an ardent supporter of romance novels and my books in particular until her premature death. It's especially appropriate that I continue to dedicate to Peggy The Last Viking, *which celebrates the appeal of a man with calluses on his hands. Her late husband, Paul, the love of her life, was a carpenter.*

My mother once told me
She'd buy me a longship,
A handsome-oared vessel
To go sailing with Vikings;
To stand at the stern-post
And steer a fine warship,
Then head back for harbor
And hew down some foemen.

EGIL'S SAGA
c. 10th century

"From the fury of the Northmen,
oh, Lord deliver us."

ANGLO-SAXON REFRAIN
9th- and 10th-century Britain

The
Last Viking

CHAPTER ONE

*R*ow, row, row your boat . . .

Geirolf let out a wild Viking battle cry before burying his face in Ingrid's massive breasts.

She was woodenly unimpressed.

He roared his outrage. Then, still clutching her voluptuous figure, he jumped from the rail of his splintering, already sinking longship into the roiling seas . . . and certain death.

Ah, well, 'tis the fate of many Viking warriors, and better than most, Geirolf thought fatalistically as a whirlpool sucked him under, swirling his body uncontrollably, faster and faster, into the briny depths. *'Twill be over soon . . . even now the Valkyries should be coming to lead me into Asgard, the hall of the gods, where a grand feast surely awaits me in the afterlife. Leastways, I hope 'tis Asgard, and not Hel. After all I endured this day, I misdoubt I deserve the underworld.*

Still holding his breath, he hugged Ingrid closer—his companion in death—and chuckled silently. *Mayhap this night I will get my very own bedmate with breasts as magnificent as yours, sweet Ingrid.*

But then some instinct moved inside Geirolf, perchance the warrior reflex. He'd been trained from boyhood to fight to the bitter end. He would not yield now like a wet-nosed pup!

Nay! Damn the gods! I am Geirolf Ericsson of the noble Yngling clan. The blood of kings runs in my veins. I am a master shipbuilder and a fierce soldier. I will not die yet. Honor demands I complete my pledge-mission for my father. Lives depend on me. I ... refuse ... to ... surrender.

Kicking out with powerful thrusts of his legs, Geirolf escaped the whirlpool's briny grave and rose swiftly, like a dolphin, to the surface of a strangely calm sea.

With a toss of his head, he cast the wet swath of his long hair over his shoulder. And, to his great surprise, it was Ingrid and her glorious breasts that kept him afloat, bobbing gently on the ocean waves. Ingrid—the outlandishly carved figurehead of a buxom, blonde-haired goddess.

More than three years past, his brother Jorund had given him, as a coarse jest, the wooden sculpture of a woman's upper torso to embellish the prow of his newest dragonship, *Fierce Wolf*. Fortunately, Geirolf had been able to grab onto the figurehead when his vessel began to shatter apart moments ago.

Geirolf laughed joyously at the irony. Saved by a woman's tits. His mother, Lady Asgar, a Christian of Saxon birth, would say it was the One-God's just retribution against her youngest son's wild life of licentiousness. His father, Jarl Eric Tryggvason, ever the Viking, would hoot with laughter at the lewd paradox. Geirolf's latest leman—sweet Alyce of Hedeby—would cluck with disapproval, then merely smile her pleasure at his being alive, no matter the means.

He gave Ingrid's left nipple—the size of a fat, sundrenched grape—a quick lick of salty appreciation. And hoped belatedly that he didn't get a splinter in his tongue.

By the fading light of the Demon's Moon—the odd celestial apparition that had drawn him to this dangerous location—

he gazed fondly at his stiff companion and relaxed. His fate was in the hands of the heavenly beings now. He could only believe that Odin had chosen to deliver him from that evil Storr Grimmsson, the villainous outlaw who'd killed or captured his entire crew of loyal sailors a sennight ago, sparing only Geirolf to a crippled vessel and stormy seas.

Pondering all that had happened to him, Geirolf decided that the Norse All-God must have some other destiny in mind for him. Thus resigned, he gave himself up to the rhythmic current.

He knew not where he was, long ago having lost his star bearings under the exotic aura of the Demon's Moon . . . surely farther west than any Viking adventurer had traveled afore. Even Eirik the Red. He would have much to tell the skalds at his father's court in Vestfold. Of a certainty, the skilled storytellers would weave sagas telling of his great bravery for eons to come. *If* ever he returned, that is.

Nay, he would not think doomful thoughts. *I must return,* he vowed, rubbing one palm over his wide leather belt, grasping the heavy clasp that hid the sacred talisman. Otherwise, there was no point to the endless journeying. No point to the bloody battle with Storr. No point to all the lost lives. *Yea, I must return the relic to its rightful place, as directed by my father.*

With a long sigh, he fought his fluttering eyelids and a soul-deep exhaustion. He was so weary and battle sore. If only he could rest for a moment. But, nay, he had to be alert for omens, for any sign from the gods that would steer him toward his future.

At dawn, Geirolf forced open his bleary eyes—he must have dozed, after all—and saw his sign. *Thanks be to Odin!* It was a half-completed longboat sitting on a grassy knoll atop a craggy cliff. Just waiting for him.

"Come, Ingrid," he shouted jubilantly to his figurehead

companion, tucked now under his left arm. With renewed vigor, he swam for shore as the sun began to rise. "There is the ship that will take us home. *Destiny*. Yea, I will call it *Fierce Destiny*."

MAINE, A.D. 1997

Wanted: Viking carpenter, cheap . . .

"No way! You are *not* putting breasts on the figurehead of my ship," Meredith Foster declared, shaking her head indignantly.

Her grad assistant, Mike Johnson, gave her an impatient scowl as he rolled up the sketches he'd prepared for her approval. "Now, now, Dr. Foster. I've researched the figureheads of tenth-century Viking ships, and it wasn't unusual to have a favorite goddess adorn the prow."

Meredith tapped a pencil on her desk and peered at him over the top of her reading glasses, trying to determine if he was serious or not. The ex-Marine, who still clipped his blond hair in a short G.I. cut and wore old U.S. Army T-shirts with his jeans, had a dry sense of humor. And he often ribbed her, thinking her much too serious and overly engrossed in her work.

"It was just as usual to have animal heads, *Mister* Johnson. Give me a dragon, or a serpent. No buxom bimbos."

He grinned.

"And don't think I missed the fact that this particular woman looks a lot like Pamela Anderson," she added. In the few months she'd come to know her handsome grad assistant, a doctoral candidate in Dark-Age Norse culture, he'd made no bones about the fact that Pamela Anderson was the one woman he'd most like to be stranded with, just about anywhere. Sometimes, she suspected that he talked about the movie sex symbol to cover his pain over losing his young wife two years before in a freak skiing accident. "Remember, we're going for historical accuracy here. And Pamela Anderson is pure anachronism."

Mike rolled his shoulders in a "Hey, it was worth a shot" shrug, and then tried another tactic. "I could always put a bra on the babe."

Meredith lifted a brow. "My friend, a Wonder Bra and a forklift wouldn't hold up the pair you've drawn on those blueprints."

Mike's eyes widened with surprise at her unaccustomed playfulness, but he came back real quick. "How about if it's a male figurehead and another kind of . . . endowment? Then, would it be okay?"

"Not even if it was a hot Scotsman in a kilt."

They exchanged warm smiles, and Meredith was glad she'd relaxed her standard formality with Mike. It felt good, for a change, to act . . . well, normal.

"Besides, we have more important concerns right now," she noted. "Spring break is about over, and we still haven't found a competent carpenter to head the project. Now that the temperate weather is here, I'd like to resume building."

With a nod of agreement, the young man slid into a chair in front of her desk, bracing one ankle on a knee. "I worked with your grandfather for over a year on the 'Trondheim Longboat Venture,' but he was the master builder. When he died last fall, everything just came to a screeching halt."

A screeching halt? Yes, Meredith knew that better than anyone. Gramps had been the light of her life, her lodestone in a world that had become increasingly lonely and alien after her bitter divorce three years before. What would she do without his sage advice and unconditional love?

"I'd be perfectly willing to take over," Mike continued,

"but I just don't have the talent to oversee all these students. I can sand wood and do grunt work with the best of them, but that's about it."

"I know, and I appreciate all the help you've given me so far." Brushing a strand of flyaway hair behind her ear, she unconsciously tucked it into the loose knot at the nape of her neck, thinking over their mutual problem. "It's too bad we got so few responses to the ads we placed in the Bangor newspapers, and none of them qualified. Maybe one of the archaeological periodicals my brother recommended will bring some interested soul out of the woodwork."

"Hey, expert carpenters want a hell of a lot more money than we can afford with nonprofit funding."

"Someone will show up," she asserted. *Even if I have to pay top dollar out of my own trust fund. Anything to make Gramps's dream come true.* "In the meantime, we can start the students on menial tasks."

"Like hand-sanding, right? With sand, the way the primitive shipbuilders did it, right?" Mike grumbled. Sanding was an endless, tedious task everyone hated.

"Right." She smiled and pushed her glasses up her nose. "And see what the woodworking shop can do in terms of an animal prow. I don't care if it's an elephant. Just no obscene body parts."

"If you insist," Mike muttered as he walked out of her office. "An elephant? Geez, who ever heard of a Republican longship? Talk about anachronisms!"

Strangers in the Night . . .

Darkness blanketed the countryside by the time Meredith had finished working for the day and was driving up the long lane to the cottage recently bequeathed to her. The one-bedroom A-frame, built with her grandfather's own hands on a desolate cliff overlooking the Atlantic Ocean, held so many memories for Meredith. As children, she and her older brother Jared and her younger sister Jillian had been shipped off to Maine each summer while their parents, engrossed in significant work as noted professors of medieval studies at Princeton University, went off to lecture, or on one research expedition or another to museums and archaeological digs.

Gram had been alive then, too, and the smells of Gramps's woodcarving and Gram's fresh-baked bread and home-cooked meals filled the house. Meredith wasn't sure if her own mother even knew how to cook, so preoccupied had she always been with her career. Not that culinary arts were an essential motherly skill. A live-in housekeeper had taken care of those domestic tasks.

Contemplating the house now as she got closer, Meredith realized how small it was, and how simple. Funny, she'd never noticed before. But then, now that she thought about it, while Gramps and Gram had slept in the upstairs loft, she and her brother and sister had bedded down in sleeping bags on the living room floor, or outdoors in warm weather next to the pool. They'd never minded.

So much love! That was what she remembered most . . . the love Gram and Gramps had clearly shown for each other, and toward their beloved grandchildren.

Now, all that was gone.

Fighting the tightness in her throat, Meredith gave a cursory glance to the half-completed longship, highlighted momentarily in her headlights. Gramps had decided to build the project on the vacant lot next to his house, rather than on the Oxley College campus, which was too far inland. Besides, Gramps had told her in his letters that his students loved to come up to the remote spot, often combining their work with picnics, or climbing down the treacherous cliff-side for a quick dip in the ocean.

She retrieved her briefcase and a small bag of groceries

from the back seat and approached the dark house. There was something so sad about an empty house at the end of the day. That was the only thing she missed about her marriage to Jeffrey.

Usually, he'd gotten home early from Columbia where they'd both been professors. In the early years—the happier days—he'd already started dinner by the time she got home. Violin sonatas by Vivaldi had been playing on the stereo. And a glass of chilled Chenin Blanc and a warm smile had greeted her as she opened the door. Sometimes, he'd even welcomed her in other ways.

Well, those days were gone forever. And good riddance!

As she opened the door to the cottage, she did get a greeting, though. And a *big* surprise.

No sooner did she step into the entryway than a rough arm wrapped around her waist from behind, lifting her off the floor, and a knife was pressed against the side of her neck. The grocery bag fell with a thud, ripping, and her briefcase snapped open, spilling its contents.

"Let me go!" she shrieked, kicking out with her sensible loafers—which she desperately wished were hiking boots—against a bare shinbone. Her flailing arms hit a thigh, and it was nude, too. And hairy. *Oh, no, the guy must be naked. Please, God, not rape!* Frightened and outraged, she screamed as loud and as long as she could, clawing at the brute's arms.

Her attacker didn't release his hold on her one iota, just muttered an incoherent breathy expletive against her exposed neck, followed by a single guttural command that sounded something like, *"Kyrr!"*

The only light in the pitch-black house came from the reflection of a roaring blaze in the fireplace in the living room up ahead, and a full moon partially visible through the French doors leading to an ocean-view patio.

A fire? Her assailant had taken the time to build a cozy

fire? She groaned, concluding that he must, indeed, be a rapist and that he planned a lengthy assault. She also recalled in a flash of terror that this was Friday night. A whole weekend stretched ahead of her in which no one would notice her absence or come searching for her.

Oh, my God! Oh, my God! Where's my Mace? To her chagrin, Meredith saw the can rolling toward the kitchen, along with three oranges, her favorite Parker pen, and a handful of change from her wallet. *Be calm. Remember your self-defense classes. Take time. Think before acting.*

Think? Hah! She was a clueless amoeba on the brain chain right now. A *screaming* clueless amoeba.

The man carried her into the living room with her legs still dangling a foot off the hardwood floor. She assumed it was a man because of his height and strength and the size of the hairy forearm crammed against her abdomen, way too close to the undersides of her breasts. Callused fingers snagged her silk blouse. He smelled of salt water, wet leather, and apples.

Apples? A quick glance showed a half dozen McIntosh apples missing from the bowl she'd placed in the center of her coffee table this morning. Their cores were thrown carelessly on the floor. *The pig!*

Meredith tried to peer back at him, but the blade at her throat prevented movement. So, still kicking and screeching, she back-jabbed him with her elbows. It was like hitting a brick wall, even though she just about knocked her arms out of the shoulder sockets with the force of her efforts.

With a curse of *"Blód hel!"* the wretch threw her to the sofa onto her back. Coming down on top of her with a suffocating whoosh, he leaned over her, practically nose to nose, brandishing the weapon, which she recognized now as Gramps's favorite carving knife. He spat out his earlier order, more clearly this time, though with a foreign accent, *"Kyrr!"*

Her befuddled mind registered the guttural word. Ancient sounding, like Old English. Having a doctorate in medieval studies, she was well-versed in Dark and Middle Age languages.

Meredith frowned in confusion, panting for air, bucking upward, to no avail. The gorilla must weigh well over two hundred pounds. And there were intimate parts of his anatomy that were becoming familiar with intimate parts of her anatomy. The possibility of rape loomed its ugly head once again.

But then, the hairs stood out on the back of her neck in warning, and a strange niggling tugged at her memory. The word and the dialect were similar to Old English, but different.

Oh, my goodness! *"Kyrr!"* was the Old Norse word for "Be still." She ought to know, having spent her honeymoon with Jeffrey a lifetime ago in Iceland where a version of the archaic language was still spoken. Jeffrey had convinced her that combining a honeymoon and research was a sensible idea. All she remembered was the cold.

He let loose with a long string of foreign words.

Heart hammering at the disconcerting pressure of his body, not to mention the danger, she puzzled over each of the separate words, deducing finally that he was asking in some convoluted combination of Old Norse and Old English, "Who are you, woman?" Her interpretation was reinforced when he added, *"Hvað heitir þú?"* which definitely meant, "What's your name?"

"Dr. Meredith Foster," she squeaked out. *A burglar fluent in medieval languages? Must be one of Mike's friends. A joke.*

"Dock-whore Merry-Death," he repeated slowly, his breath feathering against her lips. Apple breath. Mike . . . it had to be Mike, but you'd think Mike could do better than a bloomin' Johnny Appleseed. "Merry-Death," he said again, slowly, testing her name on his tongue.

She wasn't about to correct his mispronunciation, just in case he wasn't a prankster. And, yes, she'd like to kill him and Mike, too, *merrily*, for scaring her to *death*.

"Geirolf," he said, pointing at himself, *"ég heiti Geirolf."*

"Great. Now that we've got the introductions out of the way, Rolf, baby, how about getting off of me? So far, there's no real harm done, but you must weigh a ton, and you're wrinkling my best Yves St. Laurent blouse, and . . ."

Her words trailed off as he lifted himself off her and stood in one smooth motion—remarkable for a man his size. Her mouth dropped open in shock at her first good glimpse of her attacker.

A very tall male—at least six-foot-four—stood arm's length away, wearing a thigh-high, sleeveless, one-piece tunic of supple leather. The Dark Age garment was tucked in at the waist by a wide belt with an enormous circular goldlike metal clasp engraved with a writhing animal design. Etched silver armlets circled heavily corded upper arms. Jillian, who designed her own line of medieval-style jewelry, would go nuts if she saw these masterpieces. Heck, her brother Jared, an archaeologist, would be impressed, too. Even if they were reproductions, they were the finest examples Meredith had ever seen outside a museum.

His light brown hair hung down to his shoulders, damp, as if he'd just emerged from a leisurely swim. Flat-soled, leather boots covered his feet, cross-gartered up to the knee.

A Viking. Her captor resembled an ancient Viking god.

An extremely handsome Viking god.

Meredith had never paid much attention to the physical attributes of men. Raised in a scholarly home, she'd been much more attracted by brains than brawn. But, for the first time in her life, she comprehended why her female students squealed over the latest Hollywood sensation or rolled their eyes in appreciation when a particularly appealing college boy in tight jeans walked by.

Oh, my God! My hormones are regressing. She bit her bottom lip to prevent herself from saying something really stupid, such as, "Can I touch you?" But inside she was squealing like any lust-crazed teenager.

Amazing! Wherever he'd found this guy, Mike had really outdone himself. Maybe he was a male stripper at one of those female nightclubs. Oh, yeah! Vikings 'R Us.

But, no, he looked too . . . authentic. Meredith peered closer. Old scars and new wounds, oozing blood—*probably ketchup*—covered most of the exposed skin of the guy's well-muscled physique, from his massive shoulders to his perfectly formed face to his tendon-delineated calves. Despite the glower on his face and his menacing, widespread stance, the big lug was devastatingly gorgeous. In fact, he looked a lot like a Viking Age version of that actor, Kevin Sorbo, from the old Hercules program on television. Not that she watched much television, she reminded herself with hysterical irrelevance.

He raised his chin haughtily and drawled out with pure insolence a string of Old Norse words, too low for her to catch them all. Meredith didn't need a translator to know that he was asking, "Do you like what you see?" She cringed at the reminder that she'd been scrutinizing him much too long. "Not much," she lied.

He sat down on her low coffee table, knees casually widespread, and Meredith wondered—even as she chastised herself with disgust—if he wore underwear beneath the short tunic. He rubbed the fingertips of one hand over his bristly jaw as he studied her, appearing distressed, as if unable to understand her. Then he distractedly stroked the fingertips of his other hand over his belt buckle, which she could swear was solid gold.

To her bewilderment, she no longer feared the guy. In fact, she felt a deep pull of unwarranted compassion for him, even though he still held her grandfather's knife. He appeared lost, like a little boy.

He had to be an actor, hired by Mike. Hadn't her grad assistant told her over and over that she needed to lighten up? In fact, he'd given her a novel one time called *Love With a Warm Cowboy*, about a female college professor who goes out cruising for nothing more than a quick relationship with a cowboy after her longtime lover leaves her.

But enough! Fun-and-games time was over. Maybe if she threatened criminal prosecution, the jerk would end this joke and go home. Forcing a threatening tone to her voice and a deep scowl to her face, she gritted out, "Get out of my house, you . . . you rapist, or I'm going to call the police."

He blinked at her with surprise, and then glanced down at his belt with a peculiar expression. Anger quickly replaced confusion as he turned back to her. "Rapist? You call me a rapist? Hah! I am Geirolf Ericsson. My father is a high jarl in Vestfold and brother to Olaf, the king of all Norway—"

"Yeah, and I'm the queen of England," she scoffed.

"Nay, you are not. Aelfgifu is queen of all Britain, and a more timid wren there never was. I misdoubt she'll live another year. Many times has she gone through the childbed fever and yet produced but one heir for King Aethelred."

She gaped at him.

He waved a hand in the air imperiously, annoyed that she'd interrupted him. "Know this, my lady . . . I, Geirolf Ericsson, have no need to force my attentions on any wench. Women have been begging for my favors since I was an untried boy."

Favors? She rolled her eyes at his arrogance. "Listen, buster, I don't care if you're Kevin Sorbo. Get the hell out of my house."

"Your language . . .'tis odd. What is this Calf in Shore Bow?" As he spoke, a frown creased the man's brow and he continually looked down at his belt buckle, which he clasped tightly now. Then he muttered to himself, "How curious! I can understand and speak her foreign tongue when I touch the talisman."

"Give me a break," she sneered, but she realized, at the same time, that she could understand him now, too. And the bizarre thing was that she knew they both spoke different languages. A shiver of alarm swept her skin. "I don't know if this is someone's idea of a silly gag, or if you're a burglar, or a rapist, but—"

Meredith stopped speaking as she noticed a strong odor, like charred meat. Sniffing, she scanned the room, and couldn't believe her eyes. Some kind of skinned animal was impaled on a peeled stick, roasting in her fireplace. "Wh-what is *that*?" she asked shrilly. "Oh, God, is that the stray that's been hanging around my back door lately? Did you . . . did you kill Garfield?"

"Guard field?"

"Yes, Garfield, the cat."

His eyes shot up. "A cat? You think I killed a cat? And plan to eat its flesh? *Blód hel*!" Then he grinned. "'Tis a rabbit."

"Rabbit?" Inwardly, she sighed with relief. *Not a cat.*

"Yea."

Yea? What's this "yea" business? He was still grinning, as if killing a rabbit was normal. He was probably one of those NRA redneck fanatics. "Why . . . are . . . you . . . cooking . . . a . . . rabbit?" she asked very slowly, barely reining in her anger.

"Because . . . I . . . am . . . hungry," he replied, mimicking her snide pacing. "And because I'm sick of eating raw fish. Why else?"

Of course. Why else? "Hungry? Raw fish? But . . . but where did you get a rabbit?"

He exhaled loudly with exasperation, as if her questions were foolish. "I snared it outside your keep."

"Keep?"

"Your manor house. Why do you keep repeating words? Are you a lackbrain?"

"No, I'm not a lackbrain, you . . . you lackbrain." Suddenly, she thought of something else. "Where did you put the . . . other parts?" Lord, she hoped she didn't have rabbit fur and guts in her kitchen sink, especially since her garbage disposal was broken.

"I offered them to the gods, of course, in thanks for my safekeeping." He gazed pointedly at the blazing fire, a mischievous glimmer in his whiskey-colored eyes.

"I beg your pardon. Did you say that you used my fireplace as an altar to some heathen god?"

He shrugged. "I worship both gods, Norse and Christian."

"How dare you practice some pagan rite in my fireplace!"

He sucked in a deep breath. "Blessed Freya! You have a voice that could peel rust off armor. Best you shut your teeth, wench, or I may decide to sacrifice a virgin as well."

That mischievous gleam was still there in his sparkling eyes, which she decided were the color of aged bourbon. Yes, booze eyes. And that twitch at the edge of his full lips—was it a nervous tic, or suppressed amusement?

"Well, good thing I'm not a virgin then," she snapped.

He broke into a full-fledged smile, rewarding Meredith with a dazzling display of his white teeth. Her mind said, *So what?* But another part of her body said, *O-o-h, boy!*

The creep soon jolted her back to reality, though.

"I should have known a woman as long in the tooth as you are would have spread her thighs for the pleasuring. Where is your man now?"

Long in the tooth? Spread my thighs? The nerve of the chauvinistic beast! "I'm only thirty-five years old. I'll bet you're about the same, you long-in-the-tooth oaf. And I have no husband, if that's what you're asking—" Meredith immediately regretted her hasty words and backtracked. "I mean, my husband will be home soon."

He arched his brows, unconvinced. "So, you are a wanton woman—an aged wanton woman—who lives alone. Do you entertain your lovers here?" He swept her with a swift physical assessment that clearly challenged her ability to attract a lover.

She didn't care if the ape did wield a knife; Meredith had had enough. Jumping to her feet, she put her hands on her hips, demanding, "Who are you and what are you doing in my home?"

"*Ég er týndur.*" Geirolf watched the quarrelsome woman who dared to defy his commands as she assimilated his statement, word by word.

"I am lost," she translated.

His ears still rang from her high-pitched screams. Claw marks seeped blood on his forearms. And Merry-Death—the oddly named wench—dared accuse him of being a rapist. As if he would even want a woman such as she. Too tall. Too thin. Too sharp-tongued. And old. He liked his women young and soft-fleshed and biddable. Like Alyce.

He was sore tempted to toss the foolish wench into the raging sea, but he needed answers first. And, more important, he feared she might be a sorceress. On first entering her keep, he'd explored all the chambers—none of which had the customary rushes on the floor. And not a candle or soapstone lamp in evidence anywhere. Of particular interest was the room with a magic box that threw off light when the door opened. He'd found some cheese inside, but it was nigh inedible, covered as it was by an unchewable, invisible film.

If she was a witch—and those pale green eyes of hers, flashing angrily at him now, were surely witch's eyes—he would have to tread carefully. Even with the talisman, a sorceress's charm would be hard to withstand.

But Merry-Death would suffer for her insults, no doubt about that. Later, he would show her the fate of a defiant woman.

"My lady, *hvar er ég?*" he growled peevishly. "Where am I?"

That question seemed to disarm her, and her wide eyes quickly took in his many bruises, softening with sympathy. *Hmpfh!* he thought. *'Tis past time the lady thought of offering hospitality to a wayfarer in her land. And an injured one, at that.*

"Were you hit on the head?" she inquired.

He curled his lips with disgust. She obviously considered him a halfwit. "Answer, wench. Where am I?"

"Maine."

"Maine. I have ne'er heard of such place. Is it in Greenland—that new world discovered by Erik the Red?"

"Are you for real? Maine is in the northeast portion of the United States. Greenland is about fifteen hundred miles north of here."

"Hmmm. My ship went farther off course than I realized."

"Off course? More like off the globe."

"'Tis my brother Jorund's fault. He's the mapmaker in our family."

"Jared? My brother Jared sent you here?" The frown on her face—the one he would have wagered was permanently

implanted there—melted away, and before he could correct
her false assumption, she homed in on his other words. "Your
ship?"

"Thor's toenails! You sound like a parrot Jorund brought
back once from the eastern lands. Squawk, squawk, squawk.
And always repeating words." He took great delight in the
snarl that barb drew from the testy wench. "And, yea, my dragonship, *Fierce Wolf*, drifted for days, ever since the battle
with Storr Grimmsson a sennight ago. Finally, it sank. I will
miss *Fierce Wolf* mightily. 'Twas one of the finest ships I ever
built."

Merry-Death's face brightened. "You're a shipbuilder?
So that's why Jared sent you. Or was it Mike?"

He ignored her puzzling words. "Yea, I am the finest shipbuilder in the world," he boasted, "and Grimmsson will pay
with his life for the loss of my crew, as well as my ship. Ah,
well, I can easily build other ships." *Like that one outside
this keep, which will carry me back to my homeland. But best
I not disclose my plans to you yet.* "Unlike men's lives, a
boat can be replaced."

"But . . . but . . . how did you get here?"

"My ship sank," he repeated with deliberate patience, "and
I swam ashore this morn."

Merry-Death gasped. "You've been in a shipwreck?"

It took her a long time to grasp the meaning of his words,
even though the talisman was doing a fair job of translating.
Mayhap she was slow-witted, as he'd originally thought.

"No wonder you look like you've been beaten. Why didn't
you say so earlier? My God, did you climb up that cliffside?"

Finally, he would get a little blessed compassion for all
his ordeals. "Yea, and I assure you, 'twas no easy task, carrying Ingrid."

"Ingrid?" she squeaked out. "You have a woman with
you?"

"A woman?" He laughed. "You could call her that."

A flush of rage suffused Merry-Death's pale cheeks. Obviously, the wench had no sense of humor. But she had other attributes he was beginning to notice. Her hair had sprung free from the unbecoming knot at the back of her neck and spilled out over her silky, pale brown *shert*, like burnished walnut. With hands on hips, she called attention to the loose, brown men's *braies* she wore over her thin frame, and tapped her brown leather slippers.

So much brown, he mused idly. Does she try to hide her womanliness, to appear like a drab tree? Nay, not a tree, with that abundance of reddish-brown hair, and those witchy green eyes.

Oh, she was certainly not to his tastes. But she was not as barley-faced as he'd originally thought, either.

And the foolhardiness of the woman! Demanding answers of him, a high-born karl of Norway!

Hah! I'll soon put her in her proper place. "Yea, Ingrid is outside near your moat, drying out from our long swim."

"Moat?"

Her eyes didn't look quite so beauteous now that they crossed with frustration. He was convinced, the woman was feckless. "Yea, that stone ditch with the blue water."

"The swimming pool? Did you take the cover off of Gramps's pool? Oh, I've had enough of this nonsense. I can't believe you left a woman outside—probably injured—while you broke into my home to mumble incantations over a poor animal, and assault me."

Ignoring his snort of incredulity at her accusations, Merry-Death turned toward the strange glass doors and inhaled sharply at her first glimpse of Ingrid, lying breasts skyward, huge red nipples highlighted by the rays of the full moon.

"Mike Johnson, I'm going to kill you. I warned you about a bimbo figurehead," the wench mumbled; then she turned angrily, striding back toward him, about to spout more of her sharp words, no doubt. But she stopped mid-stride. "Wh- what are you doing?"

He was unbuckling the clasp at his mid-section, about to remove his belt and tunic. Tilting his head in bafflement at her panic, he tried to reassure her, "You have no reason to be fearful. I intend you no harm . . . unless you gainsay me."

"Gainsay?"

"By acting hastily."

"Hastily?"

He shrugged. "Yea, my shrewish parrot. Do not try to attack me. Or escape. Then I might be forced to lop off your head, or thrust you over the cliff."

The woman clicked her gaping mouth shut and made a gurgling sound, but apparently not at his words. Her eyes were riveted on his body as he raised his tunic over his head. Wearing only a breechclout and his ankle boots, he watched the wench back away from him in fright. Holy Thor! Surely, she had seen a naked man afore. Especially since she claimed to have no maidenhead.

"What do you think you're doing?" she stammered out.

"I'm going to bathe all this salt from my skin in your moat. Then I'm going to eat my rabbit. After that, I intend to sleep for a long time. Where are your bed furs, by the by? I couldn't find them when I explored your keep earlier."

"Put your clothes on," she directed, averting her face like a shy maiden.

Lord, he was tired of the wench's caterwauling, and her false modesty.

"Nay, I will not. And mayhap you should remove your own garments, as well." He was discovering he had another appetite besides his hunger for rabbit. In the delayed rush of exhilaration at his miraculous escape from death's talons, he felt the need to celebrate life . . . in the way of battle-weary warriors throughout time.

The wench's green eyes widened with astonishment.

"Despite your bony body and sharp tongue," he informed her, adding a smile to show the great honor he bestowed, "I've decided to take you as my bedmate whilst I am visiting in your lands."

CHAPTER TWO

☙

His longship went off course . . . WAY off course . . .

Geirolf dropped his loincloth.

Merry-Death's green eyes just about popped out of her head. She made a low strangling sound in her throat.

He chuckled with satisfaction. 'Twas the reaction of most women on first viewing his man parts. The gods had been generous with him in that regard.

"You . . . you . . ." she sputtered as he swaggered past her and through the open door.

He kept his pace deliberately slow, shoulders thrown back, so she could get a good look. Mayhap now she would appreciate the honor he bestowed in taking her as bedmate.

"Come back here," she shrieked like a banshee. "And put your clothes back on."

"Nay, in my lands we do not bathe wearing garments."

"We don't wear clothes when we bathe here, either, you idiot, but the pool heater hasn't been turned on yet. The water's freezing."

"Hah! 'Tis obvious you have ne'er taken a winter bath in a fjord in my homeland. The water is cold enough to turn a man's cock into an icicle. This can be no worse."

"But . . . but why not use the warm shower inside the house?"

He halted at the edge of the moat and dipped his big toe

in. A shiver rippled upward, all the way to his scalp, raising skin bumps in its wake. His proud staff shriveled with dread. *The coward.* Bloody hell, the water *was* freezing. "What is this 'shower'?" he inquired casually, not wanting her to think him too weak-sapped for a frigid bath.

"Come on. I'll show you. But cover yourself, for God's sake. Where did Jared and Mike find you anyhow? Some jungle?"

He halted suddenly. "I just realized something. I'm not wearing my belt."

"No kidding!"

"Your sarcasm ill-becomes you, my lady. I meant, I'm not wearing the belt, and I can understand your strange tongue."

"You're right," she agreed, looking as baffled as he felt. Her eyes skimmed downward as she spoke, and then immediately jerked back up. Scarlet flames bloomed on her cheeks.

"Do you blush, wench? Odin's breath, you do!" He liked it when she looked at him *there*. And *there* liked her scrutiny, too.

In truth, her timidity was rather endearing for a woman of her advanced years. "You'll lose your shyness once you become accustomed to me," he assured her, being in a magnanimous mood.

"No, no, no, that's where you're wrong. I'm not becoming accustomed to anything. You are going to play by *my* rules."

"Hah!"

Glaring at him ferociously, she failed to watch her step and tripped over Ingrid, letting loose a vile expletive. He was reasonably confident he knew what the exclamation meant, even without the talisman translator.

"Tsk-tsk," he said sweetly, repeating a favorite sound of his mother's, which fit this occasion perfectly. "Do you have a creaking of the bones that causes you to be so clumsy?"

She straightened in affront.

"Or perchance it is your overlarge feet?"

She gurgled with outrage.

Good. 'Tis best to put a woman in her place from the start. "And where can we put Ingrid so she will remain safe from your stumbling ways till I attach her to the prow of my longship?"

"What longship?" Merry-Death asked, rushing to keep up with his long strides.

He waved a hand in the direction of the field next to her keep.

Her green eyes shot up with surprise when she saw that he referred to the half-completed vessel. "You are *not* putting breasts on the prow of my ship. I already told Mike that. Apparently he didn't relay the message to you." She sniffed with indignation, and then his other words seemed to register. "*Your* longship? Are you serious? That boat belongs to the Trondheim Foundation and Oxley College."

"And a poor specimen it is, too. But, ne'er fear, I will right all the mistakes made thus far. 'Twill be the finest ship to sail the seas."

"You will? You can?" she asked with breathless expectation. "Are you saying that you have the skill to build a Viking longship?"

"For a certainty. I've done so many times. My ships are the most favored in the world. Kings from distant lands have come a-begging for my skill. In fact, just last year, King Aethelred of Britain requisitioned one of my *knorrs* . . . that's a larger trading longship."

"King who?" She put a hand on his arm to halt his progress. When her eyes inadvertently dropped lower to his man parts, she snapped, "Can't you at least cover yourself while I talk to you?"

"With what?"

"I don't know. Your hand."

"'Tis too small." He grinned.

"Your hand or your . . . your . . . ?"

He raised an eyebrow. "Which do you think?"

"Aaarrgh! You keep changing the subject. Who is this King Aethelred you mentioned?"

"Aethelred the Unready is the king of Britain," he explained with measured patience. "Dost recall I mentioned his wife Aelfgifu to you earlier?"

The woman put a hand to her forehead as if she suffered a megrim. "Queen Elizabeth is the queen of England. There is no king. Aethelred was king at the end of the tenth century."

"I know naught of this Elizabeth, and, yea, you are correct, Aethelred was king at the end of the tenth century . . . which this is . . . and he still is." He started to walk into the keep.

"Hold it. Are you telling me you think this is the tenth century?"

Now it was his turn to be puzzled. What an odd question! But then, she'd been asking many odd questions. "Yea. This is the year 997. That would be the tenth century."

Merry-Death burst out laughing. He saw no humor in his words. So, he could only conclude that she must be mad, as well as halfwitted.

When she finally wiped the tears from her face with the back of a hand, she informed him, "I've got news for you, buddy. This is the year 1997. Not only did your boat go off course, but it went through time. Ha, ha, ha! Lordy, wait till I get hold of Mike and Jared. They knew I was desperate, but did they have to send me a crackpot shipbuilder?"

"Nineteen-ninety-seven? Ha, ha, ha!" He mimicked her forced laughter. "My lady, have you suffered a blow to the head of late?"

"No, but I'd like to give you one."

"Have a caution with your loose tongue, Merry-Death. I sorely resent your referring to me as a cracked pot. In my country, I am a chieftain—a karl—and best you show respect for my high estate." He raised his head haughtily as he stalked past her. "And Ingrid will adorn the prow of that ship, or there will be no ship."

Drek you! . . .

Geirolf was having one of the most sensual, self-indulgent experiences of his life. A shower, Merry-Death had called it.

Standing in a cubicle with square pottery tiles on three sides and a foggy glass door on the fourth side, he allowed endless streams of hot water to wash over his body while he soaped himself with a fragrant bar and lathered his hair with a thick liquid.

Truly, the woman gave more and more evidence of being a sorceress. As she'd walked him down the corridor to her bathing chamber, she'd flicked one lever after another on the walls, which immediately set strange candles alight throughout the rooms and on the ceilings. Then she'd explained to him how the bathing room and the kitchen had running water coming into the house out of "spigots."

Well, that wasn't so remarkable. The ancient Romans with their engineering marvels had done much the same centuries ago, except that Merry-Death's spigots also emitted hot water.

And another thing passed all bounds of logic . . . a toilet. Blessed Thor! The people here had no garderobes, except in the country, Merry-Death had told him, where they called them privies, or outhouses. In this land, people relieved themselves in porcelain bowls filled with water that flushed away, miraculously, at the touch of a silver handle. It seemed a waste to him when bushes abounded outside.

Yea, Geirolf concluded, Merry-Death was, indeed, a sorceress, but everyone knew there were good witches and bad witches. She must be a good witch, he decided, because thus far he'd seen no evidence that she used her arts for evil gain.

Still, he would watch her carefully for signs. It would not do for her to cast a spell on him. Once a Black Witch had cursed his older brother for spurning her favors, and Magnus's male parts had turned purple and broke out in boils for a fortnight. His mother had claimed 'twas caused by Magnus's putting his parts where he should not have, but Magnus blamed the witch's curse.

Geirolf was so clean now that he nigh squeaked, but he poured another handful of the golden liquid into his palm and lathered up again. Then he yelled to high Valhalla for the witch's help.

Death by shampoo? . . .

Meredith was about to drop some pasta into a pot of boiling water when she heard Rolf's cry.

"Merry-Death! Help!"

Geez, the guy was loud. Lowering the heat, Meredith hurried down the hall. On the way, she cast a disdainful glance at Rolf's cooked rabbit, which lay on the kitchen table where he'd put it before going for a shower. No way was Meredith going to eat a little bunny.

"Merry-Death!"

"Hold your horses," she complained, opening the bathroom door a tiny crack, wanting to make sure he was decent before she entered. Not that the immodest brute had cared about being decent before.

He was still in the shower, groaning like crazy. Oh, no! Maybe he'd scalded himself.

She rushed over and slid the glass doors open a little bit, making sure to keep her eyes averted. "What's the matter?"

"I got drek in my eyes and I can't get rid of all these soap suds. Balder's balls! My eyes are burning. No matter how much rinsing I do, the white foam won't go away. I think I'm going blind. Did you put a curse on me?"

Meredith tried to understand his long-winded, panicky explanation. "First of all, it's Breck, not drek. That's shampoo. It belonged to my grandfather. I don't think they even make the stuff anymore. How much did you use?"

He shrugged, his eyes still closed, his face raised under the showerhead. And, criminey, he *was* covered with an ungodly amount of lather.

"Half a flask," he replied, spitting out a mouthful of soap.

"You fool, you're only supposed to use a capful. Breck is concentrated."

"How was I supposed to know this?" he grunted, combing his fingertips through his long hair, trying to blink his eyes. "Am I blind?"

"No, you're not blind. You're . . . oh, what do you think you're doing? You beast!"

Rolf had grabbed hold of her wrist and pulled her into the shower, clothes and all.

"Stop blathering like a magpie and remove the poison from my body. Now! And best you make sure I can see again or I will wring your scrawny neck, witch or no witch. Especially if my cock turns purple."

Witch? Purple? Shipbuilder or not, this guy is weird. With a harrumphing sound of disgust, Meredith soon helped him rinse off and, using a washcloth, cleaned his eyes, which were bloodshot, but not blind.

Instead of being grateful, Rolf cursed her name under his breath. That was when she noticed his eyes were riveted on her wet blouse. The silky fabric had become plastered to her body, the pale brown color practically transparent. To her horror, she saw her pink areolae and pointed nipples were clearly visible. He cursed again, and she realized that his expletive was one of male frustration, not anger.

With a swift movement, Rolf placed his hands on her waist and braced her up against the far wall. As he molded his hips to hers with erotic insistence, his mouth lowered. "What else do men and women do in these magical showers?" he breathed against her lips.

Meredith should have braced her hands against his hairy chest and shoved him away with indignation. She was a college professor. She had a doctorate degree in medieval studies. She was a principled woman of the nineties, not a brainless bimbo.

The logical side of her brain said, *Stop!* The other side of her brain said, *Hmmmm.* For once in her empty life, Meredith decided to take the illogical path. Raising her chin under the still-steaming shower, she met his lips and opened for his kiss. And Meredith was glad, glad, glad that she'd done so.

The Viking—whoever he was—played her mouth with finesse. Back and forth he rubbed his firm lips against hers until she was pliant and whimpering. Only then did he deepen his kiss, devouring her with a wild hunger.

"Three months has it been since I've had a woman," he murmured when he came up for air.

"It's been three years since I've had a man," she countered, nipping at his bottom lip. *Oh, my God! Is this really me, nipping at a man's lips?*

He grinned down at her. "Then our mating should prove spectacular."

Before she had a chance to digest that remarkable pronouncement, or say something really stupid, like "Let the games begin," he plunged his tongue into her mouth and used both hands to palm her breasts.

Her knees buckled.

His hardened penis, pressed against the vee of her thighs, held her up.

They both moaned . . . into each other's mouths.

"What is that ringing noise?" he gritted out.

Despite her passion-induced haze, Meredith recognized the telephone. For a second, she just stared blankly at the gorgeous man who stood before her, his kiss-swollen lips parted and panting. His Jack Daniels eyes were glowing with passion. His nude body ground against hers with intimate persuasion.

A stranger. She was about to have hot sex with a stranger. Had she lost her mind?

Meredith blinked at him, belatedly coming to her senses.

He blinked back at her in confusion, and she used that opportunity to shove him away and jump out of the shower. She heard him shouting after her as she ran down the hall, leaving puddles of water, but she didn't wait to hear what he said. Grabbing the cordless phone in the living room, she gasped out, "Hello."

"Mer, is that you?" her sister Jillian asked. "You sound funny."

"I just came from the shower." *Boy, did I just come from the shower! More like I almost came in the shower. Whew!*

"Oh, sorry. What's new?"

Jillian never phoned to chitchat. "What's wrong, Jillie?"

"Does something have to be wrong for me to call you?" Her voice broke mid-sentence with a little catch.

"Oh, Jillie, what now?" Meredith sank down to the sofa, and then immediately stood up again when she realized she was sopping wet. She walked a few steps and leaned against the wall, raking her fingers through her hair distractedly, hooking the wet strands behind her ears. She heard the faint sounds of Jillie's sobs. "Honey, what's wrong? Where are you?"

"I'm in London, but I might have to be in Chicago tonight."

"I thought you had to stay in London for another month,

doing that museum exhibit on Jelling Age Jewelry."

"I do. Mer, I need a favor of you. A *big* favor."

Uh-oh! Jillie was thirty years old—five years younger than Meredith—and she was always looking for favors. Two failed marriages, a bankrupt boutique, a juvenile delinquent daughter, endless lovers. On and on Jillie's troubles went. When would they ever end?

"George called me from Chicago," Jillie explained. George Huntley was Jillie's first estranged husband, a psychologist. They'd been married when they were both high school seniors, and Jillie was pregnant. "He said I have to come back immediately."

"Why?" she asked, fearing the answer.

"Gourd was arrested for shoplifting, and the police are threatening to put her in a detention home."

"Gourd?"

"That's Thea's name *du jour*. She's going through a Mother Earth phase this week."

Meredith giggled. How like her niece! Always trying to find herself. Hating her real name, Theodosia, almost from birth, she took on a different *nom de plume* every other week.

"It's her third arrest in the past five months," Jillie informed her in a rush.

"Oh, Jillie." And poor Thea. The kid had been diagnosed with everything from ADD to hostile behavior syndrome in her twelve short years of living. Meredith would probably go off the deep end, too, if she had to live with her crazy sister. And it was no kind of life for a young girl to ping-pong back and forth between schizo parents who weren't overjoyed to have her.

"George said he's wiping his hands of the kid. Said I have to come back from London immediately and be a real mother to her. No more moving from city to city. I was wondering—"

"No."

"No?"

"No, you are not shoving your problems off on me again, Jillie. It's about time you took responsibility for yourself."

"But they're going to take Thea away from me." Jillie started to cry. Her racking sobs tore at Meredith's heart. She pressed her forehead against the wall, knowing she was going to be a sucker . . . once again.

You can tell certain things about a man by the size of his boat . . .

Geirolf was angry.

No woman teased him to the point of aching hardness, then stopped mid-coupling, without an explanation. Games like those belonged to immature youthlings, experimenting with first thrills. He had long passed his majority, and Merry-Death was certainly well beyond her first bloom.

He wanted answers, and he wanted them now.

After drying off briskly, he applied the ointment she'd supplied to his cuts, then shrugged into an old pair of her brother's soft "sweating" *braies* she'd left for him, along with something called a "T-*shert*" with the words "JUST DO IT" emblazoned across the chest. He'd like to "do it" all right, and he would, too, once he'd wrung the wench's feckless neck. In the end, he put the talisman belt on as well, since it seemed to help him understand Merry-Death's peculiar language.

Finally, he stormed barefooted into the great room—something he would never do in his own keep where unmentionable items often hid in the rushes. Then, he stopped dead in his tracks. Merry-Death was talking into a little black box that she held up to her ear. A box? Well, why not? He'd heard of wizards who talked to trees, or animals, even the wind. Ah, hell, she really was a witch, then. Did he want to chance rutting with a witch?

Yea, he answered himself immediately, the evidence still lying like an anchor betwixt his thighs.

"Give me that," he yelled and grabbed the box out of her hand, intending to throw it into the hearth. But it was making a peculiar noise, like a woman sobbing. Alarmed, he raised his eyes to Merry-Death, who was trying to retrieve the object. "What is that noise?" he demanded, holding the box above his head, out of her reach.

"My sister."

"Your sister is a box?"

"No, my sister is not a box. Lord, maybe Jared really did find you in a jungle. That's a telephone, and I was talking to my sister in London."

He snorted with disbelief but still, proceeding warily, he held the box up to his ear.

"Who is this?" a feminine voice asked.

His head jerked up with surprise. "Geirolf," he responded tentatively, though he felt rather foolish talking to a box. He rubbed the talisman clasp for aid. "Who are you?"

"Jillian. Meredith's sister in England. What're you doing there?"

The box actually talked, claiming to speak from the land of the bloody Saxons. Merry-Death must be a more powerful witch than he'd thought possible. "Well, I just took a shower, but—"

Merry-Death groaned and put her head between her hands.

"A shower?" the voice hooted. "Meredith just came from the shower, too. Were you in there together?"

"Well, yea, we were both in the shower, but—"

"Give me that phone," Merry-Death hissed, but he side-stepped her clawing hands.

"What do you do for a living, Geirolf?" the box asked.

"I'm a Viking."

"A what?"

"Viking. Have you ne'er heard of *Nordmanni* . . . a Norse-man? Is everyone addled in this godforsaken country?"

"Oh, God, this is too hilarious. My sister and a Viking!" She giggled. "And where are you staying, Mr. Viking?"

Geirolf misliked the condescending tone of the woman's voice, and he refused to answer.

"Are you and Meredith lovers?"

"'Tis none of your concern who shares my bed furs." Geirolf had never been a man to boast outside the bedchamber, and he would not start now.

The box was laughing, hysterically. He threw it to the floor with disgust, and Merry-Death quickly picked it up.

"Jillie, I'll call you back later," she said. "No, he's not my lover. No, I'm not fixing you up. No, he doesn't have a big—" she looked up at him where he stood, hands on hips, and she blushed—"boat."

Hah! He would show the wench good and well, and soon, the size of his . . . *boat.*

Forget warm; this Viking was hot . . .

A half-hour later, Meredith sat at her kitchen table across from her "Viking." He filled out her brother's T-shirt and sweatpants as Jared never had. His long hair—light brown, sun-streaked with blond now that it had dried—was pulled back at the nape with a rubber band that she'd had to show him how to use.

She'd changed into another silk blouse and slacks before returning to the kitchen to prepare dinner.

Rolf sat picking at his charred rabbit, eyeing the plate of pasta sitting in front of her with a side of Caesar salad. They both had glasses of ice water.

"Are you sure you wouldn't rather share my meal? There's plenty," she offered.

He hesitated. "It looks like white worms covered with blood."

She smiled. "Yes, but it tastes delicious."

"You are not quite so plain when you smile, Merry-Death. You should do it more often." He propped an elbow on the table and braced his chin in the cupped palm, watching her intently.

Her heart lurched oddly at the backhanded compliment and his hot scrutiny. Then he spoiled the effect by adding, "And you have good teeth."

"Like a horse?"

He grinned. "Nay, not like a horse."

Nervously, she slurped one strand of spaghetti into her mouth. Not wanting to back down from the challenge in his sparkling eyes, she smacked her lips with satisfaction.

"Bloody hell! You could bring a corpse's poker to life with such a lewd gesture."

"Huh?"

He winked.

And it was as if a tingly caress rippled over her entire body. She was in big, big trouble with this guy.

"I will try one of your worms," he declared. Instead of waiting for her to get another plate and silverware, he reached across the table and picked up one strand. Arching his neck, he held it above his parted lips, like a sword swallower, then slowly sucked it into his mouth and down his throat. Holding her eyes the entire time, he licked his lips, then his thumb and forefinger.

It was the most sensual thing Meredith had ever seen a man do in her entire life. Like foreplay, but better.

"Did you like it?" she choked out.

"Immensely."

Was there a double meaning in his terse reply?

"Do you want to know what I would like even better?" he asked.

"No!" she said quickly and jumped up to get him his own place setting.

The brute just laughed knowingly behind her.

A half hour later, Rolf gave up trying to eat the spaghetti with a fork. He had tomato sauce splattered on his white T-shirt. Strands of pasta he'd tried to twirl on his fork had landed on the tablecloth or the floor. And Meredith was laughing so hard she had tears streaming down her face.

Pushing the plate aside, he growled, "I think this is a dish some woman invented to bedevil her man." Using a napkin, he wiped his face to make sure no sauce remained, then threw it to the floor, and stood. "Why do you try to punish me, Merry-Death? Because we did not complete the game you started earlier?"

"What game?" She stood as well and started to back away into the living room.

"You know. In your shower." He drew the stained T-shirt over his head and tossed it aside, then stepped toward her, a predatory, determined look in his eyes.

Meredith's traitorous eyes froze on his lightly furred chest and splendidly ridged abdomen. He'd put the wide belt with the ornate clasp on, and it called attention to his narrow waist and slim hips.

Uh-oh, here come the hormones again.

"Why did you run from my embrace, my lady?" His voice was a husky, sinful insinuation.

My lady? Feeling far from ladylike at the smoky, silent invitation in his eyes, she gulped. "Because the phone was ringing."

Every time she took a step backward, he took one forward. He stalked her. But it didn't feel threatening. It felt . . . exciting. *Oh, my!*

"And that was the only reason?"

She nodded.

"Why do you pull your hair back so severely, like, a chaste nun? You have beautiful hair."

"I do?" Meredith was behind the sofa. Rolf stood, poised to spring, on the other side by the fireplace, where the fire had burned down to embers.

"You do. When it spilled out earlier, I pictured it spread down your back, over your bare breasts, on my bed furs."

Her eyes widened at his outrageous words and her breasts peaked and began to ache.

He noticed immediately and a slow smile of appreciation spread across his lips. "Come," he said, holding out a hand in invitation. "No more malingering games."

Meredith was almost tempted. Almost. She shook her head. "I think you must have cast a spell over me with that . . . that talisman you keep talking about."

"Nay, 'tis you who have cast the spell, my sweet witch. Now, come," he coaxed, "do not gainsay me with pretenses that you do not want the pleasuring as much as I."

"I don't," she lied, even as she felt an insistent heat coil in her midsection and move enticingly downward.

"I will show you how a true Viking makes love," he vowed silkily, "and you can show me your witchly arts in the bedding. 'Tis a bartering I anticipate with great fervor."

"No, you don't understand," she protested weakly. They had circled the sofa. Now her back was to the fireplace, and he was on the other side of the couch. "We have to talk. There seems to be a big misunderstanding here."

"We can talk later. *Afterward.* And the only big thing here is—" His hand, which had been rubbing his bristled chin— he must not have shaved in days—moved lower to demonstrate.

"Don't you dare."

The progress of his hand halted midway and he fingered his belt, rubbing it in an almost erotic fashion. He was playing with her, like an overconfident cat with a helpless mouse.

But her eyes homed in on the ornate clasp of his belt, and she recalled the primitively carved figurehead from a ship's prow lying outside. Sanity began to return.

At first, Meredith had believed that this guy—this very attractive guy—had been sent by her brother, in collaboration with Mike. But maybe that was just what she had wanted to believe. Something wasn't right in this picture.

He was a stranger who'd shown up unexpectedly in her home. He claimed the bruise on his forehead came from the falling mast of his dragonship. A new wound—a shallow, six-inch slash across his back—had resulted from the sword of someone called Storr Grimmsson.

All of the modern gadgets in her home fascinated him. Not just the telephone or refrigerator or stove or running water or electricity. Even little things like ice cubes or metal cans or rubber bands.

And another thing. He knew a lot about tenth-century history. In fact, he claimed to be living in that time period, which she'd discounted as a joke earlier. But maybe he hadn't been joking. Oh, God, maybe he was an escapee from a mental institution. Some nutcase with delusions of being an ancient Viking prince.

"Listen, Rolf," she said sternly as they circled the sofa once again, "we *are* going to talk. *Now*. It's important that we get a few things cleared up."

His jaw stiffened and he seemed about to argue, but then he shrugged. "If you wish, we can talk," he conceded, "but then we *will* make love."

Her heart hammered. She was an obsessively honest person.

She'd never been coy or prone to games. "Maybe," she agreed as a blush heated her face.

"Maybe?" he questioned, tilting his head cynically, bracing his hands on his sexy hips. "Maybe?"

"Try to understand. One-night stands with complete strangers were never my style—"

"Oh, I daresay I will be here for *many* nights," he drawled. "Leastways, till my ship is completed."

"That's what you think," she retorted at the interruption. Then, flustered at the prospect of all those nights he alluded to, she went on, "I'll admit that 'Love with a Warm Viking' is looking better and better. And hard as it is for me to believe, I'm actually considering a meaningless sexual encounter. It's just that I need some answers first."

His lips twitched before he smiled lazily at her.

She hated it when he smiled lazily at her.

"Warm Viking?" he scoffed. "My lady, this Viking is hot."

CHAPTER THREE

❧

*F*alling in love with a dead man . . .

"Unleash your tongue," he said. "I am listening."

After throwing two more logs on the fire and stoking it back to life with a poker, he sank down onto the soft cushions of a narrow, bedlike structure facing the fireplace. Propping his long legs on the low table in front, he took an apple from the bowl in its center and began to chomp with a relish born of near starvation. That plate of "worms" she'd given him for dinner had done naught to fill his empty stomach.

When he looked up, Merry-Death was gaping at him and the half-eaten apple.

"What? You ne'er saw a man eat an apple?"

"Of course, I've seen a man eat an apple. It's just that you make yourself at home . . . *in my home.* You don't even wait to be asked if you'd like to sit down or eat or . . . whatever." The last word came out with a tiny embarrassed squeal.

She couldn't fool him. He knew why the wench was skittish. She was thinking about the pleasuring to come. Like a mare in heat, her body made ready for their coupling.

"By your leave, may I sit down, Merry-Death?" he inquired with amusement.

"Hmpfh!"

"Would it beggar your household if I ate one of your apples?" he added.

"Oh, really! That's not the point."

"Blessed Thor, woman talk makes my head ache. I'm tired and hungry and . . . lusty. If I must needs listen to nagging—and, yea I said *nagging*; 'tis what most females mean when they say, 'let's talk'—I want to have at least *one* of my appetites satisfied first."

The wench's open mouth snapped shut.

He smiled inwardly. Really, the wench was so easy to bait. No challenge at all to his superior talents. "Well, what do you want to discuss?" he prodded, tossing the fruit core into the exact center of the flames, where it proceeded to sizzle and throw off the delicious autumn scent of apples. She stood behind the bed-thing, glaring at him. "And, for the love of Freya, sit down so I don't have to crane my neck up to see you."

Before she had a chance to protest, he reached over his shoulder, seized her wrist, and yanked her over the cushioned backboard of the bed-thing and onto his lap, face downward. In the process, he got a close-up view of her rump before she righted herself.

His staff came immediately to attention. But then, he'd always had a fondness for a well-rounded female rump.

After he adjusted her squirming body to sit on his lap, he noticed her breasts pressing against the thin silk of her *shert*. Not that he hadn't noticed those same breasts a short time ago in the showering chamber.

"Stop looking at me like that," she sputtered, slapping at his roving hands.

But he couldn't stop looking, or roving, although he did try to conceal the smile that tugged at his lips. Next to a firm, shapely bottom, he did like a woman's breasts.

In fact, he and his brothers had engaged in a profound discussion on the subject one time—they'd been drunk—and decided that women's breasts were a gift to men from the gods. Jorund and Magnus had said that the bigger the tits the better—more to hold onto, or some such—but he believed there was allure in all sizes and said so loudly.

Then, with the wisdom gleaned from a *tun* of mead, they'd moved on to the disadvantages of bedding comely wenches.

"Winsome women are too full of themselves," Magnus had declared with a loud belch. Odd that the belch remained so vivid in his mind. "They require an abundance of flattering afore they'll part their legs."

"And plain women try harder to please," Geirolf added sagely. He couldn't remember if he'd belched or not.

"Yea, but there is naught better than a buxom wench who has enthusiasm for the bed-sport." Jorund had sighed. At the time, his brother had been smitten with the fair Else, a dairy maid, who was giving him a merry chase.

His mother, Lady Asgar, had overheard the conversation and boxed all their ears, calling them "crude, disgusting oafs."

"You crude, disgusting oaf," Merry-Death hissed at him, jarring him back to the present. "Take your hands off of me."

"Why?" He maintained an armlock around her upper body, pressing her to his bare chest with one hand, while he released the pins from her hair with the other and raked out the silken strands, down her back, over her shoulders, as far as the mounds in question. "I mislike talking intimately to a woman who has her hair skinned back like a nun," he said thickly as he buried his face in the fragrant tresses. She smelled like drek.

Merry-Death gasped.

"Do you use drek on your nether hair as well?" he inquired idly as he tasted the sweet skin at the curve of her neck.

She gasped again.

Taking her gasps as encouragement, he nuzzled her neck, then moved upward. First, he nipped the sensitive lobe of her ear with his teeth, then began to explore the inner whorls with the tip of his tongue.

The wench went stiff with shock.

He was stiff, too, but not from shock.

Meredith fought against the erotic lethargy that pulled at her senses. She felt the clasp of Rolf's belt pressing into her hip with an odd heat and wondered if it might really be a magic talisman. There was no other explanation for her attraction to such a crude man with overly sensual lips and octopus hands. Nor was there any logical accounting for an educated woman such as herself surrendering to raw impulsive lust.

But it felt *so* good. And it had been *so* long.

"No!" she insisted, mustering resistance. She managed to slip out of his arms to the other side of the sofa. Panting, she folded her arms across her breasts to hide her signs of arousal.

Rolf gazed at her, his chin lifted defiantly, passion hazing his amber-brown eyes. Then he slowly let out a pent-up breath and waited tautly for her next move.

"Who . . . are . . . you?" she asked.

"Geirolf Ericsson," he snapped, clenching and unclenching his fists, as if he could barely contain his roiling passions.

Meredith couldn't recall a time when a man seemed to want her so much. It was a heady compliment. "Where are you from?"

"Hordaland."

There he went again with those ancient words. Why didn't he just say the southwestern section of Norway—*old* Norway, to be specific? "How did you get here?" She tried not to stare at the somehow erotic movement of his flexing fingers.

"My ship wrecked," he said brusquely, obviously impatient with questions that interfered with his seductive plans, "and then I climbed the bloody cliffside to your keep."

He was repeating all the things he'd told her before. But maybe he just had his story down pat.

She ignored his sizzling glance, which pretty much said, *Now can I jump your bones?* "Who sent you?"

He shrugged.

"Are you a shipbuilder?"

He nodded, and licked his lips slowly.

And very nice lips they were, too. And his tongue wasn't so bad, either. *Oh, geez! Is he anticipating my questions winding down? Why am I having so much trouble concentrating? Could hormone overload cause a dumbing-down syndrome?* "Did you come here to finish the longboat project?" Meredith surprised herself by being able to put more than two words together intelligibly.

He hesitated, and then answered, "Yea, I believe that is why I was sent here."

"And you really can build a Viking longship?"

He flashed her an affronted glare. "Did I not say so afore?"

"How long would it take you to complete the project?"

"Well, from what I have seen, I would say that half of the work already done will have to be dismantled. Once that is—"

"It most definitely will not be dismantled."

"My lady," he said with exasperation, "do you have any intention of placing that vessel on water?"

"Of course."

"It will sink."

Her eyes narrowed angrily. "My grandfather was an expert builder. Are you saying he was incompetent?"

"Was he an expert sailor?"

"Well, no," she admitted, "but—"

"Your grandsire nailed the overlapping oak planks together adequately, but he didn't stuff the joints properly with rope. The ship is not watertight."

She inhaled sharply at that news.

"There is a saying in my land, '*Oft veltir lítil þúfa þungu hlassi.*'"

She raised a brow, refusing to ask what he meant, or acknowledge his fluency in Old Norse.

"A small leak will sink a great ship," he translated. "And here's another worry for you: The keel is off-center."

"Keel?"

"The timber beam that forms the central spine on the bottom of the ship. It is the most important element in a ship's frame. The boat will list if it's off-center."

Despite his dire prognosis, a sense of relief filled Meredith. Rolf did seem to know his craft.

"I will build this Viking ship for you, Merry-Death," he assured her, "but it will be done my way, or not at all."

What an arrogant, overconfident man! But she had no other choice right now. If he knew even half what he claimed, he would be perfect for the job. However, there was no way she'd let him control this project. She just wouldn't tell him that yet.

"Why is this ship so important to you, Merry-Death?"

His feet were still propped on her coffee table, and one long arm stretched along the back of the sofa, where his fingers played with the strands of hair lying on her shoulder. She wished he'd stop doing that. It unnerved her. Distracted her from the serious business at hand. Made her think of very unserious things . . . like, just how hot was a hot Viking?

"Because it was important to my grandfather. He was a professor of medieval studies at the local college with a special interest in Nordic culture." Once she started talking about her grandfather and the project, she lost her nervousness and the too-consuming awareness of Rolf as a man. Thank God! "All his life, Gramps dreamed about reproducing a Viking longship and actually setting sail, re-enacting one of the Viking voyages. Just like Captain Magnus Andersen did a hundred years ago."

"You are making my head ache, Merry-Death. Who in bloody hell is Magnus Andersen?"

"Andersen built a replica of the Godstad ship in 1893. To prove how seaworthy a Viking ship was, he sailed it from Norway to Newfoundland in just twenty-eight days, despite several storms. Since boyhood, Gramps was inspired to do the same, in reverse."

"Was your grandsire of Norse origins?"

She shook her head. "Gramps just believed there was much that could be learned from the Viking way of life, and especially Viking shipbuilding. This is a teaching college, and he always said that planning, hard work, and persistence, the talents learned in actually building a ship . . . well, all these things would help a student in any walk of life."

" 'Tis true, 'tis true," Rolf agreed, nodding his head.

"Gramps died before he could complete his dream." She wiped her eyes, then looked at Rolf with determination. "But I'm going to complete the project for him."

"I understand."

"You do? No one else does. Certainly not my parents, or my ex-husband."

"Though I am loathe to say so, you and I have much in common. Like your grandsire, my father gave me a mission. Until it is complete, I cannot rest."

His perception disconcerted Meredith for a moment. "Well, anyhow, that's why I'm on a one-year sabbatical from Columbia, where I'm a professor of medieval studies. I've taken Gramps's place on the staff of Oxley College until the Trondheim project is completed."

Rolf stared at her blankly.

"What?" she asked. "What's wrong?"

"Half of your words have no meaning to me. What language is this you . . . *we* are speaking?" He rubbed the clasp of his belt while he spoke, as if for luck, or answers.

"English."

"It can't be. I speak both Norse and English, which are much alike, and your words come from neither."

"Like what words?" Geez, this guy's games wore thin. Okay, he seemed knowledgeable about shipbuilding, but did he have to keep up the pretense of being a Viking? "Give me an example."

"Like profess-whore. I can hardly credit you as a whore."

"I beg your pardon," she bristled. "Professor is another name for a teacher."

"Call-ledge?"

She frowned, then laughed. "You mean *college*. That's a school . . . usually for young men and women between the ages of eighteen and twenty-two."

"Now I know you speak pure drivel. Men are long past the age of schooling by eighteen. Either they tend their own estates or fight their king's wars. And women . . . women are well into breeding by then."

"Give me a break! Listen, Rolf, I have too many problems to continue with this charade of yours. So, knock it off, and—"

"What is this made-heave-all you prattle about? Did you say you teach made-heave-all? Earlier this evening, you called yourself a dock-whore, and now you claim to be a profess-whore . . . a woman teacher? I think not."

Dock-whore? Oh, he means doctor. She should refuse to answer any more of his absurd questions, but his furrowed brow appeared genuine. Meredith was getting alarmed. He really might be a mental case. Even so, taking a deep breath, she explained, "Medieval refers to the period from the sixth to the sixteenth century. My specialty is tenth- to twelfth-century Britain."

He made an incoherent sound, which she interpreted as the usual reaction to her devoting her life to such a dull subject.

She raised her chin defensively. "I come from a family of scholars. My grandfather was an expert in early Nordic culture. My parents are famous for late–Middle Age social customs. My brother Jared is an archaeologist who has worked on the Coppergate dig in York and is currently in Norway excavating a Norse farmstead. My sister Jillian makes Jelling-style jewelry."

Rolf raked his fingers through his hair in confusion. "'Tis puzzling to me."

"Why?"

"Well, I could accept learned men studying the past, but how can they study the future?"

"What do you mean . . . the future?"

He threw his hands out impatiently. "Anytime after this year, 997, is the future, is it not?"

She tsked her disgust. "No, the period after 997 is not the future. Listen, why don't I just show you my grandfather's blueprints for the longship, and let's start from there?"

A few moments later, she stood in her small den, gathering together the oversized sketches.

"God's teeth and Odin's breath! 'Tis impossible!"

She jumped, not having realized that he'd followed so closely. Glancing back over her shoulder, she saw him gaping at the bookshelves that lined three of the walls. The fourth wall had huge casement windows that opened during the daytime onto a spectacular view of the Atlantic Ocean.

He touched one of the leatherbound volumes with reverence. "You must be very wealthy to afford so many precious books," he said in an awestruck voice. "In my world, even kings often own only one book or two."

He opened a volume carefully. Tracing a fingertip over the glossy page, he sighed. "The paintings are remarkably life-like. And the writing is strange. Not the usual ink scratchings of the monkish scribes."

"Hardly." This guy was a fantastic actor. To what purpose, Meredith couldn't imagine. But, if she didn't know better, she'd believe his fascination with books to be genuine.

"It's incredible. I understand your words when you speak, but I cannot fathom the language in these books. Is it English?"

Meredith nodded. A thread of panic caused her to back away slightly, although he did nothing menacing, other than stand there, shirtless, drooling over a book.

"Tomorrow you must teach me to read your kind of English," he pronounced with his usual arrogance, slamming the book shut.

Tomorrow. Like in one day, he expects to learn to read a language. Hah! If he thinks I'm going to waste my day pretending to give an impostor English lessons, he's got another thing coming. And even if he can't read English, what would make him think he could learn an entire foreign language in one day? Next he'll be telling me he's Einstein . . . a Viking Einstein.

Walking around the small den, Rolf picked up one book after another, poring over them, caressing their covers, murmuring soft words of disbelief or admiration. Finally, he came to a book—one written by a colleague of hers at Columbia, *The Vestfold Dig: Death of a Viking Prince.* He opened it to the center illustration and turned bone-white with shock.

"What? What is it?" she asked with alarm.

" 'Tis my sword," he said. "How can that be?"

Meredith stepped closer.

"See, the engraving is the same as that on my belt clasp."

Meredith scrutinized the color illustration of a Viking sword taken from a burial site. Its ornate hilt had an engraved design of stylized animals that was, indeed, identical to the clasp of Rolf's belt. The base of the hilt also had several runic symbols scratched onto it. She pointed to them, asking, "What do they mean?" She immediately chastised herself for asking the question. How could this jokester decipher the *futhark* alphabet?

"This weapon, *Brave Friend*, belonged to my beloved son, Geirolf Ericsson," he replied in a stony voice.

She was stunned. "Amazing," she commented, more than impressed that he could read runes, and that his words duplicated the caption at the bottom of the picture.

He flipped the page and gasped. There was a double-page illustration of a magnificent Viking longboat with a dragon prow. "Who did this? Who made a painting of my ship?"

"*Your* ship?"

"Yea, 'tis the dragonship I built last year. *Fierce Dragon*. All my ships have the word 'fierce' in their names. I intend to call my new one *Fierce Destiny*."

"I don't understand," Meredith said, rubbing the fingertips of one hand across her forehead.

"I share your bafflement, my lady," Rolf said, turning a page. "Look, look at these." He pointed to the silver armlets taken from the site and held out his arms to show the similarity of the etched motifs to his own adornments.

On and on Rolf went, examining the pages of the book, his frown growing deeper, his growls more pronounced.

And Meredith felt a ripple of fear sweep her. What was going on?

Rolf finally turned on her. "What is this book? Who wrote it? And why?"

"*The Vestfold Dig: Death of a Viking Prince*, is its title, as I said before. It's about an archaeological dig that took place about five years ago in a grave field in Norway. Vestfold was a region of southwestern Norway."

"I know where Vestfold is," he said impatiently. "I live there."

"You do?"

"And why are men digging up sacred burial sites?"

Meredith shrugged. "Archaeologists do it all the time. Thousands of Norse graves have given us the only insight we have into the way people lived a thousand years ago, since no written documents survive." She flinched when she saw the look of revulsion on Rolf's face.

"If they were Christian graves, the holy priests' hue and cry of sacrilege would reach the high heavens. Are Norse graves fair game because we are 'heathens'?"

"No, when it comes to greed . . . or, more often, the search for historical knowledge, graves become a sort of public domain."

He hugged his arms around his chest as if suddenly cold and mumbled, "Thousands of graves opened . . . who could have predicted such? 'Twould have been better if all Vikings followed the tradition of death burning." Then he seemed to remember something else. "What did you mean about this death of a Viking prince?"

This whole conversation was getting ridiculous. "I already told you," she said with exasperation. "The objects depicted in that book were taken from an ancient Viking burial site. A ship burial mound."

"Burial? Whose burial?" he asked, almost fearfully. Then added, "Ancient?"

"Well, it's believed that some powerful Viking leader had a son who died and that he erected this burial mound in his memory. There were no skeletal remains. So, it's presumed that the son died in a battle out of the country, or at sea, maybe even . . ." Her words trailed off at the absolute horror on Rolf's ashen face. "Rolf, why are you so upset?"

"He was not a prince. He was a karl . . . a high chieftain."

"Wh-what?" She shook her head to clear it. She was talking to him as if she bought all his playacting. However, the teacher in her rose stubbornly to the surface, and she explained, "Rolf, the Viking buried there died more than a thousand years ago. Ancient history."

"A thousand years?" he repeated dumbly. "Do you persist in saying this is the year 1997?"

"Of course."

"Guð minn góður!" he whispered, then repeated the expletive, "My God!" Holding her eyes, he spat out, "Not only did my ship run off course in the great waters, but it traveled through time, as well."

"That's impossible," she declared.

"What other explanation is there? Yesterday my ship wrecked and the year was 997. Today, you tell me that it is 1997."

"And you think that time travel is possible?" she scoffed.

He rolled his shoulders uncertainly. "The saga legends tell of such, but usually those adventures involved gods and the afterlife. But, yea, to answer your question, I do believe, like all good Norsemen, that anything is possible in this life."

She curled her upper lip with skepticism.

A soft moan escaped Rolf's mouth as he gazed once more at the book clenched in his fists. *"Faðir minn,"* he groaned. "My father—" he raised anguished, tear-filled eyes to hers, pleading—"my father must have prepared this burial site for me. Do you realize what this means?"

She shook her head numbly.

"I am *dauður* . . . dead."

Meredith nodded, though she didn't really think Rolf was dead, or that the man standing before her was a time traveler. No, she couldn't accept that.

Could she?

Rolf was swaying from side to side now, keening a low, savage wail of bereavement. Because of his own death? Holy cow! Over and over, he muttered, *"Dauður . . . dauður . . .*

dauður . . ." Finally, he snapped his head up, and swore, *"Hver fjandinn!* Damn it! Damn Storr Grimmsson! Damn all the gods who drew me to this place and time. Most of all, damn me for my sins, which must have brought about this punishment."

Meredith tried to put a comforting hand on his arm, but he shrugged her off. "Feel no pity for me, maiden, for I will return to my time. This I swear on all I hold sacred."

Stepping back, she watched the raging warrior who tore the rubber band from his nape and pulled wildly at the strands of his long hair in agony. He let out a primitive Viking yell, as old as time, and stormed from the room and out to the cliffs, where he proceeded to bellow his rage and grief to the night skies.

Peering through the windows, she saw him pacing along the cliff edge, tearing at his hair, beating his chest, throwing out his hands in dismay. He chanted some strange words in Old Norse. A funeral dirge?

Meredith's heart went out to the tormented man. She should be frightened, but she wasn't. Somehow she knew he posed no threat to her. At least not a physical one.

He was a stranger, really, and yet she felt connected to him in a way she couldn't define. She was attracted to him, but it was much more than that.

Tears welled in her eyes, and she felt Rolf's pain. Whatever the reason for his being here, her intuition told her that fate, or God, played a role. It was meant to be.

She went out and tried to offer solace, but he was beyond hearing or welcoming her aid at this point. Through glazed, red-rimmed eyes, he stared at her as if she were invisible. "Begone, woman. Leave me to mourn . . . alone." Turning blindly toward the house, she thought he added in a gentler tone, "A man's honor demands he show strength, even in the death farewells."

During the next few hours, as Meredith tidied the kitchen, made up a bed for Rolf on the sofa, and turned off the lights for the night, she kept glancing outside with concern. One time, she saw him kneeling with arms upraised to the moonlit sky, still chanting the Norse dirge. Another time, he raged, pounding a fist against a tree in frustrated anger.

And all the time he appeared so lost and lonely.

Finally, Meredith could no longer keep her eyes open, and she went to bed. Surprisingly, she fell into a deep sleep, exhausted by all that had happened to her that evening. Before dozing off, though, she wondered if she might awaken in the morning to find that the fierce Viking visitor had been a mere figment of her overworked imagination.

Oddly, that prospect filled her with heartfelt sorrow.

In the middle of the night, she awakened groggily, sensing a presence in her room . . . in her bed, actually. Before she had a chance to jump up with alarm, a cold arm snaked around her waist, pulling her flush against a hard male body. Although she wore panties and a nightshirt, she could feel that the body holding her was totally nude.

"No," she protested and tried to push herself out of his embrace.

"Shhh." Rolf breathed against her ear, fitting himself more closely against the length of her back, from head to heel. "I mean you no harm. Just let me hold you for a while."

She didn't want to make love with him. Not yet. The lust that had almost overcome her earlier was gone now, replaced by a new, unsettling bond that she wanted to examine more closely in the light of day. Besides, she had so many questions.

"No," she repeated. "Not now . . . not yet."

Rolf's body stiffened behind her, and his fingertips, which had been tracing a sweet path down her arm from shoulder to wrist, stilled. He exhaled softly, and Meredith closed her eyes against the enticing feel of his lips against the nape of her neck.

"I need you."

His whispered entreaty—three little words, spoken with raw, pain-ridden honesty—were her undoing. And Meredith accepted something she'd unconsciously concluded hours earlier. She turned in his arms and lovingly touched the side of his damp cheek, unable to distinguish whether the wetness had been caused by tears or ocean mist.

"I need you, too," she sighed. In surrender.

CHAPTER FOUR

※

'mon, baby, light my fire . . .
"I am dead," Rolf said with utter desolation.

Rolling over on his back, he rested a forearm over his closed eyes. By the light of an unshaded window and the lingering full moon, she saw his long hair spread out over the snowy white pillow.

Meredith propped herself on her right elbow and reached across with her other arm to place a hand against his cheek again with gentle assurance. "No. You are alive, Rolf."

Lifting his arm, he regarded her beseechingly. "Do you think so? Hmmm. I must needs yield to your better judgment on the matter. In truth, my head throbs with confusion. My body is frozen in your time, but my spirit craves the comfort of my own people. My heart is breaking. Surely those who walk in the afterlife experience no such pain."

Then he laid his huge hand over hers, which continued to caress his cheek, and guided it to his chest, where his heart thudded wildly, as if it would, indeed, burst. Rolf was bare to the waist, and from there covered by her grandmother's handmade quilt—a starburst design. She knew he was nude to the toes, but as she gazed at his magnificent body, she felt no overpowering lust. What she felt was an overpowering . . . what? Caring was the only word she could come up with to describe the emotion that swelled her heart and warmed her blood.

He was a stranger, but he was not.

She yearned to touch him and heal all his inner hurts, but she didn't even know what they were.

As a teacher, she delighted in passing on knowledge to her students. Ironically, she sensed this primitive man could teach her much, much more.

He was sent to her for a purpose, she suspected. And right now, she didn't care what the reason. She relished the gift of his presence in her life.

His bleak eyes held hers. "Make me feel alive, Merry-Death."

She tilted her head in question, her pulse accelerating.

"I am so tired and weary of the struggle. Thaw the frost that threatens to freeze my soul, Merry-Death. Please."

She nodded, unable to speak over the lump in her throat. Slowly she lowered her head, and, with her left hand still resting over his heart, she pressed her lips to his. Soft against firm. Warm against cold. He was so frozen and stiff, like death. But she would restore him, she vowed.

It was a decidedly unerotic kiss, meant to convey only caring. And, yet, it was extremely erotic, as evidenced by Rolf's quick indrawn hiss.

"Will you be my heart-friend?" he murmured. His breath was a sweet kiss in itself against her lips.

At his words, Meredith reeled as some need, long hidden and denied in her deepest soul, began to open, like the petals of a fragile flower. *Heart-friend? Was that like a soulmate? Or just a friend?*

He parted his lips, inviting more. At the same time, his arms remained immobile at his sides, palms upward, in supplication.

He didn't insist that she get naked with him. Or grab her with lusty intent. He didn't make false promises, or swear undying love. He merely waited, letting her set the pace of this loving . . . or halt it, if she chose.

Meredith found the prospect oddly empowering . . . and unique. No man had ever let her lead in quite this way, not even Jeffrey. To make all the decisions, or none. She wasn't sure what to do.

So, she deepened the kiss, testing, and he accommodated her with a slight shifting of his lips, which were no longer cool. From side to side, she moved her lips over his, exploring, till she found just the right position. Then she slipped her tongue inside his mouth, tentatively.

His heart jumped with excitement under her hand.

She smiled against his lips, and felt him smile back.

Encouraged, she pulled away and examined his face with her eyes and her fingertips: the angry bruise at his temple, which she kissed gently; the arch of his thick brows; his long, feathery, thick lashes; the sharp bones at his cheek and jaw lines; even his straight, arrogant nose.

She admired but didn't touch his wide shoulders. Nor the ridges of veins that outlined his muscled arms. Nor the many scars, old and new, that covered his skin. Not even the enticing sweep of shadow and light that marked the well-toned planes of his chest and abdomen. Instead, she savored the anticipation of touching him in all those places, eventually.

"You're beautiful," she whispered.

"Yea," he agreed, and crossed his eyes at her. For some reason, the gesture touched her deeply. Perhaps because the small sign of humor showed she was succeeding in her efforts to pull him from his despair.

"You're not chilled anymore," she remarked, running a palm up his chest to his neck, sweeping back down as far as his waist. Then stopping.

He inhaled sharply, and sucked in his stomach.

In resistance? Perhaps he'd expected her to go farther. Or perhaps he didn't want her to go so far.

"Nay, I'm not cold anymore, sweetling, thanks to you. But I am bone weary and heart sick."

Sweetling? What a lovely endearment!

Lifting his hands from their invisible bonds at his sides, he drew her into his arms and settled her against his chest. One hand wrapped around her shoulder, the other burrowed into her hair, drawing her head against him.

In seconds, with her face pressed against his warm chest, Meredith felt the slowing of Rolf's heartbeat. Then the steady rise and fall of his chest. Just like that, he'd fallen into a deep sleep.

She wasn't offended. In fact, she felt rewarded for her efforts to bring him peace.

But Meredith didn't sleep. Nor did she feel much peace that night as slumber evaded her and troubling questions niggled at her brain. Toward dawn, she slipped out of bed and drew the quilt up to Rolf's chest. One arm was thrown over his head, and a thick patch of oddly attractive masculine hair showed in his vulnerable armpit. The other arm lay across the pillow where he had been holding her only moments before.

Tears burned in her eyes as she gazed at him. Then she forced herself to turn away and went downstairs to her computer, where she intended to find some answers.

What do they say about men with big feet? . . .

It was eight o'clock before Meredith heard Rolf awaken. Soon after, she heard the sound of the shower running. She'd left a pile of Jared's old clothing for him, along with a pair of battered running shoes. They would probably be too tight.

Getting up from the computer, she went into the kitchen

to prepare breakfast. She would have to go to the supermarket soon. There wasn't much in the fridge. Deciding on French toast, she broke an egg into a bowl with milk, hesitated, then added two more eggs, figuring Rolf's appetite would probably be huge after his meager meal the night before.

When she'd prepared ten slices of French toast, she placed them in the warming cycle of her microwave, set the table, and laid out butter and maple syrup. Then she prepared a pitcher of orange juice from concentrate and turned on the coffee maker.

She could still hear the shower running, so she returned to her computer and her distressing Norse journeys on the Internet. Thus far, way too much of what she'd learned confirmed Rolf's preposterous stories. There had been a powerful Jarl Eric Tryggvason in the Vestfold region of Norway in 997, and one of his sons had been a shipbuilder and noted warrior. Eric's brother, Olaf Tryggvason, had reigned as high king of Norway at that time. Aelfgifu, queen of Britain and wife of Aethelred the Unready, had been weak and plain, just as Rolf had said. She'd died of childbed fever, possibly in 997.

How did Rolf know all this historical trivia?

Punching in her password now, she waited for her computer program to log on her access. Tapping her fingertips nervously while the computer processed her data, she made plans.

She intended to email her brother Jared in Norway, and she had some questions for Mike, as well, still not convinced that he and Jared didn't have something to do with Rolf's arrival. But she'd tried Mike earlier and learned that he was visiting some Army buddies in Bangor for the weekend.

"What are you doing, Merry-Death?"

Meredith jumped, not having realized that Rolf had come

up behind her. Placing a palm over her thudding heart, she glanced back over her shoulder and had to stifle a groan. Lord, the man was gorgeous.

Wearing the same black sweatpants she'd given him the night before, he'd donned a gray Adidas T-shirt, tucked in at the waist where his talisman belt was clasped—an incongruous combination, but somehow it fit his Viking image. He'd pulled back his damp hair with a rubber band, and he'd shaved, revealing even more dramatic good looks. Lines of grief bracketed his eyes and grim mouth, but he appeared well rested.

Never breaking eye contact, he placed his left hand on her shoulder and squeezed. "Thank you," he said huskily, and Meredith knew he referred to the comfort she'd offered the night before.

She nodded her acknowledgment and he stepped away. Then she noticed what he carried in his other hand.

"What are these?" he asked, sitting in a straight-backed chair near hers.

She smiled. "Those are jockey shorts. Underwear."

He held the white briefs up in front of him and scoffed. "Nay, they are too small to a hold a man's parts."

She scoffed back. "They stretch . . . even for the biggest *man parts*." But then she concluded, with embarrassment, that he must not be wearing anything under his sweats. *Lordy!*

"And these?" he asked.

"Athletic socks. You know—" she searched for words he would understand—"ummm . . . hose, that's the word. You put them on your feet before you put on your shoes."

He nodded his understanding, and did just that, after some clumsy efforts to figure just how it was done. Then he lifted an eyebrow and held up the last of the items he'd brought with him, Jared's decrepit sneakers.

"Those are Jared's old running shoes," she informed him, dropping down to her knees in front of him to help put them on.

"Really? Men in your country have shoes just for running?"

"Yes," she said with a laugh. It did sound funny now that he mentioned it.

"And do they have special *braies* for sitting?"

"No," she grunted out as she tried to force one of the shoes onto his foot. The shoes were, indeed, at least two sizes too small. "You must wear a size-thirteen shoe. You know what they say about Vikings with big feet, don't you?" She'd blurted out that last observation, and instantly regretted it.

Rolf looked down at her with a puzzled frown. "Nay, what do they say about Vikings with big feet? And why is your face so red?" Then a grin tugged at the edges of his lips. "Could it be the same thing they say about Saxons with big noses?"

She decided to change the subject. "Do you think you can stand to wear them? Your toes must be cramped."

He shrugged. "'Tis no worse than wet leather boots in the midst of a battle." Then he stood, did a couple of deep knee bends and ran in place for a few seconds. "Yea, I warrant a man could run like the wind in these cloth boots," he said, flashing her a dazzling, bone-melting smile. "Now show me this box you were staring at when I walked in. Blessed Thor, I ne'er saw a land with so many magic boxes."

He knew more about wood than a woodpecker . . .

A short time later, Geirolf sat blinking with amazement, trying desperately to process all the information Merry-Death and her come-pewter flashed out. "'Tis sorcery, pure and simple, of that I have no doubt, but sorcery of the most wonderful nature. Letters and pictures and all the wisdom in the world are contained in this little box . . . in the . . . what did you call it? Oh, yes, the seedy-rome."

She laughed.

He'd no doubt mispronounced one of the hellish words in this new language. "You are a mean-spirited wench to garner pleasure from my discomfit."

"It's just that you sound so cute."

"Cute? Me? Do you treat me like a lackwit pup?" He shook his head. *Cute?* "Leastways, I intend to master the magic in this come-pewter box," he snapped. "From birth, my father and mother encouraged learning about all things, in nature and in the world. 'From knowledge comes strength,' my father often said. 'Even for fighting men, the brain is as powerful a weapon as the sword arm.'"

"Your father sounds like a very wise man." Her raised brow belied her compliment.

"You are loath to believe we *heathen barbarians* relish wisdom? Nay, do not deny what shows clearly on your dubious face. I told you afore that my mother is Christian, but my father follows the old ways. At birth, he dedicated each of his living sons to the Norse gods."

"So?"

By all the saints! I'd like to wipe that smirk from her pursed lips. Mayhap a dunking in her moat would accomplish the deed. Nay, I must control my temper. For now. Until I master the secrets of all these magic boxes. "If you would bridle your wagging tongue, a man could perchance finish his tale," he told her instead. Truly, the woman could use a lesson or two—or fifty—in being biddable. "As I was relating before your interruption, my brother Magnus's birth-patron is Frey, the god of fertility and prosperity. Magnus has ten living children with his three wives, and he is the best farmer in all Norway."

"Three wives!" Merry-Death commented, as if that were the most important of all the facts he'd imparted. "Three wives!"

He waved a hand airily. "Then there is my brother Jorund, whose patron is Thor, the god of war. Jorund is the fiercest warrior in all lands."

He inhaled deeply at the sudden unhappy thought of possibly never seeing them again. Then he went on brusquely, "And my father dedicated me to Odin, the god of learning. Mayhap you have heard that the all-father sacrificed his one eye to drink wisdom from the well of Mimir?"

"A myth!" Merry-Death sneered. "Besides, you're a shipbuilder, not a scholar. So much for your father dedicating you to wisdom!"

"Ah, but I was not always a shipbuilder. From the time I reached ten winters, I fostered in the Saxon court of King Edgar, my mother's cousin. For five years, I suffered there in that snakepit of conniving noblemen, but I soaked up all that the monk teachers could provide in their monastery schools."

"Really?"

So, the wench was impressed by his learning. And she looked down her nose at his woodworking skills.

"Attend me well, my stiff-necked lady. I cherish the calluses on my palms that mark my trade. I get more pride from building a good ship than translating a Latin text."

Her face flushed at being caught in her condescension. "Oh, I never meant to imply—"

He raised a halting hand. "'Tis of no importance what you think of me. I am my own man."

"How did we get on this conversation anyhow?"

"You were no doubt rebuking me for one thing or another, as all women do."

"What was that noise?" Merry-Death said.

"I was speaking."

"Not that, you dolt." She peered at him over the top of an unusual piece of silver-and-glass jewelry she wore on the bridge of her nose and latched over the tops of her ears. Women wore diadems, or circlets, over their foreheads in his world, to hold their head rails in place. The nose was a very strange place to put an ornament, in his opinion. Ah, well, women were always finding barmy means to adorn themselves. Next they would be putting rings in their noses.

His stomach let out a growl, and he realized that it must have been grumbling for some time. That was the noise she referred to. "I do not suppose you have food to offer a starving man, other than worms?"

She smiled at the brute and led him into her kitchen. Men! Mention food and even the fiercest of them tamed down. "No, we're having French toast."

"French toast!" Rolf jeered, at first. "Many a time have I journeyed to Frankland, and ne'er have I seen such." But he scarfed down eight of the ten slices drowning in butter and syrup, drank one glass of orange juice and three cups of coffee, which he asserted must be the beverage of the gods.

Afterward, they went outside to examine the longboat.

"Do women in your country always wear men's *braies*?" he asked. "Not that I am complaining."

Meredith glanced up to see the rogue's sparkling eyes riveted on the back end of her too-tight Levis—Jillie's cast-offs, which she'd put on this morning, along with a short-waisted, white angora sweater. "No, women don't wear *braies* all the time. And we call them pants or slacks in this country, not *braies*. These particular kinds of pants are known as blue jeans. You'll have to buy a few pairs for yourself, if you don't already have them."

He looked skeptical but said nothing more, as they'd arrived at the project site. Turning immediately serious, Rolf surveyed the two open-sided, roofed shelters in the clearing. One protected the vast amount of timber needed for the seventy-foot longship, which sat uncompleted under the other shelter.

Rolf first went to the wood shed, which housed already cut, wedge-shaped planks, as well as enormous trees. Gramps had told her one time that it would take eleven oak trees, at least sixteen feet tall, not to mention a fifty- or sixty-foot tree for the keel, to make just one longship of this size.

Rolf frowned and made tsking sounds of disgust as he knelt before some of the wood, rubbing it with his fingertips, testing its weight, even smelling it.

Meredith walked up to his side. "What's wrong?"

"Who was the fool who left this wood to dry out? Every good shipbuilder knows green timber is best for the planking. Once seasoned, it becomes too brittle to work." He stood and glared at her as if she was to blame for the gross incompetence.

"There was no fool, you fool. My grandfather died suddenly last October—" Her voice broke and she couldn't immediately go on. Finally, she cleared her throat and continued. "There was no one to take over the project."

He tried to put a comforting hand on her shoulder, but she shifted away. She didn't want his pity. "All of Gramps's notes were available, and his assistant, Mike Johnson, was here, but no one really had the expertise to supervise such a project. Ever since I got here in January, we've been trying to hire someone to take over my grandfather's position, and this project."

Rolf nodded. "'Tis a question of honor."

Meredith's eyes shot up at his perception. How did he know she'd felt that way? That leaving her grandfather's dream incomplete was somehow a disgrace to his memory?

That finishing the longship would be a gesture of love and respect? Fighting back the emotion that choked her, she asked, "Can we do anything to salvage the wood?"

"Some of it," he said, "and the discarded pieces will not be wasted. They can be put to good use as rudders, blocks, clamps, and skids."

"Look at those peculiar tree limbs," she called out to him. Rolf was already on the other side, examining each of the trees and cut planks. Among all the straight trees and precisely cut wedge planks, there were some curved limbs, even forked jointures of tree limbs.

Rolf shook his head sadly. "Those are useless now. The curved timbers are needed for the ribs and knees of the ship, and the forks for tholes and keelsons, but they should have been stored underwater to keep the wood flexible."

As they moved over to the longship, Rolf gave it equally professional scrutiny. Meredith was more and more impressed with his knowledge. Wherever he'd come from, the guy was the answer to her prayers . . . well, her prayers for a shipbuilder, anyway.

Yeah, right. Like I'm not noticing all that suntanned skin and the muscles bulging under those upper-arm bracelets. Like my heart doesn't skip a beat when he smiles. Like I'm not gawking when he bends over and stretches the material of those black sweatpants.

"What did you say?" Rolf said, straightening.

"Nothing," she said, hating the blush that heated her face. The little grin that twitched at his lips told her he knew exactly where she'd been staring. "Let's go back inside and start on your English lesson. You'll never be able to read Gramps's notes or understand his blueprints unless you have a rudimentary ability to read English."

"I told you, I *can* read English," he protested.

"Yeah, yeah, yeah! We're back to the Viking prince stuff again," she grumbled as they walked back toward the house.

He swatted her on the behind and cautioned, "Best you curb your tongue, wench, or I will show you what else a Viking can do, besides build longships."

She should have chastised him for taking such a liberty, but she saw the teasing glimmer in his eyes. He was an arrogant beast, really he was. Too bad he was so attractive, as well. "Not all women are impressed with virile Viking clods, you know."

"Truly?" he asked with amazement. "Whene'er my brothers and I go a-Viking, women always fall over themselves to get to us, no matter the country. Especially Saxon women. They claim we are much taller and more comely than their ugly English men."

"Hah! The way I hear it, Vikings washed more often than Saxon men. That's what attracted the women. You didn't smell quite so bad."

He grinned. "Well, there is that, too."

There is hunger, and then there is HUNGER . . .

Four hours later, Meredith sat back in her chair in the library and stretched.

They'd made incredible progress. Rolf was rapidly learning how to read English, thanks in part to her grandfather's numerous English–Old Norse texts and software programs. Rolf must be very intelligent to grasp all the principles so easily, but Meredith sensed that it was more than that. She almost believed his assertion that the talisman had magic powers. How else could he already have mastered the alphabet and rudimentary grammar? How else could he have managed to work the computer keyboard as he studied data?

His childlike enthusiasm for learning touched her. He

didn't balk at any of her instructions, even the boring, rote drawing of the alphabet.

"Why are you so eager to learn all of this so quickly?" she asked finally. "And don't give me that nonsense about being dedicated to the god of wisdom."

He glanced up with surprise from the third-grade reader he'd been studying—one that had been hers as a child. "So I can return home," he answered simply and went back to his book.

Meredith's heart stopped at his declaration, and she wondered how she could feel such desolation at the idea of losing a man she'd just met. He meant nothing to her, other than as a shipbuilder. He was a means to an end. Once that project was completed, it would be good riddance, right?

Wrong, wrong, wrong.

She didn't know how it had happened—perhaps she was pathetically lonely—but Rolf had burrowed his way into her life and possibly even her heart in one short day. And his absence would leave a gaping hole; she just knew it would. She would have to protect herself.

"That's enough for today," she declared, reaching over his shoulder and shutting the book. "How about some lunch?"

He nodded his agreement and stood, stretching his arms wide and arching his back to remove the kinks from sitting for so long. She refused to look, already embarking on a plan of self-protection.

A short time later, Rolf leaned against the kitchen counter while she opened a can of tomato soup and made grilled cheese sandwiches. She really needed to grocery shop this afternoon.

As she moved around the tiny kitchen, he watched her every move, as if memorizing them for future reference. Maybe he was an alien come to study earthly civilization. Hey, it was no more implausible than Rolf's time-travel story.

His constant scrutiny made her unnaturally nervous. Probably because she kept remembering how he'd looked in her bed last night, how they'd almost made love.

"Tell me about that talisman," she finally said, seeking something to distract her thoughts. "How do you figure a belt clasp has magic powers?"

"Huh? What magic clasp? Oh, nay, you misunderstand. 'Tis not the clasp that is the talisman. The clasp is just a protective covering."

She turned the soup on low and put two more grilled cheese sandwiches in the frying pan, after removing two that were done. Then she gave him her full attention. "What do you mean?"

He removed the belt and demonstrated. In the back of the large, circular disc clasp was a secret lever that he sprang, releasing the back side and exposing an exquisite gold cross inside. About three inches at its widest point, the crucifix wasn't a pendant, although it probably could have been used as such. The back of the cross was rough; obviously it had broken off from another piece.

"Oh, it's beautiful! May I hold it?"

He nodded, handing it to her. As soon as he placed it in her palm, she felt its pulsing heat. She glanced up at him quickly, and she saw that he understood what she was feeling.

"What is it?" she asked.

"A gilt frontispiece that my father tore off a Bible three years past whilst pillaging Lindisfarne—Holy Island—in Britain."

Meredith put a hand to her forehead in confusion. "Wait a minute. The famous Viking attack on the Lindisfarne monastery took place about two hundred years before that, in the late eighth century."

Rolf frowned at her interruption. "This was the second attack on Lindisfarne, and—"

"Aha! You said you weren't into raping and pillaging."

He made a tsking sound at being interrupted again. "I said that my family, personally, does not indulge in rape. I ne'er said we do not pillage. Pillaging is an honorable Viking endeavor. In truth, Saxons and Franks also are quite adept at pillaging and plundering. And I did not say my father attacked the Lindisfarne monastery. The good monks left the island a century ago. Nay, my father took the frontispiece from a villager whose family had stolen the holy book afore the priests left. So, you see, 'twas not really stealing since the item was stolen to begin with."

"Go on, then," she said with a sigh of resignation. The man had an answer for everything.

"Three years past, in 994, my father joined his brother Olaf—"

"The king of Norway?"

"Yea, Olaf Tryggvason, the king of Norway. If you keep interrupting me, wench, I will ne'er finish my saga."

It was becoming a saga, all right.

"My father, a Norwegian jarl, along with King Olaf and Sven Forkbeard, the king of Denmark, banded together for a grand invasion of Britain. Ninety-four warships there were in the combined fleet—many of them ships I had built. 'Twas the most formidable Viking attack on Britain in more than a half century."

"Who won?"

Rolf shrugged. "Many of the British nobles were prepared to accept Sven as ruler, but London was defended stubbornly just the same. And, as always, there was much bickering in the Danish and Norwegian ranks. 'Twas an unnatural alliance, you see, betwixt two Viking rulers who'd been trying for years to gobble each other up. In the end, Aethelred bought their allegiance with a danegeld of sixteen thousand pounds."

Meredith was more confused than ever. "What does all this have to do with the talisman and the holy relic?"

"Sore angry was my father when he left Britain three years ago. Angry at his brother Olaf who stayed behind at the Saxon court, promising Christian conversion of all Norsemen. Angry at the weak-spined Aethelred who can be trusted only so far. Angry at the gods who failed to watch over the dead warriors. Mostly, he was angry at the Christian God since my mother had talked my father into baptism afore sailing."

"So, in retaliation, he plundered a Christian monastery on the way home," Meredith offered.

"That he did . . . except that he did not realize the monastery was no longer there." He waved his hand in a careless gesture. "So, he raided some homes instead and found their hidden riches."

Wealthy churches had been the targets of many Viking raids in the tenth century; Meredith knew that from her studies. That didn't mean she believed Rolf's story. "Go on," she encouraged, nonetheless. "Why do you refer to this particular object as a talisman? What's so special about it?"

"'Tis not the crucifix itself that is important, but the relic buried in its depths during the forging."

"Relic?"

"Yea, three eyelashes from the lid of St. Cuthbert, a former monk at Lindisfarne, wrapped around a sliver of wood. The splinter comes from the staff of Moses. He was the holy man in the Christian Bible who rid the ancient lands of pestilence through the powers of his staff."

"I know who Moses was," she snapped. "Lord, you do tell a good story. Not that I really believe there is such a relic in that cross, but assuming it's true, what is its significance to you or your father?"

"Much guilt has my father suffered for taking the sacred

relic, largely due to my mother's nagging. She believes, and has convinced my father, that the great famine that now plagues Norway can be halted only if the relic is returned to its rightful place on Holy Island. Mayhap it must be buried under the ruins of the monastery, if none of the monkish order be about.

"When the frontispiece is returned, the curse will end. My mother had a vision in which an angel told her so."

Meredith couldn't stop the derisive sound that erupted from her throat. "I'm sorry. I didn't mean to—"

"I am wont to be skeptical, too. About the stolen relic of Moses causing a famine, and its return miraculously ending the pestilence. But I cannot take the chance of being wrong. And I am honorbound to complete the mission for my father."

"So, on the way to return the crucifix to Lindisfarne, Storr Grimmsson . . . the guy you told me about . . . attacked you and stole the relic, right?"

He nodded.

Meredith was getting a headache from all this puzzling information. "So you followed Grimmsson to . . . ?"

"Iceland."

"Iceland. Of course," she said sarcastically. "And from there you chased him to these waters and got shipwrecked."

"Yea," he said brightly. "Now you understand."

Aaarrgh, Meredith shrieked silently and handed the crucifix back to Rolf. After replacing it in its hiding place and putting the belt back on, Rolf sat down at the table. She placed a bowl of soup in front of him, along with a stack of grilled cheese sandwiches and a glass of milk.

"Blood soup!"

She laughed. "It's not blood. It's tomatoes."

"These are someone's toes?" he asked with horror.

"No, you fool. Just eat the soup. It's from a vegetable, and it's good."

He did, and although he wasn't too impressed with the meal, he devoured everything, including the milk, despite his having commented, "A good cup of mead would be preferable to this child's drink."

Meredith made a mental note to buy a six-pack of beer later that day.

"Okay, listen," she said after she'd stacked the dishes in the dishwasher. She was about to tell him to go back into the den and practice his English exercises while she went to the store.

"I'm listening," he drawled against the exposed curve of her neck. He'd snuck up behind her. Darn those athletic shoes, which didn't squeak in warning.

She tried to step away, but he wrapped his arms around her waist from behind and proceeded to release her hair from its knot at the back of her head. "I love your hair," he whispered.

"So you've said before," she said, relishing the praise. False praise, she was sure. No man had ever taken particular note of her hair before. After all, even on a good hair day, it was only brown—no spectacular color—and it was straight as a poker. No feminine curls or waves.

Rolf burrowed his face in it with a sigh as he used one hand to spread its strands over her shoulders. And suddenly her hair felt thick and luxuriant and . . . beautiful.

No sooner did she register that incredible fact than she noticed that his other hand was placed flat against her stomach, like a brand of possession.

Meredith couldn't have moved if she'd wanted to.

And she didn't want to.

"I'm sorry I fell asleep on you yestereve, Merry-Death," he said softly, his lips tracing a path along her jaw to the side of her mouth, his hand moving upward from her stomach, under the hem of her sweater, to rub her bare abdomen.

She made a little mewling sound of distress. Or was it pleasure? She arched her neck back against his shoulder.

"But I'm not tired now," he whispered, and cupped one of her lace-covered breasts. "Are you?"

She practically shot off the floor at the intense, erotic sensations his gentle touch engendered. But she was held pinned against the sink counter by Rolf's lower body, which pressed insinuatingly against the back of her jeans-clad bottom.

"You need not worry about the possibility of a babe," he assured her silkily as he pulled the neckline of her sweater aside and nibbled at the sensitive curve of her shoulder.

"Wh-what do you mean?" Had he actually bitten her shoulder blade? Then licked it?

"Now, sweetling, don't go stiff on me. I just meant that I will make sure you do not breed."

"And how will you do that?" she said testily, turning in his arms. "Since you claim to be a tenth-century Viking, with no modern methods of birth control, just how will you accomplish that remarkable feat?"

"Why are you angry, Merry-Death? I think only of your reputation. Most women would appreciate the consideration."

She lifted a brow in question.

"I will not spill my seed inside your body," he explained.

Letting out a whoosh of exasperation, Meredith ducked under his reaching arms. Thank God for the ice-water effect of his words on her impetuous, irresponsible near-capitulation to his seductive efforts.

"That wouldn't be necessary, *if* we were going to make love. Which we're not. Because, you see—" she took a breath as she gathered the nerve to disclose her painful secret— "because I can't have children."

He stared at her for a long moment, and then said only, "Oh, Merry-Death, I am so sorry."

She closed her eyes briefly to hide her reaction to his sympathy. Why hadn't he said something callous like everyone else? Such as, "It doesn't matter. Having children is no big deal. You can always adopt. It doesn't mean you're less a woman." Or, worse, the remark Jeffrey had made before their divorce, "Maybe you weren't meant to have children."

Instead, Rolf had understood her pain and shared it.

When she finally got her emotions under control, she opened her eyes to see him staring at her intently, waiting out her inner struggle. He put one hand on the belt buckle and the other over his heart, holding her eyes the whole time, and all he said was, "I feel your pain."

She nodded and forced herself to change the subject. She'd decided in that split second that they both needed a lighter mood. "Good thing you've got your walking shoes on, Rolf."

"Why?" he asked with trepidation.

"We're going to the mall."

CHAPTER FIVE

⊗

When all else fails, go shopping . . .

Geirolf sat with his legs braced stiff, belted into the seat of Merry-Death's horseless, red wagon. They raced along a local road at an ungodly speed, stirring up dust in their wake.

"Slow down," he gritted out. He was going to wring her foolhardy neck . . . if he ever escaped from this box. *Box!* Thor's toenails, this was a land of boxes!

"Huh?" Merry-Death had been humming along with music that came from a shelf in the box, something she called the class-call station. "I'm only going thirty-five."

"Well, that explains it," he snapped. All the perplexing words and objects in this new land tired him mightily. He wanted nothing more than to return to his homeland, where life was simple and unmagical. He looked idly through the side window, and then looked again. "Oh, Good Lord! Stop the box, Merry-Death. Make haste. There is much danger."

Reacting instinctively, she slammed one foot against a lever on the floor and they came to a screeching halt at the side of the road. Despite the seat restraint, his forehead hit the front window and his knees banged against the dashing-board.

"What? What is it?" Merry-Death asked him in alarm.

Rubbing the already rising knob on his brow, he pointed up to the sky. "There is a huge shiny bird hovering overhead.

Surely one of Loki's vultures is about to attack. 'Tis so big it could swallow an entire troop of soldiers in one gulp. I have heard of such in the sagas."

Merry-Death scanned the area where he pointed, then giggled. "Oh, you!" She jabbed his arm in reprimand. "That's just an airplane."

Since she didn't share his concern, he released the breath he'd been holding. After she explained airplanes to him, he stared at her speechless. He could hardly credit her claims—that a machine had been invented that allowed people to fly in the air over long distances—even oceans.

Scowling at his assertion that he'd never heard of an airplane before, she started the car up again. The woman's belief that he was a liar, or worse, was beginning to annoy him. And he couldn't stop thinking about the amazing metal bird he'd just seen. As he worried his bottom lip with his upper teeth, he tried to understand. "Mayhap we should go back to your keep. I'm not certain I want to see any more witchly arts today."

She laughed gaily. "Too late now. We're there."

He wasn't exactly sure what constituted "there," something Merry-Death called a shipping mall, but she'd promised it would be amusing. He scanned the area as she drove her box off the roadway into a huge clearing where hundreds of similar boxes, of different colors and shapes, sat side by side. No ships, at all, in this shipping mall.

As she steered her box into a stall and turned off the key, he let out a whoosh of relief and then peered around with bewilderment. "When does the amusement begin?"

She ignored his sarcasm and helped unbuckle his seat belt. Grinning mysteriously, she told him to follow her. Which wasn't easy to do since he couldn't figure out how to open the bloody door of the bloody box.

They began to walk toward the shipping mall structure

when Geirolf stopped suddenly and exclaimed, "By the Holy Rood! Of all the things I have seen in this outlandish country, that is the most outlandish of all."

"What?" Merry-Death craned her neck this way and that, unable to locate the source of his incredulity.

"There," he said, pointing to an elderly woman walking with a pig on a leash. It was the ugliest pig he'd ever seen in all his born days, with a belly that drooped almost to the ground. "Is the wench taking yon hog to market?"

Merry-Death laughed. "No, that's a pot-bellied pig. It's a pet."

"A pet?" he sputtered. "Like a kitten?"

"Uh-hum. Isn't it darling?"

"Have you suffered a head blow of late?"

Moments later, they entered the glass doors of the shipping mall, and Geirolf jerked back with surprise. Every person in this world must have assembled here, and they all chattered and shrieked with good humor as they briskly walked along—singly, in pairs, and in threatening groups.

He wished he had Brave Friend with him. He felt defenseless without his sword at hand. But Merry-Death didn't appear frightened, so he trailed after her.

First, Merry-Death said she had to get some money from an aye-team machine. She inserted a square of some strange material called plays-tick into a slot, and Geirolf scoffed when he saw what came out of the wall. It was mere parchment, not coins.

She explained that, while coins existed in her country, paper, another word for parchment, counted as trading tender, as well. He accepted her pronouncement dubiously, but another distressing thought occurred to him. "I have no money with me. How will I buy clothing and all the items I'll need whilst in your land?"

"You don't have to worry—"

"I know," he said with sudden enlightenment, pulling off one of his armlets. "I can sell this for coin, can I not?"

"You could sell it, yes, but—"

"Why do you hesitate? Is it worth naught here? In my world, jewelry is a portable commodity, to be bartered or cut into pieces for money."

"Rolf, you could probably buy a small country with the money you'd get for such a priceless object. It's just that it's not necessary. There's a salary that goes with the position of head shipbuilder for the Trondheim project. Not a large one, but sufficient for your needs. I'll give you an advance."

He narrowed his eyes at her. "Are you sure? I have always paid my own way. And, for a certainty, I've ne'er let a woman care for my needs. I would not accept charity from you."

"Save your pride, Rolf. I'll let you know when your tab gets too high."

"Well, then, we are agreed," he said, slipping the armlet back on. Then, he turned with her to advance warily into the deep bowels of the shipping mall. But, he vowed, the first purchase he was going to make was a sword.

He saw several couples walk by—obviously lovers—with their hands entwined. So, he reached over and took Merry-Death's hand in his, lacing their fingers. He liked the way her pulse beat against his at the wrist.

And she obviously did, too, because she glanced up at him with surprise, but did not pull away. And the slight coloring of her cheeks betrayed how his touch affected her.

Good! He wanted to affect her. And a lot more.

"Ooh, ooh, ooh! Look at that. Isn't he adorable?" Meredith squealed and began to tug him in another direction.

"Wh-what?" he stammered, unable to discern the object of her ardor. All he saw was glass-fronted market stalls and an overabundance of people.

"It's a Great Dane. Oh, I always wanted to have a Great Dane."

"Would a great Norseman suffice?"

She started to choke with laughter at his words, and he slapped her on the back.

"Well, there is naught a Dane can do that a Norwegian can't do better," he said huffily. "And, frankly, I do not appreciate your raving on about other men in my presence."

"Rolf, a Great Dane is the name of a dog breed." She dabbed at her brimming eyes with a paper handkerchief, then indicated with a wave of her hand the forlorn puppy that sat in front of the glass window, yipping and yapping. It was probably laughing at him, too.

"I knew that," he lied and walked bravely off into the shipping mall. *Jealousy! For the first time in my life, I have exhibited that lackwit emotion. My brothers would laugh their bloody heads off. My father would say 'twas past time I suffered like all men. My mother would be arranging a wedding. I am doomed.* The next being—man or beast—that laughed at him was going to feel the bite of his sword. Once he bought a sword, that was.

The closest he came to a sword, however, was something called a laser pointer. It would have to do, for now.

Pretty in pink . . .

Two hours later, they sat at a table in the food court. Bags of clothing and other purchases were stacked at their feet.

Meredith hadn't had so much fun in years.

"Now *this* is food fit for the gods," Rolf declared enthusiastically as he finished off his sixth slice of sausage and mushroom pizza. "But what is this fondness your people have for bodily raiment? I've had my fill of trying on garments and shoes for one day."

She nodded. Actually, they'd bought more than enough to

last Rolf for now. Two pairs of jeans and a half dozen T-shirts, underwear—he preferred boxers—and socks, and a pair of work boots . . . a whopping size fourteen.

Rolf had shown a surprising fashion instinct, selecting a pair of pleated, Ralph Lauren khaki slacks and two Polo shirts, along with a pair of sinfully expensive loafers of the softest leather.

"This shopping is more tiring than a day of battle exercises," Rolf grumbled, pushing away from the table and giving her his full regard.

Meredith didn't like it when he studied her like that. It made her very uncomfortable. And he knew it. She could tell by the way he grinned, slowly and lazily. "I agree . . . about shopping being exhausting," she said, picking at imaginary lint on her jeans. "And we still have to stop at the supermarket. The way you eat, I'll need to stock up on lots more food."

"Do you say that I eat overmuch? That I am fat?" He threw back his shoulders with affront, which only accentuated his superb body.

"Hardly." He wore the plain old gray T-shirt and black sweats of that morning, along with the talisman belt, but if he got any more attention from ogling girls and oversexed women in this mall, she was going to scream. And Rolf didn't even seem to notice the pivoting heads as he strolled along because he was doing his own gaping at each of the new wonders he encountered; water fountains, ballpoint pens, aquariums. Besides, he was probably used to female adulation, looking as he did.

As they headed back toward the mall entrance, weighed down with bags, Rolf stopped suddenly.

Now what?

"Give me fifty dollars, Merry-Death, and mark it in my

book." Rolf had made her purchase a small notebook to keep track of all his expenses. His male pride again.

"Why? I thought we got everything."

"Not quite," he said and veered off to the right after she handed him the bills.

"Oh, no," she groaned, realizing that he was entering Victoria's Secret.

"Rolf," she hissed, finally catching up, her bags banging against her legs, "what are you doing in here?"

"All day we have been shopping for me, but naught for you. I want to buy you a gift." He held up a flame-red, see-through nightie. "What do you think?"

Her face heated, turning a matching flame red, no doubt. "I don't wear things like that to bed. I prefer . . . nightshirts."

"I know," he said dolefully.

"You know?" she squeaked out.

He shot her a glower of consternation. "I was tired last night, not dead."

Oh, geez, what else did he see? Or remember?

He put the hooker-style outfit back on the rack, and said idly, "In truth, I prefer you wear no bed garments at all."

As her heart started racing, he forged ahead into the store.

"These would show off those wonderfully long legs of yours." He stuck a pair of French-cut silk panties in her face. "What are they?"

"Underwear. Rolf, please," she whispered, mortified at all the attention they were getting. And, oh, Lord, was that one of her students over there—no, two of her students, Amy Zapalski and Joleen Frank?

He riffled through the assorted colors till he'd found a flesh-tinted pair edged with white lace, held it out before her as if to judge the size, and then tucked it under his arm. "Just right," he said with a wink.

Next, before she could grab his arm and drag him out the door, he said, "Aaaah," and hightailed it to the teddy section.

"What purpose do these garments serve?" he was asking a pencil-thin, blond sales clerk who'd appeared like a flash of lightning at his side.

"Those are teddies, hon. Don't tell me you've never seen a teddy before."

"Nay, never," he replied, his mouth dropping practically to the floor with appreciation as she held up one scandalous creation after another.

"That one," he said, stopping her at a pink satin, two-piece outfit, with tiny straps. Very simple and very sexy.

"What do you think, sweetling?" he asked, drawing her to his side with an arm looped over her shoulders. They'd dropped their packages to the floor back by the see-through nighties.

"I think you're crazy, that's what I think," she muttered, but when he called her sweetling, she felt warm and tingly all over. Like a schoolgirl. *Oh, Lord!*

"She loves it," Rolf told the salesclerk, who was assessing him like a giant cotton candy she'd like to inhale. He squeezed Meredith closer and kissed the top of her head.

"No, I don't love it," she argued. "It's . . . it's pink."

"And?"

"I'm thirty-five years old," she informed the brute in an undertone. "Thirty-five-year-old women don't wear pink."

"They should," he proclaimed, but by now his focus was diverted elsewhere. He was gaping at a mannequin in the back of the store wearing the undergarment sensation of the nineties.

"Bloody hell!" he breathed.

"That's it. No way! Never!" she asserted. "I draw the line at a Miracle Bra. Come on." She tugged on his arm.

"Miracle Bra," he said on a sigh, but he followed after her. While paying for his purchases, he remarked to her in an aside, "I have a brother Magnus who would buy a dozen of those, one for each of his mistresses."

She glared at him dubiously.

"He would," Rolf contended. "Magnus has a fondness for big tits."

Meredith sputtered at that crudity.

"Hi, Ms. Foster," Amy Zapalski and Joleen Frank crooned in unison, halting whatever tirade she would have come up with for the coarse Viking. The girls' eyes were glued on Rolf's bulging biceps and tight buns, highlighted when he bent down to pick up a quarter he'd dropped. Then their observation moved on to the items he was purchasing. The girls glanced from Rolf to her to the garments, and giggled.

Meredith cringed. She just knew the rumors would be flying around campus by morning. Professor in hot pink. Or would it be hot professor in pink? Or professor in pink with hot Viking?

Hungry again? Oh, that *kind of hunger! . . .*

Two hours! They'd been in the supermarket for two hours! Meredith had never spent so much time in a grocery store in her entire life.

Of all the odd things this odd Viking had encountered since arriving so oddly in her life, he claimed that the grocery store was the most marvelous. In the fruit section, he'd examined each and every different item, and she'd had to stop him from eating as he went along.

"But where does all this come from?" he'd exclaimed.

"From all over the world."

"On ships?"

"Some of it."

He'd had the same incredulous reaction in the vegetable department. "Who would have e'er guessed that so many bloody vegetables exist."

Then it was the boxes that held all the items in the store, whether they were cereals or pastas or ice cream. "I have ne'er seen a land with such a reverence for boxes."

Hmmm. She'd never thought about it before, but she guessed he was right.

And metal cans, as well, drew his fascination.

But the meat section alarmed him most. "I don't understand. What do men in your country do? What is their role? If they are not the hunters and protectors of their families . . ." His words had trailed off in dismay. "Are men not men here?"

"Men earn the money to take care of their families," she'd tried to explain. "Well, actually, that's not quite true. Today, in most families, the men and women both work. They share duties equally."

"Men are not the heads of the families?"

"The roles aren't defined like that anymore." She'd stumbled in her explanation, and she could see that Rolf was still deeply troubled. The more time they spent in the giant supermarket, the more depressed he seemed to get.

"What's wrong?"

"The excess. There's too much of everything in your land. And it comes too easy. I don't think I'd want to live in such a land. Surely, the men become soft. It's all so confusing."

Meredith couldn't argue with that.

But now, her cart was overflowing, and even Rolf's energies seemed to be flagging.

"What are those?" he asked, nudging her to look at a toddler seated in his mother's cart. The imp was eating Oreos with meticulous detail, taking the two cookies apart carefully, licking the icing with the tip of his little pink tongue, then crunching the outside wafers.

Rolf licked his lips in imitation.

"Those are Oreo cookies," she said with a laugh. Really, Rolf was like a little boy himself sometimes. She pointed to the shelf behind him.

Rolf put three packs in her cart, then added another.

There was only one more aisle Meredith needed to hit. Personal products. She bought Rolf some deodorant, having to explain its purpose.

He sniffed the open Mennen roll-on. "It's acceptable, but it doesn't smell as good as your drek."

Then she bought him a toothbrush, which he considered a good invention, though shredded twigs had done well enough in the past. She hesitated in one last section, then threw a box of condoms in the cart. Forget about pregnancy . . . a woman couldn't be too cautious about AIDS these days.

When Rolf asked what they were, she said she'd explain later. But he was persistent and sounded out the words aloud. "Tro-jan. Cone-dome."

"Rolf. Be quiet," she gritted out.

"Why is your face so red?" he asked suspiciously, looking from her to the package. He stopped in his tracks, refusing to move till she explained. After she did, briefly, he gazed at her in amazement, and then said, "And you bought only one box? Hah!" He scooped two more boxes off the shelf and threw them in the cart.

Smiling from ear to ear, he took the cart out of her hands and rolled it toward the cashier. She finally caught up with him at the checkout line.

"I'm hungry," Rolf growled. "Let's hurry home." He ran a fingertip caressingly along her jaw, tilting up her chin for a brief kiss. The husky tone of Rolf's voice and the smoky haze of his whiskey eyes told her loud and clear that his appetite wasn't for food.

And, Lord help her, Meredith shared the hunger.

And then he promised to drek her . . .

Rolf kissed her shoulder while the bag boy was stuffing their groceries into paper sacks. Even through her sweater, Meredith felt seared by his heat.

The minute they left the store, he pulled her into his embrace and pressed his lips against the inside of one wrist, then the other. The whole time, his eyes held hers with a promise that ricocheted between them.

After they'd put all the bags into the trunk of her car, Rolf backed her up against the fender, bracketed her face with his hands to hold her in place—not that she had any intention of moving—and *really* kissed her. Mouth against mouth. Insistent. Voracious. With age-old expertise, her Viking brushed and slanted and shaped her lips to fit his perfectly. Then he used his tongue to demonstrate the depth of his hunger for her. Meredith's knees would have buckled if she hadn't been braced against the car, pinioned by Rolf's body. Then he pulled back slightly and grinned, as if satisfied with his work.

She practically crawled into the driver's seat and buckled up, then inhaled deeply to calm down. Focusing on her driving, she wasn't immediately aware that Rolf had released his seat belt and moved closer to her. Too late she realized that one arm lay across the back of her seat rest. The fingertips of that hand played with the edges of her hair, and the other hand rested heavily on her knee . . . unmoving, but dangerous.

"Rolf," she protested, "I can't concentrate when you do that."

He grinned against her ear, whispering, "Exactly."

She felt his warm breath before she heard the word, and a delicious shiver traveled through the sensitive whorls of her ear, straight down through her body, making erotic pit stops along the way at her breasts and the vee of her thighs.

She moaned softly and turned off the highway onto the local access road leading to her house.

"Do you like this?" he drawled, and used the tip of his wet tongue to trace all the shell-like crevices, then dart inside.

Meredith arched her neck against the too-intense pleasure that caused her breasts to peak into hard points, and throb. "Don't," she whimpered.

"Doesn't it feel good?" he asked with surprise.

That was when she noticed the hand that had been resting on her knee was roving, a forefinger examining the inseam of her jeans.

"Open your thighs," he coaxed.

She stared straight ahead, trying to convince herself that this lonely road needed her undivided attention. But her legs parted, of their own volition.

Now, while his mouth and teeth and tongue played seductive sex games with her ear and neck, his lone fingertip traced a slow path along the inseam from knee to crotch to the other knee, then back again. Slowly. Over and over. Until she wanted to screech aloud with her increasing arousal and the urge to grab his hand and hold it where she needed it most.

"How do you feel now?"

She remained silent, not wanting to reveal her vulnerability.

"Your breasts," he said huskily, looking at her there, "tell me how they feel."

She made a soft mewling sound of resistance, never having talked like this with a man before. Besides, his teasing fingertip was still tantalizing her with its bold exploration.

"Tell me," he pleaded. "About your breasts. How do they feel?"

She nodded mutely. "Full."

"And?"

She didn't know what to say.

"Are the nipples hard?"

"Very," she confessed thickly. By now, she was creeping along at five miles a hour. She hoped no neighbors were outside to wonder what was wrong.

"Do you want me to touch them?"

She felt tears well in her eyes; that was how much she wanted his touch.

"I've wanted to touch you in that cat fur sweater all day. Every time you moved or stretched, I pictured your breasts underneath, waiting for me."

She expected he would touch her then, but, instead, he sat back on his own side. She gave him a sideways glance and saw that he was equally aroused. "What?"

"We're home," he informed her with a wry grin.

Mortified that she'd lost her decorum so badly, Meredith pulled into the driveway. She couldn't look at him now; he must be laughing at her. She released her seat belt and was about to open her car door when Rolf put his hands on either side of her waist and lifted her so she faced him on top of his lap, straddling him.

"Did you think I would end it so?" he said huskily as he adjusted her against his hardness.

"O-o-oh." She began to keen—a low, alien sound for her.

He placed both hands over her breasts and circled, crooning over the softness of the angora sweater. "I can feel your nipples," he whispered appreciatively. "They are large and hard."

She stiffened against the cataclysmic spirals of pleasure radiating out from the mounds. But, instinctively, she arched her breasts forward, her arms extended backward holding onto his knees. When he took one nipple into his mouth, cloth and all, and began to suckle, they both groaned.

A wetness pooled between her legs, and Meredith realized she'd never in all her life been brought to this point of madness by a man, clothed or unclothed. And certainly not so quickly. Or in broad daylight. In a car.

My brain must be splintering apart.

Then he moved to her other breast and, at the same time, spread his legs wide so that she moved even tighter into the cradle of hips.

It's not my brain that's splintering. It's another body part. And, damn, it feels good.

He palmed her buttocks and showed her how he wanted her to move against him.

And she did.

While she began the slow undulation he demonstrated, he held her face with his fingers twined in her hair, grasping her scalp. Just before he pulled her lips to his, she saw that his parted lips were slack with passion, his suntanned cheeks flushed, and his eyes amber pools of over-the-edge arousal.

As his tongue imitated the thrusts of his hardness against the vee of her outspread legs, wave after wave of a bone-melting climax spun out from her center and she screamed into his mouth. She tried to pull away then, it was too much, but Rolf refused to let her go as he began his own climax, grinding against her from side to side.

He made a low, masculine sound deep in his throat, and, amazingly, Meredith's arousal, once again, began to build and build and build. When he sucked on her tongue, drawing her into his mouth, and jerked against her hard . . . once, twice, three times, she exploded, her thighs trembling with the force of her release.

For what seemed like an eternity, but was probably only a few moments, the only sound in the car was that of their heavy breathing as they fought, forehead to forehead, to calm their racing hearts.

Meredith avoided his eyes. She was absolutely and utterly humiliated. What must he think of her? How could she slide off his lap gracefully and slither out of the car, without having to face him?

"Well, that certainly took the edge off my hunger." He chuckled. "Now we can take a leisurely time with the main course."

She made the mistake of looking at him then.

He wasn't laughing, or teasing. He was stone-cold serious.

She must have gawked because he chucked her under the chin playfully.

Having no way to exit with dignity, Meredith scrambled off him clumsily. "Listen, buster, there isn't going to be any main course. This has got to end right here."

"Why?"

"Because . . . because I don't do things like this."

"And you think I do?" Then, "What kinds of things?"

"Sex with virtual strangers."

"Oh, that."

"Yeah, *that*. You and I have got a business relationship, and that's all," she asserted as she opened the trunk to get the groceries. Lord, the ice cream was probably melted with all the heat they'd generated.

Remaining silent, he took several bags, too, and as they headed toward the front door, she thought, Well, finally, I've got through to the thick-headed fool. Now he understands.

But he immediately quashed that misguided conclusion

of hers by asking, "Would you like to take a shower with me?"

She went slack-jawed with disbelief. Was she talking to a wall here, or just a typical male, who heard only what he wanted?

"I'll even drek you, if you want."

CHAPTER SIX

✧

*T*hree's company, four's a WHAT? . . .

An ominous rumble of thunder followed by a streak of lightning put a quick damper on Rolf's enticing suggestion.

"Ah! Thor must be jealous of my woman-luck."

"Woman-luck?" Was he referring to her? The nerve—assuming he was about to get lucky! Or was he bragging that he'd already scored? Oh, all right, she admitted to herself, perhaps she had given him a *little* encouragement in the car. Well, okay, a lot. But that was no reason for him to—

"Yea, the thunder god throws his mighty hammer *Mjollnir* across the skies, causing lightning bolts, when mortal men offend him. The gods like to think they are the only ones blessed with the love arts."

Love arts? she mouthed silently.

"Best I be careful, or Thor will turn me into a troll." He winked at her before setting his grocery sacks on the stoop.

She hated when he winked. It made her feel all fluttery inside. And one thing thirty-five-year-old women should not be feeling was fluttery. "You already are a troll."

"Oh? You have a taste for trolls then? For a certainty, you moaned your woman-pleasure for this troll moments ago."

She made a clucking sound of disgust. "I did not."

He arched a brow. "Perchance you need a reminder." He advanced closer, running a teasing thumb over her lips.

She backed up against the door, her grocery bag clutched to her chest.

Another clap of thunder.

Rolf grimaced. "You get a reprieve, my lady. I must needs check on that timber afore the rains come."

She relaxed. But only for a moment.

As he walked toward the sideyard and the longship, Rolf called over his shoulder, "Make ready the drek. This Viking just thought of a few troll tricks."

Meredith couldn't help laughing. The light carefree sound carried on the electrified air, surprising her. When was the last time she'd bantered with a man like this? Had she ever?

With a sigh, she turned, scrabbling in her pocket for the key. Before she could insert it, though, the front door swung open. Meredith jumped back, fully expecting another Dark Age intruder to pop out of the woodwork.

"Hi, Aunt Mer," her niece Thea exclaimed as she kissed the air near Meredith's right cheek and reached for one of the grocery bags on the steps. "Great sweater, auntie, but did you know you have two wet stains on the front? Oh, don't be embarrassed. You're probably a slob like me. Genetics, don'tja know? I dropped strawberry ripple ice cream on my jeans at the airport."

Meredith just gaped, too shocked by Thea's appearance to be embarrassed over her sweater's telltale spots. What alien being had invaded her darling niece's body? And, oh, Lord! First a Viking time-traveler, now this . . . creature.

The twelve-year-old girl's straight black hair was parted in the center and hung down to her rear, outlining faded jeans and a tie-dye T-shirt. Well, that was normal adolescent fare. But normalcy ended there. Black lipliner framed her full lips, filled in with dark purple gloss. She wore so much magenta mascara, eyeliner, and shadow that Meredith was surprised the girl could raise her lids. Greenish-brown enamel covered her obviously fake, two-inch fingernails. The pièce de résistance was a tiny hoop earring in her left nostril.

"I hope you don't mind that I let myself in," Thea went on breezily. "I called from the airport but there was no answer, so I hopped a cab. Geez, did you know it costs fifty dollars to take a taxi from Bangor? I only had thirty, and, like, gol-ly, was the cabbie mad! But, not to worry. I remembered where you hide the spare key and went inside. I had to break your piggy bank. Is that okay? I gave the man twenty dollars in quarters, plus a ten dollar tip in dimes. Good thing I listen to so much grunge rock, or I never would have understood some of his swear words." Thea ended her rambling discourse with a sheepish grin.

Setting her grocery sack on the kitchen table, Thea made two more trips for the remaining bags. The whole time, she bit her trembling bottom lip. "It's okay that I came, isn't it, Aunt Mer? I mean, Jillie didn't push me on you, did she? Huh?"

Meanwhile, the girl had discovered the package of Oreos in the top of one bag and was already scarfing them down with little yumming sounds of appreciation.

"Jillie?" Meredith squeaked out, homing in on the most irrelevant of Thea's words. What she'd like to ask was why her sister hadn't told her Thea was already on her way when she'd called last night. Hah! Probably because she'd known Meredith would explode. "Since when do you call your mother Jillie?"

"After I started to get boobs, Mom said we should be more like, you know, sisters. She said she's too young to have a grown daughter. Now we can be best friends. Isn't that cool?"

Thea's sad eyes disclosed how uncool she really thought it was.

Yeah, real cool! Frankly, as far as Meredith could tell, the girl didn't have much of a bust yet, and she was far from grown up. *Jillie, Jillie, Jillie, when are you going to grow up yourself?* "Of course, it's all right that you came," she said, giving her niece's thin shoulders a squeeze. "I love having you here. You're my favorite niece, honey."

"I'm, like, your *only* niece," she said, beaming, "but my name's not Thea anymore, you know. It's Serenity."

"Serenity?" Meredith laughed. "I thought your mother said it was Gourd."

"That was last month." Thea waved the air dismissively. "Everyone kept calling me Gordie, which is so-o-o juvenile. Besides, Serenity is more New Age."

They grinned at each other.

"Aunt Mer, I promise I won't do any . . . you know, stuff . . . like shoplifting . . . or, you know, get into trouble while I'm here. I can't explain why I pull such stupid pranks anyway. I'm not really bad, you know. I'm *not*." Her eyes filled with tears as she pleaded for understanding.

"Oh, sweetie, I know that," Meredith assured her, using a tissue to dab at Thea's wet cheeks. Then, seeking to lighten the conversation, Meredith commented, "Your makeup is so . . . so—"

"Cool?" Thea asked brightly, welcoming the change of subject. "It's the latest from that new company, Urban Blight. Don't you, like, just love it? This lip liner is called Mildew, but my favorite is Slime. You can borrow it sometime."

"Uh, I don't think so."

"Jillie does. In fact, I think she stole my Puke nail enamel. I'm wearing Sludge, but it's not nearly as awesome as Puke."

Meredith put a hand to her forehead. She might just puke

herself with all these disgusting colors staring her in the face.

"Holy cow!" Thea exclaimed then, staring at something behind Meredith. "Holy freakin' cow!"

Meredith didn't have to turn around to know what she would see. The troll.

"Oh, my God! Aunt Mer, are you makin' it with Kevin Sorbo? We watched a marathon of his old Hercules shows on DVD last week. Wait till the kids in Chicago hear this. Where's the phone?"

"You're not making any long-distance calls, young lady," Meredith declared. She would think about Thea's implication that she was "makin' it" with a man later.

"Who's Calf in Shore Bow?" Rolf asked, sauntering into the room. "You mentioned him afore, Merry-Death." Leaning against the refrigerator, he dried raindrops off his bare arms and wet hair with a dish towel. The whole time he watched with amusement as the two of them watched him. For a long moment, the only sound in the room was the steady downpour of rain outside.

"You don't know who Kevin Sorbo is? Gol-ly! You look just like him. He's the actor who plays Hercules on TV. He is, like, such a boffo hunk." She blushed at her last words.

"Hercules?" Rolf frowned in confusion.

"You know, the son of that Greek God, Zeus. Hercules was so strong and brave he was called on to do all these amazing feats. Tell him, Aunt Mer."

"Greek? I'm not a Byzantine. I'm a Viking."

"A Viking? Whoa! You're, like, a pro-football player? Aunt Mer-e-dith! I never knew you were into sports."

"Just the bedsport," Rolf mumbled. "Leastways, a man can hope." The poor man was obviously confused by the whole conversation. Luckily, her niece hadn't heard his remark.

"Do you know Warren Moon?" Thea asked.

"Nay. Only the gods do war in moons. All my battles have been fought on earth, or sea."

"Huh? I meant Warren Moon of the Minnesota Vikings."

"Oh. I am of the Norse Vikings. We tend to be raiders, rather than plunderers."

"Did they sell the Minnesota Vikings to the Oakland Raiders? Hmmm. You'd think I woulda heard of that. Do you have a Super Bowl ring?" Thea checked out his bare fingers and sighed with disappointment.

"I only wear arm rings. What is a bowl ring?"

"Oh, Lord!" Meredith groaned.

"Wait a minute. You said *Norse Viking*. Are you, like, from Norway?" Thea asked.

Meredith's head shot up, and she gave Rolf a warning glance. She'd already advised him earlier when they were at the mall that it was not a good idea to tell people his time-travel nonsense.

Rolf hesitated and rubbed his belt buckle as if choosing his words carefully. "Yea, I am from Hordaland . . . the Norse lands across the sea."

"Thea—I'm sorry, I just can't call you Serenity, my tongue trips over the word—Thea, this is Geirolf Ericsson. He's come to help with the longship project. Bear with him a little, he's having trouble with the language."

"Your aunt is giving me lessons," he revealed, his lips twitching with amusement at her discomfort.

"Cool!" Thea said, already heading for the living room, the newspaper TV section in hand. "I'm on spring break for the next three weeks, you know. Maybe I can, like, help with lessons."

Three weeks? Meredith felt her stomach churn. She needed an antacid badly. Probably the start of ulcers, or something equally dire, like hormone overload.

Left alone for a moment, Rolf added with a determined

gleam in his eyes before he followed after the girl, "And I plan to teach your aunt a few things in return."

"Cool!" Thea repeated.

Never in a million years would Meredith ask what, but her imagination kicked in with a vengeance. And "cool" didn't begin to describe her vision.

Getting to know you . . .

By nine o'clock that night, Thea was already conked out in the bed up in the loft that she would share with Meredith. Without makeup and wearing a Mickey Mouse nightshirt, she looked like the twelve-year-old child she was. Meredith's heart went out to the needy girl, but she wasn't sure how to help her.

Exhausted herself by the day's events, Meredith carried a pile of linens downstairs to make a bed for Rolf on the sofa. She stopped midstep at the poignant sight of the huge man gazing forlornly into the fireplace. An elbow propped on the mantle supported his tilted head. His free hand held a poker, which he used distractedly to stir the blazing fire.

Meredith knew he was distressed by all the "modern" inventions he'd seen today, from the mall to the television, which he'd watched in disbelief for hours with Thea. But she still couldn't accept his time-travel story. There had to be another explanation.

The academic in her sought for a logical explanation. She still wanted to believe that her brother Jared or Mike had found this skilled shipbuilder for her, possibly from some primitive region where there were no televisions or malls.

She'd drawn a sketch, from memory, of the talisman belt and its hidden "relic," which she intended to fax first thing tomorrow morning to Jared, as well as Jillie and her parents. Perhaps they could do a little research on its background. Meredith was convinced that the unique object was more than a trinket. She prayed it wasn't stolen from a museum collection.

Furthermore, Meredith was considering asking Mike to check with his buddies at the local police station to see if there was a missing-person alert for some escapee from an asylum. Or a con artist on the loose posing as a Viking shipbuilder. Geez, that second possibility sounded ludicrous, even to her.

The whole time these thoughts ran through her puzzled brain, the man in question watched her silently, like a hawk, his golden eyes smoldering. Having showered earlier, he wore a pristine white T-shirt tucked into a pair of his new jeans. A rubber band held his long hair back at the nape, exposing the strong line of his jaw and the graceful curve of his neck. His big, narrow feet were bare, and looked amazingly sexy. Not that he needed any help in the sexy department. Oh, Lordy, no.

As she approached, he clucked disapprovingly at the sheets and blankets she carried. "I take it that I am exiled to sleep alone tonight."

A rush of heat filled her face. "That's right. It wouldn't be proper with Thea here. And, actually, you and I need a cooling-off period."

Raising a brow in question, he pushed away from the fireplace. "And if I do not wish to cool off?" he asked huskily. "And if I wish to finish what we started earlier today?"

He moved only one step toward her, but Meredith panicked, dropping the linens and jerking backward, stepping behind the sofa. She needed to put some distance between them. Every time he got close, her brain short-circuited.

Geirolf stopped his advance, but not because of the wench's measly protest. Every time he got close to the witch, he lost his ability to think clearly. And after all he'd seen and heard that day, more than anything he needed a clear head to figure out how to get back to his own time.

The wench thought to put him off by wearing loose *braies* and a matching oversized shirt of black silk—a type of sleeping apparel called pay-jam-hose. But he already knew what she hid beneath . . . by touch, if not yet by sight. When the time was right, she would share his bed furs—if he could find a bed fur in this godforsaken land—and she would wear the sleeping garment preferred by most Viking women . . . and men. Bare skin.

She would enoy the coupling with him, too. Geirolf had a sense about such matters, based on years of experience and a male instinct for a woman's ripeness. Merry-Death pretended tartness and an inclination to molder on the vine, but he knew better. Her juices were rising and her soft flesh yearned to be plucked.

But not yet. Not tonight. Too much depended on the fate of his mission here. His father's trust. The famine. His own honor. The warrior in him sensed danger brewing all around, and he had to be alert.

Still, the mating urge roiled his blood, and he fought to bank his appetite. Oh, he'd have the wench afore he returned to his world. But in his own good time. At his pleasure, not hers.

So, she was safe from his advances for now, shivering, foolish female that she was, cowering behind the low bed-structure called a couch. Hah! He'd vaulted many a castle wall and ship rail in his time. Did she really think such a paltry barrier could prevent his taking her?

Then, perversely, his pride rankled at her resistance to his charm. No, he couldn't allow her to think she'd got the upper hand. Women should be put in their proper place from the start. "Why do you fight your woman needs?" he grumbled.

"Wh-what?"

"You want me."

"I do not."

He snorted a laugh at her lie. "Yea, you do. Oh, your female body doesn't betray you in the same blatant manner as a man's," he said, waving downward at the joining of his thighs.

She gasped at his crude gesture.

Well, betimes a man had to be crude to make his point. Especially when the woman was stubborn. "And your arousal does not stick out from your body like a witless pole, but the signs are there for a discerning man to see. For example, the passion-mist in your eyes . . ."

She shuttered her lids.

He grinned wolfishly. "Your parted lips and heightened breathing . . ."

She clamped her mouth closed.

He grinned wider. "Your swollen nipples . . ."

She folded her arms across her chest. Too late. He'd already seen the evidence. And for just a moment he forgot why he was supposed to remain alert.

The woman was dangerous. He shook his head to clear it and dropped down to the couch. Patting the cushion next to him, he exhorted, "Come, sit beside me. You are safe from my lustful inclinations for tonight."

She balked, eyeing him suspiciously.

"Truly. Come. I must needs talk to you about the longship work. I want to start at first light, and there is much to discuss."

"What's your hurry?"

"The sooner I complete the boat, the sooner I can return the relic to its proper resting place. And the sooner I can return to my homeland. Time is of the essence."

She nodded, although he could tell she still didn't credit his explanation about time travel. Who did she think he was? An outlaw, bent on stealing her possessions, or virtue? Probably. Or a demented halfwit? Even more probable.

"Relax tomorrow. I have to be at the college by nine, but

I'll send my assistant, Mike Johnson, out to meet with you if he's around. He'll work closely with you on the project. Plus, I need to fill out the paperwork at the business office for your employment records on Monday. I don't suppose you have a Social Security number?" She studied him for a long moment. "No, I guess not. Well, Mike knows some shady characters who could probably get you fake credentials. Lord, I don't believe I actually suggested that. Me? Breaking the law? Jeffrey would laugh his head off."

"Who's Jeffrey?"

"My ex-husband."

"I don't like him."

She smiled . . . a warm, open expression that made his heart lurch. "I don't either."

"When you smile, you are not so plain. In truth, you become almost beautiful."

"Thanks a bunch." He'd honored her with that blunt honesty before. "Jeffrey said my overbite shows when I smile."

"Jeffrey is an ass. When we make love, I will draw many smiles from your lips."

Her smile faltered. "You promised," she said, edging away from him.

"I didn't mean tonight."

She relaxed. "Most men don't like women to laugh at them during sex. Jeffrey used to say—"

"Stop quoting your half-brain past-husband to me. He has naught to do with us," he growled. "Besides, you won't be laughing *at* me. You will be laughing *with* me. I intend to bring you much joy."

She lifted her shoulders hopelessly. "Arrogance comes naturally to you, doesn't it?"

He rolled his shoulders. "There is a difference between arrogance and self-confidence. I know what I know about my capabilities. Now stop bringing the conversation back to sex or I will think you have changed your mind about making love with me tonight."

She bristled indignantly. "I did not—"

"Shh," he said, putting a palm up. "Tell me how many helpmates you can provide for me. And how skilled are they?"

"Well, there's Mike, of course, and roughly two dozen students working with him, male and female. Some of them have minimal carpentry skills, but they're all eager workers. They'll follow your instructions to the letter. However, there's only one more week of spring break left. After that, most of them have full-time classes. So, they'll only be able to help for two or three hours a day, plus all day on the weekends."

"Hmmm. Perchance I will be able to finish the project in three or four weeks if I work all the daylight hours. But I must tell you, I have decided to make a second, smaller longship for myself."

"What?" She recoiled and started to stand, obviously upset. "You can't do that."

"Yea, I can. You see, at first I intended to help you build your longship, then take it for my own purposes . . . to return home."

"Oh . . . oh . . . I should have known! A thief!" she fumed, casting him a malevolent glare.

"Now, do not browbeat me. Since I have learned of your honorbound duty to fulfill your grandsire's dream, I would not do such. But that means I have to build a smaller ship for my own purposes."

"I can't charge those expenses off to the foundation. That would be stealing. Besides, we're on a tight budget as it is."

He stiffened with affront that she would think he'd steal from her now. "I will pay for my own supplies from the monies I am paid. And I will work on my own time. You will not be cheated in any way, my lady."

"I'm sorry," she said, but her apology didn't take away the

sting of her insult. "Okay, so you build two longships. I don't see any way you can get this done in three weeks, though."

"I will have to," he asserted. "When Thea and I were playing with your come-pewter tonight, I found more information on the Demon's Moon. I told you there was such an astrological happenstance the night of my shipwreck. Well, the next Demon's Moon occurs on April 28—one month from now."

"And you believe the Demon's Moon is somehow connected to a time portal that would let you return home?" she questioned skeptically.

He nodded. "And there won't be another till next year. I have to go soon if I am to complete my father's quest."

She put a hand on his arm. "Rolf, I'm not sure you're telling me the truth. But, assuming you are, chances are you can't do anything that would change history."

He stiffened, even though he knew she meant well. "I have to try."

She nodded. "So, assuming that you are able to restore the relic to its rightful place, and the famine ends, then what? Tell me what your life will be like in your . . . land."

"First, I intend to find Storr Grimmsson and put an end to his life. He and all his followers will die a torturous death for their miserable deeds. Then, I will return to my ship-building business. I own a beautiful farmstead on a fjord."

"You, a farmer? Somehow I can't picture that."

"I get much satisfaction in creating fine ships, and a lucrative living do I make in selling them about the world. In the early days, I was wont to test my vessels on trading voyages, or go a-Viking, but in recent years I have not had a yen to travel. Perchance I will go adventuring again, if the mood calls. I can see from this trip that there are many new lands to explore. Then again, mayhap this journey will kill the need to seek new horizons."

"Perhaps you're ready to settle down and raise a family."

He shrugged. "I did that afore and found no great bliss."

"You did?" she asked with surprise. "You've been married?"

"Twice."

"Twice," she parroted.

"Both wives died in the child birth. My first wife I wed when I had only seen eighteen winters and she sixteen. Ariside died of the childbed fever after delivering a stillborn babe."

"Oh, Rolf. I'm so sorry."

He rolled his shoulders. "'Tis the way of things. And it was a long time ago."

"And your other wife?"

"My second wife, Signe, died five years ago. Her labor came a month too early and lasted five days. She bled to death."

"You must have been devastated."

"Yea, 'twas tragic, their dying early and the babes ne'er having a chance. But I barely knew my wives. The marriages were arranged by my father, and I was gone much of the time."

She patted his arm. "You're young. You'll marry again."

"Nay, I will not. I have no taste for the married state, and no great inclination to breed heirs. I much resisted the last union with Signe, and only agreed when my father said it would end my blood-duty to him. So, I'll not wed again."

She blinked at him with unshed tears. Really, he thought, women went sentimental over the smallest realities of life.

"Leastways, all my appetites can be satisfied by my mistress, the sweet Alyce. She resides in the market town of Hedeby."

She sneered with disgust.

"Now, you tell me, Merry-Death. What will you do when

you complete your obligation to your grandsire? Will you stay here and be a profess-whore?"

"No," she said, still sniffing condescendingly over his mistress. Women tended to be petty in that way. "I only took a sabbatical from Columbia. I'm expected to return for fall classes."

"Expected? But what do you *want*?"

She closed her eyes briefly at the question. When she opened them, he saw bleakness and uncertainty in the green depths. "I really don't know. All my life I've done what others expected of me. My parents. My husband. Even Gramps. I can't remember a time when anyone asked me what I really wanted. Maybe . . ."

He cocked his head, waiting.

". . . actually, I do know what I want. Love."

He scoffed.

"I've always felt alone. Growing up as a child. Even when I was married. I think I would be happy to give up my career and stay home with a man who loved me, and a houseful of children . . . well, at least two."

Her eyes were misty with regret, and he remembered her telling him of her barrenness. He took her hand in his and laced their fingers, even when she tried to pull away.

"Don't pity me," she said.

"I don't."

"I can always adopt a child. Single women do that today. Maybe that's what I'll do. Stay here and adopt a child. I have a trust fund that would support me. And I could write a book—the kind my parents would consider far too frivolous." She cast him a tentative sidelong look before revealing, "I've always wanted to write a book on outrageous women of medieval times."

"I could tell you tales about a few of those."

She laughed and swiped at her eyes with a free hand. He

still held her other hand firmly, and found inordinate joy in the mere pressure of their two palms.

"What about this man who would love you?"

"There are none on the horizon, and I've been burned once. No, I'm more and more convinced that adopting a child is the answer, not hunting for a man to fulfill my life."

He wasn't convinced and he wasn't sure she was either.

Perhaps it was the odd connection he felt with this woman where their hands were joined. Perhaps it was the lustful fever that still hung heavy in his loins. Perhaps it was that mischievous god, Loki, who inspired his loose tongue. Regardless of the cause, Geirolf was as stunned as Merry-Death when he hauled her close and rasped out, "You could come home with me."

CHAPTER SEVEN

☙

*S*he was all wet . . .
    Meredith awakened the next morning to a loud pounding noise. She cracked an eye open sleepily to see it was barely daylight. Her alarm clock on the bedside table read 6:00 A.M.

As the pounding continued, she realized that it came from outside. Climbing groggily out of bed, she pulled the quilt up over Thea, who was sleeping soundly through the racket.

Her first thought as her mind cleared was, *Oh, my God, it's practically the middle of the night and that damn Viking is out there building a ship. The neighbors will call the police.*

Her second thought, following almost immediately on the first, was a recollection of the night before. *Oh, my God. That Viking actually invited me to go home with him . . . to the tenth century. And I'm tempted. I almost wish he were who he claims to be . . . sort of my very own Viking in Shining Armor.* She giggled at the fantasy.

It was absolutely ridiculous that she should feel so flattered by his suggestion. Especially since he'd immediately looked as if he was going to have a stroke when the words slipped out. And it certainly hadn't been flattering when she'd questioned him about what she'd do in his land and he'd stuttered and stammered and finally said that he supposed she could be his mistress.

As if!

Still, his proposal made Meredith feel oddly warm and fuzzy.

She lost all her warm fuzzies the minute she stomped outside in her pajamas and saw Rolf in the side yard, surrounded by the completely dismantled longship.

"Wh-what are you doing? I'm going to kill you. You've destroyed months of Gramps's work."

"Do not fret, my lady," he assured her, sidestepping her outstretched arms and holding an axe over his head, out of her reach.

"I'd like to give you 'fret,' you jerk." Meredith gritted her teeth, fisted her hands and counted to ten.

"Now, calm down, Merry-Death. I am merely starting over. In the end, it will save time. You'll see." He dropped the axe and walked over, putting an arm around her shoulders. "Wipe the tears from your eyes, sweetling. This is man's work. I know what I'm doing."

Oh, God, I hope so. "And stop calling me 'sweetling'." *It makes me feel so . . . so . . . warm and fuzzy. Geesh!* "There's no such thing as 'man's work' in society today. So cut the macho tripe."

He arched a brow condescendingly. "Really? Well, then, *helpmate*, wouldst thou carry that keel arm down yon cliffside to soak in the water?"

The keel arm he pointed to was about twelve feet long and probably weighed two tons.

"I wish I could pick the darn thing up. I know just what I'd do with it, too. I'd use it like a battering ram to wipe the smirk off your face."

Grinning wider, he stood, hands on hips in his modern

attire—jeans, T-shirt, and athletic shoes, with his hair clubbed back at the neck and covered with a baseball cap. "Were you always violent? I admire that in a woman. Like a Valkyrie, you are. Mayhap I will take you a-Viking with me some day."

"Yeah, what I really need is a little raping and pillaging in my life."

"Me, too. I can't recall the last time I engaged in some good raping and pillaging. And plundering . . . don't forget plundering."

"Don't push it, Rolf."

But his attention had already wandered. He hunkered down and was examining several slender pieces of wood, about seven feet long, which resembled tomato garden stakes. Picking up one with disgust, he weighed it in his hands, then raised it in one hand to shoulder height. In an expert move that would have put any medieval warrior to shame, he aimed it like a spear at a refuse pile twenty feet away, making a perfect landing.

"Lucky shot," she scoffed.

"Hah!" he retorted, clearly pleased at the challenge. With his whiskey eyes flashing, he did the same with five more makeshift "spears." Only then did he turn and grin at her.

"Show-off!"

"Nay, I will show you what is showing off. 'Tis a trick my father taught me." Picking up another "spear," he sauntered over and handed it to her. Then he walked ten paces away and turned. "Now, throw the spear at me."

"I will not!"

"Do as I say, Merry-Death. You won't hurt me."

"I don't know."

"Do it," he ordered. "And throw it hard, or the trick won't work."

"Okay," she agreed, not caring for his domineering attitude at all, "but if I hurt you, I'm going to kill you."

He laughed at the inconsistency of her statement, then danced from foot to foot, taunting her. "Come, Merry-Death, pretend I am your past-husband, and I have just told you of my mistress."

She needed no further provocation. She threw the spear and she threw it hard. To her horror, it was heading straight for his chest. "Oh, my God!" she shrieked.

But then, to her astonishment, he caught the spear in mid-air and, without a pause, twisted it agilely in his fingertips and flung it back at her. The darn thing whizzed right over her left shoulder.

"I would have speared you through the heart if I'd been aiming true," he boasted.

Good Lord, had he ever really done that in a battle? Had he really killed someone? Of course he had. He'd told her more than once that he was a renowned warrior, as well as a shipbuilder. But, no, no, no, that was his time-travel story, which she didn't believe.

"And this is a skill my Uncle Olaf taught me," he continued. Picking up two spears this time, he threw them simultaneously at the refuse pile, where they landed with perfect precision atop the others.

A trill of alarm went through Meredith. "You read about that in a history book, didn't you?"

"What?" He dusted off his hands and swaggered toward her.

"That stuff about King Olaf and the double spear throwing. When you told me the first day you came here that you were related to Olaf Tryggvason, I was curious. Among other things, the sagas relate the fact that Olaf had a talent for throwing two spears at once. In fact, many years after his death, a man called Tryggvi, who claimed to be his son by a foreign marriage, tried to win the throne of Norway. His rivals mocked him, claiming he was only a priest's son.

But in his last battle, Tryggvi supposedly flung two spears at once, successfully, and cried out, '*That* was how my father taught me to say Mass!'"

"Merry-Death, you make my brain spin with all these words. I know not of this Tryggvi person. Many wives and mistresses did Olaf have, in many lands, and just as many sons, legitimate and bastard alike. What is your point?"

"My point is that I want you to stop this Viking time-travel nonsense. So, you learned some dumb stick-throwing trick. Big deal! But don't pretend you were doing it with spears a thousand years ago."

"I do not lie," he said in an icy tone.

"You are not a time traveler."

"I am."

"You are not."

He held two hands up in the air for truce. "I yield . . . for now, though I do not concede the battle. We will move on to a safer subject. Let me tell you of the biggest problem I detected this morn—the location. Why did your grandsire choose this site for building a longship? 'Tis too far from the water. How will we carry the completed ship down that cliffside for launching?"

"Gramps had no choice. The college is inland and crowded for space. Gramps had this extra land here, and it seemed the logical place. Besides, it's no big deal to put the boat on a flatbed truck when the time is right and take it a few miles down the road to a docking site."

"Well, that may be, but there is also the lack of water to soak the timbers. I must needs build a water trough . . . a *big* water trough. Blessed Balder! Can you imagine how much time and muscle power it's going to take hauling pails of water up that cliffside, or from your keep?"

She snickered softly and strolled over to the side of the house. Turning on an outside spigot, she pulled the hose along with her as she walked back toward him. And the evil side of her nature—the one she'd just discovered since a certain Viking entered her life—kicked in, giving her the perfect opportunity for revenge. "Let's see you smirk at me again, Mr. This-Is-Man's-Work Viking," she jeered, and pressed the lever on the nozzle, spraying him from head to foot.

Rolf stood speechless for a moment as rivulets of water— probably very cold water—ran down his face, knocking off his cap, plastering his clothing to his body. Then a slow smile spread across his lips, just before he leapt forward, tackling her to the ground and turning the hose on her. She was the recipient of a good soaking then, and the water *was* cold.

Roaring with glee, Rolf reached out a hand and helped her to her feet. She spit out water and strands of hair from her mouth. Only then did she notice that Rolf had abruptly stopped smiling. Instead, he gazed with decided interest at her wet pajamas, now plastered against every curve of her body, like black plastic wrap.

"I thought I did not like your pay-jam-hose when I first saw them yestereve," he remarked with a lazy grin. "I have changed my mind." Then, with a shake of his head, he took her hand, leading her toward the house. "Enough of these games. You must stop trying to seduce me, sweetling."

She sputtered indignantly.

He chucked her under the chin. "Come, let us go into the keep and make a list of needed supplies. Do not dawdle now, wench."

I must be an adult here. I must not rise to every baiting word he utters. I must not stare at his behind in those wet jeans. "Have you had breakfast yet?"

"Yea, I broke fast long ago. Cookies and mead. You will have to go to the grocery mall again."

Huh? Cookies and mead? "Oh, Good Lord, did you have Oreos and Bud Light for breakfast?"

"Yea. Did I not just say so? Why is your mouth hanging open? The fare was delicious. I ate whilst watching *Sesame Street* on the picture box. Today I learned the letter X with Bert and Ernie. I've decided X is the best letter in your alphabet. Indeed, my favorite word has the letter X in it." He waited several moments for her to comprehend what word that might be, his amber eyes twinkling with mischief.

She laughed, feeling wonderfully carefree and happier than she had in ages. Impulsive.

In fact, she decided to try Oreos and beer for breakfast.

Then again, maybe she should ease into this impulsive stuff.

The real man's fantasy: power tools . . .

Geirolf had landed in shipbuilders' heaven—the Bangor Hardware Superstore.

"No kidding, man! Who are you, really?" Mike Johnson asked for about the hundredth time since he'd arrived at Merry-Death's keep hours ago, at Merry-Death's instruction. Although it was the Lord's Day, she'd gone into her off-face to work. "I mean, what man gets his rocks off over sandpaper? *Sandpaper!* Now, Pamela Anderson in a carpenter's belt, I could see. But sandpaper? You must've been living in a jungle all these years."

"What?" Geirolf replied distractedly, fingering the various grades of abrasive paper piled up on shelf after shelf. He threw a half dozen of each in his pushcart. "Do not take offense, Mike, but it appears lackwitted to me that you and Merry-Death would want to build a longship using the old methods when you have all these modern marvels."

"That's the whole point . . . to show our students the painstaking labor and perseverance needed to complete a project of this magnitude."

"Hah! The rest of you can *persevere* by rubbing sand onto rough boards and shaving wood with an adz till your fingers ache, but I am not a lackwit. I will use sanding paper on my ship."

Mike shook his head in amazement. "Professor Foster is gonna put your neck in a noose. And it's not just the sandpaper. Wait till she sees those high-tech hammers and gouging tools you've picked out. She wants this ship built *exactly* the way the primitive Vikings did it."

"The hard way, you mean. Isn't that just like a woman?" Geirolf snorted. "And who says I am primitive?"

Mike choked back a guffaw. "You're really into this Viking re-enactment crap, aren't you?"

"Nay, I told you . . . I have come from Hordaland—I mean Norway. And that is all I am free to tell you. I forswore an oath to Merry-Death not to discuss how I got here."

"Now that's real interesting, because she accused me . . . or her brother Jared of hiring you." Mike slitted his eyes, studying him suspiciously. "She practically burned out her computer this morning shooting off letters about you and that crazy belt of yours to every university in the country. Even had me run a check on you with the local fuzz."

Geirolf had no idea what a fax machine was. Perhaps Mike had meant Saxon machine. Or fuzz. Wasn't that lint found in the navel? He was sore tired of asking "What's that?" about every blessed thing he encountered in this land. He did understand letters, though. "In my opinion, that was one of the biggest mistakes your people made . . . teaching women to write. Bloody hell! You men of Am-eric-hah must be soft in the head. Now your females can not only jabber incessantly in a man's face—*Dig the moat . . . Clean the garderobes . . . Stop belching*—but they can put all their nagging on parchment, as well."

Mike laughed, rushing to keep up as Geirolf steered his cart around a corner. "And you've shared these opinions with Professor Foster?"

"Not yet," Geirolf admitted, exchanging a rueful grin with the younger man.

Geirolf liked Mike. The man, who'd seen about twenty-five winters, was dressed almost identically to him in den-ham *braies,* T-*shert* and running boots. Many of the males they'd encountered that day wore the same attire. Except that Mike's *shert* was green and had U.S. Army printed on the front. That was the name for Am-eric-hah's military force, Geirolf had learned. Mike had been a warrior for three years before going back to school, which was very strange to Geirolf's way of thinking. A grown man needing more education?

And his hair! The young man had clipped his blond tresses—there must be Nordic blood in his family—down almost to the scalp. A gee-eye buzz cut, he called it. Geirolf had never held with that biblical notion that a man's strength was in his hair, but it did keep a man warm on a cold Norse night when there was no wench available for the bedding. What could Mike have been thinking? A woman must have talked him into such a foolhardy action. Probably that Pamela Anderson creature who had Mike salivating at the mere mention of her name.

Mike had already told him that his father and mother had died years ago in a wheeled box accident, and his wife had passed away two years past whilst skiing. Geirolf decided he would have a man-to-man talk with Mike later and help steer him on the better path of masculine behavior. Mayhap he would even show him how to win that Pamela Anderson seductress to his bed.

Geirolf had spent the morning, after Merry-Death had gone to the call-ledge, working on his English-language skills with Thea. The girl, who looked much better without her face paint, had found a child's "primer" on the Internet, which helped him tremendously. Then they'd watched two hours of *Sesame Street* on a public television merry-thong to solicit money. Geirolf wished he had more time; he would relish nothing better than to meet the mischievous Ernie, who felt like a newfound friend to him in this alien country. Ernie's appearance was unlike that of any child he'd ever seen, but he had big ears like his brother Magnus, and that endeared the "boy" to him.

With the help of the talisman belt, Geirolf already had mastered the rudiments of the English language. He only needed to touch his belt on occasion now when out in society to translate odd words or phrases—the ones not found on *Sesame Street* or in the grammar texts. Such as the words that drivers of the other wheeled boxes yelled at Mike when he cut in front of them. Or the words to the songs Thea's music box played so loudly . . . lyrics as peculiar as the ill-named musicians. 'Twas a curious country where men were grateful to be dead. Or a woman was merry in death. Thea was home now, painting her finger and toenails with Black Plague, and blasting the air with the raucous music.

Now his attention swerved in another direction. "Oh, Holy Thor, I think I am in Asgard," Geirolf said enthusiastically. He soon learned that they'd entered Am-eric-hah's version of Valhalla, a real man's paradise—the power-tool section of the hardware store.

Mike hooted and sniggered at his fascination with the power tools, but Geirolf could not care. He would give his entire treasure chamber at home for half of these tools of the gods. In the end, it took Mike almost an hour to drag Geirolf away. Only a reminder of wasted time recalled to him the urgency of his mission. So, it was with a sigh of regret that they pushed their cart up to the wooden box . . . a counter . . .

where the store worker took their money and put it in another box . . . a cash register.

Geirolf's eyes were glazed over when Mike finally pulled him from the store with their purchases. 'Twas a miracle . . . all the extraordinary power tools that had been invented. There were saws that moved by themselves. Drills to bore holes in even the hardest wood with no effort. All powered by something called electrice-city, which Geirolf intended to research on the come-pewter when he returned to Merry-Death's library. Mike had even told him of huge shovel machines, called backhoes, that could dig an entire moat in one day. Geirolf knew a few Saxon kings and aethelings who'd pay a fortune for such.

"Don't look so glum, Rolf." Mike's lips twitched with mirth as he dumped their packages in the back of his wheeled box. Mike's riding vehicle was different from Merry-Death's. It was blue, and only the front seat was covered by a roof. The back portion was a long, uncovered box—*What else!*—for hauling things. "When we get back to Professor Foster's house, you can watch those two DVDs we bought—Bob Vila's *This Old House* and Tim Allen's *Home Improvement*. They'll teach you everything you ever wanted to know about modern tools."

When they reached the dirt road leading up to Merry-Death's keep, Geirolf convinced Mike to let him drive his box. After several rough lurches and skidding accelerations, he mastered the technique. And it was a truly exciting experience, speeding along at what Mike said was ten miles per hour. 'Twas like the rush of exhilaration after a fiercely fought battle, or the rush of another kind after a fiercely played bout of bedsport. By the time he came to a screeching halt in front of Merry-Death's door, Mike was alternately bracing his outstretched arms on the dashing board and laughing uproariously.

Merry-Death stood on her front porch, hands on hips, eyes flaming angrily. Thea, in war paint that would do a Scot warrior proud, stood beside her, smiling from ear to ear.

"Isn't she magnificent?" Geirolf said, inhaling sharply.

"Who?" Mike slanted him an incredulous glance. "Thea?"

"Of course not. Do you take me for a despoiler of children?"

"Professor Foster? You think Professor Foster is *magnificent*?"

Geirolf nodded, feeling the usual heaviness in his loins and a strange fluttering in his heart when he gazed at her.

"Professor Foster?" Mike repeated with stunned disbelief. "You've got the hots for my boss? You must be nuts. I mean . . . don't get me wrong, I like Dr. Foster. She's a really nice person. But *magnificent*? No way! Now Pamela Anderson . . . that's what I call magnificent."

Geirolf shook his head adamantly. "You are young, Mike. Like a horse with blinders, you are. You weigh a woman's value only with your eyes . . . and your cock."

"So?" Mike grinned. "Works for me."

"Foolish boy, there is more . . . much more."

Shopping sure does whet the appetite . . .

Meredith couldn't believe her eyes. It was six o'clock and not only had Mike and Rolf been gone all afternoon, but Rolf was driving the truck. Even though it was Sunday, she'd decided to go into her office, where she'd run into Mike. She'd asked her grad assistant to go to her house and meet the new shipbuilder on the project. She hadn't expected him to take off on some great adventure . . . and certainly not to put the Viking behind the wheel of a truck.

She was going to wring Mike's neck. Then she was going to tackle the big guy, the one who'd been causing her grief all day as inquiry after inquiry brought no answers concerning his identity, only more questions.

"Where have you two been all day?" she snapped as the two men approached, laden with bags imprinted with the Bangor Hardware Superstore logo.

"Shopping," Rolf answered blithely, leaning down to give her a quick kiss on the lips in passing. "I missed you, sweetling," he whispered against her gaping mouth.

The casual gesture zapped Meredith speechless. She forgot momentarily why she was so angry and worried. *He kissed me. Just like that. He kissed me. In front of Mike and Thea. Oh, Lord, he kissed me. As if he had every right in the world.*

Mike just chuckled.

Thea giggled.

Rolf gave Mike a knowing look and winked.

"Aaarrgh!" Meredith said, coming to her senses. "I've been so worried."

"'Tis e'er the way of women . . . to wring their hands when their men are off to battle."

"Battle? Battle? You were shopping."

Rolf waved a hand airily. "'Tis the same thing."

Mike dipped his head sheepishly. "I'm sorry, Dr. Foster. I should have called, but we got sort of, uh, delayed in the power-tool section of the hardware store."

Rolf sighed. "I am in love . . ."

Meredith's heart lurched. *He met some woman in the hardware store? And fell in love at first sight? Oh, isn't that just like a man? Snag one woman, then go trolling for another. No, no, no! What am I thinking here? He hasn't snagged me. Uh-uh!*

". . . with power tools," Rolf finished with a speaking grin. He'd obviously recognized her dismay.

"Wh-what?" she sputtered. Somewhere along the way, Meredith had become lost in this crazy conversation.

"Rolf has discovered the grown man's dream toy—the power tool," Mike declared with dry humor.

"Tonight we will watch Bibveela and Timalley on the picture box. Then you will understand," Rolf explained, pulling two DVDs out of his bag.

"Bob Vila and Tim Allen," Mike interpreted. In an aside to Meredith, he mouthed, "Who is this guy?"

Meredith's brain swirled, but one important fact seeped through. There was no other woman. Later she would contemplate the uncalled-for relief that flooded her. For now, she blustered, "Come inside. Dinner's ready, and I have lots to discuss with you two. You'll stay, won't you, Mike?"

"I wouldn't miss it for the world," Mike said, still chuckling. "I can't wait to see your reaction when Rolf expounds his philosophy on feminism." Looping a free arm around Thea's shoulder, he started into the house. "Great makeup, by the way, kid. I don't know about the earring in the nose bit, though. Doesn't Kleenex and stuff get caught there?"

"Oh, Mike! You're always kidding," Thea twittered.

"I hope we're not having worms again," Rolf grumbled, patting Meredith on the rump as he passed.

She barely stifled a squeal of affront.

"I have a ferocious hunger," he continued. "A side of roast boar would be a welcome repast right now. With a slab of manchet bread. I don't suppose . . ."

She laughed. "We're having chili and sourdough biscuits. Take it or leave it."

What's a "Tool Man"? . . .

"I talked to my brother Jared today. He said that he didn't send you here," Meredith informed Rolf as she ladled out his third helping of chili and Mike's second. She was going to have to retrain herself to cook in volume.

"Did I not tell you so afore?" Rolf retorted, still disgruntled that she hadn't stopped for more beer. "How's a man to eat a meal without mead to wash it down?" He'd been grumbling throughout dinner. "Especially this spicy provender."

"So, who told you that I wanted to hire a shipbuilder?" Meredith threw the question out nonchalantly, hoping to catch Rolf off guard, but she saw Mike and Thea raise their heads alertly, and immediately added, "Oh, never mind. You're here now. I guess that's the most important thing." She would have to pick a better, more private time.

The phone rang then and Meredith went into the living room to pick it up. Her usually immaculate home was a shambles. Thea's clothes were scattered about. A bag of microwave popcorn sat on the coffee table along with an assortment of CDs, not to mention an array of cosmetic products that would turn Mary Kay purple. In the corner was a neatly stacked pile of Rolf's new clothing, as well as his leather tunic and boots that she'd cleaned for him. Outside, the hideous, big-breasted female prow still lay on the patio.

Meredith groaned and picked up the phone on the third ring. "Hello."

"Mer? You groaned. What's wrong?" a female voice asked in a rush of concern.

It was her sister Jillian. "What's wrong? I'll tell you what's wrong, Jillie. I've got a twelve-year-old girl here who should be with her mother. I've got a Viking longship to build before the end of the semester. I've got a master shipbuilder who thinks he's a real Viking and who honest-to-God expects me to sit and watch *Home Improvement* on TV with him tonight. And, if that's not enough, I've got to decide what the hell to do with my future once this project is completed."

Jillie let out a long breath of relief. "Oh, is that all? I thought it was something serious."

Meredith groaned again. "If this isn't serious, what is?"

"I'll tell you what's serious, sister dear. It's that sketch you sent me today of a medieval ornament."

Meredith was instantly alert. She'd emailed the sketch today to Jillie, her brother, her parents, even a colleague at Columbia.

"I've spent the whole afternoon in the archives of a museum library. That belt clasp is magnificent! What materials are used? Oh, don't even try to describe it to me. I'm coming back to the States. I've got to see this in person. We could have the breakthrough of a lifetime. As big as the Dead Sea Scrolls or King Tut's tomb. Well, maybe not that stupendous. But we're talking major fame here, hon."

Meredith held the phone away from her face and stared at it, dumbstruck. Her sister was interrupting her museum work in London, not to come help her child, but to case out some ancient hunk of jewelry? And what was this *we* business?

"Are you listening to me, Mer?"

"Huh?" Apparently her sister had been jabbering away.

"I should be able to get away from here in two days. In the meantime, could you take photographs and email them to me? Or more detailed sketches if photographs would make the guy suspicious. Whatever you do, don't let that guy, or his belt, get away. Steal them if you have to."

"Are you crazy?"

A dial tone was her only response.

Meredith glanced toward the kitchen where Thea was twittering gaily with Mike and Rolf as they stacked the dishes in the dishwasher and cleaned off the table. Thea's mother hadn't even asked to speak to her, or asked about her well-being.

She was blinking rapidly to prevent tears from brimming over in her eyes when Rolf walked toward her. Waving the two DVDs in her face, he said, "Stop looking so weepish, sweetling. We are going to learn all about power tools." Meredith put her face in her hands, but not before Rolf added,

"And I've got dessert." Somewhere he'd found another bag of Oreos. Maybe they sold them in the hardware store. Thea and Mike followed with four glasses of milk.

Jeffrey would have a heart attack if he could see her eating junk food. He was a devout advocate of the "good nutrition feeds the brain" mantra. And junk TV was an even worse no-no. Unlike her parents, she and Jeffrey had had a television in their home, but he would have put a block on any channel showing anything as lowbrow as Tim Allen.

Meredith cringed at that sudden, unwelcome memory, and then straightened with resolution. Starting right now, she was going to stop that creep Jeffrey from ruling her life. "Great!" she said, plopping down to the couch. "I can't wait." And she really meant it, too.

An hour later, though, Meredith's stomach churned. And it wasn't just the Oreos and milk on top of chili and sourdough biscuits. It was Rolf and the effect TV had on him. The Viking stared, transfixed, at the TV screen, howling with delight, along with Thea and Mike. Oh, Bob Vila had held his attention, but the *Home Improvement* klutz was the true hit.

"Look at this, Merry-Death. Tim is building a man's toilet. It has a reclining La-Z-Boy seat and a footstool and a built-in stand for his mead and cigar. Is that not hilarious?"

Yeah, hilarious.

"What's a cigar? Can we buy some cigars tomorrow, Mike?"

"Sure," Mike said.

"Yech," Thea said.

"Absolutely not," Meredith said.

On and on, the episodes went. And Meredith realized that she'd created a monster—a Viking whose hero was Tim Allen of *Home Improvement*.

Rolf turned to her and sighed, "I think Tim must be one of your modern gods. Even his companion, Al . . . he is surely one of the lesser gods."

"Hardly."

Rolf finally clicked off the switch on the remote and looked directly at Meredith. "I have a wonderful idea."

Meredith's queasy stomach roiled in foreboding. Mike and Thea waited expectantly; they treated Rolf as if he was a god himself and the words he spoke were golden pebbles of wisdom.

"Let us invite Tim Allen to come here and help us build our longship."

CHAPTER EIGHT

Some family ties are meant to be broken . . .

It was ten o'clock, and Meredith was still on the telephone—this time with her mother and father.

Seated at separate desks in the office they'd fashioned for themselves years ago in the walnut-paneled library of their Princeton home, her parents managed to harangue her with a three-way phone conversation.

How many times over how many years had Meredith been called into that inner sanctum to account for her frivolous ways? As if she'd known how to be frivolous! Had she ever really lived up to their high standards of personal and academic excellence? No matter how hard she tried to please them, she was as much a failure in their eyes as Jillie, who didn't try at all.

Meredith's queasy stomach roiled, probably portending an ulcer. Coward that she was, instead of fighting back, she took refuge in calling up the invisible wall that screened out their condemnations. If she refused to listen, they couldn't hurt her.

Meredith instead concentrated on the sounds of Thea moving around upstairs, preparing for bed. Outside, the rhythmic rasp of sandpaper against wood reflected Rolf's obsession to work till he dropped so that he could hasten his trip home. When Meredith considered his inevitable departure, a dullness of spirit weighed her down. Why, she couldn't imagine. Rolf had been in her life only two days, and yet he filled such a need in her . . . one she still didn't understand and certainly never realized was there.

Who was he? And why had he come into her world? There had to be a reason.

"Do you hear me, Meredith Ann?" her mother chided. "You were a daydreamer as a child. Apparently you haven't lost the nasty habit. Pay attention, dear. This is important."

"Now, Lillian, don't upset the girl," her father interrupted. Her father always referred to her as "the girl." She wondered if he knew how offensive that sounded. Probably not. "The girl doesn't understand the importance of the information she transmitted to us this afternoon. She never did take her work seriously enough."

"She's probably still fixated on that worthless ex-husband of hers. I told you from the beginning, Herbert, that their marriage would never work. Didn't I?"

"Yes, Lillian, you did."

"I was never impressed with Jeffrey's Mensa I.Q. After all, he was only a graduate of a state university. And vain . . . my goodness, that mustache of his was a clear giveaway."

"Well, now, Einstein had a mustache, Lillian. We must be tolerant."

"Hmpfh! Einstein didn't chase after young girls and impregnate them. Einstein didn't toss his wife aside because she couldn't have babies. Einstein didn't—"

"Enough!" Meredith shouted into the telephone and surprised even herself. In a softer tone, she said, "I have to go. Is there a reason for your call?"

"I don't care for your tone at all, Meredith Ann," her mother said icily.

"The girl always had a problem with self-control," her father agreed.

"Just like Jillian."

"Aaarrgh!" Meredith contributed.

"The reason we called," her mother said with exaggerated patience, "is that your father and I discussed the conversation we had with you earlier today, after you sent the email. And while we still think the workman you hired is incorrect in his statements about tenth-century events, he poses some interesting hypotheses."

"Such as his impressions of Queen Aelfgifu. And details about the courts of the Saxon King Aethelred in Winchester and King Olaf in Norway during the tenth century. Even ship purchases made by noble personages of that time," her father added. "Did you say Ralph came from Norway? Well, there was constant traffic then between the Norse lands and the Northumbrian trading center in Jorvik. Perhaps Ralph stumbled onto some long-hidden documents—"

"Or Old Icelandic runic stones that give new data on Dark Age culture," her mother interjected hopefully. "If Ralph can read the *futhark* alphabet, as you claim, that in itself is remarkable."

"Not Ralph, Rolf."

As usual, her parents steamrolled over her. This time they didn't even acknowledge the correction.

"Workmen often uncover vital artifacts and don't recognize their importance. Remember those ancient scrolls, Lillian? The ones that Egyptian stoneworker had stuffed in his wall?"

Meredith could hear the ring of excitement in her father's voice. The thrill of a possible new discovery was the only thing that could provoke such ardor. Certainly his children never had. The only time he'd ever shown her any affection was a gruff hug as a teenager when she received 1500 on her

SATs, which was immediately dampened by her mother re-minding him that Jared had gotten 1550.

"Your father is right. The man is probably just an illiter-ate braggart, as many of those workmen at archaeological sites are, but one never knows. The pretentiousness of his calling himself a Viking, though, is so . . . so . . . plebian."

"Huh? I never said he was an archaeological worker. I said he was a Viking shipbuilder," Meredith broke in.

The collective snicker at the other end of the line was a vocal condemnation of her mental faculties.

"Did the girl just use that despicable word?"

"Yes, she did, Herbert. I thought we broke her of that trait long ago."

"What word?" Meredith asked.

"Huh?" her father informed her with icy distaste.

"Father," Meredith said with sigh of exasperation, "I'm thirty-five years old. You can stop correcting my speech."

"Be that as it may, girl, we'll be arriving on Saturday."

"Wh-what?" Meredith squeaked out. This was the first she'd heard of their coming to Maine. Her stomach pitched, and bile rose to her throat. *Saturday? Six days from now? Oh, Lord!*

"Please make arrangements for us to have a rental car waiting at the airport, Meredith Ann. And try to find decent hotel accommodations nearby."

"And whatever you do, girl, don't let Ralph escape until we have a chance to interview him."

Escape? How could I stop Ralph, the big galoot. I mean, Rolf, the big galoot . . . from doing anything he wanted? "I thought you were off to Bombay."

"Tsk-tsk, girl. Focus, remember? Bombay was last month. No, we're attending a symposium in Hamburg on Monday. 'The Social and Political Implications of Lime In Tenth-Century Garderobes.' We'll only be able to stay in Maine for two days."

"No, no, no . . . wait a minute. This is not a good idea," Meredith protested. But already her parents had tuned her out.

"Make sure you pack the tape recorder, Herbert, and plenty of cassettes."

"Yes, Lillian. And don't forget the camera. We might want to take photographs of that medieval belt clasp."

"*Purported* medieval belt clasp, Herbert."

"That goes without saying, Lillian." Her father sniffed.

They never even noticed when Meredith hung up the phone with a faint good-bye.

No sooner did she put the cordless phone on the table than it rang again. Meredith pressed a button engaging the answering machine. Enough was enough for one day.

"Hi, Mer. Jared here. I talked to Jillie tonight, and we agree you've got a live one there. Call me first thing in the morning. I have a million questions for you to grill this guy. He's probably a fraud, but that belt is . . . well, if it's what I think it is, it could be a missing link in an important segment of history. And the ship's prow sounds equally fascinating. Be careful, though, sis. Archaeological theft has become an international problem. You don't want to mess with criminals. Call me tomorrow. Oh, and did I tell you, I might be able to fly in next week? I'm due for a vacation anyway."

Archaeological theft? Could Rolf be a criminal? No, she decided immediately. But what had Jared said in the end? He might be coming here, too? Oh, Lord!

She took a big swig of Pepto-Bismol before heading outside to talk to her criminal-in-residence. Wait till he learned about all the company that would soon be converging on them.

Better yet, wait till they found out a "blue-collar worker" was living with her.

* * *

It was an invitation she couldn't extend . . . yet . . .

"Rolf, why don't you call it a night?" She walked up to Rolf where he worked industriously, sanding the bare-bones framework of a smaller longship that he'd already erected. The pungent odor of freshly cut wood drifted on the wind. "Mike will be here with the student workers by nine A.M. You've been up since before dawn. Come on to bed now."

He stood in one lithe movement, dropping the sandpaper to the ground. "Is that an invitation?" He regarded her gravely as he swiped a forearm across his forehead. He wore only jogging pants and athletic shoes, and, of course, the talisman belt. But that was all. Despite the coolness of the spring air, perspiration glistened on his face and shoulders and the wide, enticing expanse of his chest. By the light of a full moon, she watched, captivated, as one bead drizzled from his chin down his breastbone, slowly, slowly, slowly toward the belt clasp.

"Well?" he prodded with a knowing chuckle.

Snapping to attention, she shoved a glass of cold iced tea into his hands. "No, that wasn't an invitation. That's an order. You need to rest, or you'll be of no use to me."

He grinned at her inadvertent double entendre as he took a small sip of the beverage, testing. Anything other than mead usually held no appeal to his taste buds. Finding the drink palatable, he tilted his head back and drank it down in several long gulps.

And Meredith got to admire the sleek lines of his profile. Strong nose and chin. Graceful neck. Full, wet lips.

"Love with a Warm Viking" was looking better and better.

Rolf placed the empty glass on the ship's frame, and then leveled her with a hard glare. "An order, do you say? Hah! I take exception to your assertion of authority over me. In truth, my inclination is to do the opposite just to prove you cannot bend me to your will with mere words. Know this, my lady. Geirolf Ericsson takes orders from no one."

"Now wait a minute. Somewhere along the line, you managed to convince yourself that you're in charge of this project."

"Oh?" His jaw went rigid, his voice decidedly tense.

"Maybe it was when you 'led the charge' at the mall. Maybe it was when you bought all those modern tools at the hardware store, against my orders. Maybe it was when you dismantled all my grandfather's hard work, without permission. Maybe it was when you moved into my house big-as-you-Viking-well-please. But understand this, buster . . . I'm drawing a line in the sand. I'm the employer. You are the employee. And from now on you take my orders."

Rolf shook his head with disbelief. "Have a caution, wench. You pass the bounds of bravery and enter into the realm of foolishness with your lackwit female prattle."

She literally growled. "And stop calling me wench."

"I'll call you wench and much more, if I choose." He leaned down so they were practically nose to nose. "You ask when I convinced myself of my greater authority. Well, I'll tell you, *wench*."

His warm breath feathered Meredith's lips as he spoke. A shiver assaulted her, but she refused to back away. Actually, she couldn't have moved if her life depended on it, so mesmerized was she by his nearness.

"Mayhap I took control because I am Geirolf Ericsson, son of Eric Tryggvason, high jarl of Hordaland, and I was born to lead," he told her. "Mayhap it was when the gods led me through this hellish time hole to a willful lady whose tongue outruns her good sense. Mayhap it was when I saw the half-brain job done on the longship and knew I could correct the mistakes. Or mayhap—" he hesitated and ran his tongue over his upper lip with deliberate sexual innuendo, "or mayhap it was when I turned you into a mewling kitten of surrender in that wheeled box of yours yesterday. With a few mere kisses, at that."

She gasped at his reference to her lapse in sanity. And how like a man to place undue importance on her indiscretion!

Rolf grazed her trembling lips with his knuckles as he straightened. With a laugh, he added, "Imagine how it will be when we finally couple, sweetling. Do you think then that you will lead the play? Hah! I think not. The man leads, the woman follows. 'Tis the way of nature and e'er has been."

Meredith sputtered with outrage. Any warm feelings she'd had melted away at his chauvinistic words. "You . . . you overinflated macho pig. You arrogant, overbearing, Stone Age Neanderthal. I wouldn't *couple* with you now if you were the hottest Viking in the world."

"Oh, you will not say me nay forever," he assured her with supreme self-confidence. "Your protests signify naught when your eyes blaze invitation."

"They . . . do . . . not."

"You think to gainsay me with peevish challenges of my every directive. You mistrust me when I tell of my past and how I got to your godforsaken land. Well, my lady, you are the false one. You lie to yourself when you say you don't want me. You want me with a growing passion, on that I would wager my long sword. And you will have me and my *other* sword," he said, gesturing crudely to his groin, "or you may not have me, if *I* choose."

That was the last straw. The jerk had crossed over the line. "You're fired, mister."

"Fired? Oh, I am fired, for a certainty. So fired I could take you now, on the ground, and plow you to *Hel* and back."

"Not that kind of fired, you lech. You're dismissed. No longer employed on this project. I don't want you here anymore."

Meredith inhaled sharply at her own harsh words. Her blistering fury had caused her to lash out without thinking. She wished she could take back her words, especially when Rolf drew himself tall with wounded pride. "I didn't mean—"

He put up a halting hand. "Dismissed, you say? You don't want me, you say?" His words hit her like daggers. "So be it!"

With heart pounding and eyes misting with tears, Meredith watched as Rolf stormed toward the house. And presumably out of her life.

He bent her to his will, but then she snapped back . . .

The wench was looking whey-faced and miserable when she came into her homestead a short time later, but he did not care. No one—man or woman—insulted his honor and walked away unscathed. If she were a man, she would be dead now . . . or sorely bruised.

"Rolf, I'm sorry if I offended you," she stammered out.

He could see that her pride had been damaged as well, and that the words came hard. *Good.* He'd removed his modern raiment and donned his leather tunic with the talisman belt. Now he was setting aside the comfortable running boots and pulling on his stiff leather, cross-tied boots. Let her be reminded that he was a Viking, not some weak-sapped modern man that she could push here and there like a lump of dough.

With a sneer of distaste, he realized that already his manparts felt a chill without a loincloth. And he would no doubt have blisters on his heels from the chafing of his skin boots, which had shrunk in the ocean brine. *Bloody hell! A few days in this strange land and I am getting soft.*

She put a hand on his aim. "Rolf—"

"Unhand me," he said stiffly and stepped away. He had to be careful. The wench muddled his senses every time she got within a hairsbreadth of him. *Oh, wonderful! Now her eyes are filling with tears. Here it comes. She will try every feminine wile to bend me to her will. But I won't abide such cajolery. I won't!*

Taking one of the silver armlets from his upper arm, he handed it to her. "This is recompense for the money you have advanced me. I will no longer be working on your longship."

She tried to give it back but he sidestepped her.

"When Mike arrives in the morn, I'll give him the other armlet. Perchance he can find a money broker who will purchase it so that I'll have enough funds for food and supplies to complete my longship."

"Are you crazy? Those bracelets are probably worth several hundred thousand dollars."

He shrugged.

"Listen, I spoke hastily when I came outside because I was upset. My whole family just announced that they're coming here."

"Why did you not deny them your consent?"

Her head snapped up as if that thought had never occurred to her. *My brother Magnus is right. Females do have lesser intelligence.*

"They didn't ask."

He snorted with disgust. "No trouble did you have in finding the words to castigate me."

"Oh, you just don't understand. My parents badger me with politely spoken condemnations. My brother takes advantage of my fondness for him. My sister banks on my guilt and sense of responsibility." She rolled her shoulders helplessly. "It's easier to give in than argue with them."

"'Tis never easier, or best, to give in without a fight. It sets a precedent, and forever after you are easy prey for those who would chip away at your armor."

Her face brightened at his understanding. "That's exactly what has happened. They use me."

"Just as you were using me?"

Her face fell. "No. Of course not. Well, no more than you were using me."

He had rolled up several blankets and was now tossing some apples and several biscuits into their center. "If you do not mind, I have borrowed these blankets till I can purchase some bed furs on the morrow. The food I will need to break fast since you have warned me against snaring any wild game and cooking it on an open fire."

"Wh-what? You're still going? But where?"

"Just outdoors. I'll sleep under the stars near my longship. Even though I no longer work on *your* project, I must needs complete *my* boat to return home."

"You're going to camp in my yard?"

"Did I not say so?" *Yea, Magnus had the right of it where female intelligence is concerned.*

"But . . . but . . . what will people think?"

"Unlike you, I care not what other people think of me."

Scarlet patches bloomed on her cheeks. "I said I'm sorry."

"I heard you, wench . . . now and afore. And 'tis too late for apologies." He studied her for a long moment, reconsidering. "Do you take back the words?"

"Yes. I mean, which ones?" She wrung her hands nervously, looking everywhere but at him. "No, you're not dismissed," she finally mumbled with ill grace.

"Ah," he said, folding his arms over his chest, waiting till she was forced to meet his gaze. "And the other words?"

"The other words? Oh, yes, well, of course I need you for the project."

He shook his head. "Those were not your exact words, my lady. What you said was, 'I don't want you.'"

"I just said I needed you for the project. Darn it! What do you want from me?"

"The truth. Do you want *me*?"

A soft moan escaped her lips, hitting him like a potent aphrodisiac he did not need. "Yes, I want you, but I'm fighting the desire, strenuously."

He grinned. Her heightened breathing and flushed skin told him that she wanted him, even without her reluctant confession. Why did she hesitate? "Mayhap you think too much, sweetling," he said tenderly, skimming his fingertips over her parted lips.

She inhaled sharply. Did she experience the same shimmering heat that shot through his hand, up his arm, and out to all his sensitized body? "Have you ne'er chosen the impulsive path?" he asked thickly.

"Never."

"More's the pity." He stepped closer.

She backed away from him, hitting the wall. As skittish as a colt she was . . . or a mare in heat, he observed inwardly.

"Stop smirking," she ordered and slapped at his reaching hand, which had already loosened the brooch confining her hair in a tight knot at the nape of her neck. Immediately, the mahogany tresses blossomed out and the scent of drek filled the air.

He braced his hands against the wall on either side of her head and loomed over her. "Why do you tremble, Merry-Death? You have naught to fear from me."

"You don't intimidate me," she said, raising her prideful chin. He knew she resisted the temptation to duck under his arms and bolt from his presence like a cowardly rabbit. Her courage was impressive, and foolhardy. For her fate was sealed now that the hunt was on. If naught else, Geirolf was a talented hunter.

"Ah, then you tremble for me," he said, his voice husky. The first rule of the hunt was to disarm the prey. He leaned closer and brushed his lips along the line of her stubborn jaw.

"Wh-what? I do not."

"Liar. Already your body makes ready for our mating." He ran a calloused palm over one silk-covered breast, then the other.

She rewarded him with a whimper.

"Your hardened peaks bespeak the lie, m'lady." While his hand was in the vicinity, he flicked open two buttons on her silk *shert*. Two, that was all. Parry and retreat, another rule of the good hunter.

She stared at him like a doe caught before the bowman's arrow. He refused to break eye contact. Even the wildest beast of the forest could be mesmerized thus by a good huntsman. After a long pause, he opened one more button. Then another. Her *shert* gaped open, exposing her breasts.

He did not touch her. He just looked, and looked.

Under his smoldering scrutiny, the rose-tinted nipples bloomed, growing and straining against the lace cups of her undergarment.

His throat went dry, and a fierce shudder rippled over him. 'Twas not a good sign. The stalker must always be in control. At first, he could not speak. When he did, his voice came out hoarse and barely recognizable. "Do you ache for my touch as much as I ache to touch you?"

Her emerald eyes looked up in appeal, but he was beyond benevolence now. Blood roared in his veins and pounded in his lust-infused brain.

When it became clear he would not relent, she nodded.

"Say the words," he demanded.

Her pale face turned pink with embarrassment, but she yielded. "Touch me," she whispered. "Please."

He needed no more invitation. Looping a finger under the front band between her breasts, he pulled forward, tearing the garment. Her breasts burst free, and they were glorious, perfect globes of creamy skin and dusky areolae.

With a groan of pure ecstasy, he cupped each breast from underneath, raised them even higher, then lowered his head to take one nipple deep into the hot cavern of his mouth, suckling deeply.

She screamed, a high-pitched wail of agonizing pleasure.

Had ever a man heard such a sound from his woman and not felt as one of the gods . . . blessed? In reward for such homage, he gave equal treatment to her other breast and had to hold her upright as her knees collapsed with weakness. With a laugh of triumphant joy, he scooped her up in his arms, prepared to carry her outdoors where they could couple in private.

She did not protest. Not once. Instead, she curled against his chest and buried her warm face in his neck. The smell of drek surrounded him, and Geirolf exulted. 'Twas wondrous, this feeling of man-woman as they prepared to make love.

"I am so pleased that you surrendered, sweetling," he said huskily against her ear as he nudged the door open with his hip. "I feared you wouldn't agree that I am heading the project."

"Wh-what?" Her body went stiff as a warrior's pike. "You misunderstood. I'm heading the project. Not you."

She scrambled out of his arms. Her eyes were still slumberous with passion. Her hair flowed every which way in wild disarray. Her nipples continued to glisten from his kisses. But her mood was fast changing. That was more than obvious when she braced her hands on her hips and scowled at him. "I was surrendering my body, not my authority."

He stepped back. "I'll not work for you, Merry-Death. Either I head the project, or I'm not involved at all. No more of this 'I am the employer, you are the employee' business. No more bloody orders."

Her shoulders slumped. "That's one concession I can't make. I direct the Trondheim Venture. I give orders. That's the way it has to be."

Like ice water from the North Sea, her words dashed his excitement. How could he have misread her body signals? Damn her, and damn all willful women who would not bend to a man's better judgment. She gave him no choice. "Then we have naught else to say to each other." With that, he stormed down the steps, picked up his blanket roll, and left the keep.

His pride was still intact.

His heart was not.

CHAPTER NINE

❧

Who's in charge now, baby? . . .

Two days later Thea was on the patio painting bright red nipples on Ingrid when Meredith arrived home. The girl had already given Rolf's figurehead a base coat in a flesh tint where the flaking "skin" was exposed. Now she was refurbishing Ingrid's finer points.

"Hi, Aunt Mer."

Meredith could barely hear her niece over the music blasting from the CD player at her side. The raucous musicians were named some ridiculous appellation like Nine Inch Screws, or was it Nine Inch Nails? Whatever. The lyrics were incomprehensible, though undoubtedly vulgar. Meredith's parents were just going to love Thea's music; their tastes ran more to medieval dulcimer.

"What are you doing home so early, Aunt Mer?"

"Mike called and asked me to come talk with Rolf again." His exact words had been, "Beg the man, Dr. Foster. We're in deep shit here." Meredith leaned against the patio door and continued, "Mike said he and the college kids aren't making any headway on the project. They're bungling more than they're building. Meanwhile, Rolf's ship is going up like gangbusters."

"Rolf is, like, so cool, Aunt Mer."

Cool? Hardly the adjective I'd use. "He's nice," she conceded.

"Nice? Nice? Peanut butter is nice. Rolf is, like, industrial. Can't you make up with him?"

" 'Making up' isn't what this is about, honey." Just then, Meredith noticed that her niece wasn't wearing her usual grunge makeup. *Hallelujah! One fewer thing for my parents to complain about.* "You have beautiful skin, Thea. *Really* beautiful skin. I never realized how pretty you are."

"That's what Rolf said. He made me stand in front of a mirror, first with my makeup, then without. And he didn't tell me which one was better. He just asked me which one I prefer. Because that's the most important thing, you know. Not trying to impress other people. Just being happy with myself."

Was Rolf's counsel to Thea supposed to be a not-so-subtle message for me? Meredith wondered. "Well, that's very good advice, sweetie, but what brought that discussion on?"

"Oh. I'm not sure. We have lots of talks. Rolf never treats me like a kid. He says children become adults when they're only twelve years old in his country." Thea put her paintbrush down and tilted her head in concentration. "Now I remember. We were talking about his sister Katla. She married a Viking prince from Normandy when she was only thirteen—they marry young in his country, you know. Anyhow, Katla was always unhappy with her hair. Like, it was so blond it was almost white. So-o-o, one time she dyed it with walnut juice." Thea giggled. "It took six months for the stain to work out of her hair. And her forehead. And her hands. In the end, it turned out that her prince lo-o-oved her white-blond hair. That is such a totally cool story, don'tja think?"

Oh, yeah! I wonder why Rolf doesn't share these per-

sonal reminiscences with me? Hah! Maybe because I never believe anything he says. Maybe because I ignore him most of the time. Or try to. "I'm glad you now recognize the importance of natural beauty. I notice you still have the nostril earring, though."

"Hey, let's not take this inner beauty stuff too far. Besides, Rolf said that if you can wear jewelry on your nose, he supposed my nostril ring wasn't so bad."

"Huh?" *Geez, did I really say "huh?" Again? I'm regressing here, big time.*

"Rolf thinks those silver-rimmed spectacles you wear perched on your nose are a kind of nose ornament. Like my earring." Thea's eyes danced merrily as she related that information.

They both laughed companionably then.

"Have you had lunch yet?" Meredith looked at her watch. It was only twelve-thirty, and she hadn't accomplished anything at her office. She might as well stay home today. Work on some lesson plans. Shampoo her hair. Ogle Rolf.

"No thanks, Aunt Mer. Rolf is making all of us a Viking feast outside on an open fire."

Meredith immediately stiffened. Oh, Lord! "Not . . . oh, please don't tell me it's going to be fresh-killed rabbit."

Thea smirked. "Rabbit? Geez, Aunt Mer, where do you get these ideas? No, he sent Mike and some of the college girls to the supermarket. They couldn't find a cauldron or spit anywhere, though, not even in WalMart. They finally bought some cast-iron contraptions from an antiques store. Mike bought some old furs for Rolf there, too. They are, like, totally awesome."

"Furs?" Meredith said weakly. What next?

Meredith didn't have to wait long to find out.

Sniffing the air, Meredith realized that Thea had been telling the truth. The scent of food cooking on a wood fire wafted through the air. She wondered idly if there was an ordinance against that sort of thing in this neighborhood. Maybe not.

"By the way, Aunt Mer, I hope you don't mind. Mike put an extension cable on the TV so that we could watch *Home Improvement* DVDs outdoors. He'll bring the TV set back in later."

Meredith shook her head at the irony. Primitive cooking on an open fire and television.

"Rolf is totally buggin' over that program, you know. In fact, Aunt Mer, he's, like, adopted Tim 'The Toolman' Taylor as his hero. Isn't that so cool?"

Yeah! Real cool! Another thing my parents are going to love.

"Is it true that Grandfather and Grandmother Foster never had a television set when you and Mom and Uncle Jared were growing up?" Meredith noted that Thea had taken to calling her mother "Mom" again, and not Jillie. Another change for the better.

"It's true, hon. 'Junk food of the masses,' our parents called TV. To this day, they don't have a television."

"Yuck! They are such brainiacs."

That about says it all, Meredith agreed.

"Wait till they get a gander at *Home Improvement,*" Thea remarked with a mischievous grin.

Meredith grimaced. "The show that epitomizes male chauvinism and stupidity, that glorifies working with the hands, rather than the brain. Oh, Lord!"

"Like, I can't wait," Thea said enthusiastically.

"I can," Meredith said and put a hand to her forehead. It seemed she had a nonstop headache these days. "Do we have any Extra-strength Tylenol left, Thea?"

"Nah, you emptied the bottle last night. You know, when

Rolf walked out of the shower in his, whadjacallit, loin-cloth." Thea grinned again.

Even though Rolf refused to stay in the house, or eat with them, he couldn't quite give up his showers. He insisted on paying Meredith for the use of her bathroom—a ridiculous ten dollars a shot. She suspected that he was in and out of the house repeatedly during the day when she was at the office.

"Yo, Dr. Foster. You and I have got to have a heart-to-heart," Mike asserted, coming from around the side of the house.

Meredith's jaw dropped practically to her chest.

Mike was wearing a long-sleeved, collarless, deerskin tunic that hung down to mid-thigh and was belted at the waist with a three-inch tool belt. His bare legs led down not to a pair of flat-soled boots, like Rolf's, but instead to hiking boots with no socks. The image was ludicrous considering Mike's close-cropped blond hair.

"What in the name of God are you doing?" Meredith asked, barely stifling a giggle.

A flush stained Mike's cheeks, but he raised his chin haughtily. "Rolf said it would be a good idea for all of us to dress the part to make this a truly authentic project. By the way, toots," he said, addressing Thea, "where's your Viking babelet gown?"

"In the house. I didn't want to get paint on it," Thea answered, looking up at Mike adoringly.

"Ahem!" Meredith coughed, drawing Mike's attention back to her. "I thought Rolf was refusing to give you any advice."

"He is . . . on the longship project. But he doesn't mind sharing information on the Vikings themselves."

"How big of him!" Meredith observed snidely.

"Rolf was right, Dr. Foster. Everyone feels more in the spirit of the project when they're dressed appropriately. And isn't that what your grandfather really wanted from this project—to teach young people about another way of life?"

"Well, maybe," she conceded, sticking her head around the corner. Sure enough, the dozen or so students were dressed like Mike and Rolf. Some wore the same collarless, thigh-length tunics over tight-fitting trousers, with the shirts gathered in tightly at the waist with huge belts. A few had simple capes thrown over one shoulder and attached with round metal pins, instead of the traditional ornate Viking brooches. Their modern "brooches" sported such logos as, "Go Eagles," or "Long Live the Grateful Dead," or "Party Night at Sigma Nu, You Might Get Lucky," and even one that said, "It's Not the Way You Fish, It's How You Wiggle the Worm."

The college girls looked darling in braided hair and long-sleeved linen shifts covered with calf-length, open-sided Mother Hubbard-style aprons attached at the shoulders with garish bronze brooches.

"Where did they get all this stuff?" she asked, turning back to Mike.

"Some of them went to the local Society for Creative Anachronism. Some to Goodwill. But mostly the kids made their own outfits. The fabric was real cheap, and the belts and brooches are just dollar-store items," he said defensively, giving Meredith a clue that the money had come from the project kitty.

She relaxed. "Well, I suppose—"

"Would you have any problem with our using the damaged lumber to build a longhouse out by the swimming pool?"

"Wh-what? Absolutely not. Where's Rolf? I want to talk to him. Now! What happened to his tight time schedule? A longhouse! Oh, I'm going to kill him. Where is that damn Viking?"

"Must you shriek all the time, Merry-Death?" Rolf said, coming up behind her. Mike and Thea hurried off, leaving her to face the man alone. "Truly, every seagull from here to Iceland has flown away with all your caterwauling."

Because she'd had to present a progress report at a faculty meeting that morning, Meredith wore a black silk peplum suit with a knee-length skirt, nylons, and high-heeled pumps. Even as he criticized her "caterwauling," Rolf leaned lazily against the house, arms folded over his wide chest, and made a sweeping assessment of her outfit. It was hard to miss the appreciative widening of his whiskey eyes at the vast stretch of exposed legs.

"I was not shrieking," she said, disconcerted. "I merely said . . . Rolf, are you listening to me?"

"Huh?" His eyes were still riveted on her stockings, not to mention her fitted jacket and the modest cleavage where a single pearl on a gold chain nestled. Then a slow grin crept over his lips. "Just how high do those scandalous hose go?"

"High enough," she snapped, her face flushing with heat. "Really, my attire has nothing to do with . . . aaarrgh! . . . what are you doing?" This time she really was shrieking.

Rolf reached an arm downward and was proceeding to lift the hem of her skirt to check for himself on the hosiery.

She slapped his hand away and told him, "It goes to the waist, and it's called pantyhose. Now, can we get back to the reason for my coming home—to talk to you?"

"Hmmm," he murmured, his attention now centered on the pearl pendant. "I have an emerald necklet in my treasure casket at home . . . bartered from a Rus trader in Novgorod. I would give it to you if I could. 'Twould match your beautiful eyes, sweetling." He flicked the pearl with a forefinger.

Her bare skin underneath felt seared by his brief touch. "Oh." She sighed involuntarily.

"Oh," he said at the same time, throatily, with obvious surprise. Then his amber eyes went heavy lidded and smoldering. In an instant, the brush of his forefinger across her skin had acted like the abrasion of a match, striking instantaneous fire in them both.

Alarmed at the sudden wave of turmoil that flooded her, she backed away, through the patio door and into the house.

He followed after her, drawing the door shut and clicking the lock in place.

She backed into the corner by the fireplace, out of view of any who might pass by outside. Did she do so accidentally, or because she wanted privacy to be alone with Rolf? Had he missed her as much as she'd missed him these past two days? Did he want her as much as she was beginning to want him?

With arrogant presumption, Rolf snaked one hand around her nape and used the other hand to haul her hips up flush against his. And, oh, Lord, he had missed her. A lot.

"I don't think—" she started to protest.

"That's right, dearling, don't think," he finished for her. Incorrectly, of course, but Meredith couldn't manage to get the words out to set him straight. Rolf had lifted her by the waist and pushed her against the wall, her high heels a good foot off the floor. With his hips holding her in place, belly to belly, Rolf proceeded to do what he'd intended all along.

With a rumble of supreme male determination, he ran his callused palms over her silk stockings, from the creases of her knees, over the backs of her thighs and buttocks, up to the waist, hitching her skirt up along the way.

"I'm going to have dozens of snags," she choked out.

"Yea, you are good and truly snagged now, wench," he misinterpreted and undulated against her once in demonstration. Bolts of white-hot arousal shot out from that point to all her extremities, and Meredith blinked with wonder. She hoped her eyes weren't bugging out.

Then he pulled away for a second to allow space to hike the skirt up to her waist in front, too. He flipped up his tunic as well so there were only her pantyhose and the thin fabric of his loincloth separating them. Before she could slip down to the floor, his hips were back in place, locking her to the wall like a rag doll.

"Who is in charge now, Merry-Death?" he said huskily against her ear, reminding her of their ongoing battle.

Even his hot breath felt like a caress, but she refused to answer. It was so unfair of him to carry their differences over the longship project into this personal arena.

He laughed at her unspoken resistance to his question, and Meredith feared he would take it as a challenge.

He did.

Bending his knees slightly and canting his pelvis forward, he fitted his arousal with perfect accuracy into the vee of her legs. Her senses reeled and a soft whimper escaped her throat.

"Was that an order I just heard, Dr. Foster?" he asked, taking her hands, which had begun to push against his shoulders, and raising them above her head. Lacing her fingers with his, he placed them against the wall.

She shook her head. "Is this how Vikings go about raping and pillaging? Is this how you subdue your captive women?"

"Nay, this is how," he replied silkily.

And Meredith comprehended even before his head began to descend that she'd stepped into his trap.

"Wet your lips," he demanded.

She should have refused. Instead, she obeyed. Her only satisfaction was his quick intake of breath.

He nodded with approval, and then coaxed, "Part your lips."

She obeyed.

His erection lurched against her. "Arch your neck and raise your mouth to meet mine." His order this time was a barely discernible whisper.

He took her lips then with a savage intensity, catching her moan in his open mouth. Rapaciously, he forced her lips wider to take his thrusting tongue. To her shock, Meredith found herself welcoming his rough invasion, drawing on his tongue, kissing him back. Never breaking the kiss, Rolf molded her mouth with wet, clinging expertise. He directed her without words on how to make her lips pliant, how to please him most.

When the pulsing sensation between her legs began to throb and spiral outward with delicious agony, portending a too-hasty, too-violent climax, Meredith tried to tear her mouth away and tighten her thighs together. "No!" she cried out.

Understanding far too much, Rolf nipped her bottom lip with controlled aggression. "Shhh, sweetling, let me." It wasn't a request.

"But I don't want . . . oh!" Somehow in her passion-induced state, she hadn't realized that her hands were still raised above her head, voluntarily now, while his hands had been busy undoing the buttons on her jacket. His golden brown eyes glittered with erotic excitement as he gazed at her lace-covered breasts, then eased the fabric aside.

He didn't have to order her to bow her back and thrust her aching breasts forward. She did so out of a primordial need for his male touch. And, oh . . . *o-o-o-h!* . . . it took a mere flick of his callused fingertips over the swollen nipples for her to whimper and spread her legs, wrapping them around his waist.

With a guttural growl, he put his hands on her nearly bare buttocks and rocked her, first gently, then hard, hard, hard till the agonizing pulse grew and grew and grew. They both exploded against each other in a wild rush of overwhelming ecstasy.

At some point, Rolf's legs must have given way for she awakened from a brief swoon—the first of her life—to find herself on the floor, with her legs still clamped around his waist. He looked stunned.

She was pretty stunned herself. And mortified beyond belief.

You can't win an argument with a hard-headed Viking . . .

Geirolf leaned against a tree and watched Merry-Death through slitted eyelids as she skittered amongst her students. She'd resisted Thea's urging to change into an extra Viking gown, and instead donned a pair of jeans and a huge sweating *shert* emblazoned with, "I Am Woman, Hear Me Roar." He smiled as he read the message. He already knew how she could "roar."

He much preferred her in the garment she'd worn earlier— the one that exposed her long legs and a good portion of her bosom. Or the cat-fur sweat-her she'd worn to the shipping mall several days past.

He wouldn't tell her of his preferences yet, though. At this moment, he was not pleased with the wench. Oh, she talked to the young people in a normal tone of voice about the project and other sundry matters. They sat about the fire nibbling at the meal he had provided for them on wooden trenchers: chunks of beef swimming in a thick gravy served over slices of unleavened manchet bread, which they called pita bread in this land. And she laughed gaily when admiring their attire, but he knew the gaiety was forced. The wench was as nervous as a cat on hot coals. And with good reason.

She'd escaped his clutches after their near coupling an hour past. But not for long. He knew it. And she knew it.

Geirolf couldn't believe he'd spilled his seed in his breech-clout like an overeager youthling. For the second time. The wench with her wanton hose had seduced him into an over-powering loss of control. And his release, though not attained in the mode he would have preferred, had been gloriously exquisite. Whilst he misliked the woman's ability to turn his brain to gruel and his bones to butter, he could scarce wait to see what their actual bedding would be like, if this fore-taste was any indication.

"You're not eating," she commented, coming up to him finally. He noted that she maintained a good distance be-twixt them, as if she thought he might pounce on her.

Mayhap he would.

"I would prefer to finish the meal you offered, then took away afore I had a chance to fully . . . ah, indulge." His words brought a stain to Merry-Death's cheeks, which amazed him after her uninhibited display such a short time ago.

"Well, that was a—" she gulped—"mistake. Not to be repeated."

He laughed, causing several students, as well as Mike and Thea, to glance their way. For her ears only, he whis-pered, "Nay, not a mistake. And, for a certainty, to be re-peated. Again and again and again. Except *I* intend to lead the loveplay in future. *I* intend to give the orders."

"It seems to me you gave enough orders already," she blurted out, and he could see she wished the words had never escaped her lips . . . lips that were still swollen and bruised from his kisses. That reminded him of how much he enjoyed kissing Merry-Death. The way she responded so readily. The ardor with which she returned his deep kisses. The kit-tenish purr she emitted when—

"Stop that! Stop it right now!"

"What?" His forehead furrowed with puzzlement.

"Looking at my mouth like . . . like . . ."

He arched a brow. "Like a hungry man?"

She moaned. "Rolf, this is serious."

"Yea, 'tis."

"No, I mean we have to behave in a more serious, professional manner. I came home from the office today to talk to you about our differences over the project, and instead—"

"Instead you enticed me with your harlot hose. 'Tis how women throughout the ages have attempted to settle differences with their menfolk. Tsk-tsk! Somehow, I expected more of you, being a *professional* woman and all."

"I did *not* entice you," she snapped indignantly. "You're the one who assaulted me. No wonder you Vikings have a reputation for raping and pillaging. It must come naturally."

"Assault? Do you say I assaulted you? Is that what you called it when you moaned your need into my mouth? When your green eyes turned molten with appeal? When you locked your warrior thighs about my hips and knocked me to the floor?"

"Warrior thighs? Warrior thighs?" she sputtered, shoving a palm into his chest, and then immediately stepped back when she saw the students gaping at them.

"Ah, you misread me, wench. Warrior thighs are an asset for a woman. Better to clench man and horse alike."

"Aaarrgh!"

"Your nipples are peaking."

She looked down in horror, then cast him a disparaging scowl when she realized he could see nothing beneath the huge *shert*. "They are not."

"Mayhap I am mistaken."

"*Mayhap* your brain is lodged between your legs."

He grinned. "For a certainty."

"You're impossible."

"Yea. 'Tis one of the things women love about me."

"Do all Vikings have overinflated egos?"

He pulled a face at her. "You confuse self-importance with self-confidence."

"Are you going to take over the project again?"

"Are we changing the subject?" He laughed.

"Yes, we're changing the subject. Look at this," she stormed, waving a hand in the air toward the two unfinished long-ships. "Mike and the students barely have a framework up for the project vessel, while yours will be done in no time."

He shrugged. "With my time freed from *managing* the project, I've been able to spend all the daylight hours working on my boat. And, of course, I have no reservations about using sandpaper and modern wood fillers. Tomorrow I'm going to have Mike take me to Hardware Heaven again—"

"That's Hardware *Superstore*," she corrected.

"I know that, wench," he said, tweaking her nose, "but to a man who works with his hands, it is indeed heaven. As I was saying, I intend to buy some power tools. Mayhap a drill and an electric saw. And duct tape. I have heard that duct tape is man's best friend." He jiggled his eyebrows at her.

"You are *not* using modern tools on my longship."

"Tsk-tsk-tsk! You are not listening, my lady. These are for my longship, not yours." He tapped his front teeth pensively. "I just had a wonderful idea. Mayhap I will make another purchase, too. A motor. Yea, I will be the first Viking with a power motor in my longship."

"You . . . you—" she fought for words "—you wouldn't!"

"Merry-Death, Merry-Death, Merry-Death, you disappoint me. When will you learn not to rise to every bait a man throws your way? Nay, I'll not spoil a good ship with a motor. However, I've been studying the motor in Mike's wheeled box, and since he got me a sew-shall sack-your-tea document today, along with a travel pass—a passport—I am contemplating . . ."

His hesitation should have given her a clue.

". . . getting my driver's license tomorrow. And buying my own wheeled box. A car, not one of those trucks that Mike prefers."

"Oh, my God!" Merry-Death used the expression over-much when talking to him. It no doubt meant he overwhelmed her with his wisdom and cunning.

"Perchance, do you know a good wheeled-box mart where . . . ?" he started to ask, tentatively.

Merry-Death narrowed her eyes suspiciously at him. He loved her sea-green eyes, even when narrowed shrewishly.

". . . where a Viking could purchase a . . . longcar?"

She made a choking sound before spinning on her heel and stalking toward the keep. To search for another of those magic pills of hers, he would wager. Let her cure her head megrims any way she could, for she will not plead an aching head later when he came presenting his own magic. And his magic wasn't in a pill.

CHAPTER TEN

✧

He knew how to snare a woman . . .

Meredith's sister Jillian swept into their lives that evening like a summer storm over his beloved Vestfjord Valley. All bluster and no substance.

She wore tight black *braies* of a stretchy material that would surely catapult her all the way to Iceland if a man pulled on the waistband and let go. On top, her breasts strained against a silky white *shert* that went down to her thighs and wrists but was cinched in at the waist with an oversized, metal-studded belt. Several opened buttons provided an impressive cleavage filled in with a handsome gold-and-amber necklet similar to those made by the Coppergate artisans in Jorvik. Matching loops hung from her ears, which were exposed by the oddest hair. The color was the same dark reddish-brown shade as Merry-Death's, piled atop her head in disarray, but strands of gold ran uniformly through it. He didn't think the sun could produce such an effect.

Mike and the students had left for the day, and dusk approached as Jillian hugged Thea over and over, then sent her outside to carry in the vast amount of baggage she'd brought with her. Turning to him and Merry-Death, Jillian asked bluntly, "So, are you two lovers?"

"No!" Merry-Death said.

"Yes," he said at the same time.

Jillian looked at each of them, her crimson lips curving up with amusement.

" 'Tis a question of definition," he explained, ignoring Merry-Death's coughing fit.

"We are *not* lovers," Merry-Death said emphatically and speared him with a sidelong glare. "I hired Rolf to work on the longboat project. He's a shipbuilder from . . . Norway." She'd warned him in a nervous rush when Jillian's hired box drove up earlier that he was not to discuss time travel, ancient Vikings, or anything that would cause her sister to know his true identity. Not that Merry-Death believed his explanations. And he didn't appreciate her referring to him as ancient, either.

He wagged an admonishing finger at Merry-Death. "Nay, you misspeak our relationship. I was hired to *direct* the project. Is that not so, my lady?"

A speaking silence ensued in which Jillian mouthed the words "My lady?" at Merry-Death, and then narrowed her eyes, watching them far too closely.

He no longer required the talisman's magic to help him translate their strange language, except for the occasional tongue-twisting words. Although he'd always mastered foreign tongues with ease, he was certain the relic had helped speed his lessons this time.

Finally, Merry-Death's shoulders slumped with resignation. "That's right. Rolf is directing the physical work on the project, and I'm handling the paperwork and liaison with the foundation committee. We're . . . partners." Her last word came out tentatively, and she held her breath, waiting for his reply.

Damn, but the woman was willful. He should take an excessive time contemplating her impertinent claim. But compassionate man that he was, he nodded, and she released a sigh of relief. Later, she would pay for testing him so.

"Mom, where do you want this luggage?" Thea asked, huffing into the room, overloaded with leather boxes of all sizes named for the biblical hero Samson.

Jillian raised a questioning brow at Merry-Death, who said, "Upstairs. You can sleep with Thea. I'll use the sofa."

Jillian's eagle eyes then swerved to him in speculation.

"Rolf prefers to sleep outdoors under the stars," Merry-Death answered for him.

Geirolf made a soft snorting sound of contradiction as he passed Merry-Death on his way to relieving Thea of her burdens. She put a halting hand on his arm and whispered, "Will you help me, really? Will you resume work on the project tomorrow?"

"Yea."

She tilted her head in surprise at his swift compliance.

"All you had to do was ask, sweetling. Not order."

"Sweetling? How quaint!" Jillian observed.

"Oh, you are the most exasperating man!" Merry-Death said.

He grinned at her and couldn't resist leaning forward to steal a quick kiss from her parted lips.

"Not lovers, huh?" Jillian hooted.

He jerked back. Merry-Death had a way of making him forget where he was. And how could it be that his lips tingled from that mere touch? Amazing. How much more intense would the tingling be if some other parts of their anatomies connected?

"Lordy, lordy, you two throw off more sparks than a bonfire."

A rush of pink flooded Merry-Death's cheeks.

He winked at her, envisioning a hundred different things he could do to make her blush even more. He could scarce wait.

Merry-Death jutted out her mulish chin, not her most attractive feature. As she stormed past him, leading the way to the stairs, he remarked to Jillian, "Your sister needs a lesson in the womanly arts . . . how to be more biddable."

Merry-Death stumbled but didn't look back.

Jillian chortled with laughter.

Thea was walking up the stairs, backwards, in front of them all, grinning from ear to ear.

"You see, Merry-Death gleans all her learning from books, whereas her real-life education is sadly lacking."

"How interesting!" Jillian opined.

Merry-Death snickered and muttered something about Vikings who were full of themselves.

"You see, men in this land have a perfect hero to emulate—"

"Oh, no!" Merry-Death exclaimed, scowling at him from the upper corridor.

"Tim the Toolman Taylor!" Thea whooped.

Jillian joined Merry-Death in the hallway, her mouth forming a little circle of astonishment.

"Your hero is Tim Allen, the actor on *Home Improvement*?" Jillian asked incredulously, and then burst into another fit of laughter, throwing an arm over her daughter's shaking shoulders. Even Merry-Death put a hand over her mouth to stifle a smile.

Why did these thick-headed women not understand the heroic qualities of the much-maligned Tim?

When Jillian's laughter finally subsided into mere giggles, she slapped her thigh with delight. "And who, pray tell, Mr. Viking, would be the heroic equivalent for women? Who should we emulate to become more—what did you call it?— biddable?"

He did not much relish their laughter at his expense. And,

really, females were all half-brained, chirping for explanations about every bloody thing. Well, he would enlighten them, good and proper. "Martha Stewart."

"Martha Stewart!" all three women chirped in unison.

"Yea. I watched her on the picture box this morn whilst breaking fast. By all the gods, she is a wonder. In less than an hour, she baked twelve loaves of bread, poured concrete for a rock garden, pruned an apple tree, and crocheted a tablecloth. And not once did she badger a man to come to her aid."

"Is this guy for real?" Jillian asked Merry-Death.

"I'm not sure."

"You women could learn much from Martha. In truth, 'tis what I told Pamela Anderson yesternoon when she complained about her busy schedule."

"What did you just say?" Merry-Death shrieked.

Really, if he were not so smitten with the wench, he would have to tell her that her voice made his eyes water betimes.

"You talked to Pamela Anderson?"

"Did I not just say so?"

She put a hand to her forehead in that eternal female pose of "My lot in life is suffering and woe . . . and men are the root of all evil." It was a good sign, in his opinion. She was weakening. "Where . . . how did you talk to Pamela Anderson?"

"On the telephone. What a marvel that black box is!"

"Why did you call Pamela Anderson? And how in God's name were you able to get her number?"

"Hah! 'Twas not easy, I will tell you." He put the travel cases on the floor and leaned into the corridor wall. "You know that Mike yearns for this woman, though I cannot see her appeal. Too coarse, if you ask me. And I must confess, Merry-Death, I do not believe she was born with blond hair. My sister-by-marriage, Gilda, looks just like Pamela, except—"

"Aaarrgh!" Meredith shrieked, *again,* causing his eyeballs to flinch. Next would come the watering. "Will you get on with your explanation."

He cast her a disapproving scowl, and continued. "Mike wants the woman, and I was showing him how a Viking would handle the snaring."

"Snaring? Snaring? Are you talking about snaring a woman?" Merry-Death sputtered.

"Exactly how is this snaring done?" Jillian was not quite so appalled at the notion of men snaring women.

"Straightforward. No muddling about with milksop pleas or sweet virginal dalliances. Just tell the woman, 'I want you.'" He thought for a moment. "Or else just take her. That is, of course, another method. Some women don't want to be asked. Yea, that is my usual strategy. 'Twas my mistake with you, Merry-Death. Too much muddling."

"God, I'm glad I decided to come," Jillian chortled. "You are going to be so-o-o good for my sister."

"Well said!" Geirolf commented enthusiastically. Then he went back to their previous discussion. "Pamela cannot come to Maine, unfortunately. She is acting out a story for the TV box. But she invited Mike to come visit her in Holly-Forest."

"Tell them who else you called, Rolf. Tell them," Thea urged, jumping up and down with glee.

He brightened. "Oh, did I forget to inform you, Merry-Death? Tim and Al are coming here to help with your longship project. They will bring a picture box crew with them, too, to make a flummery, a pretend story, about Tim building a longship in the courtyard of his keep."

Merry-Death went speechless, her lips trembling with words that would not come out. In truth, she resembled his Great-uncle Bjolf when about to have a fit. No doubt she was overcome with awe at his ability to adapt so well to her country. He puffed out his chest, continuing, "And Tim's over-lord will pay you. So there! You may thank me later for adding to the sorely depleted coffers of your project."

"Tim and Al?" she squeaked out. Leastways, she did not shriek this time.

"Tsk-tsk. You are not paying attention. Tim Taylor and Al Borlund."

"You've been making all these long-distance calls on my phone?" she inquired weakly.

"Yea. And believe me, I had to make dozens of them afore I got the correct numbers. Agents. Picture Guilds. Ted Turner. Tart-tongued upper-ate-oars."

Merry-Death put her face in her hands. 'Twas a favored gesture of hers when talking with him. "I want an aspirin."

"Ass-burn? Now? Well, well, well, Merry-Death! It sounds rather perverted to me, and your timing is odd—" he paused for only a moment "—but I'm willing, if you are." He threw his arms out in invitation.

Jillian and Thea howled so hard tears streamed down their faces, but Merry-Death stared at him as if she'd been poleaxed.

Sometimes, he decided, 'twas wise to poleax a woman. In one form or another.

When Vikings fall, they fall hard . . .

Hours later, Geirolf sat drinking mead at the scullery table while Jillian endlessly examined his belt clasp under a magnifying glass. She'd done the same with his arm rings before that. For some reason, he didn't mention the hidden relic, which was revealed only when a secret bead on the gold work was pressed just so. From the very beginning, he'd told all to Merry-Death, without hesitation, and yet he'd held back with her sister. How curious!

But he didn't want to dwell on such ruminations now. He was bored. And in a rare lustful mood.

Oh, the lust itself was not rare, but the fierceness of his need for Merry-Death was becoming nigh overwhelming.

Merry-Death had gone upstairs a short time ago with a glass of wine to soak in something she called a bubble bath. He would like to see that. Yea, he would.

Instead, for the past hour, he'd listened to Jillian ooh and aah over his belt clasp, when he'd much rather have Merry-Death ooh and aah over another of his possessions—a mite lower down his belly—and clamoring for attention.

"Why are you glaring at me?" Jillian asked.

He refused to answer and grabbed his belt out of her hands. "'Tis time for sleep. I must be up at first light." The last thing on his mind was sleep.

"I'm not very tired," she said, slitting her eyes at him. "Why not leave the belt with me to do a few more sketches? I can return it to you in the morning."

Hah! No doubt she planned to scramble off with the talisman in the dead of night and place it under guard in some dusty museum. Or sell it to the highest bidder. "Nay," he asserted emphatically, "you have examined and scribbled enough."

The flash of vexation in her eyes, which she quickly masked, told him that slyness was second nature to her. She cared for herself and her own greedy ambitions first and foremost. That was evident in her neglect of her daughter. Not to mention her current flirtatious fluttering of eyelashes and not-so-accidental brushing against his body parts.

He was buckling on his belt and walking toward the outside door when she called after him. "My sister isn't woman enough for you, you know. I would be the far better choice."

His step faltered and he turned slowly. "What a faithless wretch you are. Does family mean naught to you?"

She shrugged. "I love my sister . . . Oh, don't look down your nose at me, Viking . . . I *am* fond of Mer—in my own way." She stretched her arms over her head, presumably to remove the kinks from her long sitting, but more to tempt him with her form.

It was a very nice form, but he felt no inclination to see more of it. Or to try her charms.

Still she persisted. "I've never made it with a Viking before. Have you ever done it with a jewelry maker? We have really good . . . hands." She gave him a slumberous meaningful glance and flexed her fingers.

He shook his head with disgust. "'Twould seem some things ne'er change. In every land and every time, a snake in the grass is still a snake in the grass. You are cut of the same cloth as that biblical Jezebel."

"Don't be such a judgmental prude. We're talking about a little hanky-panky, not a freaking marriage. Besides, it's plain to see that you and Mer haven't done the deed yet, and probably never will, if I know my sister."

Angered by her perfidy, he stomped back to the table and jabbed an admonishing finger into her chest. "Whether we have or not, she is the woman of my choice, and she is your blood kin. Have you no shame?"

Jillian's face flushed red at his rejection. Then she threw her hands up in surrender. "Hey, it's your loss, buddy. You'll see. Mer is sweet and all that. Too sweet, actually. Some men get turned on by that niceness, but they soon lose the itch when they realize how unimpressive she is. A wimp."

"A wimp?"

"Weak."

"Are you demented? Merry-Death is the strongest woman I have e'er met. Well, aside from my mother. Whate'er obstacle the fates throw in her path, she meets the challenge with the mettle of a seasoned warrior. Ne'er does she run from her honor-bound duties." He addressed the last remark to her pointedly, referring to her lack of maternal responsibility.

"You don't know Mer as well as I do," she said, glossing over his criticism. "She's always trying to please. Always failing. I learned a long time ago not to dance to the music of other people's dreams, but Mer is still running in place, trying to memorize the right dance steps."

He cocked his head in puzzlement.

"From the time we were kids, my parents set such high standards for us. Impossible standards. Jared, our older brother, came closest to meeting the grade. He had the best marks in school. The most serious personality. Never got into trouble. If Mer is boring as a rock, Jared is a concrete tomb."

He bristled at her disparaging words, but Jillian jabbered on. "Jared was super-intelligent. He moved out when he went to college and never came back. But the damage was already done. He's become a clone of Mother and Father . . . an academic workaholic with no social life."

"And Merry-Death?" he asked. Despite his misgivings about listening to this loathsome woman's prattle, he wanted to know more about Merry-Death's past . . . why she was so skittish with him.

"Meredith was pathetic, even as a little girl. Somehow she got the idea that our parents would love her if she met their standards."

He made a grunting noise of disbelief. "Parents do not set conditions on their love."

She arched her brows in disagreement. "Ours did, and still do. And while Jared has flown the coop, and I stopped jitterbugging to their tune long ago, Mer is still trying to please them . . . to earn their love."

His heart ached with sympathy for Merry-Death. Having been raised in a loving household, he cringed with sympathy at the cold atmosphere that must have formed her early years.

"Mer did the same thing with Jeffrey, her husband," Jillian went on spitefully, and Geirolf's ears pricked up. "She smothered him with love. Oh, I know that he left her for that young bimbo he was screwing, and I know he got the girl pregnant, but there's no question in my mind. If Mer had been more of a woman, Jeffrey never would have left. Even if she'd been able to pop out babies like Pez candies. As I said, she's pathetic."

Geirolf stiffened angrily. "Mer is all woman. Any person who fails to see her worth is blind. Furthermore, there's strength, not weakness, in the fealty she lavishes on those she loves."

"You use the most archaic language. Where did you say you were from?" Jillian's forehead creased with concentration as she studied him. "Anyhow, I don't know who you are, or where you've come from . . . *yet*. But I do know that you find me attractive."

He exhaled wearily. So, they were back to the seduction. His lack of interest should be more than evident.

"I saw the way you stared at me earlier," she argued. "You turn me on, too, Viking, in a primitive way."

His lips curled with revulsion at her lack of loyalty toward her sister and the too-blatant invitation to share her bed. "A man's pole will rise to most any bait, but it takes a woman with more than surface beauty to hook the fish. You, my lady, are a poor fisherwoman."

"And you think Mer is better in the sack than me?" Her mouth slackened with incredulity. "Listen, if you're worried about Mer, she doesn't have to know. We can go outside. I don't mind sharing a sleeping bag."

"I use bed furs."

"Even better."

He groaned at her perseverance. "Cast your hook else-where, my lady," he chided. "This fish is taken."

Her eyes widened as if suddenly enlightened. "Good Lord! My sister has landed herself a Viking. The nerd and the stud." Jillian leaned back in her chair and scrutinized him as if he'd grown three heads. "You're in love with my sister."

"Nay, I am not," he denied. *Am I?* His heart began to thud madly as he pondered the outlandish suggestion. *Is it true?* "Why would you say such?" he blurted out, wishing instantly that he could bite back the question.

She smirked as women are wont to do when they believe they have won some battle with a man, though why his af-fection for her sister should count as a sign of defeat for him he could not fathom.

"I suspected it the first time I saw you together. You can't keep your eyes off Mer."

"I doubt that I watch her overmuch," he demurred, "al-though she *is* pleasing to the eye." He resolved then and there, to keep a close rein on his traitorous eyes in future. "Besides, a man looking at a woman does not signify love."

"You touch her every chance you get."

"Now, *that* I know to be a falsehood. I am very careful about touch—" He caught his mistake at once. Had he really revealed a conscious—or was it unconscious?—effort on his part to control his impulse to touch Merry-Death?

"And the way you defended Mer to me a little while ago . . . well, anyone could tell you must love her."

"You mistake chivalry for some romantic notion," he said with finality and departed huffily from the house. The bothersome wench's laughter followed after him.

Regardless of his protests, Geirolf was unable to stop

thinking about Jillian's suggestion. Deep down in his soul, he feared she might have discovered something he hadn't realized himself.

Girding himself with resolve, he vowed, *Nay, I do not love Merry-Death. I will not allow myself to fall in love with her, or any other lady.*

But in that moment, he knew. Somehow, some way, he had managed to fall in love for the first time in his life. And the recipient of his reluctant affections was almost a thousand years younger than he.

How could that be?

I do not want this.

What future could they have? None. He would return soon to his time, alone.

Alone. Why, after all these years of cherished freedom, does the solitary life no longer appeal?

Well, 'twas for the best, he decided, laying out his bed furs near his half-completed longship. She was too different from him. And it wasn't just their disparate cultures and times. She worked with her mind; he worked with his hands. She dreamed of a quiet family life; he carried the blood of Viking adventurers. She deliberated too much afore making decisions; he acted on instinct. He liked Oreos, she preferred pasta worms.

Ah, but what would it be like to mate with a woman he loved? With Merry-Death?

That enticing image lingered. And lingered. And lingered. It would not go away as he tossed about restlessly in his bed furs, unable to sleep.

I am doomed.

On the other hand, he made much ado over naught. Perchance if he said the words aloud—nay, not aloud—perchance if he said the words in his head, he would see how foolish the proposition really was. So, that's what he would do, Geirolf decided. Scrunching his eyes closed, he clenched his fists, fortifying himself for the ordeal.

He might have been preparing for a brutal battle, or a dousing in the frigid North Sea.

I love Merry-Death, he said, testing. Then, it was as if a volcano erupted in his brain. The words poured out in an unending stream, like lava. *I love Merry-Death, I love Merry-Death, I love Merry-Death, I love . . .*

With that terrifying recognition, another equally terrifying prospect occurred to him. Was it possible that his destiny was not to replace the relic?

Was Merry-Death his destiny?

Rub-a-dub-dub, can a Viking fit in her tub? . . .

It was midnight and Meredith was still basking in her grandmother's deep, footed bathtub—an extravagance her grandfather had provided for his beloved wife when putting in the large modern bathroom with its shower stall. Thank God for his extravagance. And his love.

She kept a thin stream of hot water running, and every once in a while dumped in more scented oil to replenish the bubbles, using her big toe to release some water so it wouldn't overflow.

Oh, the memories of Gram coming upstairs at the end of the day for her nightly soak. The secret smile she and Gramps used to exchange. The scent of roses permeating the small house.

Was that why Meredith had continued to buy the same bath product over the years, although she hadn't dared use it when Gramps was in the house for fear it would bring him too much pain? Did she associate the fragrance with love? Jeffrey had detested the perfumed oil. Too flowery. She adored it.

Taking another sip of white wine from the crystal glass on the tub ledge, Meredith leaned her head back, her hair dangling in a wet swath over the back edge. The house was quiet. Jillian had stopped in a half hour ago just before going to bed.

Even Jillie hadn't been able to upset her tonight with her prodding questions about Rolf, his background, where he came from, her feelings for him. On and on she had grilled her, but for once Meredith had stood her ground. "Tomorrow, Jillie. Tomorrow, I'll explain it all to you." So, Jillie had gone off to sleep with her daughter.

For the first time in days, she felt at peace. No cares about the project. No worries about her personal future. No compulsive need to think and plan each little aspect of her life and work. No being on constant guard against Rolf's tempting presence. Maybe she should take life like this soothing bath . . . go with the flow.

The door clicked open behind Meredith and she realized that her sister hadn't gone to sleep, after all. "I hope you're not going to renew your interrogation, Jillie. Hand me a towel, will you? My skin is beginning to feel like a prune."

"Now that is something I would like to test for myself." A deep masculine voice chuckled.

Geirolf feasted on the sight before him. Merry-Death let out a little squeal and tried to sink deeper into the water as he neared the tub. *So, this is a bubble bath. Bloody hell, there are a few things about this land I would not mind taking back with me to the past. Bubble baths. Power tools. Merry-Death.*

"Shhh," Geirolf said, coming up to the side of the tub. "We would not want your sister storming in here to the rescue. No doubt she would launch a fierce assault to protect your virtue."

The cynicism of his tone must have alerted Meredith. She studied him for a telling moment, then exclaimed, "Oh, good heavens! My sister put the make on you, didn't she?"

Her lack of jealousy surprised him, giving him no time to fabricate a story. "'Twas naught of importance."

"Hah! Maybe not to you. Listen, Rolf, you've got to understand my sister. She gives the impression of being overconfident, but deep down she's insecure. My parents always made us kids feel . . . well, lacking. Jillie's method of handling the continual criticism was rebellion . . . and cockiness."

He shook his head at her. "You are amazing, Merry-Death. I cannot credit your making excuses for your sister's guile. She attempts to lure your man into her bed, and you call it a trifle. Well, I consider it more than mischief, I tell you."

"Rolf, you are not 'my man.' You are just . . . Oh, never mind. And you're right. I do make too many excuses for Jillie. Do you know—" she hesitated, and then divulged "—I suspect that she made a play for Jeffrey while we were married."

And that weasel Jeffrey probably succumbed. Poor Merry-Death! Always the victim of those she loved most. Before he had an opportunity to offer solicitude, she went on. "What are you doing here anyway?"

"I thought perchance I would take a shower," he lied.

"Liar!" She laughed. "You've already taken two showers today."

He raised a brow. "You've been counting the number of showers I take. Hmmm. Mayhap you have been imagining yourself in there with me."

"I have not," she said indignantly, a becoming color suffusing her cheeks. A good guess, he decided with immense satisfaction. She *had* been picturing them both thus occupied. "Besides, you can't just walk in here when I'm taking a bath. You're going to wake everyone up."

"No one will know I'm here if you soften your voice. Has anyone e'er told you it has a decided screech to it?"

"Rolf, you've got to respect my privacy."

He could tell he made her uncomfortable. She made him uncomfortable, too. "Hmpfh! With all the people coming in and out of this keep, when do you and I get to have some much-needed privacy? It occurs to me this is the only chamber with a lock on the door."

Looking askance at the bubbles that were starting to diminish slightly—not enough, to his mind—she reached over to a low shelf and poured a dollop of liquid into the tub, causing more bubbles to erupt. At the same time, she lifted a big toe from the water and flicked a silver lever, which immediately caused water to gurgle out. Then she flicked her toe in the opposite direction.

"*Blód hel!* Do that again and you will have one large Viking in the tub with you."

"Do what again?" She cast him a startled sidelong glance.

"That exotic trick you just did with your toe." He smiled at her. His wench was very talented. He wondered idly what other talents lay hidden beneath her prim exterior.

"Stop smiling at me like that."

He smiled wider.

"And stop staring at me. It's not decent. Oh, what are you doing?"

After locking the door, he'd pulled a short stool closer and sunk down onto it wearily. Then he stretched out a hand to the bottle of bubble lotion, placing it at the opposite end of the ledge, out of Meredith's grasp.

Meredith studiously avoided looking at the hem of Rolf's tunic, which rode up when he sat down, knees spread, exposing way too much hairy calf and thigh. "I asked you a question. What are you doing here?"

Resting his elbows on the side of the tub, he smiled lazily. She hated it when he smiled lazily. "Waiting for the bubbles to evaporate," he said.

"Oh," she squeaked out and sank a bit lower in the tub.

Now, he was tracing a forefinger through the thick layer of bubbles, making a path of letters that immediately melded together. "I-L-O-V—"

"Wh-what are you doing?" she asked in a panic. Surely, he hadn't been writing what she'd thought she'd seen.

He jerked back his hand, as if just realizing what he'd been doing. "Practicing my alphabet," he said.

Liar.

"Mayhap you would like me to practice my letters on your skin. Prune skin, did you call it when I walked in?"

She closed her eyes as a tingling awareness passed over her, almost as if he were actually tracing the words on her flesh . . . words she yearned for and at the same time resisted with her whole being.

"Merry-Death," he said gently, a note of desperation in his voice, "do you tingle when I touch you?"

Her eyes shot open. Could he read her mind now, too?

"Not when I touch you intimately, but just in passing. Like that fleeting kiss I gave you earlier? Did you tingle then?"

He gazed at her with such abject bleakness as he asked the question.

She frowned with confusion. "What's wrong, Rolf? Why are you asking me these questions?"

He shrugged. "'Tis something your sister suggested to me."

Meredith bristled. "Was that before or after she attempted to jump your bones?"

The grimness of his expression lightened and he chucked her playfully under the chin. And she did tingle, darn it.

"After."

"Well, then, what did my sister suggest that has turned you so grim?"

He was back to tracing letters in the bubbles with seemingly idle concentration, but she could tell that he was deeply troubled by something . . . something Jillie had suggested to him. What could it be? Meredith had no deep, dark secrets.

He lifted his head and held her eyes. "She said . . . she said that I am in love with you."

That was the last thing Meredith had expected. "I . . . I . . ." she sputtered. What she wanted to say was, "Are you?" but she didn't have the nerve. For some reason, his answer was far too important to her.

Tears welled in her eyes, and she turned her face toward the wall. Her vulnerability was crushing her. Not so much because she was naked and he was not, but because she felt so . . . needy.

With a forefinger against her jaw, he forced her to face him. "I denied it . . . at first."

At first? Oh, my God!

"But I fear that Jillian made a wise assessment."

"She did?" Meredith's white knuckles clutched the sides of the tub in desperation. If she didn't hold on tight, she just might sink and drown in two feet of water from the sheer passionate lethargy that swept her torso. "What are you saying, Rolf?" she whispered.

"I think . . . Nay, I cannot hide behind cowardly words of hesitation," he confessed huskily. *"Ég elska þig."*

"What?"

"I love you," he translated in a low mumble. Then louder, "I love you. May the fates have mercy on us, but I do. I love you, Merry-Death."

CHAPTER ELEVEN

She was slippery as a fish...

"You love me?" Merry-Death choked out.

The scarlet flush of arousal on her face faded to pale cream, and her luminous eyes widened with anxiety. If her white-knuckled fingers clutched the tub's edge any tighter, she might break through the porcelain.

Geirolf wasn't offended. He understood her panic. Had he not fought the same urge to run like the wind when Jillian first suggested to him that he loved Merry-Death?

Regaining her composure, Merry-Death laughed. It was a false laugh, one of those unattractive sounds people make to cover their real emotions. "Ha-ha-ha," Merry-Death said. "Great joke, Rolf, but you don't have to give me that old line. I've already decided to have an affair with you. So you don't—"

"You have?" Grinning at her from where he remained perched on a stool, chin propped on his steepled hands, he could scarce keep from jumping into the tub with her—tunic, boots, and all. But first, he had to make himself clear. "'Tis not a line, as you name it. 'Tis a statement of fact. I wish 'twere not so—we have so many obstacles in our path. I do not want to love you, Merry-Death, but there 'tis. I love you."

She made a kittenish mewl of distress, and he couldn't

tell if she was pleased or not. Since he'd never uttered those three dreaded words to a woman afore, he had no experience to draw on.

"I'm telling you, Rolf, you don't need to soft-soap me to get me in your bed. You won that battle days ago."

He chuckled. "But I would much relish soft-soaping you, sweetling, if the exercise even remotely resembles drekking you."

A smile twitched at the corners of her lips—lips that he anticipated kissing very soon and very thoroughly.

"Have I told you how much I enjoy the scent of your drek, almost as much as the flowery bath oil that permeates this bathing chamber? I will ne'er smell roses again without thinking of you."

Merry-Death's head snapped back, and she gave him an uneasy look. Why would she be surprised that he cherished the fragrances associated with her? But he had another question. "What is this 'affair' you have decided to have with me? Is it a perversion?" he asked hopefully. Meanwhile, he trailed his fingertips idly through the dissipating bubbles, giving him a murky vision of the glorious body beneath.

"You are outrageous," Merry-Death proclaimed, but she didn't seem sad about that. "An affair is a fling, a casual relationship that both parties know will end in a short time."

Geirolf drew himself straight. "Nay, there is naught casual in my sentiments for you. Do not dismiss me in such a light manner, my lady. It demeans what I offer you."

"And what, exactly, are you offering me?" she inquired tentatively.

"My heart."

"Oh, Rolf." Her eyes filled with tears . . . happy tears, he would wager. She started to say more, but then stopped. "Look, this isn't the place to discuss this. Would you turn around so I can get out of the tub?"

He grinned. "You may certainly stand, but I'm not such a lackwit that I would turn away."

"I'd feel more comfortable talking to you on an equal basis, fully clothed."

"I could remove my garments," he offered.

She tsk-tsked at him, just like his mother. Well, not exactly so. The dreamy expression on her face was far from maternal, praise the gods!

"Come, Merry-Death, stand and let me dry you off. Then we'll see about the business of . . . uh, discussing."

She sank deeper into the tub, her chin skimming the water's surface. The stubborn wench!

"Coward!" he taunted.

Her eyes flashed green fire for a moment before she stood with a whoosh, splashing water over the rim. He wanted to clap or give words of praise for her bravado, but his tongue stuck to the roof of his mouth, and his arms lay frozen at his sides.

She was magnificent.

Standing stone-still in knee-deep water, she stared boldly back at him, allowing him to study the lines of her trim body. Like a Byzantine marble statue she was, all sleek planes and enticing curves. With her wet hair combed back and her proud chin held high, she presented a face that was not beautiful but nicely formed. Flawless skin. High cheekbones. Straight nose. Thick arched brows over crystalline green eyes. Full, kissable lips. Nay, he amended, she *was* beautiful . . . to him.

Her breasts were round and firm, the size of pomegranates, the nipples and surrounding areolae a lovely shade of dusty pink. He adored her breasts and would show her how much—later.

She was slender, but not overly so. A narrow waist tapered out to full hips that framed a flat stomach and indented navel.

He promised himself an extended exploration of that territory with his hands and tongue, mayhap even his teeth. Yea, teeth would be interesting.

He forced his eyes to move on to long, clean-shaven legs that joined at the most enticing spot of all, a patch of dark brown curls glistening with wet drops from her bath. His own groin tightened as he looked at her there, wondering at all the hidden secrets she harbored and would ultimately reveal to him. 'Twas a heady, heady prospect.

"Well?" she demanded. The word came out brashly, but he could tell she needed affirmation of her appeal. Oh, foolish, foolish maid, that she did not know.

He paused, seeking the perfect compliment, but she misread his hesitation.

"You jerk," she hissed and catapulted herself at him over the edge of the tub, reaching outstretched hands for his throat. She hit harder than he expected, prompting him to fall backward off the stool. They both landed on the floor, her on top of him, with a loud thud.

He held onto her affronted body with an armlock around her waist as she tried to squirm away. Then he began to laugh, but immediately bit his bottom lip, tucking her face into the curve of his neck, when he heard a sharp rap on the door.

"Mer, are you okay? Did you fall?"

Merry-Death raised her head, though he held the rest of her body, chest to legs, flattened against his. "I'm okay, Jillie. I just slipped on a loose . . . rug."

I will show her just how slippery a "rug" I can be.

"I was about to say that you are beautiful . . . magnificent," he whispered into her ear, licking the shell-like lobe in the process. It tasted so good, he did it again.

She groaned.

"Did you just groan?" Jillian asked, apparently still standing in the hallway. "You *are* hurt. Let me in, Mer."

He started to inform Merry-Death that her fingernails digging into his shoulders were piercing the skin, but she slapped one hand over his open mouth. And he soon forgot the insignificant pain as she turned slightly toward the door, lifting her breasts inadvertently closer to his face.

Holy Hel and Blessed Valhalla! What a sight!

"I was groaning because I'm tired and it's an effort even to put my nightgown on, Jillie. Go to bed."

In one expert move, Geirolf took her by the waist, shifted her slightly up his chest, then immediately clasped her flailing arms by the wrists in his one hand behind her back. He used his other hand to mold her bare buttocks, fitting her against his hardness. Then he wrapped his legs around her calves and spread them apart ever so slowly.

Her eyes nigh popped out, and the pulse in her neck jumped. With a motion of his head toward the door, he cautioned that they might not be alone yet. He couldn't have spoken aloud if he'd wanted to, so lightheaded had he become.

"Jillie? Are you still there?" she croaked out.

While her attention was diverted to her sister, he used the opportunity to pull on her wrists, still enclosed in his fist resting on her rump. The movement induced her shoulders to bow backward and her breasts to arch forward in invitation.

He was never one to deny himself such an invitation.

"I'm worried about you," Jillian said through the door.

He leaned his head up slightly and flicked his tongue over one hardened peak, then another. Merry-Death made no sound, though her lips parted and her belly lurched against his.

"I told you I'm not hurt," she told her sister. The whole time, their eyes were locked in a fiery exchange.

"Oh, I don't mean that. I mean about you and this Viking character. He's strange."

This strange Viking character began to lave wet circles around her areolae and taut nipples, first with the flat of his tongue, then the pointed tip.

Merry-Death's breathing escalated to panting as she tried to twist out of his embrace.

"He could hurt you, Mer," Jillian continued.

"I don't see how." Meredith snorted, though she gave him a meaningful glance that implied there were different kinds of "hurting." To punish her for the silent reprimand, he took one nipple and areola deep into his mouth and began to suckle with a rhythmic fervor. With each erotic pull, a delicious shiver passed from his tongue to his loins. He suspected there was pulling and shivering going on in her body, as well.

"Well, all right then. We'll talk in the morning," Jillian said. The shuffle of her departing feet faded down the hallway.

Merry-Death probably wasn't aware her sister had left, so stunned did she appear. He had that effect on women ofttimes. Gasping, she closed her eyes and threw her head back, giving him even greater access to her breasts. At the same time, her hips began to undulate against him.

It would be over afore he began if he wasn't careful. Twice now, the witch had seduced him into losing his seed in his *braies*. It would not happen again, he vowed.

Releasing her hands, he rolled over, causing her to land on her back with him on his side bending over her. Numb with passion, she gazed up in confusion. "Wh-what?"

He put a fingertip to her lips. "Shhh. The time isn't right for our joining. There is much we need to settle first." He gave her numerous little kisses in between his words.

She gaped at him blankly, and her breath still came out in gasps. He shared the turmoil.

Passing his palm over a heaving breast, he skimmed her stomach, resting the heel of his hand against her nether hair, the fingers delving into her woman dew. He nigh keened with male triumph that he'd brought her to this state so swiftly. "Before we talk, do you want me to bring you to your ecstasy?" His fingers moved against her slickness till they found the bud of her pleasure, swollen with need.

Her thighs trembled before she stammered, "A-alone?"

He puzzled over her question till he realized she was asking if they'd bring each other to mutual satisfaction. Or couple. "Yea. Alone. Just you." *For now.*

"You idiot!" she exclaimed, shoving him aside and scrambling to her feet.

Now it was his turn to blink in confusion. He sat on the floor with his knees drawn up to his chest, watching with bafflement as Merry-Death grabbed a fleecy robe from a wall hook, sliced him a quelling glare, unlocked the door, and shot away from him, faster than an arrow from a crossbow.

He would never understand women. How could Merry-Death's mood have altered in such a short time from happy tears over his avowal of undying love to scowling condemnation? Was it a woman quirk? A female tactic to drive men mad?

Or could he perchance have mishandled the situation?

Was there ever a more impressive declaration of love? . . .

Quickly, before Rolf could follow, Meredith extinguished the living room lights and crawled under the sheets of her makeshift bed on the sofa. She didn't want him to see how shaken she was. She didn't want him to see the tears that wouldn't stop flowing.

She heard the shower running upstairs. The dolt! She boiled

with frustration, and he was cool, calm, and collected enough
to take another of his leisurely showers.

How could she have been such a dope . . . falling for that
old line? *I love you, Merry-Death.* Hah! There was nothing
of love in his working her up like a wind-up Barbie, then
having the nerve to tell her they wouldn't be making love . . .
that he'd be pressing her buttons, but not participating himself. She felt pathetic and unfeminine.

It was probably some kind of power play. A form of Viking
torture. Another example of her trying too hard to please,
and falling short. Pathetic. She was pathetic. He *had* been interested in the beginning, she knew he had, but somewhere
along the way he must have decided she wasn't all that exciting. *What else is new?* The challenge for him had faded
away with her surrender. But Rolf had pitied her in the end
and he'd been willing to finish her off. Oh, the humiliation
of it all!

Suddenly, one lamp light clicked on, then another. Rolf
stood over her, water drizzling from his wet hair, which was
raked back off his forehead and behind his ears. Water also
drizzled down his body . . . a body that became alarmingly naked and menacing and fully aroused when the towel
wrapped around his hips accidentally unknotted and slipped.
He started to catch it, then shrugged and let it drop to the
floor.

Aroused? But he didn't want me.

Grinning when he caught her gawking at his . . . ah, mid-
section, he drawled, "Even a cold shower couldn't bank my
lust for you."

Huh? "You said you didn't want to make love with me."

"I said no such thing," he asserted, and then burst out
laughing. Pointing downward, he chuckled, "Merry-Death,
Merry-Death, tsk-tsk, how can a woman with your education
be so naive? In truth, how could anyone with a lick of sense

misinterpret *this*." His laughter escalated to deep belly guffaws.

She began to blubber in earnest under the onslaught of his ridicule, causing him to notice her tears for the first time.

"Blód hel!" he cursed, and scooped her up in his arms—sheets and robe and all. Then he swiveled his body so he plopped down on the couch with her on his lap. She kicked and flailed and clawed, to no avail.

"Leave off," he hissed, and maneuvered his torso so she was sandwiched between the back of the sofa and him. There really wasn't room on the narrow cushions for two people, and certainly not when one of them was six-foot-four and over two hundred pounds, with an added rock-hard appendage poking her belly.

She stilled but continued to show her resistance by glaring at him . . . between sobs. A lot of good that did. He raised one of his hands, which had been imprisoning hers at her sides, and used a thumb to wipe the tears from her cheek. It was useless. No sooner did he erase one than another took its place.

With a cluck of reproval, he asked, "Why?"

She raised her chin, refusing to open those wounds again. To her surprise and dismay, though, she blurted out, "Because you don't want me." *I am pathetic, pathetic, pathetic. Next I'll be begging him to make love to me.*

"I love you, Merry-Death. How can you think I don't want you? Is this a language problem we are having? Shall I fetch the talisman belt?" While speaking, he'd distractedly opened the front of her robe and taken her left breast in a wide, callused palm.

And it felt so-o-o good. Was she acquiring a taste for calluses now? *Oh, lordy, yes!* Were her tastes becoming as plebian as her parents said? *Yep!* Oh, geez, did she say . . . no, did she think, "yep?" *Yep.* Would she be ogling blue-collar workers at construction sites, like that guy in the diet Coke commercials? *Probably, if they have long hair and washboard stomachs and tushes that . . .*

While her mind was regressing, Rolf watched her and absentmindedly drew wide, abrasive circles over her breast. Every bone in her body began to melt, one calcium particle at a time. She wanted to slap his hand away, but she forgot how.

"Do you do everything you darn-well-Viking-please, without asking permission?" she asked in a suffocated whisper.

"Yea."

She shuddered under his ongoing caresses.

"Let me," he implored thickly. "Let me give you pleasure. After that, we can talk with a modicum of rationality about . . . so many things important to us."

Was he saying she was irrational? "Aaaarrgh!" she shrieked and gave him a harsh shove against the chest. Caught off guard, he fell off the sofa and onto the floor.

Startled, Geirolf peered up at the wench with shock. He ever did love a good battle and his Merry-Death was giving him a fair chase. She'd knocked him right on his arse. With a grin, he congratulated her. "Well done, sweetling." Then he launched himself at her afore she could scramble away. This time, he tossed her over his shoulder and carried her into the scullery where he flicked on the light lever, and then dropped her into a chair. "Sit," he ordered, "and do not move."

He went back to the great room where he found a pair of sweating *braies*. A man could scarce carry on a serious discussion when naked and lustful. On second thought, he scrounged through the small chest Merry-Death had given him for his belongings till he found a pair of the tight jaw-key undergarments men wore in this land. He needed something to bind his raging man-root if he wanted to speak in more than a drooling drivel to Merry-Death.

Returning, he sat in a chair on the opposite side of the table. Her robe was tucked neatly around her body now, but if she thought she presented a prim and proper picture, she was sorely mistaken. Her drying hair wisped out in wanton disarray. Her cheeks were flushed with anger and brush burns from his night-time whisker stubble. Her eyes glittered with glorious fury.

"I love you," he said, taking her hands across the table.

Her shoulders slumped. She tried to pull out of his grasp, but he laced their fingers and held firm. She averted her face.

"Look at me, dearling." When she did, reluctantly, he asked, "What is amiss? Does my love displease you?"

"You don't love me, and saying you do out of pity . . . that's what displeases me."

"I have ne'er told a woman I loved her afore. . . . Oh, do not look so skeptical. I have not. Therefore, if I fumble with my words, you must make allowance. 'Tis new territory for me."

"Rolf, I'm thirty-five years old. I'm not a raving beauty. When I walk down the street, men seldom give me more than a passing glance. I'm not a scintillating conversational-ist. My sense of humor is about nil. I devote my life to study in boring, cryptlike libraries. I can't have children. So, when a man like you says he's fallen in love with me . . . Well, pardon me, but I'm not buying it."

He shook his head sadly at her self-assessment. Pulling their laced fingers up to his face, he kissed the knuckles of one of her hands, then the other. Her indrawn breath, quickly suppressed, ricocheted down her throat and lungs and out to her extremities. He knew that was so because he felt it in the rapid beat of her pulse where their wrists were joined. With great effort, he placed their hands safely back on the table where he wouldn't be tempted to kiss more than knuckles.

Searching for the right words, he began tentatively, "I have met more beauteous women, 'tis true, and have enjoyed tumbling a few of them. Nay, I will admit, more than a few."

Her lips twitched to hold back mirth at his stumbling admission. 'Twas a good sign, this half-smile.

"But my heart ne'er thundered like Thor's mighty hammer when one of them walked into a chamber," he continued. "The blood did not drain from my head, leaving me dizzy and gasping for breath at a mere smile from one of them. I did not tingle when one of them brushed my skin in passing."

"Tingle? You?" She hooted with disbelief.

"Yea, you may smirk if you choose, but I have taken to tingling. My brothers would make great sport of teasing me if they knew of the malady, I can tell you. And the skalds would write a saga poking jest at me. 'Geirolf the Tingling Shipbuilder,' or some such."

She did smile then, a full-blown smile that transformed her face and touched his heart. He closed his eyes and counted to ten. *"Einn, tveir, þrír, fjórir, fimm, sex, sjo, átta, níu, tíu."* Upon regaining his composure, he went on. "As to your not having a sense of humor . . . I cannot credit that. You are funny to me. In fact, I cannot recall having smiled or laughed so much in all my born days as I have this past sennight with you."

She squared her chin, unconvinced. The stubborn wench!

"You point out your less-than-exciting profession. Well, I know naught about that. When Jillian called you boring earlier—"

"My sister called me what?" Merry-Death squealed and tried once again to escape from his renewed clasp, no doubt to go attack her sleeping sister.

Her ferocity amused him mightily. "What I started to say was that, when Jillian called you boring, I told her she was blind."

"You did?"

"I did."

Her open face revealed the inner struggle her mind was

waging with her heart. Unfortunately, he must hurt her before all was reconciled betwixt them. "Lastly, you are barren."

Meredith recoiled under his harsh statement.

"You told me of your infertility afore. Do not ever mention the subject again. 'Tis of no importance."

She sighed. "Rolf, I don't understand any of this."

"Do you believe that I love you?"

He held her gaze till she answered in a whisper, "Yes."

Releasing a sigh of relief, he leaned across the table and kissed her lips, briefly. Then he sat straight in his chair, all businesslike. "So, we have settled one issue. Now, the next important hurdle. Who am I? Tell me, Merry-Death, who is this man who sits across from you, professing his love?"

"I don't know. I honestly don't know."

"See. That is one of the biggest obstacles we have to overcome before taking any further steps, including making love. And we will be making love, sweetling. Do not doubt that."

"Are you saying that you didn't want to make love with me upstairs because I don't know who you are?"

"Exactly! Well, partly."

"Then tell me. Who are you?"

"Merry-Death, I do not lie. You must concede. When I tell you that I come from the past, you must accept it as truth."

"But it's impossible," she cried.

"'Twas hard for me to credit, too. But there it is. Until you trust me fully, we cannot . . . proceed."

"But—"

"I could spend days telling you of my land and my time. I could describe, in detail, the Norse and Saxon courts and all their peoples. Their dress. Their language. The politics and the everyday living. I could fill in the gaps in your history books, and correct the mistakes they contain. Eventually, you would believe that I am Geirolf Ericsson, born in the year of our Lord nine-hundred-and-sixty-two on a Norwegian fjord to a Norse jarl and a Saxon lady. But we do not have days to waste, and I much prefer that you trust me on my word alone." After his long-winded declaration, he waited for his words to sink in to Merry-Death's obviously troubled mind. Finally, he insisted on a reply. "Who am I, Merry-Death?"

"Oh, no!" she whimpered. There were tears in her eyes as a dawning acceptance unfurled. Then, with a firm voice, she said, "You are Geirolf Ericsson, a tenth-century time traveler."

He nodded, too overcome to speak. Her trust meant more to him than he'd realized.

"I'm not sure why I believe you, Rolf. Or when I accepted that you were telling the truth. Maybe just now. All I know is there have been too many little-known historical details you've volunteered that have turned out to be true. But, in the end, it comes down to intuition. Going with the heart."

"Thank you," he said softly.

She pulled their clasped hands across the table and reciprocated his earlier gesture, kissing each individual knuckle with slow, painstaking care. The whole time, her eyes clung to his with some mysterious message. He felt the tingle everywhere, even in his ears where he could swear tiny bells were ringing. When she was done, she set their hands back on the table.

"You haven't asked me the most important question of all," she informed him. "If you think those other things were impediments to overcome, you must know there's an even bigger one ahead."

He cocked his head. There were so many questions, but he wasn't sure which she referred to. Except . . .

Oh, dear Lord, how could he have failed to consider *that*? Insecurity was new to him and unwelcome. He did not favor the unsettling queasiness in his stomach at the possibility of rejection. *Oh, please*, he prayed to all the gods, Christian and Norse alike, *do not let me have come so far, only to fail.*

Her face was blank now, revealing nothing. Would she keep him in suspense forever? "Well?" he rasped out.

"Well what?" Oh, she was a cruel wench, torturing him with knowing delight.

"Do . . . do you love me, Merry-Death?" His voice was so raw and low, he was not sure she heard him.

But she did.

"With all my heart, Viking. With all my heart."

CHAPTER TWELVE

Viking men have special talents . . .

Meredith reeled under the euphoria of her own words. *I love him. I can't say why. I don't know when it happened. But I do. I love him.*

"I love you," she whispered in wonder.

He stood and came around the table to take her into his arms. His fingertips gently cupped her face as he adored her with his eyes. "I love you, too, heartling." The kiss he pressed lightly on her lips was soft and sweet and full of promise. She could tell he restrained himself from deepening the kiss or holding her more intimately. Why? Her mind swirled in confusion under his intense scrutiny.

But then she noticed the tears that filled his eyes. He swiped at them with a man's embarrassment. "I ne'er expected love to feel like this. You make me tremble with so many new feelings. I want to scream my joy to Valhalla. And I want to weep with the exquisite pain."

"Oh, Rolf." There were no words adequate to express the depth of her emotion. "Let's . . . let's go somewhere private where I can show you how much I love you. I want . . . I need to make love with you, sweetheart." She tried to wrap her arms around his neck and pull him close.

He groaned and, with a quick kiss, took her by the forearms and set her at arm's length.

"What?" *Oh, geez, is he going to reject me again? I don't think I can take much more of this ping-ponging back and forth. Want you, want you not.*

"Wipe away that wounded look, Merry-Death. Do not for one moment doubt my desire to mate with you."

"But?" Meredith tried to sound angry but her voice came out wobbly with insecurity.

Rolf groaned again, and his jaw worked with a silent effort for control. "Come," he said, leading her into the living room where he adjusted the sheets on the sofa. "Lie down."

When she did, expecting him to join her, he instead tucked her in tightly up to the neck, arms bound at her sides. Alone. He was putting her to bed *alone*. Then he knelt on the floor beside her.

"Sweetling, please, I beg you, help me do this right."

"I didn't say anything."

"Ah, but you did. Your eyes reproach me for being a rascal, which I am not. I am trying my best to follow the noble path." He put up a halting hand when she started to protest. "Two days ago—nay, two hours ago—if you'd suggested we have a . . . what did you call it? . . . a fling, I would have been on you faster than lightning. And we would have enjoyed each other's bodies. Immensely."

"Then what's the problem?" She moaned, trying to wriggle her arms out of her sheet strait-jacket to reach for him.

"Shhh. Behave yourself, wench." He feathered a fleeting kiss across her lips and chuckled. "Did you feel the tingle?"

"I'm looking for a hell of a lot more than a tingle."

"Tsk-tsk," he teased. "A coarse tongue is uncomely in a Viking woman."

She told him in one explicit expletive what he could do with his Viking women.

"Surely you know that I have no desire to do *that* with any woman but you at the moment. Patience, my love," he cautioned with a smile, "though I must admit that your eagerness flatters my ego. No, no, no, do not turn willful on me now. And sticking out your tongue is another thing that is ill-favored in a Viking woman. Truly, you must learn to curb your waspish impulses."

"Let . . . me . . . up . . . now," she demanded.

"Nay. Lie still till I explain."

"You are driving me crazy. Are we or are we not going to make love?"

"You must be crazed if you would ask that. Of course, we will make love. But not tonight."

He had to subdue her then, bearing down on her shoulders. Otherwise, she would have slapped him silly. The man was turning her into a basket case.

Finally, she calmed down, and Rolf began again, "When we exchanged vows of love, it changed everything. Before, our coupling would have been a mere sating of lust. A form of 'Love with a Hot Viking,' as you once mentioned. Now, it will be much more. Lust, to be sure. 'Love with a Hot Viking,' to be absolutely sure. But, in addition to that, methinks love merits a different, more tender handling."

Meredith clamped her lips together, resisting the urge to ask Rolf to elaborate on his insane logic. But her eyes threw daggers at the infuriating man.

"If we were in my land, my father would go to your father and ask for your hand in marriage."

She giggled at that ridiculous notion. A Viking jarl entering her father's staid library? No doubt replete with furred mantle and battle axe. Then she inhaled sharply. Marriage? She hadn't expected that. But she liked it. A lot.

"There is naught of amusement in formal wedding negotiations, Merry-Death. A legal wife is distinguished from a concubine by the bride price her husband's family pays for her."

Meredith didn't like the sound of "price." It made her feel like chattel. "And if my father refused?"

"I would have you anyway." He grinned at her with heart-stopping arrogance.

"Are you . . . are you asking me to marry you?"

"Yea . . . nay. Damn, I am bungling this badly because I care too much."

Bungling? This guy's bungling could charm the socks off a nun.

He took a deep breath before resuming. "If we were in my homeland, I would get down on my knees—" he looked pointedly at his kneeling position—"and pledge you my troth . . . man to woman. The Viking way. 'Tis as valid in the eyes of the gods as any Christian marriage."

"I want to touch you so badly." She whimpered under the sweet caress of his words.

He denied her plea, soothing her with a butterfly stroke of his fingertips across her lips. "But that wouldn't satisfy my family, especially my mother. Banns would be called up and down the fjords throughout Norway, and a grand wedding feast would be planned. Each week, I would send a new and more wondrous present to entice you to my bed—fine jewelry from Byzantium, sable furs from the North Seas, fine silks, a newly foaled Saracen colt, fragrant oils from the east. When the fated day arrived, we would wed in the loud and boister-ous way of Norsemen throughout time, and then say our vows afore the priest who serves my mother's chapel. The celebra-tion would last two sennights."

She smiled at the splendid picture he painted.

"But we are not in my time, or my land, and ne'er will be." He sighed. "Leastways, not together."

Ripples of panic drew her alert.

"So, I must improvise."

"This is the future, Rolf. Couples today rarely wait till marriage to consummate a relationship, especially when engaged, or committed."

"Ah, but I am not a man of the future."

Geez, this is a new twist. A man insisting on celibacy before marriage. But I kind of like it. Yes, I do. He'd better not make me wait too long, though. "We could be married by a priest, or a justice of the peace, here in Maine."

"Nay, I am the man. I must provide. We'll have a wedding, to be sure, but it will be that of a Norse man and woman. A personal ceremony—man to woman—not a religious one. A ritual of the heart."

A ritual of the heart? What a wonderful expression! God, this man is really smooth. Or he speaks from deep emotion, which is a soul-staggering prospect. She blinked back tears. "When?"

"Two, three days at most."

She moaned.

He chuckled. "Anticipation is not a bad thing, sweetling."

"Easy for you to say," she snapped.

"Nay, not easy at all," he said somberly. Then he released a breathy sigh of resolution. "But I must make preparations first. The wedding garments for us both. My bride gift. The ritual bed furs. The marriage longhouse."

"I don't need all those things, Rolf. And if you go out and kill some animal to give me a fur, I swear I'll kill you." But then she caught the last of his statements. "Oh, no, no, no. I told you before. No longhouses built on my property."

He smiled and patted her arm. "We shall see. Mayhap just a small one. A few discarded planks from your ship, some wattle and daub, a thatch or turf roof, a center hearth, a bed— most important, a bed. A sweat-house would be nice, too . . . just a tiny one, a hut, really. I don't want to anticipate *too* much."

"You . . . you . . . you . . ." she sputtered.

"Overwhelmed, are you, dearling?"

"I'll show you overwhelmed," she raged.

"You will? Ah, I can scarce wait. Will it be a sexual trick?"

"Let me loose," she demanded.

He tightened her linens, instead. "Is it wise to turn your face so red, my love? I don't want you to swoon with the vapors afore we settle our other obstacles."

She went still with suspicion. "What other obstacles?"

"The divorce."

"I beg your pardon. You asked me to marry you only a few moments ago. Now, you're planning the divorce. Oh, no! You're not talking about a prenuptial agreement, are you?"

"Prenuptial what? Oh, that. Nay. I meant that I will be leaving your land in a few short weeks, and—"

"You intend to leave? But I thought—"

"You thought I would stay now that we have acknowledged our love?" he finished softly.

She nodded.

"It cannot be. My mission remains the same. I have to return the relic as I promised my father. I've been researching tenth-century Norway in your library and on the Internet. There *are* references to a famine late in the tenth century."

"That may well be, but I keep telling you, I don't think you can change history."

"Mayhap not, but what of changes *within* history?"

She waited for him to explain.

"Since the books give no date when the famine ended, perchance my intervention will cut it short by months or years. And there is another concern." He worried his bottom lip with his upper teeth as he contemplated something that clearly alarmed him. "I discovered in one of your history tomes that Aethelred, the slimy bastard, intends to slay all

Norsemen in Britain five years hence, in 1002, including the Viking settlers and hired soldiers in his own service. Amongst those to fall under his blade will be the sister and the brother-by-marriage of King Svein of Denmark. Duty compels me to give my fellow Vikings fair warning of Aethelred's evil designs."

"Now, that *is* changing history. And you must know, if you read farther into those texts, that there will be massive retaliations against Aethelred in subsequent years. And ultimately, around 1017, a young Viking knight, Cnut, will conquer all of Britain. England will be under Viking rule for twenty-five years after that. So, in a sense, what goes around, comes around."

"I am unfamiliar with this go around-come around rule. I just know I must return to my homeland, to complete the circle."

"Then I'll go with you," she decided suddenly.

His expression hardened. "It cannot be."

"You made the offer to me before," she pointed out.

"Yea, but that was afore I loved you. I'm not even sure that the Demon Moon time hole will work for me. And I would never, ever risk your life in the effort to perform my mission. Besides, you'll have your own grandsire's quest to carry through when I'm gone. I can build your longship, but I'll not be here for the sailing."

"So, what does all this have to do with a divorce?"

He swallowed with some difficulty, and then proceeded, "When I am gone, I do not want you to grieve . . . leastways, not overlong. In time, you'll want to wed again." He raised a palm to stop her objections. "That's why we'll exchange only the Norse vows. No Papist rite, which is more binding. Divorce is simple in my society. A mere declaration of intent afore witnesses and a stating of the grounds for complaint."

"Like?" she said through gritted teeth. Lord, he was a thick-headed ass if he thought she'd do any such thing.

"Any number of just causes. Impotence, the woman wearing men's *braies,* the man donning feminine apparel, miserliness—"

"I'll bet a wife's being barren is one of those just causes."

"I thought I told you not to mention that subject again. By the by, did I neglect to tell you, a willful wife is one of the biggest reasons for divorce?"

"How about a husband who refuses to listen to his wife?"

"That, too," he said with a grin.

"So, Mr. I've-Got-It-All-Planned, you intend to marry me, bebop off through time to your home, divorce me, then—"

"Oh, nay, I ne'er said I'd be divorcing you, sweetling. I have no intent of doing that. I'll not wed again, that I vow. I but wish for your freedom."

This was the most ridiculous conversation. "Will . . . will you come back?"

"I could try, but, nay, my guess is 'twould be impossible."

"And how about your mistress, that sweet Alyce from Hedeby tart?"

He shrugged. "I cannot promise celibacy for life. Nor would I expect it of you."

Meredith felt as if she'd been dealt a sucker punch to the stomach. "You are so incredible. You tell me you love me in one instant and that you're leaving me in the next. Well, I won't stand for it."

"You have no choice, dearling."

"Oh, I have a choice all right. I may not be able to stop loving you, but I can refuse to make love with you. And I sure as heck am not going to marry a guy who intends to desert me a few weeks later."

"They can be the best weeks of both our lives," he pleaded.

She surged upward with anger and desolation. When he tried to push her back down this time, she bit the heel of his hand.

"Ouch!" he griped, but didn't give way, even when she drew blood.

She sank back down and closed her eyes. She couldn't bear to see even that tiny wound on his hand and know that she'd caused him pain, however small. "I won't marry you," she repeated in a dull monotone, with her eyes still closed.

"Yea, you will."

"And I won't make love with you now." Making love with Rolf, and then giving him up would hurt more than never having him at all. "And none of your sweet talking will move me, either."

He laughed with supreme self-confidence. " 'Tis said that a Norseman, when his sap runs high, could move the earth."

"Go away, Rolf. I want to go to sleep now." She needed time alone to ponder all that had happened tonight and to brace herself for the days ahead. Days when she would have to fight her feelings for Rolf. Then those days when he would no longer be here.

"I'll stay with you till you fall asleep." He got up off his knees and nudged her hips over so he could sit on the edge of the sofa. She scrunched her eyes tighter. "Mayhap I could tell you a bedtime saga. Nay, I know; I'll regale you with little hints of the ways in which Viking men make love to their brides."

Oh, no!

"You do know about the famous Viking S-spot, of course."

A snicker was her only reply.

"You doubt my word? Ah, you will pay for that, wench,

in good time. But, truly, Norsemen have long been known for their prowess in the bedsport, and—"

She snickered again, continuing to keep her eyes closed. She wouldn't give him the benefit of seeing the hurt in her eyes.

He tapped her chin in reprimand. "Part of our prowess is due to our fit bodies, no doubt—"

"No doubt."

"Sarcasm ill-suits you, my love," he remarked, "but there are some who attribute our prowess to the . . . ah, secrets."

Secrets? What secrets? When he didn't carry on, she cracked one eye only a teensy bit, but he noticed. It was the cue he'd been waiting for. The rat!

Chuckling, he clarified his outrageous assertion with great gusto. "Being adventurers, we Norsemen travel far and wide—"

"And along the way, rape and pillage every female in sight."

"This raping and pillaging accusation has become tiresome. What I was about to say is that, in our vast travels, we have learned many secrets of lovemaking. Secrets we pass down in our families. Secrets that draw women to our beds like honeybees."

"Don't think for one minute I'm going to hop in the sack with you because of some sexual secrets. Buzz off and find another place to scatter your pollen, you oversexed . . . insect. This bee isn't interested."

"Ha-ha-ha! I am laughing at your jest. See, Merry-Death, I told you that you have a sense of humor."

"Well, I'm not laughing now, and this is no joke. You either stay in Maine, or I go home with you. And that's that."

"Nay."

"Yes."

"Nie þýðir nei," he said sternly. "No means no, and that's final."

"Not in my vocabulary."

He inhaled and exhaled several times with exaggerated loudness. "Mayhap I should share one of the secrets with you to change your mind. Just one, do not beg for more. But you must promise not to reveal it to any other."

She rolled her eyes at his persistence.

To her horror and amazement, he went into graphic detail about some erotic foreplay that involved tongues and ropes and immense size and remarkable out-of-this-world staying power.

"You lie," she accused. No one, man or woman, could do what he'd just described.

He arched a brow with displeasure. "Did I not tell you that I never lie? If you cannot credit that secret, mayhap you will be more believing of the 'Hot Oil—Cold Sword' secret. That one is for more accomplished warriors in the bed-sport." He grinned at her. "I have done it many a time."

She clucked at his overinflated ego. Really, if she weren't so angry, she'd have to admire his adorable charm. "Go away, Rolf. I will *not* marry you." She rolled over, facing the back of the sofa.

"Have you e'er made love in bed furs, Merry-Death?" he asked in a silky rasp. "There is no better sensation in the world for a woman, I am told, than the caress of the furs at her back, and the seductive torment of her lover's furred skin at her front. I would give you that experience."

A thrum of excitement whisked through her.

"And then, of course, we shipbuilders have particular talents."

"Oh, Lord!"

"It comes from working with our hands. We love to touch . . . and touch . . . and touch. The skin on our fingertips has become so sensitive. Have you e'er made love with a man who bears the calluses of his trade, Merry-Death? I would warrant you have not." He paused, the sound of his breathing heavy in the air. "It is a pleasure beyond all others, this I promise you," he ended on a whisper.

She turned back, facing him. "Don't do this to me, Rolf."

"I love you, Merry-Death," he said fervently, leaning forward to lay his warm lips against hers. "I cannot promise you a perfect manifestation of this love. I can guarantee no future for us. But this I do swear; I will do the best I can to make you happy in the days we have. No man could do more."

With that, he stood and walked away from her. At the patio door, he stopped. Over his shoulder, he repeated, "I love you, Merry-Death."

"And I love you, Rolf," she choked out. But he was already gone. And Meredith got a foretaste of the slow death she was going to suffer when he abandoned her for good.

Beware of men with plans . . .

A whirling dervish hit Maine the next day, and its name was Geirolf Ericsson. Now that he had a mission, he worked with a feverish intensity. And his mission, in this case, wasn't the return of the relic. The mission was—*Heaven help me*—her.

How would she ever be able to resist him?

When she came home from the college at six o'clock, Rolf and Mike were glaringly absent. But the progress made on the project in just that day of Rolf being back on the job was phenomenal. Although Rolf's ship appeared much the same as the day before, the college longship—which they'd christened *Fierce Eagle* after the school mascot and to complement Rolf's *Fierce Destiny*—had a skeleton framework standing proud on the stocks, highlighted by an impressive fifty-foot keel. Even the stem and stern had been hand-riveted on. Rolf had been right. Already this ship looked much sturdier and more finely crafted than Gramps's had.

She'd left for work at seven, having a pile of project paperwork to tie up and lessons to prepare for classes, which resumed on Monday. Before her departure, she'd studiously avoided even a glimpse of the side yard where she could hear Rolf working. Coward that she was, she'd feared facing him after their monumental disclosures of love the night before, followed by his infuriating opposition to a future for the two of them. But she wouldn't be able to dodge him forever.

She began to walk around the site. There were more of the students than ever before—at least three dozen. Apparently, as word of the project spread, more young people volunteered their time. Meredith had received three phone calls this morning at her office from area newspapers wanting to do feature stories on the Trondheim Venture. That should garner even more support.

To her dismay, Meredith had also found a message on her answering machine from the producer of *Home Improvement,* which she'd yet to return. And, even more incredible, Mike had a message from Pamela Anderson. "Hey, Mike. Just calling between scenes to chat. Later, babe. Pam."

Strolling farther, she glanced at a crude worktable set up at the side of the house, above which several papers had been tacked on a makeshift bulletin board. Apparently students had been organized into work groups, following detailed schedules for their duties that Rolf must have printed off from her computer. Cutting of planks. Wood shaving and sanding. Cooking. Weaving of wool and animal hair for caulking. Making wood nails. Trough for water soaking of timbers. Drying of skins.

Huh? What skins? What drying?

One sheet listed SCA Activities. Wait a minute here. When

did the Society for Creative Anachronisms get involved
this project? When she'd asked for their help last mont
they'd been uninterested. To her amazement, the schedu
listed hands-on workshops, lectures, exhibits and whatn
on such things as Saga Telling: A Skaldic Tradition; Tent
Century Costume; Quern-Made Bread; Soapstone Craft
Medieval Fabrics; Viking Handheld Looms; Pennanul
Brooches: A Norse Trademark; The Pattern-Welded Swor
Dragon-ships and Sea Wolves. And they were all to be he
on her property over the next few months.

There was a sealed envelope on the table with her nam
"Merry-Death," written in almost childlike pencil handwri
ing. With her heart thudding, Meredith opened it to find
carefully folded sheet of notepaper with only one senten
on it. "I love you." There was also an erasure at the botto
that she was able to decipher—one that Rolf had wisely d
cided was inappropriate in this circumstance. "Did you bu
more mead?"

Tears filled her eyes. *Oh, Rolf, you are going to be a ve*
formidable foe in this battle of wills.

She forced herself to stop daydreaming and move arour
the clearing. "Hi, Jerry, Pete, Frank," she called out. Havir
been in Maine the past three months, she knew many of th
students by name.

"How's it goin', Dr. Foster?" they replied, setting dow
their axes and wiping their sweaty foreheads with bare for
arms. Most of them were shirtless, a fact not missed by
number of female students, whose eyes followed their ever
movement with appreciation.

She waved them back to work and watched for a few m
ments as they engaged in the ancient method of clink
shipbuilding. The boys, all athletically fit, were energet
cally splitting logs along the radii to create wedge-shape
planks—as many as sixteen from one log—much like th

slices from a round cake of enormous height. These "clove boards" would be overlapped to form the sides of the longship.

"You're home, Aunt Mer," Thea said cheerily as she ambled up to her, a toddler on one hip. The baby wore denim coveralls and the cutest little black-and-white checkered athletic shoes. At Meredith's uplifted brows, Thea explained, "This is Teddy. He belongs to one of the SCA ladies." She pointed to the other side of the clearing, where several women were stirring a huge caldron over an open fire.

Holy cow! That kettle would hold enough stew to feed an army, which it appeared she was accumulating here. "Dinner?" she asked.

"Nah. Soap," Thea said. Her niece was wearing a long gown in the Viking style, the white chemise covered with the open-sided apron. Her dark hair was neatly plaited into two braids, and not a speck of makeup marred her perfect complexion. All this was a great backdrop to her nose ring.

Soap? she mouthed silently. What did soap have to do with the building of a Viking ship? But whoever was responsible for this transformation in Thea deserved a huge hug.

Unfortunately, or fortunately, she suspected who the big lug was, and no way was she going to risk giving that lug a hug, big or otherwise. Not unless he agreed to stay here in the present or take her with him to the past.

"Would you mind holding Teddy for a while, Aunt Mer? He weighs a ton. And I hafta go check on the boar."

Gladly, Meredith took the child into her arms. He gazed up at her, blue eyes wide with curiosity, thumb stuck in his adorable mouth. Meredith closed her eyes. Babies always made her feel this way. Teddy, meanwhile, was tugging on her hair, causing the pins to come loose. He giggled as one side of her upswept hair flopped down. "What boar?" she squeaked out finally, opening her eyes to see Thea eyeing her new hairstyle with amusement.

"It's not really a boar. There were none in any of the butcher shops we called this morning, can you believe that? Not one single boar! But Rolf said boar tastes similar to pig. So, we're having a pig roast tonight," Thea announced joyfully. "It's been cooking all day in a pit we dug filled with hot stones and wet leaves. I'm so glad I came here, Aunt Mer. I'm having such a cool time."

Thea started to walk off, but Meredith grabbed her shoulder with her one free hand. Teddy's sticky fingers were working on the neckline of her cotton knit sweater, stretching it out as far as it would go. "Whoa, Thea, hold on. Where are Mike and Rolf?"

"They were here till about two o'clock. Then Rolf said he had lots of shopping to do." Thea averted her eyes with those last words.

"What kind of shopping?" Meredith asked suspiciously.

"Gee, how would I know?" Thea exclaimed, but she still wouldn't make eye contact.

Meredith took Thea's chin in her hand and forced her to face her. "What's going on, Thea?"

"Is it true that you and Rolf are gonna tie the knot?"

"No!" she said too quickly and too vehemently, her cheeks immediately heating with embarrassment.

"Rolf said I could be, like, a witness. That's the same as a bridesmaid in a Viking wedding, you know."

Meredith groaned.

"Did you see the roses yet?" Thea's voice was hushed with awe.

Uh-oh! "The . . . the what?"

"Roses." Thea pointed to the back of the house. "That's, like, the most romantic thing in the whole world. I told Phoebe and Cora in Chicago this morning, and they said it was, like, totally buggin', even better than the time Brad Pitt . . ."

Thea's chatter droned on, but Meredith had already spun on her heel and was stomping toward the back of the house, the side facing the ocean. Teddy, propped on her hip and hanging on by one hand around her neck, had managed to work his other grubby little hand inside her shirt, tugging gleefully till one bra strap broke. The neckband of her shirt had lost its elasticity under his insistent jerking and now hung off one shoulder.

Thea scurried after her, informing her in a rush, "Oh, and I totally forgot to tell you. Mom up and took off this morning. She just left a note saying she was, like, called out of town on an emergency. She said she'd be back, but, you know Mom, maybe she will and maybe she won't."

Who cares what my sister does now? Who cares if this baby turns my clothes to shreds? Who cares if half of Maine is overtaking my yard? I have more important worries.

Meredith stopped dead in her tracks when she turned the corner. Dozens, literally dozens, of rosebushes had been planted around the patio and the wood foundation of what Meredith feared was going to be a Viking longhouse. The plants were large and small, budded and full-flowered, ever-blooming and late blooming, long-stemmed and climbing, but already the scent of roses filled the air. And Meredith couldn't stop the tears that overflowed her eyes.

Teddy took one look at Meredith's tears and began to wail himself. She rubbed his back distractedly till he ceased sobbing and tucked his face sleepily into her neck.

Meredith scanned her wonderfully transformed backyard. Rolf must have suspected how much the rose fragrance meant to her when he'd entered her bathroom last night. Somehow, he'd known. Oh, God, how she loved him!

Before she walked away, Thea informed her softly, "Rolf

said he wanted you to remember him, forever and ever, whenever you smell roses."

Meredith sighed.

"And he said it's your first bride gift."

CHAPTER THIRTEEN

§

He didn't play fair . . .
"Let me take Teddy."

Mike came up to her and took the sleeping child from her arms with an ease that startled her for a young bachelor. Teddy blinked his eyes at the man nestling him onto his shoulder.

"How ya doin', cowboy?" Mike playfully patted his well-padded rump. Amazingly, her grad assistant was wearing an Oxford collared shirt and jeans *and* a pair of black-and-white checkered running shoes that matched the miniature ones on the boy's feet.

"Mike," the child murmured contentedly before nodding off again.

"Do you know Teddy's mother well?" Meredith asked. It was a personal question she wouldn't have asked just a few days ago.

"Sonja?" Mike squirmed under her scrutiny.

Meredith glanced off in the distance where a blond-haired woman in Viking attire raised her hand and waved at them before resuming her soap-making demonstration. Meredith remembered her now. Sonja Wareham. A divorcee and new assistant professor. Although she'd only met her a few times at college functions, Meredith recalled her as being very nice. Rather quiet and serious, but definitely nice.

Was it Mike's contact with Sonja, who was an active SC
re-enactor, that had gotten the organization involved in tl
project?

Mike's ears turned red. "We've dated a few times."

"Well, well, well," she teased. "Apparently, your taste isr
as atrocious as I thought." Teasing was another thing she
always avoided with her employees. *Why?* she wondered nov
Was her reserve a trait she'd picked up from her parent:
The them-versus-us mentality separating people into classe
whether they were lines drawn by intelligence, money, birtl
or occupation.

"Hey, just 'cause I lick my chops over a jelly donut doesn
mean I can't appreciate a bagel once in a while."

Meredith laughed. "I don't think Sonja would apprecia
being compared to a bagel. And by the way, the jelly donut le
a message for you on the office answering machine."

"Oh, that," Mike said, his ears burning redder. "I thin
she's more interested in Rolf than me."

Why did that not surprise Meredith?

"Oh, no!" Mike said. "Rolf's gonna cut out my loos
tongue."

"So, where is the matchmaker from Valhalla?"

"Out front, unloading the truck." Mike started to wal
away.

"Whoa!" she said to his back. "Where have you two been'
His shoulders slumped as he realized he wasn't going t
escape so easily. Turning, he asked, "Is it true that you tw
are gonna get hitched?"

"No!"

Mike's blue eyes widened. "Rolf seems to think so."

"He doesn't listen to me, that's why."

"Honest to God, Dr. Foster, he's convinced that you're i
love with him. I mean, you wouldn't believe all the stuff h
bought today because he's so crazy in love. And he thinks—

Crazy in love? "Mike, I never said I didn't love him. I do, even though we've only known each other a few days. But I won't marry him." Was she really telling Mike about her intimate feelings? It was so . . . inappropriate. "I won't marry him," she repeated nonetheless.

"I wouldn't be so sure about that," he muttered.

"What?"

"Oh, nothing. Damn, I'd better tell you some of what we did today before you hear it somewhere else and come after my butt."

She folded her arms over her chest, waiting.

"Remember when Rolf tried to give you and me his silver arm rings in exchange for money and our help? Well, we both gave them back, but today Rolf insisted I take him to an upscale antiques dealer in Bangor." He took a deep breath while he unconsciously rubbed Teddy's back; then he informed her, "He sold one of them for a hundred and fifty thousand dollars."

Meredith gasped. "That man is so stubborn. I told him not to do that. Over and over, I told him. But he doesn't listen. I think he's been eating too many Oreos. They're eroding his brain and clogging his ears."

Mike's mouth twisted with amusement at her vehement response. "The dealer said he'd give him three hundred and fifty thousand for the pair, but he refused. And the dealer practically went into a drooling fit over the belt, which Rolf insisted was not for sale under any circumstances."

"Oh, Mike, he probably could have gotten three hundred thousand for just one arm ring by putting it up for auction at Sotheby's or Christie's."

"Rolf knows he was lowballed, but he said he didn't have time to haggle. And, man, when it comes to making good use of time, that guy is a black belt shopper."

"Exactly what did he buy today?" She already knew about the roses, but what else?

Mike waved a hand airily but he wouldn't meet her eyes. "Let's suffice it to say, we've been to jewelry stores, landscapers, car dealers, seamstress shops, furriers, a farm . . ."

She groaned, but had no time to press the issue because a loud noise diverted her attention to the side of the house—the side away from the shipbuilding enterprise. With the roar of a revving engine, a flatbed truck was backing up slowly, easing its way past the swimming pool, toward the longhouse.

"Oh, no! Please, don't tell me—" She jerked around to address Mike and saw that he was already gone. The coward!

Turning back to the truck, she got her second shock of the day. Well, actually, her zillionth shock of the day. The driver of the truck was none other than Rolf. She braced an arm against the house for support.

The man was a thousand years old. He didn't have a modern identity, except for the fake one Mike had obtained for him, let alone a motor vehicle license. Even so, he was driving a . . . well, practically a semi, for heaven's sake. And it was loaded down with long rectangles of precut sod. *Sod?* Her eyes shot to the longhouse foundation.

He wouldn't.

She gawked at Rolf behind the wheel of the truck.

He would.

Cutting the motor, he jumped down from the truck and sauntered over to her. If Meredith hadn't been speechless before, she was now. Wearing Gucci loafers, a white Polo shirt, pleated Ralph Lauren slacks, and, of course, the talisman belt, he was so handsome he made her teeth hurt. A new addition was a small leather fanny pack, probably to hold all his loot. His hair was pulled off his face with a rubber band at the neck, which showed off his deep tan, especially when he favored her with one of his dazzling white smiles.

"Merry-Death." He greeted her in a husky whisper before lowering his mouth to kiss her.

Hel-lo! Meredith said in her head. *Is anybody home? I'm supposed to be resisting this guy. I'm supposed to be laying down the law. I'm supposed to . . . oh!*

She averted her face at the last minute, and he kissed her neck instead, which didn't bother him at all. Chuckling, he propelled her, body to body, up against the house and nibbled at the curve where a pulse began to thump against his warm lips.

Who knew the neck was an erogenous zone? Oh, my. "You are not building a longhouse, Rolf," she protested on a whimper.

"Whate'er you say, dearling," he agreed, and then grinned when he got a gander at the stretched neckline of her shirt, which left one shoulder bare. "You have the nicest garments, Merry-Death," he drawled, fingering the edge of the neckline till it slipped even lower. "Will you wear this for me one day with your wanton hose? Or with those sheer pan-tease I bought for you at Victory's Secret?" Meanwhile, his teeth were nipping the curve of her neck.

"Stop it!" she demanded. "There are people all around here."

As usual, he heeded only what he wanted. "Was there a strong wind at the college today?" He'd just taken note of her half-up, half-down hair style, and he was smirking.

"No, I got a new hair stylist," she snapped. "Mr. Ted."

Over his shoulder she saw Mike, who'd returned after changing his clothes. He still wore jeans and the checkered sneakers but had donned a leather Viking tunic on top, belted at the waist. He was directing some college boys where to unload the sod.

The sod. Jolted back to the present, she shoved Rolf away. "I am *not* going to marry you, Rolf. So cut all these seductive moves. Are you listening? I . . . am . . . *not* . . . going . . . to . . . marry . . . you." It had been a nonstop refrain of hers the past two days. He'd been unwilling to budge on his plans to leave her eventually; so, she'd been equally resolute in her refusal to marry him. She glared at him now.

"You are wearing your wanton hose today," he observed, his eyes flashing appreciatively. "For me?"

She was wearing stockings, but she'd deliberately chosen a calf-length skirt and a sedate, short-sleeved cotton sweater. Definitely unwanton. She glared even harder at him. He was filtering her words again.

"You have lipstick on your teeth," he commented irrelevantly.

"What?"

"Would you like me to lick it off?"

She put a forefinger to her front teeth and started to rub till she remembered something. "I'm not wearing lipstick."

"Oh." He grimaced in one of those it-was-worth-a-shot expressions.

At her raised eyebrow, he explained sheepishly, "Whilst we were driving home from Bang-whore, Mike regaled me with tidbits from a book he bought. *How to Seduce Wenches in Ale-Houses,* or some such. That remark about lipstick was one of the lines guaranteed to break the frozen water. Since you were scowling so at me, I figured 'twas worth a try."

"Mike was telling you how to pick up women in bars?" She laughed. "Take my advice, Rolf. Stick to the Viking charm. It'll get you a whole lot farther."

"It will?" He smiled. "Well, that is what I told Mike."

"Aaarrgh!" She'd just noticed that Mike and the students were continuing to unload the sod. When he'd come back a few moments ago, she'd been about to order him not to touch the stuff, but somehow she'd gotten distracted. "Put that sod back on the truck, right now. Rolf, I mean it, you're not building a longhouse."

Mike and the students halted their work and glanced

questioningly at Rolf. He shrugged. "Whate'er Merry-Death says. After all, 'tis her bridal home." With an exaggerated sigh, he added, "Mister Burgess will be so-o-o disappointed."

"Mister who? Oh, no! Don't tell me. You're not talking about Frank Burgess, the foundation board member."

"Yea, that's the one." He beamed. "He came to visit this morn."

"That does it. Now we're going to lose our funding. Frank Burgess is the most cantankerous, short-sighted, hard-to-please, stingy man I've ever met."

"Frank? Cantankerous?" Rolf frowned. "Why, Merry-Death, surely you misjudge the man. He was very amiable. In truth, he was so impressed with the progress on the project that he donated the sod for our longhouse. I invited him to the wedding."

Putting aside her dismay over his issuing wedding invitations when there wasn't going to be a wedding, she leveled disbelieving eyes on Mike, who nodded. "It's true. The old fart actually smiled today. I didn't think he knew how."

"He asked if he and his wife, Henrietta—who e'er heard of naming a girl child after a chicken?—could volunteer on the weekends. 'Twould seem they are cooking book collectors. Is that not an odd thing to collect, Merry-Death? And they would relish trying some of their made-heave-all recipes here," Rolf elaborated. "Especially was Frank impressed with all the Norse activities blossoming about the site. In addition to the shipbuilding, of course."

"Speaking of blossoms—" she began.

"Ah, you noticed the rosebushes," he said, making a surreptitious little hand gesture to Mike to continue unloading the sod. Before she could chastise him for that sneaky action, though, he looped an arm around her shoulders. He was being entirely too familiar around Mike and the students. She tried to duck away, but he held her tight to his

side. "With all the nagging you have lashed me with sinc
arrived, I thought perchance you'd missed them."

"How could I help but notice the rosebushes, Ro
They're all over the place," she sniped unfairly. She regr
ted her hasty words when she saw the wounded expressi
on his face.

"You do not like them? But I thought—"

She moaned. The man had a knack for putting her on t
defensive and making her forget why she was so angry
him. "I adore them."

He immediately brightened. "Come, see this one, swe
ling." He pulled her over to the foundation of the longhou
and what would presumably be the front door. A small bu
with one single blood-red bud—so dark it was almost black
held prominence. "'Tis called Norse Rose," he told her in
hushed voice. "Do you think 'tis an omen?"

She closed her eyes on a shudder, fighting hard to qu
the new and wonderful emotions swirling through her bod

"Are you gladdened by my first bride gift?" he asked w
touching vulnerability.

Against her better judgment, she opened her eyes a
almost staggered under the sensual assault in his smoky amb
gaze. "I'm delighted with the roses," she conceded in a su
focated whisper. Straightening with resolve, she added, "I a
not going to marry you, though."

"Whate'er you say, dearling." With an arm still wrapp
around her shoulders, he hugged her closer and kissed t
top of her head, then walked her toward the shipbuildi
area. He spoiled the whole conciliatory pose, however, wh
he palmed her behind and confided, "I bought a barrel
dried rose petals today to spread on your bridal bed."

"I am *not* going to marry you."

"Whate'er you say, dearling."

And when she went to her bed that night—the one s

shared with Thea since Jillie was gone once again—Meredith
saw a little velvet box on her pillow. With trepidation, she
opened it to find an exquisite gold pin in the form of a rose.
On one of its finely detailed petals perched a bumblebee that
was sucking on the flower's nectar. Taped to the inside top
cover was a tiny piece of paper, folded a dozen times into a
one-inch square. When she finally got it open, a sob escaped
her lips. With a tremulous smile, she read the one-word pen-
cilled message, "Bzzzzz!"

How could she resist a man who made her smile? . . .

It was already approaching dusk on Friday when Meredith drove up the road to her house.

Thea was babysitting tonight so that Sonja and Mike
could go out to dinner and a movie. Her niece would be back
by midnight, but Meredith wasn't taking any chances. Rolf
would make sexual mincemeat of her if he got her alone for
more than an hour. So, employing the weapon women have
been using throughout the ages to ward off aggressive men—
hiding—she'd stayed intentionally late at her office, then
had done some unnecessary shopping at the mall and supermarket.

She felt a bit guilty, knowing Rolf would be chagrined
that she hadn't taken him to the mall with her. It was one of
his and Thea's favorite places.

As she pulled into the driveway, Meredith noted that the
students had left for the day, but the house was fully lit, as
well as the side yard with its floodlights. How different it
was from the dark, lonely house she'd approached just one
week ago! It seemed impossible that she'd only known Rolf
for seven days.

She could see him now in jeans and T-shirt pounding
away on the project ship. The man never stopped working.
He was obsessed. In more ways than one.

She blinked away the tears that filled her eyes, knowing the inevitable day would come when she'd drive home like this and he'd no longer be here. How could he have become such an important part of her life in such a short time? Was their love destined, as Rolf believed?

In any case, he'd been a godsend to her in at least one respect. Since he'd reassumed control of the shipbuilding project three days ago, it was moving along at a surprisingly rapid pace. His small ship, *Fierce Destiny,* was almost completed, thanks to his fifteen- to twenty-hour work days, though there was much finishing work to be done. And the new Trondheim vessel was fully framed out and ready for the planking. *Fierce Eagle* was going to be a spectacular ship, as great as any of its Viking forebears. Once the students returned to classes next week, they wouldn't be able to come out so often; so, she was elated to see so much done this week.

With the brisk efficiency of a born leader, Rolf had taken over management of all the various activities related to the ship construction and its ancillary Viking projects. But, even as he concentrated his efforts on his job, overseeing the students and working hands-on himself, he was relentless in his crusade to win her over. Among the arsenal of weapons he employed, the most obvious were the bridal gifts that he lavished on her.

"Rolf, I can't accept this," she'd said Wednesday when he slipped an engagement ring on her finger. It was a heavy gold ring of intertwining wolves, the center stone being the yellow citrine eye of the beast in profile.

" 'Tis not the traditional-style betrothal ring in your land," he'd explained huskily, "but it seemed perfect when I saw it in the antiques dealer's shop. Some refer to Vikings as sea wolves, and Geirolf means wolf in my language, you know."

I know, she'd thought, but what she'd said was, "I will *not* marry you."

"Whate'er you say, dearling."

And somehow the ring had stayed on her finger.

Then came the soft-as-silk bridal bed furs yesterday. He'd caught her in the kitchen before she'd left for the college. No hiding that time.

"Sable? You thick-headed dolt! Do you ever listen to anything I say? I will never—absolutely, positively never—sleep on the fur of some poor endangered species."

"Ah, but you must look closer, sweetling. 'Tis a high-quality fake fur. See, I do listen to you."

"Hmpfh! Well, anyhow, I will *not* marry you."

"Whate'er you say, dearling."

"What's that I smell on your breath? What have you been eating?" she'd asked then. His lips, and hands, and body, were never far from her when they were in a room together. It was as if he had a homing device implanted in his brain with a magnetic pull toward her. Or maybe it was implanted in another body part.

"Ah, I have discovered another food from the gods . . . almost as good as Oreos." He'd held a sandwich in front of her face.

She'd sniffed. "Peanut butter?"

"Yea. Thea introduced me to this delicacy. At first, I thought 'twas a prank she played on me. My tongue stuck to the roof of my mouth, but she advised me on the proper method of making the sand-witch. The key is in the jam, you know?"

"It's not a very filling breakfast," she'd said dubiously.

"Oh, but I've had ten," he'd countered brightly.

"Don't tell me . . . washed down with beer?"

"Of course."

She'd laughed then, something she did a lot these days. He might frustrate and infuriate her with his insistence that they would marry and then part, but he also brought a smile to her

face. It was hard to hate a man who made you smile. N
that she even remotely hated him. Lord, no. Just the oppos

So, now it was Friday—their anniversary, in a way. S
cringed to think what outrageous bride gift would greet I
now.

Oh, who was she kidding? She could hardly wait.

He wanted a certain body part made of steel . . .

Meredith was putting groceries away when Rolf came
The first thing he did was kiss her . . . thoroughly. It w
what he always did, whether there were people about or n
He claimed he couldn't help himself, any more than he co
resist touching her. She no longer resisted . . . his kisses,
least. She enjoyed them too much. She probably had a sex
homing device, too.

"Why did you go to the food mart without me?" he co
plained, nipping at her shoulder as she shrugged out of I
arms. Then his eyes latched onto a bag with a mall store i
print. "And the mall, too! Oh, you are a cruel, cruel wom:
I will have to think of some suitable punishment."

She edged away from him with a sidelong glance of tre
idation. One never knew what this Viking would do. T
last time he'd decided to punish her for some transgression
probably snickering at a remark Tim Allen made on his n
ronic show—he'd tickled her till she giggled like a school g
then caressed her till she'd felt . . . well, not like a scho
girl.

"I need to take a shower. Mayhap you should drek n
like a slave girl."

That's a punishment? "No way!"

"Why do you resist me so, Merry-Death? You say y
love me."

"I do," she said wearily. "Rolf, we've been down this ro

before, and we always hit the same pothole. Either you stay, or I go with you."

"'Tis impossible."

"Then, I will *not* marry you."

"Stubborn wench," he muttered with disgruntled resignation.

But she knew he hadn't given up. Not by a Viking longshot.

"Your sister called an hour past," he informed her as he rummaged through the sacks till he found what he'd been searching for. Oreos. If he stuck around much longer, Meredith was going to buy stock in Nabisco.

"I'm not surprised. She called me three times today at the office. She's persistent, if nothing else." Jillie was obsessed with Rolf's belt ornament and arm rings. She was trying to convince him to lend them to her for testing through the Metropolitan Museum in New York where she was now. In fact, Meredith suspected she was meeting with publishers there as well, lining up book deals, expecting Rolf to give her enough material to fill its pages. In one of their conversations, Jillie had let slip a tentative title, *The Last Viking.*

"I know she's your sister, sweetling, but she's becoming tiresome. I but wish to build my ships and spend my remaining time with you."

"Just ignore her."

"Hah! Her bothersome pestering has passed the bounds of my endurance. I am loath to offend any member of your family, but I must tell you, I hung up on her this time, blood kin or no."

"Good for you!" she congratulated him, and then added with a self-conscious grin, "So did I."

"You did?" Rolf seemed inordinately thrilled at such a monumental discourtesy on her part. He was always telling

her to be more assertive, to stop trying to please everyo
Well, she'd taken the first step today, and it felt darn goo

"Would you stop doing that?" she grumbled. Rolf
separated the Oreo cookie into two halves and was lick
the icing off with slow pleasure. You'd think it was an ero
experience for him. Maybe it was.

"What?" He peered up at her, all innocence, but then
tongue took one more long swipe, and his golden brown e
danced merrily. He was doing it on purpose. Before
could berate him, he said, "I have another bride gift for yo

She groaned. "I will *not* marry you."

"Whate'er you say, dearling."

While Rolf went outside to get the bride gift—the m
didn't listen to her at all—the phone rang. She went to ansv
it in the living room, where Rolf had considerately starte
cozy fire for her. Probably because he planned a cozy sed
tion. Picking up the phone, she hoped it wasn't Jillie again
her parents, who still planned to arrive tomorrow afterno
Oh, joy!

"Hello," she said with mock cheerfulness.

"Hello, is that you Meredith?"

She froze with shock. Jeffrey?

"Meredith, are you there?"

"Yes, I'm here. What do you want, Jeffrey?"

"Well, you don't have to be rude," he griped, reducing
to a child who'd never learned proper manners. "I thou
we had an amicable divorce. I thought we were still frien

Friends? Amicable? Divorced men must live in anot
world. "Great hearing from you, Jeffrey! How's the fami
What do you want?" she said snidely.

"I was thinking of taking a drive up to Maine and—"

"No!" she shouted in panic. But then she worried tha
might sound as if she still cared for him. In the words

Thea, *As if!* She took care to modulate her voice as she went on. "Why would you want to come to Maine? You always hated it here when we were married. Too rustic for your tastes, you said."

"It still is, but there are some ... uh, professional ideas I'd like to hash over with you," he said, as if picking his words carefully. "You and I always brainstormed well on academic issues."

"Professional work? Would you be bringing Nookie with you?"

"That's Cookie," he bristled.

Meredith knew only too well that the bimbo's name had been Corinne Cookson. "Nookie, Pookie, Cookie, big difference!"

"No, Cookie can't come."

"Oh, why is that? Bad case of the zits? Too much homework? Diaper rash?"

He inhaled sharply. "She's pregnant again and her doctor advises against traveling."

Meredith swayed under the pain, as if she'd been punched in the stomach. Pregnant? Again? And Meredith couldn't have even one child. Oh, life was so unfair! "When's the baby due?" she was unable to stop herself from asking.

"Three weeks."

"Three weeks! And you're going to leave her alone while you traipse up here to Maine to ... what did you call it? Brainstorm? Give me a break! Oh, no! Don't tell me you're looking to have an affair on the side now that your wife is indisposed? That would be a sad irony, wouldn't it? You had your affair when we were married because I *couldn't* have kids. And now you have an affair with your ex-wife because your present wife *can* have kids."

He said a foul word, and lashed out indignantly, "I don't want you *that* way."

Meredith's cheeks heated with embarrassment. We he'd certainly put her in her place, as usual.

"What's wrong with you, Meredith? You were never malicious before. Jillie was right. She said you were und the influence of some unsavory character. You always we too trusting. You need a keeper, if you ask me. Why don' come up there, and—"

"Jillie? You've been talking to Jillie?" Meredith shrieke Putting a hand to her face, she realized that she was cryir Why did Jeffrey always have this effect on her? And was it just like Jillie to enlist Jeffrey's help in wearing her dow They were both probably planning book deals, gree amoral animals that they were.

"Merry-Death, what ails you?" Geirolf said with conce as he walked into the living room. Tears were streami down her face, and her hands were trembling as she talked someone on the telephone. Another one of her family mer bers, he would wager.

Angry with her kin, who continued to badger her, ar frustrated with Merry-Death's failure to stand up to ther he tossed the boxes he was holding onto the sofa. "Give r the bloody telephone," he snapped, moving closer to her.

"No! Oh, no, no, no!" Her weepy eyes dilated with horr at the prospect of his speaking with whomever was on t other end of that talking box. Furious, he grabbed the pho from her hand. "Who is this?" he growled.

"Jeffrey Foster. Who the hell are you?"

"I am Geirolf Ericsson, Merry-Death's betrothed. Wh did you say to cause her to weep, you bloody whoreson?"

"Wh-what?"

"You heard me good and well. Know this, you blac hearted bastard. You tossed aside the best woman in tl world, but a better man has picked up the pieces. Do not pr sume to change your lackbrain mind now."

"I don't want Meredith. Whatever gave you that idea?"

"I know her for the treasure she is—that's what gave me that idea."

"Hot damn! She must have developed a few sexual talents since I've known her to make up for her other . . . deficiencies."

A fierce rumble of outrage rolled up from his chest, emerging as the noise warriors often made before entering battle. "If you were here now, you cowardly cur, I would wring your neck and feed your scurrilous tongue to the ravens."

"You're a lunatic. Let me talk to Meredith."

"Apparently you have a hearing problem. Do not ever call Merry-Death again. Do not intimidate her. Do not belittle her. Do not come within a hide of her manor."

"You have no right to order me around. Who do you think you are, you . . . you illiterate lowlife?"

"I am the man who will lop off your head in a trice if you so much as look at my woman again," he snarled and slammed down the phone.

It took several moments for Geirolf's berserk temper to pass. 'Twas always thus when the war fever hit, giving him the blood surge necessary to fight off his enemies. When he came to his senses again, after several deep, panting breaths, he noticed Merry-Death staring at him. Her eyes were wide with unshed tears and recrimination. *Recrimination?* That brought his rage back with a vengeance.

Advancing on her, he wagged a finger in her face. "Wench, when are you going to learn to defend yourself against your enemies, instead of cowering like a pup? What will happen when I am gone? Who will fight your battles for you then?"

"Why . . . why . . . you dolt! I don't need you to be my knight in shining armor to settle a disagreement, and that's all it was. Not some major fight. Jeffrey and I always disagree. And, frankly, if you want to know the truth, you big,

thick-headed oaf, I had already told him off before y
jumped into the fray."

"You did?" His anger immediately dissipated and w
replaced with a heart-wrenching desolation. Her tears m
have been caused by the love she still harbored for this pa
husband. He could scarce breathe over the lump in
throat. "Dost still love the man then, Merry-Death?"

"Huh?" She was in the midst of wiping her eyes with
clean-axe when he asked his question. The scowl she ga
him then put him in the same class as donkeys and thi
skinned melons.

"Your tears," he pointed out. "Since you do not weep
cause of some offense given by your past-husband, the te
must come from your . . . love." His voice quivered on
last word. He turned away from her to conceal his weakne

"Are all Vikings idiots, or just you?"

Some time the wench was going to push him too far w
her insults. He turned slowly. She was standing with
hands braced on her hips, which were covered with tho
infernal men's *braies* again, even though he'd told her ma
a time that he much preferred garments that required t
wanton hose. If she loved him, she would want to please hi
wouldn't she? Hell, she tried her damnedest to please ever
one else in the world. But then, he'd just learned that she s
loved her past-husband. "Damn your impertinence, my lac
And damn you for leading me about like a smitten yout
ling."

"Rolf, I don't love Jeffrey, and probably never did."

"Do you tell me true, Merry-Death?" His heart lurch
with hopefulness. Bloody hell, he abhorred his vulnerabil
where this woman was concerned. 'Twas a weak link in
manly armor, to be sure.

"He's a creep and I pretty much told him so."

"Then why were you soaking the carpet with your tears

"Because he made me so mad. And because I was relieved to finally express my true feelings to him."

"Oh." Did that mean he'd made a fool of himself? Not in hurling harsh words at the brute on the phone, but for accusing Merry-Death unjustly. "I'm sorry, sweetling. I behaved like an ass."

"Hmpfh! That's for sure."

He was too happy that he'd been wrong in his ill-conceived conclusions to chide her for concurring. "Come, sweetling, let me show you my bride gift." He took her hand and tugged her toward the bed-couch. Of course, his fingers tingled where their skin met.

Her hand flinched with surprise at the contact of their palms and he knew that she felt the tingle, too.

"Do you think our nether parts will tingle when they meet?" he asked expectantly as he handed her a white rectangular box with the words "Meako's Fine Hand-crafted Clothing" imprinted in gold letters on top.

Meredith's mouth dropped open. That remark was outrageous, even for Rolf. When she didn't answer immediately, he glanced up from where he was opening another box, noticing her shock. She closed her mouth, but not before he also noticed her obvious interest in his question. He winked at her, and Meredith felt butterflies take flight in her stomach.

"Open your bride gift," he urged her.

"I will *not* marry you," she repeated in her now familiar refrain and he gave her one of those "Yeah, yeah, what else is new" looks. But her curiosity got the better of her, as he probably knew it would, and she lifted the lid, then peeled back the gold tissue paper. He had commissioned an exquisite Viking-style wedding gown to be made for her. "Oh, Rolf."

"Do not even think of weeping again," he warned her. "I have had more than enough emotional upheavals today."

She wasn't sure if he referred to her emotions or his. "I

will *not* marry you," she said again, but even she recognized how weak her voice sounded.

She held the fantastic garment up, and the flickering flames from the fireplace cast dancing lights on its shimmering folds. The undergown was a long-sleeved, collarless chemise of gossamer white linen gauze, ankle-length in front and pleated and slightly longer in the back. The wrists and circular neckline were edged with bands embroidered with metallic threads of green and gold and white against a red background. The silk overgown, open-sided in the Viking style, was a deep crimson with matching bands of embroidery at the hem and neckline. Here, the colors were reversed, a white background with crimson, green, and gold threads. The embroidery design was a series of intertwining roses. Two rosebud shoulder brooches were enclosed, along with a gold link belt to be worn loosely at the waist, more in Saxon than Viking fashion, which normally was unbelted at the waist.

"Rolf, it's beautiful, but why do you keep giving me these gifts when I tell you—"

"Come see what I purchased for myself," he interrupted, gesturing at the box he was opening. "'Tis my wedding raiment. I would not wish my betrothed to outshine me overmuch on that day," he teased.

She sighed with admiration. His outfit was a pitch-black, long-sleeved overtunic of softest wool, mixed with cashmere, which would hang to mid-thigh or slightly lower. The tunic would be worn over a pair of slim trousers of the same fabric and be held in at the waist by his talisman belt. Both the tunic and a white silk-lined mantle were embroidered with the same band of roses as her gown.

"If I were going to marry you, which I am not, I couldn't ask for anything more perfect," she said honestly. "Thank you."

"You are more than welcome, sweetling, but save your thank you for our wedding night."

She groaned. The man was a brick wall.

"But let us set aside our differences for now. It's almost eight on the clock, and you know what that means." He pulled her over, gave her a quick kiss, shoved her down on the sofa, and then said, "Shhh."

She shuddered with distaste. *Home Improvement* was coming on the television.

When the show was finally over and one of those exercise infomercials came on, Rolf watched with a concentration he usually reserved only for his favorite toolman. "Could it be?" he murmured and turned on her as if enlightened. "Could it be that the reason you resist me so much is because I have a—" he hesitated, grimacing with horror—"a physical defect? Something women of your time favor, but men don't develop in my world?"

Rolf defective physically? I . . . don't . . . think . . . so. "Well, now that you mention it . . ." she teased, tapping a forefinger thoughtfully on her chin.

"Well, why didn't you tell me from the start?" he said grumpily. "I could have ordered one of those machines from the come-her-shall and been working all this time to correct my flaw. Bloody hell, my brothers would make great jest of this if they knew a woman had spurned my favors because of some ill appeal. You may not have noticed, but I have a certain arrogance about the way I look."

"I hadn't noticed." Then she took pity on him. "Rolf, I haven't the faintest idea what you're talking about."

He jerked his head toward the television where some fitness expert was spouting off about how to firm up the gluteus maximus muscles. Her eyes shot to Rolf with sudden understanding.

"You have resisted me mightily because I do not have . . . buns of steel."

She burst out laughing and couldn't stop even when he

stood and glowered at her. Finally, she was able to choke out, "Rolf, I have no idea whether you have buns of steel or not."

Which was a big mistake.

Pivoting 180 degrees, he dropped his sweatpants to the floor and asked over his shoulder, "What do you think?"

He wasn't wearing any underwear.

"And *Nordic* Trak—did you see that? They have a machine for Norsemen alone. We must have some special deficiency."

Once she pushed her eyeballs back in their sockets, she sputtered, "I think you have nothing to worry about in that department."

But what she really thought was, *I am going to have some very strange and very vivid dreams tonight.*

CHAPTER FOURTEEN

&

Vikings love to give gifts . . .

"*Aaaccckkk!*" Meredith screamed when she opened her front door the next morning to get the newspaper. Parked in her driveway, tied with a huge ribbon, was her latest bride gift, one of those 1950s classic convertibles with winglike back fenders. It was as big as a Viking longboat—probably got about one mile per gallon—and it was (Meredith shuddered) pink.

Rolf came rushing from the side of the house, hair all disheveled, bed furs thrown over his bare shoulders. He wielded one of the long wooden "spears" he'd improvised the other day. And he couldn't have looked fiercer if he were a true Viking warrior about to do battle.

"What's amiss, my lady?" he said, pivoting his head this way and that, scanning the area. "Where's the enemy?"

Once she snapped her gaping mouth shut, she pointed to the left. "*What* is that?"

"Do you say your keep is safe from attack?" His body relaxed when he comprehended that no imminent danger loomed, but he cast her a disapproving scowl. "Have I mentioned afore, you have a shriek that would drive a sane man mad? You would do well, my lady, to hear the saga that skalds tell in our lands about a boy who cried dragon once too often."

"Don't you mean the boy who cried wolf?"

"What wolf?" Once again, he was surveying the ya
this time ridiculously searching for a wolf.

"Never mind." She tapped her foot impatiently and in
cated with a motion of her head that he hadn't answered I
question about the pink monstrosity in her driveway. It v
probably a vintage Mary Kay car.

"Oh, that." He shrugged. "I couldn't find a suitable ho
for you on such short notice."

"A horse?" she squealed.

"Besides," he said with an open-mouthed yawn, "did y
know they have zone laws that prohibit you from buildin
barn on your property? I am planning to appeal to a hig
authority . . . mayhap even the king. Is King Clinton the o
sovereign you have in your land?"

"A barn? A barn? Don't you even think of building a ba
That longhouse is bad enough. And if you dare to phone
White House, I'm going to disconnect our telephone servic

"Whate'er you say, dearling." His mouth turned do
in one of those sad-sack moues, and he said with boy
hurt, "Methought you favored the longhouse now 'tis ni
complete."

She snarled and Rolf dropped an arm heavily around I
shoulder, drawing her back into the house. Once he realiz
that the pout wasn't going to cut it, he advised, "Settle dov
Merry-Death. You need to relax more. 'Tis good you're ta
ing the day off from working. You've been much too hig
strung of late." His seeming consideration flew out the wind
when he added, "No doubt it stems from sexual frustration
I learned that word on *Sesame Street*."

"You . . . never . . . did."

He cocked his head. "Oh. Mayhap so. Well, it must ha
been the *Dr. Ruth Show,* then." He waved a hand airily. "Lea
ways, 'tis a well-known fact that when the sap runs, the s

must run. Denying the body juices their free course clogs the pores and muddles the mind."

"You are incredible." She laughed.

"I know," he acknowledged, beaming at her.

Actually, Meredith was glad to have the day off. Once she'd vented her newfound assertiveness with Jeffrey last night, she'd gone whole hog and called her parents, telling them in no uncertain terms that they were unwelcome in Maine. Despite vehement protests at their carefully laid plans being destroyed by her insensitivity, she'd held firm.

Rolf had been so proud of her.

Thus encouraged and under the influence of a rush of adrenaline, she'd called Jared and given him the same message. Much more conciliatory, he said he was buried in work anyhow.

So, with her schedule unexpectedly free, Rolf proclaimed a vacation day for the project, inviting her to go on a calendar event with him . . . a date. Since it was Saturday, she agreed, but only if Thea, Mike, Sonja, and Teddy could go with them, sort of a four-pack of chaperons.

They decided to visit the zoo.

Would she consent to be his love slave? Oh, yeah! . . .

Meredith's first date with Rolf was a disaster.

As they headed for home later that afternoon in the pink mega-car, a morose Rolf stared blindly out the window, watching the landscape pass by. Mike was driving, with Thea in the front seat beside him. Meredith sat in the back with Sonja and Teddy on her right and Rolf on her left. They'd put the top up when the air turned cool and talk had been impossible over the roar of the motor and the wind, not to mention the mortifyingly loud muffler.

She slipped a hand in Rolf's—something she didn't often do. "I'm sorry, Rolf. It never occurred to me that a zoo would upset you so much." They'd all observed from the beginning that the zoo experience revolted Rolf, but Teddy had been enjoying himself so much they'd stayed.

Rolf turned bleak eyes on her, the bourbon color flashing with outrage. "How could civilized people torture animals? 'Tis surely an affront to the gods, caging wild beasts so."

She pursed her lips pensively. "I never thought much about it before, but The Silver Oaks Zoo is one of the most reputable in the country. Believe me, there are zoos that treat their animals in an inhumane way, but this isn't one of them."

"Don't they have zoos in your country?" Mike asked over his shoulder.

Meredith tensed. Rolf had never discussed his time travel with anyone but her, though she sometimes caught Mike looking at him strangely. Who wouldn't? Despite his mastery of the language, he used enough 'tis'es and 'twas'es to make anyone suspicious. And some of his ideas were definitely archaic.

Rolf made eye contact with her and took heed of her unspoken warning. "Nay, we don't cage our animals." It seemed that was all he would say, but then his jaw jutted out angrily. "You are Christians. Your Bible says all creatures have dignity and a reason for existing. What dignity do you leave animals when they are gawked at day and night, with no privacy for body functions? Even their mating is observed, for the love of Freya!"

"It's not all entertainment, Rolf," Meredith told him gently. "Scientists study the animals in captivity. And sometimes they learn things that help mankind."

"Then I say 'tis too high a price to pay," he stormed. "Damn the scientists!"

Meredith cringed, wondering if he put her in the same class as those scientists.

"But you have nothing against hunting, do you?" Sonja inquired, sincerely trying to understand.

"'Tis different," he said, folding his arms over his chest and slinking lower in the seat with exasperation. "All animals, man and beast alike, fight the battle for survival. There is no shame in the hunt and chase."

He gazed imploringly at Meredith. "Didst you see that aged Bengal tiger, Merry-Death? His eyes spoke to me. 'I have no pride,' the beast said. 'Warrior to warrior, I ask you. Give me peace.'"

"That is so totally awesome," Thea interjected. "Like I never heard of anyone talking to animals before, except maybe Walt Disney."

"If I'd had *Brave Friend* with me, I would have put my trusty sword through the tiger's heart. 'Twould have been a blessing, too."

Mike and Sonja exchanged worried glances. Thea chortled, "Wow!" And Meredith breathed a silent prayer of thanks that she'd laid down the law when Rolf had suggested going back to the antiques dealer to buy a sword.

"Many a time have I seen polar bears in their 'natural habitat,'" he continued. "Tell me true, Merry-Death, dost think that regal white-furred creature in the zoo was fooled by a mock glacier?"

"Some sociologists contend there are layers in all civilization," Mike speculated tentatively. "You know, animals and humans fall into classes—by wealth, or birth, or physical fitness, or whatever. Aren't some species supposed to dominate others? Isn't that what the whole Viking way of life was about?"

Rolf inhaled sharply. "You haven't studied enough, Mike, if you conclude thus. 'Tis true that Norsemen invade other countries and subdue their peoples, but that is because our own lands have become so overcrowded or are terrorized by brutal kings. We seek new lands to settle. This raping and pillaging word-fame is unearned by most Norsemen, I tell you."

"But the Vikings took captives, Rolf, remember that," Mike reminded him with reckless bravery.

"Ah, but we don't put our slaves in cages. We don't treat them as freaks of nature. We allow them to earn their freedom. And best you remember that the Saxons and Franks take captives, as well."

"Gee, Rolf, you talk as if you're a real Viking," Sonja said with a giggle.

"Yeah," Thea put in.

Mike waited expectantly for his answer.

Rolf rolled his shoulders. "Who can say what is a *real* Viking."

"Rolf comes from a region where they practice the old ways," Meredith hastily explained. "Sometimes they forget it's the twentieth century."

He sliced her a reproving glare. The constant pretense annoyed him, she knew, but, luckily, he said nothing more.

Meredith sighed with relief. If nothing else, the visit to the zoo had brought home to her the danger of Rolf's presence in the twentieth century. Fortunately, Rolf hadn't told anyone, other than her, about his time travel. If he had, and if by some remote chance, someone believed him, scientists would cage him as surely as they did those wild beasts in the zoo. And he'd be treated as a freak, too.

She perceived another thing, too. It was necessary for Rolf to return to his time for a reason besides his father's mission. If he stayed here much longer, eventually he'd let something slip. There were too many hazards for him in this land and time.

"Blessed Thor! You're going to weep again. Over my growling, of all things! 'Tis naught to cry about, sweetling," he said, pulling her close. Then he whispered in her ear, "If you are going to cry when I roar, what will you do when I bite?"

She blinked away her tears and smiled. "Bite you back."

He howled with amusement. "I scarce can wait."

He wasn't laughing fifteen minutes later when they entered the house. Mike had taken Sonja and Teddy home, and Thea skipped upstairs to play her music. Too late, Meredith saw that she was trapped between the refrigerator and an angry Viking.

"Wh-what?" she stammered at the menacing figure he posed, fists clenched at his sides, his lips white with vexation. "Do you want something to eat or drink?"

"Nay, Meredith, I do not."

"Then what do you want?" He was closing in, inch by inch. Girding herself with resolve, she refused to shiver. But inside, she was shivering like a bowl of Jell-O.

"You."

Oh, boy! "I will *not* marry you," she insisted, "under your conditions." She assumed that was the cause of his sudden fury.

"Whate'er you say, dearling," he drawled with a mocking grin.

It wasn't a grin to engender warm, fuzzy feelings.

"What's the problem, Rolf?"

"Mike isn't the only one who knows naught of Vikings," he went on in a voice whose calmness contrasted ominously with his take-no-mercy eyes. "You two study Norsemen in your books but fail to see us true."

"I don't understand."

"Nay, you do not. That is a certainty. You have caged the wild beast here, Merry-Death," he informed her, pounding his chest with one fist, "but it is about to break free."

The quiver in her stomach escalated to an earthquake. "Are you trying to frighten me?"

"Do I?"

"No."

He smiled, but it was more a feral baring of the teeth.

"Foolish wench. I realized today that I have allowed mysel
to be caged voluntarily, chained by my excessive lust for you
I have played the tame pet for you overlong. 'Twas my mis
take, granting you time to give your free consent to our join
ing. Enough! If you will not be my wife, then you will be m
thrall."

"A slave?" she twittered nervously.

"Yea, a love slave," he said softly. "How do you view th
prospect of being a Viking captive? Hmmm? Subject to m
every whim?"

"Stop playing games with me, Rolf." She tried to edg
away, but he put a palm on either side of her head, his arm
braced tautly. She had the coolness of the refrigerator at he
back and the heat of an aggressive male at her front. It wasn'
an entirely unpleasant experience, she admitted to herself.

"Mayhap, slave, I will keep you naked till you bend t
my will. Or wearing the scant garments I choose." His eye
took note of the angora sweater she'd donned earlier at hi
request.

A mistake, she discerned now as he licked his lips slowly
With anticipation?

Did he suspect that she'd also put on the Victoria's Secre
panties he'd bought for her?

He did, she saw as his hot scrutiny briefly settled there
She was wearing loose linen trousers, but he knew. He knew

"Put your hands over your head, thrall," he demanded.

"What?"

"Do you question your master's authority, slave?" he sai
with lethal calmness, taking a steak knife from the counte
and pressing it against her throat. "A recalcitrant slave mus
be punished."

She wasn't really frightened, except perhaps of the thud
ding of her heart. She surprised herself by doing as he'
commanded, raising her hands to the top of the refrigerator

where she grasped the edges of a casserole dish. But, despite her compliant pose, she tossed her hair over her shoulder in a gesture of petulance.

"Ah, a defiant slave," he cooed. "Are you wanting to be tamed, wench?"

She shook her head. *Do I?*

Before she realized his intent, he eased the small knife inside the neckline of her sweater, first to the left, then the right, slitting the straps of her bra. He did the same from under the hem in front, cutting the center band of her undergarment. With the flick of his fingers, he pulled the wispy lingerie out and dropped it to the floor.

"Nay, do not move," he ordered when her hands began to lower.

Holding her eyes, he undid the button of her slacks. The rasp of the sliding zipper echoed loudly in the silent room. In an instant, the fabric slithered down and pooled at her ankles. She was bare from ankle to waist, except for the French-cut, flesh-colored silk briefs.

The slight hitch of his breath was his only sign of appreciation.

"A beautiful slave girl is a highly prized commodity," he said in raw tones, dragging the hem of her sweater downward so the sensuous fibers abraded her bare breasts. The tautened material outlined her uplifted breasts, whose nipples blossomed into hardened peaks as he watched. He released the hem, and the elasticized material sprang back into its original shape. He repeated the procedure several times till her nipples ached for more. The touch of his calloused fingertips came to mind.

"Rolf," she whimpered and lifted her arms higher, bowing her chest outward in invitation.

"A slave does not address her master," he reprimanded,

running the backs of his knuckles over the tips in a too-quick motion. She wanted more.

"Spread your legs," he said, "as far as you can."

Restricted by the pantlegs at her ankles, she could only separate her feet so far. But it was enough. Her feminine folds parted, exposed against the silk crotch of her panties.

"Good." Rolf stepped back.

Meredith couldn't believe her eyes. Instead of taking her in his arms, as she'd expected, he walked away from her and sat in a chair on the other side of the table. "Do not think of moving, slave, or it will not go well for you," he informed her in a thick rasp. Then he leaned back in the chair, arms lying loosely in his lap, legs sprawled forward, and he studied her like . . . like a possession.

The kitchen clock ticked the seconds away. Thea's rock-'n-roll beat created a rhythm that was echoed in the throbbing of her nipples and the heated place between her legs. It was a vulnerable, seductive position he'd placed her in, but oddly, she didn't feel demeaned. She felt extremely excited.

Whatever label she took on—wife, lover, friend, slave—she was Rolf's. Well, that wasn't quite true. They were still at a stalemate concerning his plans for their future. He was leaving in a few short weeks, and she was going to be devastated. Better the small pain now than the agonizing pain later.

"I will *not* marry you," she cried. And she meant it.

"Whate'er you say, dearling." He grinned. And he didn't mean it.

"What I say is that I want you to touch me," she snarled with frustration.

"Where?" he asked with amusement, though she noticed his knuckles were white where they now clasped his knees.

"Everywhere."

"Greedy wench." He laughed.

"So, do the Vikings have male captives, too?"

"For a certainty."

"Do female Vikings ever have male slaves?"

His eyes lit up with understanding at the train of her questioning. "Yea, some do."

"Hmmm. Perhaps you might be willing to reverse roles and—"

"Aunt Mer," Thea shouted from upstairs, "what's for dinner? I'm starved."

Rolf swore softly at the interruption, and Meredith scurried to pull up her slacks and hide her damaged bra.

"Yea, Merry-Death, I am starved, too." Rolf strolled over to help button her slacks because her fingers were trembling so. Their eyes locked for a moment before Thea came barreling into the kitchen.

It wasn't food he was hungry for, and Meredith shared the hunger.

With a chuckle, as if reading her mind, Rolf swatted her on the behind. "Never fear, sweetling, a Viking always satisfies the appetite of his lady."

She clucked at his play on words, and he winked at her.

"Of course, a Viking man partakes heartily of the feast, as well. We are renowned for our lusty appetites. Then, too, we are equally renowned for our hospitality." He paused dramatically. "'Tis not polite to let a lady eat alone."

Some ex-es deserve to be ex-es . . .

All hell broke loose that night, and the dispute she and Rolf were having over marriage faded in importance.

Bam!

Meredith jackknifed into a sitting position in her bed. Thea, as usual, slept like a rock. Maybe it was just a dream. No, she'd been dreaming about male anatomy. Specifically, Viking male anatomy of the gluteus maximus variety.

Bam!

"Oh, my goodness! It's a gunshot. And it's coming f[rom] the side yard," she murmured.

"What was that?" Thea slurred sleepily.

"Nothing, honey," Meredith said, already up and rush[ing] for the door. "Go back to sleep. I don't want you com[ing] downstairs. Do you hear me?"

"Um-hmmm." Thea rolled over and fell back asleep.

Meredith took the steps two at time and didn't bothe[r] snap on the lights or grab a flashlight as she unlocked front door and hurried to find . . . she didn't know what. ' sounds of raised voices, grunts, and tussling emanated o[mi]nously from outside. Some peril threatened them; she sen[sed] that much.

What if . . . ? Oh, gee, a little more than a week ag[o] stranger from another time had invaded her home. Mayb[e] whole darn shipload of time travelers were storming keep now. She fought back a wave of hysteria at that ridi[cu]lous notion and rounded the corner of the house.

"Oompfh!" She tripped over a black-clad body and alm[ost] fell. There was only a half-moon tonight, and all she co[uld] make out was dark shoes, pants, gloves, and a ski mask gun lay on the ground near the open hand of the unmov[ing] perpetrator.

A gun? Oh, my God! Was he dead?

One of Rolf's wooden spears rested where it had lan[ded] near the person's head. Having no point, the stick could have broken the skin's surface. At least, she didn't think But maybe a head trauma from a blunt object thrown w[ith] force might be fatal. She should check for a pulse. No, no. First, she had to find Rolf.

Scuffling noises, accompanied by guttural curses, ca[me] from the back of the house. She picked up the spear a[nd] rushed forward. Another black-clad figure, much bigger t[han] the one she'd just found, wrestled on the grass with Rolf, who wore only a pair of jogging pants. Rolf must have been sleeping in the longhouse tonight.

In delayed reaction, she gasped, then put a hand over her mouth and screamed.

Startled, Rolf looked up and shouted, "Go back, Merry-Death. 'Tis not safe. I'll handle these assailants."

The attacker took advantage of Rolf's surprise and managed to scramble free, raising a gun. And, oh, dear Lord, he was aiming it at Rolf. Acting instinctively, Meredith grasped the spear like a baseball bat and swung. It was heavier than she'd expected; so she didn't have much momentum. To her dismay, at the last minute, the creep ducked. And she hit Rolf smack across the stomach.

"Oompfh!" Rolf fell backwards on his butt and the assailant's gun went off accidentally. The bullet didn't seem to have hit anyone.

For a brief second, Rolf and the attacker gazed at her as if she was a crazy woman. She was. But Rolf was in danger, and she couldn't let anything happen to him. Weaponless now, she made a leap for the jerk with the gun, but he spun about and with a twist of his body had an armlock around Meredith's neck. He pressed the gun to the side of her head.

Rolf stood warily. "Don't harm her," he pleaded. "I'll give you whate'er you want. Be careful. No one has to be hurt."

"The belt," the man demanded in a muffled voice. "Drop it to the ground, and step back."

A sense of something familiar or not quite right about the gunman nagged at Meredith, but she couldn't puzzle it out now. "Don't do it, Rolf. He's bluffing." *At least, I think he is.*

"One more word and you're dead, bitch," the obviously disguised voice said against her ear.

Rolf didn't pay any attention to her. He'd already unbuckled his talisman belt. It fell with a clunk. Then he took two steps backwards.

"The arm ring, too," the thief ordered.

Arm ring? Since when does your everyday burglar know that is an arm ring? Most people would call it a bracelet, or silver arm band. But "arm ring" is a medieval term. Recognition hit her like a ton of bricks. *Jeffrey! The bastard!*

Uncaring of the risks, she wrenched herself out of his arms by elbowing him hard, then swiveling and delivering a sharp knee to the groin. His gun went off again, right against her head, but Meredith realized at once that, although her ears were ringing, she hadn't been injured. The weapon must contain blanks.

With a groan, Jeffrey bent at the waist, clutching his precious jewels. By then, Rolf was standing. He picked up the spear and whacked Jeffrey over the head, knocking him unconscious.

Rolf grabbed her by the forearms and demanded, "Are you all right?" She nodded, and he hauled her into a bone-crunching bear hug. "Woman, I'm going to wring your neck in a few moments for taking such a foolhardy chance. But right now, I'm so happy you're alive." His voice cracked at the end as he lavished tiny kisses of euphoria all over her face and neck.

"Oh, Rolf, I was so worried. I thought . . . Oh, sweetheart, I love you so. And I thought I'd lost you . . . already. I mean, too soon. Oh, I don't know what I mean." She was sobbing and kissing him at the same time.

"Shhhh," he crooned, and then straightened with concern. "We've got to get these two inside and restrain them. Open the patio door for me, Merry-Death." Bending, he heaved up the body with ease, even though it must be very heavy for him, and threw it over his shoulder like a sack of flour. "I know not who these knaves are, but you can be sure I will soon find out," he growled.

"Well, actually—" she stammered, shifting from foot to foot.

Rolf had started to walk toward the house with his living baggage, but he paused and turned back to stare at her.

"You know this man?" he asked icily.

What? Did he imagine she was in cahoots with the burglars? Geez! "It's . . . Oh, I know this is hard to believe, but it's—"

"Spit it out, Merry-Death."

". . . my ex-husband."

Rolf said a very foul word, then pointed toward the side yard. "And who might that be? His pregnant wife?"

"No. I'm not sure. Oh, God, this is so awful." She began to weep.

"Hell, the tears again!" he stormed. "Merry-Death, this man weighs more than a butchered boar. Speak up. Who's the other miscreant?"

"My sister. Jillie," she said in a small voice.

"Blód hel!" he swore, then put his free hand to her face and whispered, "Oh, Merry-Death. I'm so sorry." He was the one who looked as if he might cry then—for her.

Forget Land of the Lost, this was Land of the Lunatics . . .

Much later, they still sat about Merry-Death's great room, trying to determine what to do with the culprits squirming on the sofa under his scowling scrutiny.

"I vote for throwing them off the cliff," he grumbled, but Merry-Death—kind-hearted soul that she was—urged, "Stop kidding, Rolf. What we have to decide is whether to involve the police."

"Give me a break, Mer," Jillian said, examining her fingernails with unconcern. Apparently, a major tragedy had occurred in the course of her falling—she'd broken a fingernail. "You wouldn't want the publicity. Besides, I could sue that barbarian over there for attacking me." She rolled her shoulders and winced for effect.

What a game she played! Pretending to be hurt when his "spear" hadn't even broken the skin between her shoulder blades. Then he pondered her words. "Are you calling me a barbarian, wench? You, who planned a siege of your own sister's home?"

"Shhh, Rolf," Merry-Death cautioned. "She's right. I don't want to call the police, but not to protect my reputation or hers. Thea has to be protected."

"That's another thing," Jillian complained. "You had no right to have Mike come here and take her away. She's my daughter and—"

"Jillie, that's the most self-centered thing I've ever heard you say, and that's saying a lot. How could you have wanted Thea to witness this? Don't you care if she knows you're a thief, or worse?"

"Don't be so melodramatic, Meredith," Jeffrey chimed in. "We're not thieves. We would've returned the belt and arm ring after we'd done the testing and written the book. Sometimes, Meredith, you're too damned stubborn for your own good. If you'd been reasonable when Jillie and I talked to you—"

With a roar, Geirolf went for the man, arms outstretched, but Meredith held him back. "Please," she begged.

He halted, for her sake, but he lashed out at her past-husband, "Put a lock on your coarse tongue when you talk to my betrothed, or I will cut it out with great relish."

Bloody hell, Geirolf decided, they thought and talked too much in this land. What they needed was less brain gnashing and more body gnashing. They'd been sitting for more than an hour drinking coffee. Well, the rest of them drank coffee. He swigged mead from a long-neck bottle. After three cups of coffee, he'd told Merry-Death he was going to piss black if he drank any more of the strong liquid.

Jeffrey had made a foolhardy remark then about his "crudity," and that was the first time Geirolf had split his lip. The second time was when the bastard dared to ogle Merry-Death's rump in her tight jeans whilst she bent to pick up a piece of firewood. Merry-Death had done her tsk-tsk routine at Geirolf then and refused to go upstairs and change into something more modest—like a tent.

After they'd brought Jeffrey and Jillian into the house, Merry-Death had gone to her bedchamber to soothe Thea and change from her sleeping *shert* into a sweating *shert* and the den-ham *braies*. Good thing she wasn't wearing the cat sweater . . . *that* he wouldn't have allowed, no matter her resistance. The visual, and tactile, delight of the cat sweater belonged only to him. In fact, he was going to destroy it before he departed this land.

He groaned inwardly at the thought of his inevitable separation from Merry-Death. He couldn't imagine how he would survive the rest of his life without her. But he was also more adamant than ever that he would leave her behind after tonight's incidents.

When he'd seen the scoundrel holding a gun to her head, Geirolf's blood had run cold. He'd thought he'd lost her then. And it was all his fault. He'd brought the talisman belt here; he would take it away.

And there was naught she could say that would convince him to take her with him. Especially not now. He would never, ever risk her life again. And definitely not with the almost-certain death associated with the Demon Moon and the shipwreck whirlpool. The time porthole was never intended for the likes of her.

Besides, what if he were able to take her back? And what if he were killed in one of the incessant battles with the Saxons? How would she survive alone in another time?

Merry-Death glanced up at him and his uplifted bottle

with an anxious frown from where she sat on the raised hearth near his feet. He patted her head, assuring her he would behave—for now—because she asked. She had withstood his request for mead, at first, saying she wanted him to keep a cool head. Hah! A tun of mead couldn't make him any more furious than he was now. And if he chose to beat the villainous cur to death and cut off the bitch's nose, as he sorely yearned to do, then a cup of coffee wouldn't hold him back. But Merry-Death's fervent plea had held him back—for now.

He leaned against the fireplace and took a long swig of mead. Every time he hoisted the bottle, he saw Jeffrey's upper lip—the one covered with a thin milksop mustache—curl with distaste. The man had a death wish, he really did, daring to cast condescending eyes his way.

Merry-Death put a hand on his calf. No doubt she would latch onto his ankle like a puppy if he lunged for the two lackwits who sat guiltily on the couch-bed. They'd run like the wind if he turned his back.

"Can we get on with this?" Jeffrey asked testily. "I have an appointment at noon with my department head. You remember Dr. Preston, don't you, Meredith? He came to our wedding."

A rumble of outrage rolled up from Geirolf's chest, but it was Jillian who put up a forbidding hand to him this time. Addressing Jeffrey, she said, "You are a solid gold-plated ass, Jeffrey. Put a lid on it, or I'll cut out your tongue." She spoke to Merry-Death then, a contrite expression coming onto her face. "You're well rid of the jerk, Mer. Really. He's a weak, two-faced, sniveling bastard, and I feel sorry for the woman who has him now. Really."

"You have no room to talk," Jeffrey spat back at her. "You're nothing but a bitch in heat, except you've got the hots for fame, not sex."

"Could we please stop all this bickering?" Merry-Death

interjected shrilly, and Geirolf could see that she was approaching the limits of her endurance. Hauling her to her feet, he cradled her in the curve of his shoulder, and whispered into her hair, "Go up to bed, dearling. Let me handle this."

She shook her head. "It's my problem. I brought them here by sending them sketches of your belt clasp."

"Nay, sweetling, I brought danger to you by coming to your home in the first instance."

"Son of a bitch!" Jeffrey cursed, gaping at the loving picture of Merry-Death in Geirolf's arms.

"Could you two save the billing and cooing for later? I have a plane to catch in Bangor at five A.M.," Jillian snapped. "Either call the cops, or let us go."

"Yea, 'tis time to stop dawdling," Geirolf agreed. "We will not involve the legal authorities. That has been decided. Am I correct, Merry-Death?"

"Yes."

"What destination does your flying machine have, Jillian?"

"Flying machine? Huh? Oh, I'm going back to London. Jeffrey was going to take the belt and arm ring to the Met to be dated, though God knows why I trusted him. Chances are he would have hocked the things and taken off for some tropical island to screw a few dozen nubile native girls."

"Bitch!" Jeffrey seethed at her, spit flying.

"Bastard!" she countered, making a point of wiping the drool off her face with a tissue.

"Aaarrgh!" Merry-Death said.

"Damn, but you two deserve each other," Geirolf opined.

"Jillie, what about Thea? She's supposed to be back in school in another week. Will she be going back to her father in Chicago, or to London with you?"

"Hell if I know," Jillian said morosely. "Oh, don't go getting all uptight and sanctimonious on me, Mer. I'm not sure what to do with her yet. And let's be honest, isn't the best place for her right now here with you?"

"You would give up your child?" Merry-Death stared at her sister incredulously.

"No!" Jillian shouted, but then softened her voice. "Maybe . . . I don't know. Maybe I could give you guardianship . . . for a while. Oh, Mer, I do love Thea, but I'm so damned screwed up, and George has remarried. His new wife has two kids of her own. It's just such a mess." Jillian ended by bursting into a long sob. Then she began to blubber in earnest.

Merry-Death slipped from his arms and went to her sister. Both of them were hugging and crying now.

"Aaarrgh!" Geirolf said then.

"I'll second that," Jeffrey added with a shiver of disgust.

"I need another mead," he grumbled, heading toward the scullery.

"I think I'll have one, too," Jeffrey said, standing.

Rolf stiffened. He didn't want the companionship of this swinish past-husband of the woman he loved. But then he shrugged. He had surely landed in a country of lunatics, and he feared he was becoming mad himself.

Beware when a Viking says, "So be it!" . . .

An hour later, Jeffrey and Jillie stood at the front door, preparing to leave. Meredith was emotionally drained and physically fatigued beyond endurance.

Despite the despicable acts that they had planned, there would be no legal repercussions for the two of them. They'd promised not to try their dirty tricks again, or spread the word about the belt on the academic grapevine. That was the way Meredith wanted it, and Rolf had grudgingly conceded. She wasn't entirely certain that he'd been jesting when he suggested they throw them off the cliff.

"Are you sure you won't reconsider, Rolf?" Jillie tried one last time. "Honest, I would return the belt to you. It could be so important to science and history."

"Leave off, Jillian," he ripped out.

"Won't you at least allow us to interview you?" Jeffrey tried. Rolf was right. The jerk had a death wish. Anyone looking at Rolf's stormy face could see Jeffrey was treading in treacherous waters. "I still don't understand who you are, or where you've come from. But your description of—"

With a snarl of irritation, Rolf shoved Jeffrey and Jillian out the door and slammed it loudly after them. Then he turned the key in the lock and swung her into the circle of his arms, swirling her in a circle. "Alone, at last," he said joyfully into her neck.

Almost immediately, he set her on her feet near the stairs. Holding her by the upper arms, he studied her face. "You are going to fall over with exhaustion, my sweet. Go to your bed and sleep. I already told Mike there will be no work on the morrow; so, you can sleep late."

"Well, I don't know. . . . Oh, okay."

But he didn't let her go just yet. Leaning down, he kissed her tenderly on the lips, then he kissed her hungrily. Finally, with great restraint, he held her away from him again. She felt like a rag doll, no longer capable of common sense.

"I must know, Merry-Death," he began somberly, "will you wed with me?"

What? Where did that question come from? After all they'd been through that night, it was the last thing on her mind.

"We've been at cross-purposes over this issue for days, and 'tis time to blister or bleed, as I told Jeffrey and Jillian earlier. Will you give your free consent to marry me?"

"Will you take me with you when you leave?" Her tone was weary because she already knew the answer.

"Nay, I cannot," he sighed.

She sighed then, too. "If that's the case, the answer is no. I love you so much my heart aches with it, but I can't marry you, Rolf. I can't."

He gazed at her for a long moment, and then nodded. "So be it, then." He gave her another quick kiss and proceeded to walk away from her.

So be it. What does that mean? So be it, I give up? I don't think so. Or is it, so be it, now you'd better beware?

"Rolf?" she questioned as he walked around the room clicking off lamps. "Rolf, what do you mean, 'So be it'?"

He didn't speak. A slow smile curved his mouth but never reached his icy eyes. It wasn't a smile that said, "Okay, baby, have it your way. I give up." No, his smile said, "Watch your butt, baby. You are in deep Viking trouble."

Meredith was almost afraid to fall asleep that night. If she'd been living in another time, she'd be calling out her knights to man the ramparts, pull up the drawbridge, and prepare for battle. She giggled at the thought. But just before deep slumber overtook her, the oddest line occurred to her. It was a famous Anglo-Saxon refrain in the ninth and tenth centuries:

"From the fury of the Northmen, oh, Lord deliver us."

CHAPTER FIFTEEN

❧

Some days are just doggone hard...

"RUFF! RUFF!"

Meredith's eyes shot open to bright sunlight and a rumpled bed. Had someone been shouting, "Rolf! Rolf!"?

Disoriented, her sluggish brain slowly registered that she'd just awakened from an exceptionally deep sleep and that it was very late. A quick glance at her alarm clock showed it was almost eleven o'clock. *Eleven o'clock!* She couldn't remember the last time she'd slept that late, if ever.

"RUFF! RUFF!"

The noise came from downstairs, followed immediately by Rolf muttering, "Oh, shit!" or was it, "Oh, no! Shit"?

The loud barking noise, not someone shouting "Rolf," was what had awakened her, she realized. *Barking?* Before she had a chance to assimilate the implications of barking, she heard thundering footfalls running down the hallway, around the living room, and then up the steps.

"Come back here," Rolf yelled. "You'll spoil the surprise."

The surprise—about a hundred pounds of dirty white fur on a creature that resembled a cross between a sheepdog and a small bear—barreled through her doorway, took a flying leap, and landed on top of her, causing her to fall back on the pillow. Then the animal, which wore a bright red bow around its neck, proceeded to lick her face and neck and hair with a wet tongue the size of a man's tie. Dog hair was flying everywhere.

"Dog, get off Merry-Death. She's sleeping," Rolf said irritably, coming into the room.

Dog propped his front paws on her shoulders, pinning her to the bed. The rest of his body sprawled over her like a living rug.

She leveled a glare at Rolf. "You are in *big* trouble."

"Oh, you're awake, sweetling."

"No, I'm sleeping with my eyes open," she snapped. "What makes you think the racket you two made lumbering around downstairs didn't wake me up? What makes you think the sound of barking wouldn't wake me up? Did you expect me to think it was you barking? And what makes you think a dog the size of a horse lapping my face like an ice cream cone wouldn't wake me up?"

"I think Dog likes you," Rolf declared brightly, sitting on the edge of the bed near her.

"Hah! What's wrong with its eye?" It must have been injured in an accident, because one side of its face was twisted upward, leaving its right eye half closed and its mouth elevated off-center in a harelip fashion. The result was that the dog looked as if it was winking and grinning all the time.

"It ran into a cow that didn't appreciate having its face licked. Dog is a very affectionate fellow, and very sensitive." He said this last in a hushed whisper. "So, we must be careful what we say about his appearance."

"Rolf, I don't want a dog."

"See, you've hurt his feelings."

The dog didn't seem any different to her, except . . . oh, geez, was that a tear in its eye?

"You must not judge him by his minor imperfections, Merry-Death. In my opinion, his defects will not detract from his being a fierce guard dog for you when I am gone."

"Guard dog! This animal couldn't guard its own tail," she sputtered and refused to think about Rolf's when-I-am-gone remark. "You're taking this dog back where you got him."

"I can't."

"Why not?"

"They'll kill him if I take him back."

She groaned and tried to sit up. Rolf helped her by pulling the dog by its ribbon collar. Finally, the dog gave in and decided to favor Rolf with a good face slobbering.

"Who'll kill him?" she asked against her better judgment.

"The animal shelter where I purchased him. Nobody wants him. Is that not incredible, Merry-Death?"

They both looked at the dog, which jumped—plopped would be a better description—off the bed and ambled around the room, sniffing. Probably searching for a fire hydrant. Then, with a frenzied yipping, the dog discovered the full-length mirror on the back of the closet door and began barking ferociously at itself. Its contorted face gave it a comical expression, as if it was making weird faces on purpose.

"You said once that you always wanted a Great Dane, sweetling, but I just couldn't bring myself to give you such a mongrel breed. Danes are really not so great, you know."

She started to laugh, then stopped. "What's that smell?"

"Dog needs to take a bath," he admitted sheepishly. "I'll put him in your tub once you're finished."

"Finished what?" she asked dubiously.

"Your bridal bath."

He planned to wed her and bed her, in either order . . .

Once again, Meredith was soaking in a tub full of rose-

scented bubble bath. There were a few major differenc
this time, however.

Number one: The bath salts came from a basket of expe
sive powders and oils Rolf had presented to her as anoth
bride gift . . . after he'd carried her kicking and screami
into the bathroom, followed by the wildly barking gua
dog.

Number two: The bathroom door was locked from the o
side. Rolf had told her that, if she'd been in his land, the ladi
of his family would massage aromatic oils into her body af
the bathing. It was a ritual to prepare her for the marria
bed. Since he was without female relatives, he'd insisted th
either she anoint her own body, or he'd do it for her—whi
was highly inappropriate for a betrothed, apparently. Eith
way, the door wouldn't be opened until she'd completed t
task, or asked for his help. *As if!*

Number three: Her Viking bridal gown was laid out ov
a chair near the door. On top was the pink Victoria's Sec
teddy Rolf had bought for her last week, the only underg
ment he would allow. "You will don the gown, or be wed r
ked. It matters not to me. In truth, there is appeal in the latte

"You are a brute."

"Yea, I am. But I'll not bend on this, Merry-Death. V
will be wed this day."

"Even if it's against my will?"

"Even then," he'd said adamantly. "My father captured r
mother in a Saxon raid. She was wedded and bedded wit
gag in her mouth and her body restrained with ropes."

"I don't believe that for one minute."

"Believe it, my lady."

You could say it was a carpenter's massage . . .

An hour later, he knocked on the door of the bathing cha
ber. "Are you ready, Merry-Death?"

No answer. "Damn, she is going to be willful to the end," he commented to Dog, who lay guarding the locked door. Even Geirolf had to admit 'twas an odd position for guarding: The animal was stretched out flat on his stomach with his four paws spread wide. He'd been snoring wheezily, but he cracked open his one good eye upon hearing Rolf's voice. "Well, the die is cast, Dog. A man must set the pattern of authority with his woman from the start, or suffer thereafter."

The beast agreed with a growly rumble and then yawned loudly, stumbling to his feet, watching Geirolf unlock the door.

Meredith had completed her bath, apparently, but that was all. With wet hair combed off her face, she stood on the opposite side of the room, wearing her fleecy robe, instead of her bridal garments. And she dared to raise weapons at him. In one hand, she held a long-handled bath brush and in the other a can of hair spray. "Go away, Rolf. You can't bully me."

He lifted a brow. "Dost think to deter me with those? Think again, my lady."

She, too, saw the weakness of her weapons and dropped them to the floor. "You're not a violent man. Don't do this. You won't like yourself in the morning."

"Who says I am not a violent man?" Then he asked, "Didst thou perform the anointing ritual?" A quick glance at the basket of oils showed that none had been unstoppered, except the bubbling one he'd dumped in her bath water. He made a tsking sound at her. "Foolish, foolish wench, to test me so."

Dog ambled in then and Meredith released a little squeak of disgust as he sniffed at the toilet and began to lap up the clear water inside. "Bad dog," she scolded and reached over to shut the lid in his face.

Unrepentant, Dog padded around the small chamber, snuffling here and there. When he reached the half-full tub, he went up on his hind legs, paws on the edge, to see better. And slipped head first into the rose-scented bath water.

"'Twould seem Dog is going to have his bath sooner than later," Geirolf remarked dryly as the ungainly beast splashed water on the wall and floor and even the ceiling while he tried to get a firm footing. The whole time, he was barking, "Woof, Woof, Woof."

"Oh, this is ridiculous! He's going to scratch the veneer on the porcelain. Do you know how hard it is to get one of these things reglazed?" Merry-Death sliced him a glare as if it was all his fault. "You hold the beast down while I soap him."

Ah, now this was a step forward he hadn't anticipated. She'd asked for his help.

Within a short time, Dog was soaped and rinsed and dried off with big towels. Smelling sweetly of roses, the disgruntled dog stood in the middle of the chamber and shook his fur, scattering drops like a summer rain. Then he squished over to the door, gave Geirolf a wounded look, and waited.

Geirolf opened the door to let the dog out, then immediately locked it behind him again.

Meredith was kneeling on the floor cleaning the tub when she heard the door click shut. "Not again, Rolf," she chided him, recognizing that he was now going to deal with her.

"Again."

She stood and wrapped her now sodden robe tighter about her body. Her green eyes flashed defiance at him.

He inhaled deeply with regret. Why did she fight the inevitable? Was it a woman thing? "Take off your robe and lie on the rug," he told her as he picked up a small flask of oil. There was a hand-woven carpet, now slightly damp, on the floor beside the tub. He unfolded a dry towel and spread it over the rug.

"No," she said, backing up.

"Do you say me nay, still?" he asked wearily, and made short work of removing the garment, pushing her to the floor face down and restraining her by sitting lightly on her buttocks.

Meredith was calling him some coarse words that did not bear repeating. And she was flailing her arms and legs, to no avail.

He uncorked the flask and poured a small amount of the oil into his palm, then warmed it by rubbing both palms together. It was rose-scented, of course, but a light fragrance mixed with other essences. Not overpowering.

"I asked you this question afore, Merry-Death. Have you e'er made love with a man who has calluses on his hands?"

She stopped flailing.

"Methinks 'twill be especially pleasing to be anointed with fingers and palms carrying the hardened marks of a workman's toil. Do you take my meaning, Merry-Death? Soft oil, abrasive skin?"

She seemed to stop breathing. He was fairly certain that was a sign that she understood his meaning.

Moving the wet swath of her hair to the side, he began massaging the oil into the back of her tense neck and delicately carved shoulders. "I have ne'er done the anointing, Merry-Death. So, you must tell me if I am too rough."

She moaned and bit her bottom lip.

"Was that a good moan, or a bad moan?"

She declined to answer. He'd expected naught else.

As he rubbed the oil into her arms, from shoulders to fingertips, and underarms to endearingly fragile wrists, he talked softly of the day he'd mapped out for her. "'Tis traditional to exchange the wedding vows afore witnesses, but I've no fancy for others beholding the ignominy of a reluctant bride. Thus, our ceremony will be a private one . . . man to woman."

He saw that she was about to protest, again, but then pressed her eyes closed tightly, dark lashes fanning out against pale cheeks. As if that would shut out his words!

"Tomorrow, or the next day if you prove particularly recalcitrant, we'll have a wedding feast, with witnesses. In truth, next weekend might be best. More people could come." He'd moved lower and was oiling her back and ribs and waist. The small of a woman's back had always had a special allure to him, and he took extra care with that enticing indentation.

"Rolf, give it up. This is the twentieth century. You can't make me marry you if I refuse."

"Watch me, sweetling."

"I don't want this . . . this farce."

"You will yield in the end, that I promise."

She muttered something about arrogant, conceited Vikings while he switched positions. Still resting on her rump, he faced the opposite direction. Starting with the soles of her feet, which he learned were very ticklish—he stored that information for later—he worked his way up her long legs, stroking her ankles, calves, the backs of her knees and thighs. She was making little mewling gasps.

He forced himself to talk again, to divert his attention from his hardening arousal. "I called Mike this morn and told him there will be no work on the morrow, and perchance not the following day, either. Depends on how long it takes to—"

"You had no right, Rolf. Tomorrow is the first day after spring break. I have classes to teach."

"'Tis no problem," he apprised her airily. "Mike said he can substitute for you, especially since you left such detailed lesson plans." He shifted himself slightly backward to rest on her back and focus on her buttocks. Over and over he kneaded the satiny globes till they glistened and grew pink.

Only once did he allow himself the pleasure of inserting his fingers into the cleft, pressing downward. Already her woman dew was rising, slippery and warm.

"Ah, sweetling, your tongue may say you want me not, but your body speaks another language." With that, he rose to a kneeling position, flipped her over onto her back, and sat back down, now on her stomach. He began to work on her legs, undaunted by her fists pounding his back.

"Let me up," she squealed. "I'll finish the anointing business myself."

He paused and gazed at her over his shoulder. "And will you give your free consent to the wedding vows?"

The foolhardy wench balked.

He shrugged and continued massaging her legs, stopping at the soft curls that joined her quivering thighs. He was saving that delight for last.

When he turned and straddled her from the other direction again, she tried to rear up and shove him off. He used a pair of her sheer hose hanging from a metal bar nearby to tie her wrists behind her back, then drizzled the oil over her breastbone, between her breasts, over her stomach and into her navel. With meticulous care, he massaged the oil into her flushed skin, above, around, below her breasts.

"Dost want me to touch your breasts?" he inquired solicitously.

She averted her face to the side, her eyes scrunched tight. The traitorous hitch of her respiration and wildly beating heart gave her away, though, not to mention the hardening of her rosy nipples and the swelling of their surrounding areolae.

He delayed giving her that satisfaction . . . yet. She needed to be punished. He needed time to control his raging urge to consummate the marriage here and now, afore the vows.

When he'd massaged everything except for those most

erotic spots he'd saved for last, he sat back on his haunches and stared at her. She was so beauteous to him. The fierceness of his passion for her both frightened and exhilarated him.

He ran an oily forefinger over her parted lips and she cried out softly, as if in pain. Turning her head, she looked at him directly, her eyes green pools of desire.

Holding her gaze, he poured a dollop of oil over her breasts and massaged them in wide circling sweeps, moving the entire mounds. Each time his callused palms passed over her hardened peaks, her eyes grew wider and her breathing more shallow.

He shimmied lower and poured the remainder of the fluid into her woman hair.

She gasped.

He allowed himself a brief exploration of that territory, fingering the oil into the curls, then between her legs where its slickness mixed with hers. He could bring her to her rapture now, but he knew from past experience that she would resent that. So, with a long sigh, he stood and helped her to her feet.

Clasping her by the shoulders, he said, "I love you, Merry-Death. Will you wed with me?"

Her face went soft for a moment before she whispered, "Will you take me with you when you go?"

He groaned inwardly at her unwavering insistence on the impossible. He shook his head sadly.

"Then, I will *not* marry you." Her eyes had become flat and unreadable as a North Sea mist, and rancor sharpened her voice.

"You have set the course of my actions by your words, Merry-Death. So be it."

"So be it? Does that mean . . . does that mean you've given up?"

He could see conflicting emotions on her face. She wanted him, but she didn't want him. But how could she ask such a lackwit question? He gave her a disbelieving look—the type he and his brothers had been practicing on thick-headed females since boyhood—mostly those who'd doubted their prowess.

And all he said was, "Hah!"

It was the wedding of the century. All the centuries . . .

A short time later, Dr. Meredith Foster stood in a Viking longhouse, wearing her crimson-and-white wedding finery. She was about to exchange nuptial vows, against her wishes, with a magnificently garbed Viking nobleman. With restless energy, Rolf was laying out ritual items on a small table.

Although it was mid-afternoon, the interior of the longhouse was dim, having only one glassless window and a door. Rolf had set a fire in the central hearth where smoke escaped through a hole in the sod roof. The structure was built in the Viking rectangular style, with the sides curved inward slightly. In the early days, this design was favored because it would have been roofed with an upturned longship. This one was a small dwelling by any Norse standard, only twelve-by-twenty feet, and far too confining when a virile, tightly coiled male Viking was taking up too much of the space.

Meredith wasn't gagged, but her hands were restrained behind her back around a support beam. She hadn't come willingly. A dark cloud of determination had settled over Rolf as he'd dressed her himself and carried her outside, unmoved by her screeching threats.

"'Tis time, Merry-Death," Rolf said, carrying the small table over to her side. On it he'd arranged a goblet of wine, an ornately jeweled knife, a gold-braided cord, a hammer, a polished stone, and a bowl of wheat seeds.

Standing before her, he was hardly recognizable as the

man she'd come to love. And it wasn't just the jet-black richness of his tunic and slim trousers, with the talisman belt and the incongruous fanny pack defining the trimness of his waist. Nor was it his golden brown hair spilling over his shoulders, unbound. No, it was his whole demeanor. He was commanding, rigid, his square jaw visibly tensed, his muscles bunched with a fury that she feared would soon be unleashed on her.

He was very, very angry that she still resisted him.

He was pure Viking warrior now, not the gentle shipbuilder she'd come to know. Raising both arms above his head, he began to chant some primitive words in Old Norse. The whole time, he stared blankly through the window, out to sea.

Then he relaxed, and translated for her. "I call out to God and man, family and friend. Come witness today the marriage of Geirolf Ericsson and Merry-Death Foster."

"Why didn't you call out to the police, too? Maybe they'd come and rescue me from a maniac."

"Your willfulness will only make it harder for you," he said tautly. "Heed my warning, you stubborn wench. Every second you waste this day in thwarting me will be paid for tenfold."

She wasn't afraid of him. She knew he wouldn't hurt her . . . not physically, anyhow. Not that she didn't believe he had some punishment in mind. "Rolf, don't do this."

He looked pointedly at her mouth, and she knew that she risked being gagged if she kept on protesting.

Now his long fingers cradled the goblet of wine. Speaking in English, he prayed, "Odin, we draw this nectar from your well of knowledge. May you bring us the wisdom to deal well with each other in this marriage journey we begin today. Especially give Merry-Death the wisdom to know when to give up the fight."

"Hah!"

He took a sip of the wine, then turned the goblet, pressing it to her lips so she could drink from the same spot. The cold metal seemed to carry the seductive heat of his mouth.

After she'd sipped the ruby liquid, he gave her a satisfied nod, and picked up the hammer. "Thor, god of thunder, I take in hand your mighty hammer, *Mjollnir*. This I pledge: I will protect my wife from all peril. I will use the fighting skills learned at your feet to crush her enemies. Let it be known forevermore. Her foe are now my foe. My foe are her foe. The shield of the Yngling clan is now *our* shield." With that, he raised the hammer and crushed the stone.

Meredith jumped and Dog jerked his head up. Dog gave them an inquisitive glance from his good eye, then went back to sleep.

Next, Rolf moved to the bowl of seeds, taking a pinch between his thumb and forefinger. "Frey, god of fertility and prosperity," he began.

Fertility? Meredith stiffened and tried to step away, but she was hampered by the beam at her back.

Giving her a reproving scowl, he sprinkled some of the seeds over her breasts, as well as his own chest, and continued. "We implore not fertility or great wealth in this marriage, oh, great Frey. What we seek, instead, is that you bless us with the richness of love . . . and an abundance of passion." His lips twitched at that last, though he remained unsmiling. She suspected passion wasn't part of the traditional ritual.

The lout! Okay, the *adorable* lout, Meredith admitted to herself. She was melting with each word of the poignant ceremony, as he'd probably known she would.

After that, he took the knife, walked behind her, and ran the razor-sharp blade over the skin of her inner wrist. Peering back over her shoulder, she saw a thin line of blood im-

mediately appear. She gaped at it in horror. "You a*
barbarian.

He cocked an eyebrow. "Didst I e'er say otherwise?"
sliced his own wrist then and took the gold cord, bind
their two hands together, wrist to wrist. He worked from
awkward position, having to secure his left hand to her ri
behind her back—certainly not the way the ceremony
intended to go, she was sure. This position also caused
to be standing very close to her, hips and thighs touch
His warm breath fanned the side of her face.

"As my blood melds with yours, Merry-Death, so s
my seed. From this day forth, you are my beloved." He t
her chin in a firm grip and forced her to look at him. See
that her eyes were brimming with tears, he clenched his
then jutted it out imperiously. He probably thought she c
because she was so unhappy. The dolt! "You will repeat
words after me now," he charged.

*Hmmm. We'll see. I haven't done what you've ordered
far.*

"With this mingling of our blood, I pledge thee
troth . . ."

*Well, that wasn't too bad. I guess I could concede
much.* "With this mingling of our blood, I pledge thee
troth," she said. To her chagrin, her voice came out wob
with emotion.

He sighed, as if relieved that she wasn't going to m
this any more difficult. "From the beginning of time, to
end of time . . ."

She repeated the words softly, "From the beginning
time, to the end of time."

". . . let it be known that I, Geirolf Ericsson, give
heart to thee, Merry-Death Foster."

A little sob escaped Meredith's throat at the beauty of
declaration. Could she say this? She'd be pledging a lot m

than her troth. She'd be promising to love him forever. But that was a given. No matter how arrogant or overbearing his demand that she marry, then divorce him, she would never stop loving him. So she said the words, with her own interpretation, ". . . let it be known that I, Meredith Foster, give my heart and soul to the damnedest Viking in the world, Geirolf Ericsson."

Rolf let himself smile now. "It is done."

"What's done?"

"We are wed," he said, leaning forward to press a soft kiss against her lips.

"We are?" She wished he would kiss her longer, or deeper, but he probably feared she'd nip his tongue off. She just might. She realized belatedly that he'd won this battle of wills, after all. "Is it permitted for the bride to bite her husband?"

"Only in the bedsport."

"Don't think that I've surrendered."

He grinned. "The heavens would collapse first, I warrant."

"How about untying me, oh sarcastic one?"

"Will you still fight me, oh obstinate one?"

"Probably."

"Good," he laughed. "Every warrior loves a good battle. It makes the victory all the sweeter."

"That was just a skirmish. Don't think you've won the whole campaign."

"Hardly."

"We're not really married," she snapped when he wouldn't argue with her. "There isn't any court in the world that would recognize it." *That was a mean thing to say. Shame on me. The ceremony felt very, very real to me.*

"Ah, Merry-Death, you should not have said that." His nostrils flared with anger.

"Why?"

"Because now I will have to prove to you that we are

wed, as well as punish you for all your transgressions this day."

He bent over and removed his boots, threw his cape, talisman belt, and fanny pack to the hard-packed dirt floor. He was in the process of lifting his tunic over his head.

"Wh-what are you doing?"

He tossed the tunic to the floor, giving her an eyeful of wide shoulders, ridged abdomen, and tendon-delineated arms. But that wasn't all. Without hesitation, he released the ties at his waist and let the trousers fall to his ankles. Stepping on one foot, then another, he kicked them off his feet and away. Apparently, his wedding outfit went only so far. No codpiece, breechclout, boxers, or jockey shorts in sight.

Meredith's mouth went dry. She'd known he had a good body. She just hadn't known how good. The firelight and the late-afternoon sun filtering through the window cast golden shadows on his tanned skin. And there was a lot of it. Narrow waist and hips. Flat stomach. Muscular legs and chest with their furring of brown hair. And . . . oh, my, my, my . . . Rolf had been justified in feeling overly confident about his physical endowments.

Slack-jawed, she repeated her earlier question in an embarrassingly squeaky voice. "Wh-what are you doing?"

He smiled then, a bone-melting, dazzling display of white teeth and raw sexual promise. He moved closer . . . so close she could feel his male heat. His answer came in a thick whisper against her parted lips. "Preparing for battle."

CHAPTER SIXTEEN

Your body is a wonderland . . .

"Battle? Ha, ha, ha!" A little shiver ran visibly over her. She wished Rolf would smile or do something to assure her he was just kidding.

He did smile, but he did it while kneeling in front of her. Oh, my God, she stood fully dressed and a naked man—a very aroused naked man—knelt at her feet. If she was a sexual fantasy kind of woman, this would rank as a real X-rated Kodak moment.

"Are you about to pray for my forgiveness?" she choked out.

"You would like that, wouldn't you, wench? Best you fortify your ramparts, my lady of the running tongue. This warrior is about to lay siege to your every portal. And you have ne'er seen the likes of a Viking with the war fever, I wager."

"Aren't you being a little melodramatic? . . . Oh, no, stop that." He'd lifted the hem of her gown, reached up and jerked the tap pants of her teddy all the way down and off.

She thought she heard him mutter, "There goes the moat."

But who was paying attention? She was more interested in the fact that her gown remained hitched up to the waist, held by his hands on either side of her hips, leaving her bare to his view.

He moaned.

She moaned.

"Now you have done it, Merry-Death," he gasped out.

"Me?" she squeaked.

"There should have been a prolonged bout of love-play on our first nuptial bedding. You deserve gentle words and sweet caresses. But, bloody hell, you made me wait overlong," he informed her in a guttural rush. "Too damn long!" He hoisted her by the waist, cupped her bottom, canted her hips outward, and plunged inside.

She screamed.

He stilled.

There wasn't any real pain. She'd been ready for him since that blasted anointing exercise. But he was so big and she was so tight and she hadn't expected his entry and, oh, God, it was Rolf, the man she loved who was filling her for the first time, and if he didn't stir soon she was going to scream again.

His forehead, beaded with perspiration, pressed against hers. His eyes were closed, and he gulped for air. "Did you feel that? Oh, hell, did you feel that?"

"What?"

"A tingle. How can that be? I'm tingling *there*."

She tried to focus *there*—an impossibility when so many incredible sensations assaulted her everywhere. "Lord, I feel it, too. Maybe . . . maybe the talisman's magic slipped and lodged—"

He started to laugh, but it came out more like a gurgle since his teeth were grinding with restraint.

"Untie my hands," she whimpered as she lifted her legs, wrapping them around his waist, trying to adjust their position so her body could accommodate his size . . . and the tingling, which was really becoming . . . uh, disconcerting.

At first, she didn't think he'd heard her, but he reached around and undid the silk cords. She curled her arms around his shoulders, and he walked her to the built-in bedstead against the wall. In one fluid motion, he tumbled her to the bed furs, still imbedded in her.

Every cell in her body tingled.

For several long moments, he just lay on top of her, panting. When he raised himself on extended arms, he studied her face. "Did I hurt you?"

She shook her head.

"Am I too heavy?"

She shook her head again.

"Do you want me to stop?"

Another shake of the head, this one rather vehement.

"Why won't you talk to me, dearling?"

She swallowed a nervous giggle. "I . . . can't."

He raised an eyebrow. When understanding dawned, he grinned.

So, he considers my overstimulation funny? "Why aren't you moving?" she grumbled.

"The same reason as you," he clipped out. "I can't."

His words excited her. And her inner folds spasmed around him.

He groaned. "Betwixt the tingling and your pulsing, this will be a one-stroke coming if I move now."

"I don't pulse."

Another spasm.

"You did that apurpose," he accused.

Oh, geez, this was embarrassing. "No, my body is just trying to accustom itself . . . to your . . . to you."

"Oh," he said with sudden understanding. Then he broke into an arresting smile. "I can help you adapt to me, and take more."

Take more? I . . . don't . . . think . . . so. "No, I don't think . . . a-h-h-h-!"

He arched his upper body back on one extended arm with his hard penis motionless inside her. With his other hand, he reached down between their bodies and began to strum the slickness, back and forth.

She raised her hips up high, spreading her legs more. And wailed in one endless stream of "Oh, oh, oh, oh . . ." at the intensity of the sensations convulsing through her in ever-widening spirals.

To her amazement, her inner folds did expand, and Rolf grew inside her. And he still wasn't moving, darn him.

He waited for her to open her eyes before he gripped her head in both hands and said fervently, "I love you."

"I love you, too."

"Don't you dare cry now," he ordered as he began to move at last.

At last, at last, at last, she thought as he pulled out almost all the way, then slammed in. Three or four or ten times, he pummeled her with his long strokes. She couldn't keep count. It wasn't very many, but her body was climaxing over and over and over each time he hit her pubic bone, and she was sobbing and screeching and hitting his shoulders each time he withdrew.

He might have been making noises, as well. In fact, she was pretty sure he was. He threw his head back, the veins in his neck almost popping, and lunged in one last time, spurting hotly to her womb. And in the end, he did cry out, and she caught his cry with her open mouth.

Oh, my God! Meredith thought just before she passed out.

"Guð minn góðþur!" Rolf said just before he passed out.

Several minutes later, she awakened to feel Rolf's dead weight on her. It wasn't unpleasant.

The low masculine exhale he released with excruciating slowness could have been of pain, or exquisite satisfaction. She was betting on the latter.

He rolled over to his side and took her with him. Lifting her one leg over his hip, he remained inside her. Not hard, but not soft either. He kissed her tenderly, then savagely. Then he laughed with utter joy.

She hid her fiery face in his neck, belatedly embarrassed over her uninhibited behavior.

"Do you blush now, wanton witch? Odin's teeth, you do!" When he saw that she was unsure of herself and the propriety of her performance, he added with a tweak of her chin, "Methinks the anticipation proved too much for both of us, sweetling."

Gritting his teeth, he eased himself out of her, and chuckled when her hands fluttered with involuntary distress at his disengaging too soon for her taste. "You are a greedy wench, and overeager," he teased, "but I wouldst try *all* your charms, and your garments impede my efforts."

He murmured words of astonishment at what had just happened between them as he undid the shoulder brooches on her overgown and removed the gold-link belt. It was short work after that for him to maneuver her clothing off, but not too short, because he paused and whispered compliments to each body part he bared.

Oh, he was a smooth lover, this Viking was, knowing instinctively what many modern men still didn't understand— that women need to feel good about their bodies to enjoy making love, even if their attractiveness is only in the eyes of their lovers.

By the time she was naked, her entire body felt heated by his torrid, worshipful perusal. She couldn't stop herself from asking hopefully, "Again?"

"And again and again and again," he promised, holding her down at his side when she would have leapt from the bed with mortification at having expressed her craving aloud. "But this time we'll go slow. This time will be for you, sweetling."

And who was the last time for? But she decided to keep that revealing question to herself.

"You must needs be punished first," he warned with silky eroticism as he trailed his fingertips from her knees to the joining of her thighs. She was lying flat on her back now like a rag doll. "Hmmm. Mayhap your first penance—"

"Penance?" she said breathlessly. "First?"

He smiled. "—shall be honesty in the loveplay. You will tell me with words, as well as actions, what pleases you."

And that's punishment? "You tricked me, Rolf. I never intended to marry you, or make love," she stormed. "Maybe you're the one who should be punished."

"Hmmm." He tapped his chin with a forefinger as if seriously considering her reproach, then agreed too quickly, "All right. But later."

His callused fingertips brushed over the tight curls between her legs and he sighed.

A feeling of light-headedness flowed over her at that feathery caress. And Meredith thought there should be a dissertation written on the merits of calluses. And the carnal beauty of a man's sigh.

"Drops of moisture from our first mating linger here," he pointed out huskily, "like morning mist on seaside grass."

Her eyes shot wide. Blood roared in her veins and her brain went blank at the seductive praise. She tried to roll over to hide herself, but he wouldn't allow that modesty.

"Or wouldst you prefer I start here?" He placed his fingertips against her lips, and her neck arched for his kiss. But he was already skimming his fingertips lower, a straight tantalizing line from her chin, over her breastbone, down her abdomen and waist, over her navel, to her thighs again. A violent shiver passed over her.

His lips turned up appreciatively. "Where, Merry-Death? Where do you want my touch first?"

With a soft mewling cry, she took his hands and led them to her breasts. Although he hadn't touched them since the anointing, the rose-hued nipples were still hardened into pebbles of arousal and the slightly paler areolae were puffy with desire. She ached for him there.

Instead, he nudged her legs apart and braced himself on outstretched arms. His erection pressed against her thigh and his hips pinned her against the bed furs, but a half-foot of space separated her breasts from his chest.

"Caress me with them," he coaxed in a voice so thick she could barely comprehend his meaning. When understanding dawned, she wondered if she had the nerve.

She did.

With the support of her elbows, she bowed her back upward and moved her breasts, back and forth, across the bristly hairs on his chest. The magnitude of agonizing pleasure was so great it set off a chain reaction through her body. He couldn't help but feel the thudding of her heart and the quiver in her thighs. Rolf had been right when he'd insinuated one time that there was nothing more sensuous for a woman than the friction of bed furs at her back and her lover's chest hairs at her front.

He made a hissing sound through his teeth. "Don't stop."

Again and again, she swept her aching breasts across the abrasive hairs. When she dropped back, unable to stand the pressure building in her breasts for a different kind of succor, he raised himself to a kneeling position between her knees.

"You were serious about punishing me," she said. "This is pure torture."

"Ah, but have you not heard? There is no ecstasy without agony." With that enigmatic Norse philosophy, he lightly fingered her nipples. She whimpered at the surge of sensitivity lodged in their centers. By the time he lowered his mouth and touched the tip of his tongue to her left nipple, she was clutching the bed furs in her fists and stiffening her legs. He did the same to the other breast, then leaned back to study her again.

"No," he said disapprovingly. "Relax." He forced her to unfist her hands and waited for her thighs to untense. Then he took her breasts, one after the other, into his mouth and suckled on her with a punishing rhythm.

"I feel as if I'm caught in the eye of a hurricane," she confessed as waves of pleasure rippled out from the pumping of his open mouth encasing the whole of her nipple and areola.

"Yea, you shall be as a ship on the roiling seas," he said, laughing, "and I'll be the gale wind that brings you tribulation, and the greatest thrills."

His words frightened her a bit, and she tried to push him off. She scratched his back. She flailed her legs. But he wouldn't stop. Then the hurricane broke, and she was hurtled into a frenzied climax under the onslaught of the tempest.

When her vision cleared, she saw him sitting on his haunches between her outspread legs, watching her, and waiting.

"You make me blush when you look at me," she protested weakly.

"You make me tremble when you look at me," he countered hoarsely.

Her cheeks burned under his all-seeing scrutiny, and she suspected that her "punishment" had barely begun. Although his whiskey eyes shimmered with passion and his ragged panting was a testament to his excitement, she sensed that the maddening man intended to torment her much, much more before he gave himself relief.

He arranged himself on top of her, a flat weight of domination. His big hands framed her face, and he murmured against her lips, "And dost my lady favor kisses, as well?"

"Yes." She smiled against his parted lips.

At first, his kisses were slow and thoughtful. A tactile exploration of molding lips and gliding tongue. But soon the kisses took on the character of controlled aggression as he bit her bottom lip, then sucked it into his mouth for soothing. He tunneled his fingers in her hair and held her firm as he took her mouth with a savage fervor, prodding her lips open with his thrusting tongue. Wet and clinging, she succumbed to his forceful seduction.

"I can't stand any more," she pleaded finally.

He tore his mouth from hers, fighting for air. Sitting back on his haunches again, he surveyed her, then nodded his approval. "Be strong, my lady, for the invasion has scarce commenced."

She paled but had no time to consider his implied threat, because he was already moving to another erotic territory. He hooked his arms under her knees and spread her legs wide and high with a rolled bed fur under her hips. Legs draped over his arms, she was open and vulnerable to his eyes and fingers and mouth.

"I would taste the pearl of your arousal," he whispered, and even his breath against her there caused the distended bud to swell and unfold. He kissed it softly, and she bucked upward. From then on, she keened a continuous dirge of sweet agony as he plied that center of sensation, its surrounding slick folds, even inside her, with his tongue. Probing. Fluttering. Laving. Stabbing. Sucking. So abandoned was she that she didn't even realize when the rolled bed furs had been removed from under her hips or that Rolf was poised to enter her.

"Tell me," he demanded huskily as he pressed a scorching kiss of possession against her mouth.

"I love you."

He drove into her, and it was he who cried out then as her body stretched and stretched to accommodate his size. "You feel like velvet fire licking at my staff," he gasped as he pulled out, then drove in again, long and slow and sinfully pleasurable.

"And you feel like hot marble," she whispered back, surprised that she could play this game of sex talk.

"I want to reach the heart of you," he ground out and plunged deeper.

She gasped against the assault and compelled herself to relax and take more of him.

"Your woman dew anoints me like molten lava," he told her as his long, slow strokes shortened into pummeling thrusts.

She should have been embarrassed at his truthful words. But she could only focus on the increasing pressure between her legs. She spread her thighs wider and levered her hips high so that when he reared his neck back and battered into her one last time, she burst into a million shards of pleasure. Even when he buried his face against her neck and murmured, "I love you, Merry-Death," she continued to pulse around his limpness.

She felt shattered, deliciously sated, and very much in love.

Hey, sweetling, wanna drek? . . .

Geirolf couldn't believe his good fortune. He'd always been a man favored with woman-luck, but this . . . this mind-splintering ecstasy his new wife had showed him . . . well, truly the gods had cast their gift of approval on him this day.

He tickled her nose with the edge of a bed fur. She twitched but pretended to sleep. He moved the bed fur lower, tickling a pointed nipple, and her eyes flew open.

"Mer-ry Dea-th," he drawled out. "I have a wonderful idea."

She moaned and rolled over to bury her face in the furs.

He followed, conforming his body to the back of her. They fit together very nicely.

"Don't you want to hear my idea?" he purred, placing a palm against her stomach and hauling her back more tightly into the cradle of his hips.

"Your ideas are too . . . punishing," she complained, but he knew she was more than pleased with his sexual torment. He knew *he* was. "How long did you let me sleep?"

"Oh, a half hour or so."

"A half hour!" she exclaimed and turned to gape at him with incredulity. "And you have *ideas* again so soon?"

"Yea. It comes from being a Viking . . . and creative . . . and—"

"Insatiable?"

"That, too." He laughed and picked her up in his arms, carrying her out of the longhouse, into her keep, and up the stairs. Dog followed them. No doubt, Dog figured they were going to have a feast, or mayhap an orgy.

She shrieked when she saw that it was still daylight, barely past the dinner hour. "Someone might see us running around naked," she chided him.

"Nay, no one will dare return till I give the word. I threatened to lop off the head of the first person who steps on this property without my consent."

"You didn't," she said, drawing back slightly to peer at his face.

That gave him his first full daylight glimpse of her breasts and womanly nest. He stumbled and almost swallowed his tongue.

Seeing the direction of his gaze, Merry-Death clucked her reproval and tucked her pink-stained face back into his neck. 'Twas one of the things he cherished most about his new wife, her innate modesty contrasted with a sexuality that could blister his manroot at twenty paces.

When he finally set her on her feet, Merry-Death peered up at him questioningly. How could she not know what was next on his carnal calendar?

"Drekking," he informed her brightly.

Rock the boat, baby . . .

Toward morning, Rolf awakened her again. "I want to show you something," he whispered in her ear.

"I've seen it five times already," she groaned into his chest.

"Six times," he corrected her. "Didst thou forget the nude spear-throwing lesson?"

"How could I forget?" She turned and looked up at him— her husband. And her heart swelled and overflowed with love for him. His hair was pulled back now in a rubber band. His firm lips were slightly swollen from her numerous kisses, some of them surprisingly aggressive. From the flames of the nearby hearth, which he must have recently stoked, she saw reflected in his amber eyes a fierce passion for her, and a soul-rending tenderness. Love. She saw love in his face, and for that she felt blessed by all the gods, his and hers alike.

She had capitulated to Rolf's seduction. She wasn't resigned to giving him up in a few short weeks, but this night had been too glorious for her to argue. Not now, anyway.

"So what's this *thing* you want to show me?" she teased, putting her hands to his neck and pulling his head down for a kiss.

"Sunrise," he murmured against her lips, "on the prow of a dragonship."

"Naked?" she asked, nibbling his bottom lip.

"Yea." He grinned. "And rocking."

"Rocking?"

"Um-hmmm," he answered, taking a few nibbles of her bottom lip, as well. "Did you not know that the prow of a ship dips and rises, dips and rises, in the open seas?"

"But your ship isn't on the open seas."

"Ah, you've not been listening to me, Merry-Death. Tsk-tsk. Did I not say we Vikings are creative?"

No chicken dance at this wedding . . .

Thea returned to the house the next day, and the wedding feast was held the following Saturday. Meredith insisted that it be a small affair—Thea, Mike, Sonja, the students, and a few SCA members they'd gotten to know. It was probably mean of her, but she'd balked at having Jillian or her parents present. And Jared was too far away to come.

Meredith had harbored many doubts about their having a public celebration of their wedding. It was going to be very difficult to explain Rolf's disappearance in a few weeks. But she was glad now that she'd given in to his urging for a public wedding. The vows they'd exchanged just a few hours ago before his long-ship had been beautiful . . . a memory to treasure forever.

A short time ago, she'd gone into the house to get more manchet bread. Now she stood leaning against the post of one of the colorful, open-sided tents, watching the scene unfolding around her. Everyone was dressed in Viking or medieval costume. Musicians played authentic melodies on dulcimers, lyres, and panpipes.

Rolf, splendidly attired in his lush black tunic and *braies,* the talisman belt sparkling in the sunshine, was demonstrating for Thea one of the dances done in his country. The young girl, who should have been more comfortable doing the boogie, or whatever the dance du jour, giggled and followed his steps with enthusiasm.

Rolf had talked Meredith into signing papers to take over temporary guardianship of Thea, and the girl was already enrolled in the local junior high school. Meredith suspected he'd been so persistent because he feared for her state of mind when he left her behind. But she wouldn't dwell on those depressing ideas today.

Rolf glanced up suddenly and caught her staring at him. He'd told her as dawn broke today that the best thing about making love in the morning is that you feel like you have a secret all day long. He was right.

The rogue winked, as if reading her thoughts.

She took the bread over to the cooks and asked about the progress of the Maine lobsters and side of venison being baked in a pit filled with layers of moist grass and red-hot rocks. She tasted the skyr, a form of Norse cheese curd being made on the spot by Frank and Henrietta Burgess. The elderly couple, obviously still in love after all these years, also showed her how they'd prepared the flat oak cakes baking on the open fire.

"It was a beautiful ceremony," Henrietta gushed, tears brimming in her eyes.

"And I congratulate you on a job well done with this project," Frank added. "When your grandfather first formed this foundation, I had reservations. I never envisioned that the project would encompass so much more than just the shipbuilding and voyage. Though that in itself is an admirable achievement."

Meredith's jaw dropped open in astonishment at the praise coming from this unexpected quarter.

"What you've pulled off here, my dear, is a true learning experience for college students," he went on. "History, culture, sociology, language, anthropology—"

"Don't forget women's studies," his wife piped in.

"That, too." Frank laughed. "But, really, Meredith, I'm hoping you'll consider staying here in Maine and making this a continuing project."

"Oh, I don't know about that."

He put up a hand. "Now, now, just think about it."

She nodded and proceeded around the clearing, pondering that interesting suggestion. As she stopped and chatted with the various people, all dressed in period costumes as required in their invitations, her gaze kept returning to Rolf, again and again. And each time, he was watching her, love shining openly in his eyes.

This time he walked up to her and linked her hands with his, drawing her over to the side. Dog came trotting after him.

"What is *that* in Dog's mouth?"

"Oh," Rolf said, unconcerned, glancing down at the huge mutt, "it's Oreos."

"You fool! You shouldn't be feeding a dog cookies."

"I shouldn't?"

"No. Especially not chocolate. It's better if he eats the dry dog food I bought for him."

He pondered a moment, but then seemed to disregard her opinion. "Have you e'er sampled that dog meal, Merry-Death?"

"Have you?" she choked out.

"Well, of course. Dost judge me so cruel that I would give your pet something I wouldn't eat myself? And I tell you true, it tastes worse than dried cod on a North Sea voyage."

She retched.

He chucked her under the chin. "I was jesting with you,

Merry-Death. I fed only one Oreo to Dog because he loves them, just as I do. Almost as much as I love you."

Now that was a love declaration for the poetry books. And the heart. Love and Oreos.

Really, she thought, you gotta love a Viking.

CHAPTER SEVENTEEN

✣

X, Y, and Z mark the spot, not to mention the famous S-Spot . . .

For the next three weeks, their love blossomed and unfurled like the sails on the Viking longship that neared completion in her yard.

Meredith had never been so happy in all her life, or so miserable. She often awakened in the middle of the night and wept silent tears, knowing the sands of her happiness were slowly sifting away.

She didn't question his decision to leave anymore. In a way, she understood. But she didn't want to put a damper on the little time they had left, so Meredith tried to put on a cheerful face even as she was self-destructing inside. With increasingly exposed nerves, she walked a tightrope whenever in Rolf's company.

"Was I wrong to have forced you into this?" Rolf asked as he pulled her closer into the cradle of his arms. They were lying side by side on the sofa. Thea had gone to the mall for some Sunday afternoon hanging-out with girlfriends she'd met in the neighborhood. Dog snored contentedly in the corner on his very own bed furs.

"Watching the zillionth episode of *Home Improvement*? Yes, you were wrong. Tsk-tsk," she tutted, pointing at the

TV screen where Tim Taylor was explaining to his wife Jill why big breasts were God-given male magnets.

"Not *that*," Rolf chuckled, and then turned serious. "Was I wrong to force you into marrying me? Was I wrong to force you into sharing these last weeks together, knowing we had no future?" He took her chin in hand so that she had to meet his gaze. "Mike speaks often of the pain of losing his wife, even after two years, but he says that having her, for even a short time, was a blessing, something he would ne'er regret. I thought . . . well, I thought 'twould be the same for us. Now I wonder, though, if I erred in judgment."

Meredith stiffened and would have bolted if she weren't trapped against the back of the sofa. Rolf was going to insist on the conversation she'd been avoiding for weeks, ever since their marriage.

He saw her panic and soothed her by gently stroking wisps of hair off her face. The loving concern in his golden eyes tore at her heart strings and brought tears to her eyes.

"Don't, sweetling. Don't," he coaxed hoarsely, kissing her eyelids closed.

"No, you weren't wrong, Rolf," she confessed with a sigh of resignation. "I wouldn't have traded these wonderful weeks with you for anything. Marrying you—" she gulped to get the words past the huge lump in her throat "—marrying you was the best thing I've ever done in my life."

"'Tis the same for me, dearling. Sometimes . . . sometimes—" He fought for the right words. "It's as if I have so much caring for you here that my heart nigh bursts." To demonstrate, he put her palm against his chest, where his heart thudded under her fingertips. "I ne'er imagined loving a woman—*really* loving a woman—would feel like this."

She couldn't have spoken if she'd tried.

Rolf continued. "Time races so fast these days. I even un-plugged your wall clock in the scullery yestermorn. 'Twas lackwitted, I know, to play such games with myself, as if I could stop time." He shook his head sadly at his whimsy. "At night, I lie awake looking at you as you sleep. I have this over-powering urge to grasp each moment . . . to store the memo-ries."

"Hah!" she said, trying to lighten Rolf's sober mood, though his words touched her deeply. "You probably just needed a breather between bouts of making love. You are insatiable, you know?"

"Do you complain, my lady?" he grumbled with mock ferociousness, arching a brow.

Even though he jested, it amazed Meredith how vulner-able he was and how much reassurance he needed all the time. Despite their vast differences, they were alike in that regard.

"Not in the least," she answered, blinking back tears as she traced the line of his strong jaw with her fingertips.

"Well, I should hope not," he said huffily, leaning down to take a chastising nip at her exposed shoulder. She was wearing only the pink teddy, and Rolf a pair of white boxer shorts covered with red hearts—a post-wedding gift. "Espe-cially since I shared with you the secret of the famous Vi-king S-spot, which even you agreed was far superior to your modern G-spot."

She laughed and jabbed him playfully in the ribs. How many times these past precious days had they made each other smile in the midst of making love? Meredith had never realized that sex could be so much fun. "You've spoiled me, Rolf. I don't think I'll ever be satisfied with any other man now."

His face went somber again. "I feel the same, heartling."

"You'll probably be boating right off to Sweet Alyce the

Slut the minute you get home." She'd intended her tone to be teasing, but her voice broke at the end.

"Nay, I'll not be seeing Alyce again. That I vow to you."

"Oh, Rolf, don't make me promises like that. I don't expect you to be celibate for the rest of your life. It will be hard for me when you go—very hard—but—"

"Shhh," he said, kissing her lips lightly. "I wish I could spare you the pain. If I could stay, I would. If I had not made an oath to my father—"

"No," she said, putting two fingertips to his lips. "You can't stay. I know that now. There's no sense playing the 'what-if' game. You'd become like a caged animal in a contemporary setting, always pretending, always lying for fear someone would connect the dots of all your strange words and perspectives on history."

"Do you say I could not adapt?" he asked, bristling.

She shook her head at his pride. "Oh, you might change, adapt to these times, lose your primitive, Viking identity. That would be nice for me . . . a way to keep you here, but—"

"'Twould certainly be true to the tradition of my fellow Norsemen, who have no trouble melding into the societies of the countries they settle. 'Tis why no separate Viking culture has lasted through the centuries, I warrant."

"Believe me, Rolf, I've thought about ways you might be able to conform to modern society. A 'Last Viking,' so to speak."

He grinned. "Lust Viking?"

"You silly fool! I said 'Last Viking,' not 'Lust Viking,'" she remarked dryly, "though it would be an appropriate appellation in your case."

"Last or lust. It matters not. If I had no obligations to the past, I *would* stay, Merry-Death, do not doubt that. And I'd manage to adapt. For you, I could do anything."

"But would it be what you really wanted? I'm not even

sure anymore that it's what I want. Think about it. You in a three-piece suit, carrying an electronic organizer. You mowing the lawn and jogging off extra pounds on a Stairmaster. You playing golf or speeding about the ocean in a powerboat. You buying insurance and growing old."

Rolf had rented a sailboat the day before to take her and Thea out for an afternoon on the ocean. If ever Meredith had doubted his expertise with boats, or his love of the open waves, she knew better now. He wasn't a man who'd accept being landlocked for long.

She sighed deeply. "As much as I yearn for you to stay, I just can't picture you in any modern role."

He sighed, too. "'Twas the same when I tried to imagine you in my time. You cracking ice off a fjord stream in the midst of winter to tote water into my farmstead. You taking on the subservient role of women in my society. You waiting idly at home whilst I go off a-Viking or trading. You cooking over a hearth. You growing old far too young under the strain of a harsh life."

Meredith knew he painted a deliberately bleak picture. He failed to mention cold winter nights when they'd be bundled together under the bed furs. Or the fact that he would take great joy in introducing her to the beauty of his land. Not to mention the fact that she could go on trading voyages with him. And what if . . . oh, what if she were able to bear his children in another lifetime?

She exhaled wearily. It was useless to dream of the impossible.

"The bottom line is, you can't stay," Meredith said firmly, hoping to put an end to the discussion. "You would start to hate yourself for what you'd consider a dishonorable choice—reneging on your father's mission, letting hundreds of people die in a famine that you might be able to stop. As ridiculous as the notion is that a restored relic could halt an act of nature,

I can't argue the point. After all, a talisman belt and a mystical occurrence in the sky caused you to travel through time."

"I have to go back," he agreed.

"And the alternative—my traveling in time with you—is equally impossible. I accept that now."

He patted her hand comfortingly. "The celestial fates decreed my adventure, and I feel certain they designed the time portal for me, and me alone."

"You don't have to convince me anymore, Rolf. When you asked what I'd do if I were able to travel back with you and then you died, I asked myself whether I would want to live in the tenth century without you. The answer was 'no.' Bad enough being abandoned in the twentieth century!"

He flinched at the word abandon. "Then you're reconciled to my departure?" he asked.

She nodded.

"'Tis as a noted philosopher once said. 'Tis better to have experienced the joy of love, despite the pain of parting." He paused and tilted his head in concentration. "I think 'twas Will-son, the neighbor on *Home Improvement* who spoke the words. Or was it Ernie on *Sesame Street*? I misremember now."

She frowned, and then burst out giggling. "Oh, you dolt! That was Tennyson, and the exact quote is: ' 'Tis better to have loved and lost than never to have loved at all.' "

"Tennis-son, Will-son, Ernie"—Rolf waved a hand dismissively—"they are all great thinkers, like the skalds of my time." Then his eyes twinkled mischievously at her as he trailed a forefinger from the center of her chin down her neck, over her breastbone, skimming the silk fabric of her teddy till his fingertip pressed into her navel. "Have I shown you the famous Viking X-spot?"

Had he ever! "About five times. Or was that the equally famous Viking Y and Z spots?"

"Which are not to be confused with that age-old S-spot, of course," he reminded her.

She grinned sadly at him, finding it harder and harder to banter when her heart was breaking. "I must say I'm rather partial to X."

"Ah, well, 'twould seem a Viking's job is ne'er done." He sighed as if vastly overburdened. Then, jiggling his eyebrows at her, he boasted, "Did I e'er explain how a Norseman practices his alphabet?"

Meredith laughed then. But inside she was crying.

Some partings are sorrow without a lick of sweet . . .

By the following week, Geirolf's longship, *Fierce Dragon*, was completed, and the major portion of the Trondheim Venture vessel had been finished, as well. Oh, the school project had many weeks of finishing work to be done, but Mike and the students could handle that type of labor themselves. They'd even contracted with a skilled sailing expert from Annapolis, Maryland, to captain the vessel in August, when it would be launched for the voyage to Norway.

But he wouldn't be here then. Tomorrow, the Demon Moon would appear again, and he would be gone.

He should have been elated that the day had arrived at last. Instead, he was dying inside at the prospect. Unbelievably, this time and place—mostly, this woman, Merry-Death—had become his home. But he was trying his best to hide his inner turmoil from Merry-Death. He didn't want to spoil their remaining time together.

Leaning on a braced elbow in their bed furs, he watched his wife sleep. Four times this night he'd made love to her with feverish desperation, and he would wake her soon to cleave onto her one last time. Though he would never admit as much to Merry-Death, he'd coupled more times with her these past weeks than he ever had with any one woman, and still 'twas not enough.

He'd prepared methodically for his time travel tomorrow night. His small longship had already been transported by truck to a docking site a few miles down the coast.

He'd mapped out a route whereby he would be able to maneuver his small ship with a single mast, wooden rudder, yardarm, and square sail. He needed no modern compass, knowing from years of experience how to map his journey by following landmarks, stars, the presence of certain seabirds and their lines of flight. He wished he had the traditional two ravens to carry aboard, both to appease the gods and to give notice of nearby land, but, to his amazement, there were no ravens available for sale in Maine. If he hit a storm, he'd never manage on his own. But, from the start, this mission had been in the hands of the gods. So be it now.

Assuming the time travel worked, he'd be back in his own time twenty-four hours from now. Would it be the same night then as when he'd passed forward, or would it be a month later? Would he find some of his men drifting at sea? Or would he make a solitary trip to Greenland, or even Iceland, where he'd hire on men to sail with him to Britain and then his homeland?

He'd already lost one month's time chasing after Storr Grimmsson. If he'd lost another month with his time travel, and it took another month to return to Britain, that would be three months since he'd left his father's side. How many of his countrymen would have lost their lives in the famine during that time? Would an earlier end to his mission have made any difference?

So many questions! It was all such a risky venture. Impossible, really. But his coming here in the first place had been impossible, too.

All Mike and the students knew was that they were taking the ship out for a trial run tomorrow afternoon, that it
would be anchored, and that he wanted to stay aboard overnight by himself to test its watertightness. Mike and the
students would return to shore on motorboats he'd leased.
Presumably, they would find the wreckage of his ship and
conclude he'd drowned.

Not a completely believable explanation, but it would do.
He hated the distress this deception would cause Thea,
Mike, and the students, but he saw no other alternative.

Like a man preparing for his death, he'd made arrangements this past week for when he would be gone.

Thea—who slept even now in the keep bedchamber whilst
they were in the longhouse—would live with Merry-Death;
so, his wife would not be alone. He'd checked and double-
checked the Trondheim ship and pecked out numerous notes
to Mike on the come-pewter keyboard so that it could be
finished without his supervision. And he'd helped interview
the man who would captain the vessel on its journey to Norway this summer.

All of the modern purchases he'd made, especially the
power tools, he'd instructed Merry-Death to give to Mike.
He still thought Merry-Death should accept the *Home Improvement* show's offer to participate in her project, but the
stubborn wench dug in her heels when it came to his idol,
Tim Allen.

There was one contingency he'd been unable to control.
Even though Merry-Death claimed to be barren, he'd hoped—
in fact, he'd prayed—that his seed would take, even knowing
he'd never see his own babe. He would have given her that
gift, gladly. Especially after they'd watched the *Starman* video
about a man from another planet who'd given an earth woman
his child in parting. And if travel through time was possible,
why not the miracle of birth? But, alas, Merry-Death had

told him earlier today that she suffered stomach cramps, the beginning of something called pea-amiss. In one day or two, her monthly flux would arrive, she'd explained.

So, all was set in motion.

Except for Merry-Death.

Had he been selfish to take her for his wife, knowing he would have to leave? Never had he expected their parting to be easy, but how could he have anticipated the magnitude of the love that had grown between them in such a short time?

Without words, he'd perceived Merry-Death's internal agony these past weeks as the minutes and days flew by. And because she loved him, she'd kept her torment to herself . . . as he had. Even her outward appearance had altered as she'd lost flesh, unable to eat. He feared she would fall apart emotionally when he left. She was strong, but even the strongest sometimes couldn't withstand the forces of pain. For now, he had his father's mission to keep him going forward, day to day. But when that was complete, he wasn't certain he'd want to exist without her at his side.

"Please, God," he prayed to her Christian deity, "help my wife through her grief, now and after I am gone." He thought a moment, and then added, "And please help me endure her loss."

"Did you say something?" Merry-Death asked as she awakened sleepily and saw him leaning over her. She reached up to pull him close. In that brief moment, between sleep and consciousness, she forgot the horror that awaited her.

Strands of Rolf's long hair formed a golden brown canopy about her shoulders and face as he stared dolefully down at her, reminding her—as if she needed a reminder—that there was so little time left. The candles burning on a table near the bedstead cast flickering shadows, making Rolf appear ethereal . . . a dream. Perhaps that was all he'd ever been, a dream she'd conjured up to fill her lonely life.

He kissed her tenderly as he moved on top of her and then, without any preliminaries, inside. His shoulder muscles bunched as he braced himself on extended arms.

No, he wasn't a dream.

She moaned softly as he pulsed, then expanded inside her, and, foolishly, she wanted to clench her inner muscles and lock him in place, to keep him with her forever. The molten heat of him seared her delicate folds, and she melted around him. It was love, not chemical energy, though, that flowed back and forth like an electrical current between them where they were joined.

She put her hands on either side of his face and whispered, "I love you, Geirolf Ericsson. Never forget me."

Lowering his head, he murmured against her lips, "Ah, Merry-Death . . . heart of my heart—" He paused as his grainy voice shook with emotion. "I will love you forever. I will never forget you."

Their lovemaking took on a dreamy intimacy then as each tried to show the other with touch and soft, disjointed endearments how very much they loved each other. For an hour and more, they caressed and kissed and tried to soothe their unspoken pain. In prolonging their mutual satisfaction, they made memories that would prevail through the centuries.

Tears filled both their eyes in the end as husband and wife made love for the last time with their bodies. They would love each other eternally with their souls.

They lay unsleeping, weeping silent tears, as dawn broke with a brilliant splash of color into their long-house. Rolf instructed her to destroy the dwelling where they'd been so happy when he was gone.

The abyss of despair is deep and dark . . .

Geirolf stood, legs widespread for balance, steering

Fierce Dragon by means of a side rudder fastened to the starboard quarter. It was a primitive though effective instrument that could be manned by a single member of the crew in any weather with just a small line to aid him.

Sixteen of the students, boys and girls alike, were stationed at the oarlocks. They would continue to row rhythmically to the count called out by Mike, the crew leader, till they reached the open seas where the sails would be unfurled. Females never manned Viking ships in his day, but Merry-Death and Mike had argued that the college would never accept less than equal opportunity on this project.

Equal opportunity amongst the sexes! Bloody hell, 'tis a concept to boggle the mind.

They were moving slowly away from the wharf, still crowded with dozens of spectators and news scribes who had surprisingly shown up to see them off, even though this was only intended to be a trial run on the smaller longship.

Many leave-takings had Geirolf experienced in his thirty-five years—from father, mother, brothers and sister, friends and lovers—but nothing had prepared him for the devastation of this leave-taking today. Even now, he strained for one last glimpse of Merry-Death standing at the forefront of the throng. Her proudly erect figure grew smaller and smaller as the distance widened between them. But then, to his horror, he saw her tightly coiled composure shatter as she collapsed to her knees on the ground. Thea and Sonja were immediately at her side, comforting her. He yearned to go back and soothe her himself, but his die was cast in another direction.

Too soon, the longboat passed a bend in the shoreline, and he could observe his beloved no more. A crushing weight slammed against Geirolf's chest, and he, too, sank to his knees.

"Rolf, are you all right?" Mike asked, rushing to his side.

Embarrassed, Geirolf stood quickly and grabbed for the

loose rudder, surreptitiously wiping his damp eyes. "I slipped on a wet spot," he lied. "'Twould seem I must regain my sea legs."

Mike accepted his explanation with a dubious nod and told one of the students to pick up the row calls. "Something weird is going on here," Mike said, bracing his hands on his hips and throwing his shoulders back with defiance. Geirolf was dressed in the Viking attire he'd worn on his arrival, but Mike and the students wore shorts and T-shirts for this rehearsal. "How 'bout explaining what the hell this caper today is really about?"

"We've been over this before," Geirolf said wearily.

Mike put up a halting hand. "No, don't feed me any more bullshit about your staying alone on the ship overnight to test its watertightness. This boat is sealed tighter than a drum, and you know it. More important, you and Dr. Foster are acting as if you never expect to see each other again. What gives? Really."

Geirolf stiffened. "Leave off, my friend. You tread recklessly into the realm of my personal life, and I do not appreciate the intrusion."

Mike stiffened, as well. "I care about Dr. Foster, and I care about you, you son of a bitch, though you've been behaving like a horse's ass the past few days—"

Geirolf raised a brow at the young pup's audacity.

"Damn it, man," Mike raked his fingers through his short hair with exasperation, "on the shore back there, you two looked like Bogart and Bergman in the last scene from *Casablanca*."

He understood Mike's reference. He and Merry-Death had watched a video of the famous moving picture last week. Merry-Death had insisted on renting a so-called "chick flick" after he'd compelled her to watch two hours of America's Cup races.

"I am far handsomer than that Hump-free character," he said with a laugh.

"If you consider me a friend, then don't cut me out, buddy," Mike insisted somberly, refusing to accept his attempt to change the topic of conversation.

Geirolf shook his head grimly. "Desist this line of questioning. There are things best left unexplained. I will say this, though, my friend, if e'er . . . if e'er any thing should happen to me, I trust that you will look after Merry-Death."

"You know," Mike said, cocking his head to the side as he studied him, "there are times when I almost think you're a real Viking."

"Have I e'er said otherwise?"

"No, but—"

"Enough!" Geirolf asserted; then he grinned at this new-found comrade whom he would miss sorely. "So, tell me true. Will you pursue this Pamela creature till you gain the bedding? I heard that she phoned you repeatedly this past week."

Mike glared at him, not wanting to drop the subject. But then his shoulders relaxed with resignation. "Nah."

"Sonja?"

Mike shrugged. "I suppose."

"But they are so different. Not that I'd argue in the buxom wench's favor. I suspect Sonja is by far the better choice."

"Hey, sometimes a guy looks for a babe to put a little extra crispy in his corn flakes, if you get my drift," Mike said, his lips twitching with amusement. "And sometimes he finds there's just as much snap, crackle, and pop in his own backyard."

Geirolf burst out laughing at that analogy. 'Twas one his brothers would enjoy when he relayed it to them . . . with a few medieval modifications, such as oat cakes in place of corn flakes. Yea, male thinking was the same throughout the ages, he concluded, though Merry-Death would have called it male *chauvinist* thinking.

Corn flakes made him think of his favorite food, Oreos, and that brought his thoughts back to his wife, who had chided him often on his "fixation" with the modern delicacy. As Mike returned to his duties and he resumed his steering—they needed only to go out about a half-mile—his mind wandered over the many important events that must fall into place in order to make the time-travel reversal succeed.

And, in the course of those meandering thoughts, he wondered idly if there might be some sign he could give Merry-Death from the past to let her know he'd arrived safely in his own time. With macabre humor, he came upon a most creative idea . . . leastways, he considered it creative.

He would have one of his father's skalds record a saga about a wandering Norse knight called The Last Viking who had a passion for a mythical food of the gods called orioles. Of course, most listeners would think the name referred to the colorful bird of the crow family, but perhaps Merry-Death—if she were researching the old sagas as she was wont to do and if she came upon this particular one—would recognize the play on words as a coded message to her.

Hah! He was grasping at threads when what he needed was a rope to pull him from the abyss of desperation. He was destroying the woman he'd come to love with this time-travel adventure. His own life, once the mission was complete, would be worth naught.

What logic was there in this madness? Why had he been sent through time if he was to be catapulted back? Why had he been given true love for the first time in his ill-begotten life, only to have it yanked away? *Why, why, why?* The questions hammered away in his brain to the tempo of the rowing chant.

Trust in God, a voice in his head said.

Geirolf's chin shot upward and he glanced around to see

if anyone else had heard, but, nay, Mike and the students w
going about the business of rowing the longship out to se

Which God? he asked silently.

He thought he heard a chuckle in his head, but that v
impossible. *Give me a sign*, he pleaded, nonetheless.

A seagull passed overhead and dropped an ignominic
"sign" on the deck near his feet.

'Twas not a good omen.

CHAPTER EIGHTEEN

*B*eer and Oreos: food of the gods . . .

The time travel had failed.

Geirolf realized that fact the next day as he swam toward shore in the early-morning hours. He recognized in the dawn light the coastline south of Merry-Death's home with its modern dwellings scattered along the clifftops. It was still 1997, not 997.

There had been a Demon Moon the night before. A crack of lightning had struck his longship, causing it to splinter apart and sink. He'd been sucked into a whirlpool, just like the first time. When he'd risen to the surface, clutching his faithful Ingrid, he had no way of knowing if the time travel had been reversed. Not until the morning light.

Everything had been a replica of his previous experience, but the time portal had remained closed to him. Why?

"Well, Ingrid, what the hell do we do now?"

Geirolf heard the sound of a motor and studied the horizon till he saw two fishermen in a motorized pleasure boat approaching. "Hey, buddy, had an accident?" a man wearing a Minnesota Vikings cap called out with concern.

Vikings? The irony of it prompted Geirolf's lips to curve up in a rueful smile, despite his uncomfortable position in the frigid water. "Yea, my boat capsized."

"Hop in, then," the other man said. He was wearing a Baltimore Orioles cap.

First, Vikings. Now, Orioles. If Geirolf wasn't so damned cold, he'd laugh at the humor of the "signs" bombarding him at every turn.

"We'll give you a ride back to shore. You can call the Coast Guard from there. Are you all right?"

Nay, I am not all right. "I just need to get out of this water and think."

Hauling him up, they alternately studied the figurehead and him, taking special note of his leather tunic with the talisman belt and his cross-tied boots. Ingrid's bosom got a fair share of their attention, too. The men didn't look devious, just quizzical. They handed him a pair of dry sweating pants and shirt and a wool blanket, which he wrapped around his shivering body.

He hesitated to ask, but had to, "What year is this?"

"Just call me Chuck," said the Orioles man, who then guffawed, "It's 1997. Don't worry, fella. A good dunking will do that to ya. Makes the brain fuzzy. My brother-in-law almos' drowned las' year, and he couldn't remember his girlfriend's name fer a month."

"Harry never did know Betty's name," the Vikings man, who identified himself as Bruiser, chortled. Then he turned good-naturedly to Geirolf. "Hey, mister, wouldja like a beer?"

Now there was a Vikings man after a Viking's heart.

"Care fer a pretzel?" the Oriole offered, as well, holding out an open bag of salted brown sticks.

Geirolf shook his head. "I don't suppose you have any Oreos?"

"Of course. Ain't nothing better'n beer and Oreos in the mornin'," Bruiser opined. Truly, a man of discriminating taste. And another "sign," Geirolf concluded.

Chuck pointed the long-neck bottle of his mead at the figurehead resting near their feet. "Who's the bimbo?"

"Ingrid," he said, taking a gusty swig of the cold brew.

"Great tits," Bruiser remarked. Norsemen always did have superior discernment in that regard.

"She'd look great over the bar in my den, next to the Coors sign. Wouldja like to sell her?" Chuck asked.

Geirolf erupted into laughter then and couldn't stop. Ingrid was going to be the life, or death, of him yet.

Men are men, no matter the age . . .

It was afternoon by the time Geirolf shook hands with his rescuers in a nearby village.

"I thank you for your help," Geirolf said.

"Hey, no prob," Bruiser bellowed over the sound of the surf, clapping him on the back. "And don't worry 'bout us spillin' the beans to anyone 'bout rescuin' you. We understand a guy wantin' to get away from his little woman fer a while." He winked at Geirolf in a manly fashion.

"Exactly where didja say that Viking S-spot is, again?" Chuck added, also clapping him on the back. And winking.

On the boat ride back to shore, the men had been complaining about their womenfolk watching too much Oprah. And he'd offered his opinions on *Home Improvement*, to which they'd agreed heartily. The conversation progressed then to the ill advice offered on all those television talk shows, which caused women to nag their hardworking husbands when they arrived home. That was when Geirolf had told them that the surest way to silence a woman's complaints was to show her the famous Viking S-Spot.

Chuck and Bruiser, both duly impressed, had said he ought to have his own TV talk show.

He'd demurred humbly.

They'd scoffed at his offer of money for their services

after helping him transport Ingrid to a boat-rental mart where she was now stored in a locker. He'd scoffed at their suggestion that he go to a hospital for care.

He needed no healer, modern or otherwise, to tell him what was wrong with him. He was lost between two worlds. That was why he'd urged them not to speak of his rescue. He needed time to figure out his latest dilemma.

Air travel was scarier than time travel to this seasoned traveler . . .

That evening, Geirolf lay with his arms folded behind his head as he reclined on a bed in the village's sole travel lodge—Swifty's Motel and Pizzeria. The only good thing that could be said about the dreary room was that it contained a "gel" bed that vibrated in a most delicious manner when four coins were inserted in a metal slot. He wished Merry-Death were here to share the experience.

Fortunately, Geirolf had forgotten before the boat launching to give Mike his leather belt pouch, which contained fifty thousand dollars. In fact, he'd given Merry-Death all the money earlier, despite her resistance. She must have put it back in the pouch considering it demeaning, as if he were paying for her services. Foolish wench!

He hadn't spent much time studying modern currency, but he assumed fifty thousand dollars must be a great deal of money, because when he'd pulled the wet roll out at the lodge desk to pay in advance for the fifty-dollar room, the clerk's eyes about popped out. Villains abounded in any century, and he'd decided to lock his door tonight and prop a chair under the handle as a precaution.

The question now was, what should he do?

The time travel hadn't worked this time. But that didn't mean he wouldn't try again. And again. And again. Till he prevailed.

Could he go back to Merry-Death and put her through another, or repeated, partings of the type she'd experienced yesterday? Could he be so cruel?

But wasn't it even more cruel to be alive, in her time, and not let her know?

No, he decided. It was more cruel to cause the same devastating grief over and over, like opening a bloody wound.

He had to figure out what had gone wrong last night and how to do it right the next time. Idly clicking on the television, he gasped, then fell back on the gel bed.

There stood a ravaged Merry-Death staring back at him from the screen.

"Has the Coast Guard found a body yet?" a newsman called out to her.

Merry-Death flinched before answering in a choked whisper, "No." She was speaking into a microphone being held in her face—a face that seemed to have aged overnight. Her hair was tangled and uncombed, her eyes bloodshot and underlined with dark circles. Creases of pain bracketed her eyes and mouth.

This is what I have done to her. What kind of love is it that causes so much misery?

Flanking her on either side were Mike and Thea, who appeared equally distraught. Tears filled their eyes.

"What effect will this disaster have on the Trondheim project?" another reporter inquired. Apparently the press conference had been in progress for some time. "Will the voyage this summer be cancelled because of the potential danger to the students?"

"Absolutely not!" Merry-Death exclaimed, pulling herself upright with indignation. "The lightning that struck Rol . . . Mr. Ericsson's longship last night was a freak accident . . . an act of God. It will have no bearing whatsoever on the continuation of the Trondheim Venture."

Geirolf gave Merry-Death a mental salute. His wife was stronger than she appeared at first glance. She would survive; he could see that in her quick flash of anger.

"But don't you think it's odd that the lightning storm didn't hit anywhere else in the region?" the first reporter interjected.

Merry-Death shrugged. "You'd have to ask a meteorologist, although it's always been my understanding that storms at sea are erratic."

A woman newsperson tried to push forward, but when she was thwarted, shouted, "Is it true that Mr. Ericsson is your husband? How are you feeling, Mrs. Ericsson, about the death of your new husband?"

Merry-Death's eyes went wide with horror at the woman's crass question, and Mike put an arm around her shoulder, answering for her, "That will be all for today, folks. Any further questions should be directed to the college public information office. Thank you."

With that, the picture faded away and moved on to a commercial for feminine products. Talk about crass!

Well, that settles it, then. If Geirolf had even remotely been considering a return to Merry-Death's keep, that possibility was wiped out now. Not only would such an ill-considered action subject his beloved to the continual grief of his partings, but now he realized that future attempts to use the time portal would jeopardize the Trondheim project.

What should I do? Where is the answer to this puzzle? Why did my time-travel reversal fail? How can I ensure that my next endeavor will be successful?

Geirolf rubbed his talisman belt and lay back, spent, on the bedstead. With all these perplexing questions hammering at his brain, he fell into an exhausted sleep.

In the middle of the night, the answer came to him.

He would go to Norway on one of those flying machines.

Perchance there he would find some answers. Not that he thought the time hole would open for him in another country. Nay, 'twould have to originate here off the coast of Maine. But, for some reason, he sensed that the clue lay in his homeland.

Thus inspired, Geirolf—knees knocking with fright—boarded a flying machine the next day in Bangor, where a taxi driver had taken him for only five hundred dollars. He'd even stopped along the way at a Wall-Mart so he could buy a leather Samson case and some clothing. Geirolf was sore tired of the strange looks he garnered everywhere he went. You'd think these people had never seen a man in a leather tunic afore.

As the flying metal bird took off into the sky a short time later, Geirolf braced himself within his seat restraints and prepared himself for what should be the most wondrous adventure of his life. 'Twas the fodder of the greatest sagas.

But he just stared dolefully out the window. All he could think was, *I miss Merry-Death.*

What was the meaning of this time-travel mission? There had to be a reason why he'd been sent here. It couldn't just be an accident of fate.

It was probably wishful thinking on his part, but deep down inside his heart, a tiny spark ignited. Thus far, he'd been reacting to the events bombarding him at every turn. For the first time, he was taking action. *Perhaps . . . oh, please,* he prayed to all the gods, *if it be possible, let me find a way that will lead me back to Merry-Death.*

"Ladies and gentlemen," a rumbling masculine voice said from out of nowhere.

Awestruck, Geirolf glanced right and left, but no one else was paying attention to the God voice. The deity must be speaking only to him.

"Welcome to the friendly skies . . ." the God-voice went on.

Friendly? One of the gods is calling me a friend? Well, that certainly is a good sign. Is it Odin or the all-God?

"I promise you a safe journey," the God-voice continued. Some of the words were not decipherable, sounding like Merry-Death's car telephone. But *safe journey*, that was surely good news. He had just prayed to the gods to help him find a way to complete his father's mission and be with Merry-Death, and the God-voice had just promised him a *safe journey*. That was as good as a promise in his mind.

Geirolf was drained from the emotional and physical battering of the past few days. But, for the first time in many sennights, he felt hopeful. Resting his head on the back of his seat, he allowed sleep to overcome him.

It was all in the hands of the gods now.

CHAPTER NINETEEN

☙

He left her a precious gift . . .

"What the hell is this?" Mike exclaimed a week after Rolf's "death."

After seven days of soul-wrenching anguish, Meredith had finally gathered enough strength that morning to log on her computer, at Mike's urging. She'd intended to retrieve the instructions Rolf had said he'd typed in related to the ship project, which was at a standstill.

But she'd found much more. A letter to her from Rolf.

It was like a message from beyond the grave. Even though Meredith knew he'd written it the week before, it still felt as if he was talking to her now, from a thousand years away.

Merry-Death, my love:

When you read this, I will be gone . . . back to the tenth century. Please, dearling, do not mourn for me. What we had for a short time was more than many people ever experience in a lifetime. A gift from the gods, to be sure.

Study the Norse sagas, Merry-Death. I will try, if I am able, to leave a message for you. Some sign that I arrived safely in the past.

I misdoubt that I can change history because of my experience in your time, but I myself have changed.

*For the better. Because of you. Surely I will be a finer
person for having my heart opened thus.*

*Please finish the longship project. I take comfort in
the knowledge that you and I will both have fulfilled
our honor-bound blood oaths. If we do not, our sacrifice was for naught.*

*Take joy in Thea, my love. Adopt children, if you
must. But do not value yourself any less as a woman
for your inability to conceive. You are all the woman
any man could desire. For a certainty, you are all the
woman this Viking will ever want.*

With all my love, forevermore,

Geirolf Ericsson

Meredith wept . . . silently, at first, then great shuddering
sobs. Mike took her into his arms, trying to soothe her with
soft spoken words and pats on the shoulder.

Thank goodness, Thea was in school and unable to witness this breakdown. Poor Thea! Even though devastated,
she was handling Rolf's "death" better than any of them.

Finally, when Meredith calmed down and they sat in the
kitchen over coffee and Oreos—for some reason, Meredith
had developed a taste for Oreos—Mike said, "We need to
talk, Dr. Foster. What's that crap in Rolf's letter about time
travel?"

Meredith sighed and told her grad assistant the whole
story. He deserved an explanation. After fifteen minutes,
she concluded, "So, in the end, Rolf planned his 'death.' His
departure from me . . . this time . . . was ordained from the
start."

"Holy hell!" Mike said under his breath, staring at her as
if she'd told him aliens had just invaded Maine. Then more
loudly, he repeated, "Holy hell!"

"Oh, I don't expect you to believe any of this," she said,

waving a hand in the air. "It was hard enough for me to accept, and I was living with the evidence."

"Actually," Mike began tentatively, "it makes a weird kind of sense."

Her eyes went wide. "You believe in time travel?"

"I never did before," Mike said with a snort of self-derision, "but there were so many niggling contradictions about Rolf. And he knew so damn much about the tenth century."

"We can't tell anyone about this," she said quickly.

Mike nodded. "If nothing else, they'd put us in a looney bin. Or close down the project." He studied her for a moment. "Do you think it's possible? Rolf, a medieval Viking?"

She shrugged, then straightened resolutely. "Yes . . . yes, I do believe."

After that, Meredith's healing progressed more rapidly, especially since she now had someone to confide in.

She studied the Norse sagas meticulously for more than a week, but nowhere could she find any with even a remote message from Rolf. But then, many of the skaldic tales had been lost over the centuries, most never having been put to paper.

Work resumed on the Trondheim Venture as a result of persuasive arguments by Meredith before the foundation board. The only stumbling block was that the Annapolis man they'd hired to captain the voyage in August had suffered a heart attack, and they'd been unable thus far to find a replacement. But, with all the obstacles Meredith had faced these past months, she considered this a minor problem.

Then, a month after Rolf had left, Meredith was delivered a tremendous shock, and her life turned upside-down again.

"But how is it possible, Dr. Peterson?" she asked, plopping down in a chair before the physician's desk. She'd gone

in for a checkup that afternoon because of persistent wei
loss and flulike symptoms of nausea.

"The usual way," Dr. Peterson responded with a v
grin. "I assume you've had sexual relations with a man."

"Of course," she said, frowning at his deliberately mi
terpreting her words. "You've seen my medical records.
know that I'm infertile . . . incapable of bearing children

"Meredith, I ran the tests twice to make sure. You're pr
nant, no doubt about it."

"But how . . . I mean, was my original diagnosis inc
rect?"

"No, I don't think so," he replied, choosing his wo
carefully. "Hell, Meredith, science isn't perfect. Unexplai
things happen all the time."

Unexplained things happen all the time, Meredith
peated in her head. *Tell me about it! I've lived the unexpl
able.*

"Call it a miracle, or call it a fluke of science. Just
happy. It's what you've always wanted, isn't it?"

"Oh, yes," she said, tears brimming her eyes.

As she walked down the Bangor street a short time la
her lips twitched with a secret smile. She kept putting a pa
to her flat stomach. *A baby! I'm going to have Rolf's baby*

She didn't know if the talisman belt was responsible
this miracle, or God, or even Rolf's Norse gods. But R
had left her with the greatest gift of all. A part of himsel

So, for Meredith, there was finally a meaning to Ro
time travel.

Finally, the key to his mission . . .

"Praise the gods!" Geirolf shouted in an attic alcove
Oslo's Vestfold Heritage Museum. His jubilant exclamat
was accompanied by a brisk rap of his victorious fist on
rickety table in front of him.

He could not care. Finally, *finally*, after one long month of searching, he had found the key that might allow him to stay in the future with his wife.

"*Mis-ter Er-ic-sson,*" a crotchety voice reprimanded. The female form of Miss Hilda Svensson was just now poking its wiry gray head up the narrow stairwell. "This is a research facility, not a beer hall. You must respect the academic environment of your fellow scholars."

Geirolf grinned sheepishly and thought about telling her he was a Viking, not a scholar. And he could have pointed out that she was the only mortal being he'd spied this past week in her three-story home, which was pretentiously called a museum, while actually housing only generations of her own family's historical books and letters. Not that they weren't valuable. In truth, it appeared as if they would provide the answers he'd been unable to find in the most prestigious libraries and museums throughout Scandinavia.

But Geirolf kept his thoughts to himself and instead stood, barely avoiding whacking his head on the low ceiling. Then, with a whoop, he gathered the elderly woman into his arms and swung her in a circle. She was an angel, really she was. Ever since he'd met the diminutive Norse woman a sennight ago, she'd opened her museum home to him, renting him a room and giving him access to her hoard of hidden papers, protected in acid-free, clear plastic covers in climate-controlled closets.

"I've found the key to my puzzle, Miss Svensson. Bless you for giving me access to your precious documents." He bestowed a loud kiss on her flushed cheek before setting her on her feet again. "Truly, you have saved my life, sweetling."

Adjusting herself prissily, though obviously pleased at his exuberant appreciation, Miss Svensson walked over to the table and titled her head toward the parchment he'd been examining. "This is it, then?"

He nodded.

"Will you be able to return to your wife now, Mr. Ericsson?" Her eyes were misty with emotion over his "estrangement" from Merry-Death, which she viewed as a romantic melodrama. Though he hadn't told her all the details, he had informed her that a separation from his beloved wife was necessary unless, or until, he found some important historical data.

"I think so," he said. "Look at this. One of your ancestors, a scribe in the service of the Norse king in 1250, has left a copy of a missing page from *The Heimskringla*."

"The *Chronicle of the Kings of Norway*?" she translated.

"Yea. 'Twas written by Snorri Sturluson afore his death in 1241."

"Is that important . . . the missing page, I mean?" Miss Svensson asked, her frail fingertips pressed against her trembling lips. She probably hadn't had so much excitement in her life for decades.

"Very! I read a copy of the book back in the United States of Am-eric-hah, but it did not say how long the famine lasted." He tapped a forefinger on the plastic, midway down the page. "This is the most important line to me. 'And in this year of our Lord, nine hundred and ninety-seven, a great famine continued to besiege the land. A thousand and more good men, women, and babes succumbed to the scourge afore a great calm swept the country the first night of the spring equinox. After that, the earth flourished again. Thanks be to God!' "

"But . . . but I don't understand."

"It's the date that's important. I cross-referenced the spring equinox of 997 with the Demon Moon occurrence of 1997, and they occurred on the same day of the month."

"And?" she prodded, her brow still furrowed with bafflement.

And that means that the need for me to return to the past ended with my being thrust through the time portal, along with the sacred relic. But he couldn't tell Miss Svensson that, without revealing all. "*And* that means that there is no longer any encumbrance to keep me from returning to my wife's side."

Except for a few more questions that must be resolved. Such as, why was I sent into the future? If removing the reliquary from Norway, or even from that time period, was enough to wipe out the famine curse, then why did the gods require my going a thousand years to Merry-Death? Why not a sennight, or a year, rather than a century? Why to a country on the other side of the ocean? And why not some other woman, rather than Merry-Death?

The twists and turns of his life were all so confusing, but still Geirolf was overjoyed at today's discovery. Standing suddenly, he flashed a mischievous smile at his marvelous benefactress, whose eyes were level with his chest. "M'lady, how would you like to celebrate with me over a horn of mead?"

To his surprise, she flashed him an equally mischievous smile. "'Twould be my pleasure, m'lord." Then she added, "Shall I open those Oreos you had me special order from the grocer?"

He threw back his head and laughed, deep and long. Her mention of the heavenly cookies was another sign from the gods, he was certain.

And so he came full circle . . .
Several days later, still scrambling for answers, Geirolf traveled over the causeway leading to Lindisfarne, in Britain. It was impossible to cross to Holy Island two hours before high tide and three hours after; so, his time was limited. But then, time was at the crux of all his troubles.

He wasn't exactly sure why he'd felt the need to come to Lindisfarne. His blood-oath to his father had ended with his discovery back in Norway that the famine had ended with his time travel. At the very least, he hoped to leave the relic in the monastery. A closure.

But there was no monastery, only the ruins of what had once been the sanctuary of its founder, St. Aidan. With the booming sea as a background and the cries of sea birds overhead, Geirolf fancied that the mournful chants of the Dark Age monks carried on the wind.

His head shot up with alarm. Had he been restored to his own time? But no, it was just the breaking of waves against the rocky shore and the trills of gulls and kittihawks.

He shuffled through the ancient remains—chiseled red sandstone boulders that had withstood the ravages of the centuries. So many changes! Nothing was as it had been in his day. *He* was not as he'd been in his day.

Geirolf was lost.

A man with no country, to be sure, but that was true of most Norsemen. Hadn't that been proven to him in his journey to the twentieth century? Hadn't he been shown that Vikings as a separate people didn't survive the ages? So, in that regard, he was no different from his fellow Northmen who searched for a new home.

But he was a man without an anchor in time, as well, and that was the puzzle that nagged at him. Where did he belong? Was he destined to travel through time till he found his final resting place?

"Good tidings, my son," a kindly voice said, jolting him back to the present.

"Wh-what?" Geirolf hadn't heard anyone come up behind him. He turned, then took a step backward.

Standing before him was a tonsured priest of indeterminate age. He wore the traditional brown robe of the monastic community, with sandals and a cowl hood. The skin of his face was smooth and translucent, his eyes a penetrating blue.

"Where did you come from?" Geirolf snapped. The tour group was up at the castle, which stood on a dramatic outcrop of stone on the other side of the island. In the distance, he saw the structure glistening like a proud jewel in the midday sun, framed by a steep rock face bright with thyme, valerian, mallow, and gillyflowers.

The holy man just curved his lips upward in a slight smile of mystery.

"Who are you?" Geirolf wished he had his sword with him. The abbot was regarding him in a most unsettling manner. And, after all, it was a well-known fact that many priestly men were as bloodthirsty as the most hardened warriors. Besides, they had good cause to hate Norsemen.

"Aidan," the man replied.

"Aidan?" Geirolf choked out. "St. Aidan?"

"Well, I know naught about sainthood," the man said, his ethereal eyes twinkling as if at some jest.

"Are you the monk who started a religious order on Lindisfarne?" Geirolf couldn't believe he'd actually asked such a question. If true, it would mean that the monk had lived here more than thirteen centuries ago. Ridiculous!

But is it any more ridiculous than my traveling here from the tenth century?

Geirolf put a hand to his throbbing head.

"Why dost thou trouble thyself about matters thou cannot control, my son?" the man inquired with compassion, his misty eyes seeming to pierce Rolf's soul. "Nothing will happen but what God wills."

Geirolf raised his eyes hopefully. Perhaps this priest, whoever he was, had the answers.

"I believe you have something for me," the monk said, holding out a palm.

A shiver passed over Geirolf's flesh. Without hesitation, he undid the clasp on his talisman belt and removed the sacred relic. He placed the crucifix in the monk's hand, which immediately closed over it. Then, with a sigh, the monk said, "It is done."

"What's done? Who are you, really? And why am I here?"

Once again, the monk just smiled softly at him. "When time comes full circle, the line will continue."

"Huh? What kind of riddle is that?"

He made the sign of the cross in the air before Rolf. "Bless you, my son."

"But . . . but . . . what am I supposed to do now?"

"Fulfill thy destiny."

"Destiny? What destiny?" Geirolf cried to the monk's departing back.

Just then, a gusty breeze came up, whipping his long hair across his face. In the second it took for Geirolf to brush the strands from in front of his eyes, the monk was gone.

"Fulfill thy destiny," the monk had said, but Geirolf had no idea what that destiny could be . . . until his gaze, still scanning the windswept coastline for the monk, snagged on a red object nestled amongst the craggy rocks. How could he have missed it?

Stepping closer, he saw a single red rose growing amid the ruins. Hunkering down, he sniffed the air permeated with the flower's scent. And then he smiled. It was a sign.

Geirolf now knew what his destiny was.

Merry-Death.

He came home, literally . . .

"Professor Foster, we have another applicant for the captain position," Mike said, poking his head into the doorway of her office at the end of the day.

Meredith's head jerked up from the papers she'd been

grading, and she glanced quickly at her watch. Six o'clock. She would have to leave soon to pick up Thea after soccer practice. She was surprised to see Mike here so late. Since he'd begun dating Sonja, he didn't hang around evenings anymore. And why wasn't he at the longship site?

But she was even more surprised to hear him announce another candidate for the longship job. They'd filled the post, albeit unsatisfactorily, the week before with a young boating enthusiast from Michigan.

"Tell him we've stopped interviewing." Meredith took off her reading glasses and rubbed the bridge of her nose. She noticed then the paleness of Mike's complexion and the way he held a fist to his mouth, as if to suppress some great emotion. "Are you sick?" she asked with concern, standing and moving to the side of her desk.

He shook his head. "I think you'll want to meet this . . . applicant," Mike insisted. "He's perfect for the job."

With that, he stepped back, calling over his shoulder, "Sonja and I will go pick up Thea at the school."

Before she had a chance to react to Mike's unsolicited offer, a very tall man started to back into the room, speaking softly to Mike as he entered. At first, all Meredith could see was long legs encased in loafers and designer jeans, and broad shoulders covered with a collarless, white linen dress shirt and a dark blue blazer.

But, no, she observed something else in that split second. Long, pale brown hair pulled back into a ponytail. Just like . . .

Her heart lurched, then pounded madly against her chest as the man turned in what seemed an exaggerated slow motion. And a pair of familiar whiskey eyes clung to hers with staggering adoration.

As blood drained from her head, a wave of lightheadedness swamped her. She grabbed onto the edge of her desk to prevent herself from fainting. She blinked once, twice, three times to make sure she wasn't hallucinating. The proof stood before her still, eyes brimming with tenderness, waiting for her recognition. A Viking, to be sure, despite the modern trappings.

A sob escaped her tortured lungs.

"Dearling," he rasped.

"Rolf!" she cried and threw herself into his arms. "You came back!"

At last! Geirolf thought when he got his first glimpse of Merry-Death. In that brief flash of time before she launched herself at him, he saw that she'd reverted back to drab brown *braies* and *shert*, and her luxuriant mahogany hair was pulled back into a nunlike knot at her nape.

He would change that soon enough, but for now he closed his eyes as an overwhelming rush of pleasure surged over him. His misery at being parted from Merry-Death had been a physical pain, he realized now. One touch from her and he was healed.

Kicking the door shut with his heel and flicking the lock with a snap of his fingers, he proceeded to lift Merry-Death more tightly into his embrace, her legs dangling above the floor, his face buried in her neck. He inhaled deeply, and the faint scent of roses filled his senses.

He was home. *At last!*

With a bone-deep sigh, he raised his head. Then he couldn't resist skimming his mouth lightly across hers. He almost swooned with the heady bliss of his lips on hers once again. Immediately, the kiss turned hungry and devouring. It had been too long. Too damn long!

Finally, she tore her mouth from his, panting for breath. She held his face in her hands and gazed at him with pure love. Tears streamed down her face from eyes that looked like liquid emeralds.

"Did you feel the tingle?" She gasped, pressing the fingertips of one hand to her lips. "Oh, God, I haven't tingled for six long weeks."

He smiled. Yes, there was a definite tingle on his lips . . . and other unmentionable body parts. He smiled wider.

Somehow, they'd moved to the desk, and she was half-sitting, half-leaning against the side with him bent over her. Rolf stretched out an arm and swept all the papers, pens, and other profess-whore-ly debris from her desk, then hoisted her up so she could lie flat on her back.

In a pinch, Vikings were known to improvise a bed for coupling anywhere. In fact, some said a Norseman could mate on a glacier if the lust was upon him, Geirolf recalled. His brother Jorund once claimed to have made love in a tree, but Geirolf hardly credited that as true.

In his haste, he didn't bother to undress her, or himself. He merely pulled her *braies* and silk panties to her knees in one swoop, buttons flying hither and yon. And he undid the snap and zipper on his jeans—Lord, these modern men knew what they were doing when they invented zippers. In the blink of an eye, he was poised over her. He would have bruises on his knees from the hard desk, but who could worry about that now? Every Viking warrior knew the best-won battles were worth a little pain.

Her eyes narrowed at him. "You haven't been tingling anyone else while you've been gone, have you?"

He tried to laugh, but it came out as a suffocated gurgle. "Sweetling, would I be on you like an overeager pup if I had been tingling another wench?"

She smiled sweetly, pulling him forward with one hand wrapped around the back of his neck. The other hand was wrapped about his man-part to guide him, thus causing stars to burst behind his eyeballs. He fought for restraint. And then—Bless the gods!—he was inside the hot, welcoming sheath of his beloved.

Between his strokes, he planted feathery kisses on her eyelids, chin, the soft pulse spot beneath her ear, her forehead, the tip of her nose. And intermingled with his kisses were soft-spoken endearments expressed by them both on how much they'd missed each other and how wonderful it was to be together again.

"You broke my heart," she whispered.

"I'll put it back together," he promised, "with my love."

"Never leave me again."

"Never!"

"I love you, Geirolf Ericsson."

"I love you, Merry-Death Ericsson."

The earth moved then as they came to an explosive, mutual climax. Or mayhap it was just the desk skidding across the wooden floor from the force of their lovemaking.

He preferred the former explanation. Another sign from the gods. In truth, he could swear he heard a clap of Thor's thunder in the distance. Or was it the Christian one-god clapping at this thick-headed heathen finally fulfilling his destiny?

As he and Merry-Death lay sated in each other's arms, murmuring their awe at the fates that had ordained their converging paths, Geirolf pondered whether it was too soon to ask Merry-Death if she had any Oreos and beer at her keep.

He should have known his homecoming was too easy . . .

Meredith couldn't believe how dramatically her life had changed in a few short hours. As they headed toward the pink convertible in the faculty parking lot, she kept looking at Rolf just to make sure she wasn't dreaming.

"You kept the car," Rolf commented with a smile, reaching over to brush a wisp of wind-tossed hair behind her ear. He couldn't stop touching her. She felt the same way.

She raised her chin defensively at his remark about the car. "I haven't had time to get rid of it yet," she lied. Although she'd protested his purchase of the horrendous car in the beginning, threatening to sell it the moment he was gone, she'd come to love the gas guzzler, which could be seen even from this distance—a football-field length away, thanks to its Pepto-Bismol color.

He laughed, and continued to ask her nonstop questions. She had a ton of questions for him, as well. What happened when he'd traveled back to the tenth century? Had the famine ended? How had he managed to come back? But she let Rolf talk first.

"I feel like I've been gone a millennium, instead of six weeks." He expelled a breath and pulled her snugly against his side, kissing the top of her head. "Tell me everything that's happened since I've been gone."

"It's been hell."

"For me, too, sweetling." He squeezed her shoulder. "Is Thea adjusting?"

"Extremely well. Oh, she's been distraught over your"— she stared at him with dismay—"death. But kids are resilient, and Thea is blooming in this environment."

"Speaking of blooming—why is your face so flushed? You're not feverish, are you?"

Meredith's heart skipped a beat. Rolf didn't know about her pregnancy yet. In fact, no one did; she'd planned to keep the secret to herself until she began to show in another month or two. She cast him a shy sideways glance. Would he be happy? Of course, he would. But this wasn't the time to give him the news. Later. She wanted the moment to be special . . . just right.

Rolf cocked his head. "Merry-Death?" he prompted.

"It must be the sun," she answered evasively, and then wiggled her eyebrows at him. "Or our lovemaking."

He nodded with arrogant satisfaction. "Just don't think of getting sick now—at least not till we've made love another ten or twenty or fifty times."

Yep, arrogance was second nature to Rolf. As they arrived at her car, she tossed her briefcase into the back seat and turned to him, lifting a skeptical eyebrow.

He winked.

"Promises, promises," she taunted, barely able to suppress a giggle at the flutter of butterflies in her stomach that his mere wink engendered. "By the way, where did you get the fancy duds?"

"London," Rolf remarked idly, about to open the car door.

Uh-oh! Geirolf thought, realizing his blunder immediately.

"London?" The soft expression on Merry-Death's face went hard as a rock. She speared him with an incredulous scowl. "You just got back after six weeks in the past, and you decided to go to London *before* seeing me?"

He'd also forgotten her talent for ear-splitting shrieks.

"What? No, you misunderstood, Merry-Death," he said, trying for a casual tone. "The time-travel reversal failed. I have been . . ." His words trailed off as he saw her demeanor become even stiffer.

"The time reversal didn't work?" she gritted out. "Are you saying that you've been around the neighborhood for the past six weeks and you never bothered to inform me of the fact?"

"Not the neighborhood, sweetling. Europe." He tried to put an arm around her shoulder. He wasn't surprised when she shoved his hand away.

"You moron! You beast! How could you do that to me? Oh, to think of the agony I've been through!" She put her face in her trembling hands. "I never thought you could be so cruel."

"Merry-Death, let me explain."

"No!" she shouted and stormed to the other side of the car, opening the driver's door. Bracing her hands on her hips, tears of anger and hurt welling her eyes, she told him icily, "I thought I was used to betrayal, after Jeffrey, but this . . . this is the worst thing any man has ever done to me. I never want to see you again. Do you hear me? It's over."

"Never!" How dare she liken him to that misbegotten past-husband of hers! He had just cause for his actions. Love for her had been his guiding light. "Merry-Death, if you would only listen. I had good reason for pretending to have died."

"Nothing—*nothing*—in this world could justify that." She slipped into the driver's seat and slammed the door. Turning on the ignition, she revved the motor, then glared at him as he prepared to slide into the seat next to her. "Out! You are not coming home with me now."

"Where should I go?" he sputtered.

"I don't know," she wailed. "I don't care."

Stung, he removed his body from her vehicle and slammed his door shut with equal vehemence. "You don't mean that, Merry-Death. Have a caution with your harsh condemnations. Some words, once spoken, can ne'er be taken back."

She pressed her forehead against the steering wheel for a moment. Then with a long sigh, she looked up at him. "I care, Rolf, but some things are more important in life."

"More important than love?" he scoffed.

"Yes. Like trust. Commitment. Honor. I need some time alone to think this through, Rolf. Don't follow me. Please."

Before he had a chance to tell her that she would be unable to reflect on the matter without all the facts, Merry-Death's car roared away in a cloud of exhaust fumes. And Geirolf's Viking pride kicked in.

Trust went both ways. Where was Merry-Death's trust in him?

And what made her imagine he would chase after her like some milksop swain? He'd suffered much these past sennights, trying to find a way to stay in her time. And did she appreciate his efforts? Nay!

Worst of all, Merry-Death had questioned his honor. That insult he could not countenance. That slur to his integrity was the verbal knife wound that hurt the most.

Well, let her come to him when her common sense returned. He was a Viking. No more would he demean himself in pursuit where he was not wanted.

It was not the homecoming he'd envisioned.

CHAPTER TWENTY

Rolf "The Toolman" Viking? . . .

"Oh, my God! Aunt Mer, hurry! You've got to see this," Thea called from the living room.

Meredith wiped her hands on a dish towel and turned down the flame under the pot of chicken soup simmering on the stove. With deliberate care, she plastered a smile on her face as she prepared to go into the other room, not wanting her niece to see how she was splintering apart inside.

It had been a week since Rolf had returned . . . a week during which pride had prevented each from approaching the other. Despite the urging from Mike and Thea, who'd both spoken with Rolf on numerous occasions—in fact, Rolf was staying with Mike—she'd refused to meet with him. Her feelings were still too raw.

And she feared for her baby. Did she want to bring the baby's father into its life if he might leave at a moment's notice? Or *choose* not to be in their lives, as he'd done so callously those past six weeks?

Meredith groaned as she saw why Thea had beckoned her into the living room. The girl was watching *Home Improvement* on the television. Dog slept at her feet, all four legs spread out.

Then Meredith did a double-take.

Was that Rolf on the screen, conversing with Tim "T
Toolman" Taylor, his friend Al, and the neighbor Wilson?

It was.

Somehow, the insufferable brute had managed to g
himself on the network program. *He'd better not be pla
ning on bringing the show here. I already warned him abo
that. He'd better not involve the Trondheim Venture. He
better not . . .*

Hah! The thick-headed fool would do whatever
wanted, as evidenced by his face being plastered on natio
wide television—just the kind of exposure she'd warned hi
could be dangerous.

Rolf was dressed in full Viking regalia: thigh-length dee
skin tunic, cross-gartered ankle boots, and a wide leath
belt with a gold buckle. In fact, the TV cast members wo
similar attire as they stood admiring a Viking longship th
sat, incongruously, in Tim's driveway.

But how had they gotten a longship on the set with su
short notice? This particular model must have come from
museum, or else it had been whipped up hastily with pl
wood and hot glue. Or duct tape—the dumb man's favori
tool toy.

"It's a show about how Tim soups up his motorboat to
a 'real man's motorboat,'" Thea apprised her hastily, givi
her a quick catch-up on what had already transpired in t
program. "When he and Al tried it out on a local lake, t
speedboat went about one hundred and fifty miles per ho
Of course, the stupid thing ran into the wharf, where Ti
met this Viking character, played by Rolf, who had ju
come in from sailing his longship. Isn't that a cool storylin
Aunt Mer?"

Yeah, real cool! Studying the screen, Meredith decid
that all the men looked ludicrous, especially Tim, wl

sported an anachronistic horned helmet. Al had a battle-ax propped over one shoulder. Wilson's face was screened by a battle shield.

On second thought, Rolf didn't look ludicrous. He looked absolutely gorgeous. As usual. Darn it!

Meredith frowned. Where was Rolf's talisman belt? Now that she thought about it, he hadn't been wearing it last week when she'd seen him, either. And he never went anywhere without that blasted belt. Unless . . .

"All I wanted to do was build a really impressive power-boat," Tim was complaining to his buddies. "I don't see why Jill is so upset. The damage wasn't all *that* expensive. Women!"

"You weren't here when she needed you," the logical Al reminded him. "Remember. Jill told you that she was having problems with her job. The boys were driving her crazy. And she needed to lose ten pounds before her class reunion next week. Her female psyche was calling for a male ego boost—sort of like the positive and negative electrodes on a battery." Al shook his head hopelessly at Tim. "Tsk-tsk! You let Jill down, Tim."

"You may have a point there," Wilson said. "Yes, in-deedy!"

"Nah! She just needs a battery charge. Ha, ha, ha!" Tim quipped. "Real men know how to keep a woman's motor humming."

"Real men? Hah! *I'm* more sensitive to a woman's needs, Tim," Al declared with an air of self-satisfaction. "That's be-cause *I'm* attuned to the feminine side of my brain. Just as you should be. Just as all men should be."

"Huh?" Tim and Rolf exclaimed.

"Where did you learn that bit of wisdom, my good man?" Wilson had moved into Tim's yard and his face was now hidden by . . . *oh, good Lord!* . . . a pair of huge breasts. Was that Ingrid he was attempting to affix to the front of the dragonship?

It was. A "real man's" figurehead, to be sure.

"Oprah," Al answered.

"That figures," Tim and Rolf said at the same time.

As he considered Al's advice, Tim's helmet slid slightly off center and his horns went askew. "But Jill should be sensitive to my needs, too. A man's got to fulfill his . . . his . . ."

"Destiny?" Rolf prodded.

I'd like to show Rolf his destiny, all right.

"Yes!" Tim concurred. "Every man has to follow his destiny." The other men nodded.

Dolts! They are all dolts.

"It's true, Tim," the sage Wilson opined. "Yes, indeedy, when I was in Pango-Pango, I learned from a village chieftain that every man has a life goal to complete . . . a destiny, so to speak. Sometimes women don't comprehend when a man's honor is at stake. Isn't that the way it is in the Viking culture, as well, Rolf?"

"Yea, some things ne'er change, no matter the culture, no matter the century," Rolf stated nervously as he shifted from foot to foot. "A man must protect those under his shield— wife, father, mother, friend. 'Tis the woman's place to demur to his better judgment."

Howard Stern Ericsson—that's who he is. The ultimate Viking chauvinist pig.

"Yeah!" the other three idiots whooped.

"If a woman loves a man," Rolf continued, addressing the camera again, as if directing his words to her, "she should have confidence in her man to follow the right path. She shouldn't dishonor him by questioning his loyalty."

But what about the man having confidence in his woman, Rolf?

"Did women nag their husbands in Viking times?" Tim

interjected, steering the conversation to a more humorous vein.

Rolf snorted, muttering something crude under his breath, which was bleeped out.

All the men, Rolf included, were laughing heartily, lifting long-necked bottles of beer to their mouths in salute to that bit of shared universal maleness.

Meredith plopped down on the couch next to Thea. "Did you know about this?"

"No. All I knew was that Rolf asked me to tape tonight's show for him."

Meredith decided she had much to think about. The men were now on the set of Tim's TV workshop, constructing a clinker-built longship.

"The most important thing is that the woman . . . uh, wood, be pliable," Rolf explained, flexing a strip of green uh, wood, that had already been cut into a wedge shape. "That allows a man to bend them in the right direction."

"Right on, man!" Tim shouted, pumping the air with a fist.

"There is naught worse than a stiff-boarded boat."

"Or a stiff-necked woman," Tim added.

Rolf grinned, no doubt patting himself on the back. "A man must be in control of his ship, steering its course," he elaborated on his macho analogy. "A boat that is off keel will list through life . . . I mean, through the seas. Rudderless." He grinned even wider.

I'm going to take care of his rudder if I ever get my hands on him again.

"A good *boat* can be a man's greatest treasure, or his greatest heartache," Rolf concluded with a sigh. "Of course, there's one sure way to stop a willful *boat* from tossing you to and fro," Rolf said casually, walking over to the wall of tools on the side of the set. Taking down an S-shaped metal bolt, he held it in the air. "Norse shipbuilders make such a device, carved from wood, Tim. Have I e'er told you about the famous Viking S-nail? Nay? Well, perhaps another time. 'Tis a sure-fire mechanism for securing a wayward boat, or, in the case of the famous Viking S-spot, putting a woman in her rightful place."

Then Rolf winked into the camera lenses.

Meredith knew—she just knew—that the wink was intended for her. A promise. The Viking lout intended to put her in her "rightful place."

What a great honor to be a man's destiny! . . .

Dusk already blanketed the countryside as Meredith drove up the long lane to her cottage the next evening. She'd just come from the airport, where she'd put her niece on a shuttle for Chicago. Thea was going to spend a few days with her father and his family—the first visit since she'd moved in with Meredith. It wasn't a trip the young girl had looked forward to, but she'd consented to a short visit, at Meredith's urging. The girl needed her father's love.

Approaching her darkened A-frame cottage, Meredith felt a sense of déjà vu. It had been a long time since she'd come home to an empty house—almost three months, in fact. That was when Rolf had first entered her life, and then Thea.

At that point, the Trondheim longship hadn't been built. She hadn't given up her tenured position at Columbia to stay on here at Oxley College. Her life hadn't been turned upside down and inside out. She hadn't been pregnant.

A solitary few days would be good for her, Meredith resolved as she parked the car and then walked to the front door. She needed time alone to make some decisions about her future and any relationship she might have with Rolf, whom she presumed was still in New York where the *Home Improvement* show was taped. Or was it L.A.? Whatever.

Mike had been decidedly mum when she'd questioned him about Rolf that afternoon, except to tell her that Tim Allen had offered Rolf a periodic guest spot on his program—a Viking philosopher role, similar to Wilson's. Apparently, the show's rating had shot sky-high last night.

She'd gone slack-jawed with amazement at the news. That was all she needed—Rolf as a TV celebrity.

"Rolf declined the offer," Mike had related.

Thank God!

As she inserted the key in the lock, a loud yipping noise greeted her. She smiled, realizing some other things were different from her lonely life of a few months ago. She wasn't entirely alone now. She had Dog.

Yippee! she thought wryly.

No sooner did she step into the entryway than a rough arm wrapped around her waist from behind, lifting her off the floor, while a knife was pressed against her neck. Time stood still, and the last three months slipped away like snow-flakes in the wind.

In an exact recap of the previous experience, she dropped her briefcase to the floor, its contents spilling everywhere. Even her words came out the same as she flailed her arms and legs, shrieking, "Let me go!"

Dog barked loudly, but Meredith wasn't sure if he was trying to scare the "attacker" off, or encourage him.

"Hljótt!" Rolf ordered the animal, who slunk off to lie down obediently in the corner. Geez, did Dog understand Old Norse?

Her "attacker" spat out the single guttural command of *"Hljótt!"* or "Quiet!" to her, as well, when she continued to scream and fight his painful hold on her. Finally, he exhaled loudly with disgust and tossed her over his shoulder.

"You want a vicious Viking, you'll get a vicious Viking," he muttered. Carrying her into the living room, where the only light came from the blazing fireplace, the wretch threw her down to the sofa and followed after her, his braced hands pinning her shoulders flat and his right hip nudging her body firmly against the backframe.

"You're . . . you're despicable," she screeched.

"Yea, I am," he seethed. "And best you accustom yourself to my baser nature, because even your screeching will not drive me away this time."

"You can't just barge into my home. A civilized man would respect my wishes and stay away," she stormed weakly.

"Like Jeffrey? *Blód hel!* Is that the kind of man you favor now?" The contempt in his voice ripped through the air.

"No!" Then, realizing she'd conceded a point, she added, "But that doesn't mean—"

He put up a halting hand and inquired frostily, "Wouldst prefer that I go back to my own time, Merry-Death?"

She shook her head, unable to speak over the torment such a possibility evoked. What a dog in the manger she was. She didn't want him here, but she didn't want him gone.

Rolf's expression softened as he stared at her. "In truth, I suspect you don't know what you want. Most of your resistance these past days stems from hurt, and I understand that. Truly, I do. I've muddled your senses with my lackwit actions, Merry-Death. Let me explain myself. Mayhap it will help."

He leaned back slightly, though still pinning her to the sofa, and she got her first good look at the "new" Rolf. He wore the same outfit he'd had on in her office a week ago—loafers, designer jeans, a white, collarless linen dress shirt, and a dark blue blazer. But his long hair had been cut. Not short-short, like Mike's, but close-clipped on the sides and collar-length in the back.

"Why did you cut your hair?" She gasped.

"I'm adapting," he said sheepishly.

A sadness rushed through her then that Rolf sought to lose his Viking persona. "Oh, Rolf, a haircut won't make you a nineties man, nor fancy clothes. You can take the man out of the Viking, but you can't take the Viking out of the man."

"That's not why I bought the clothes, nor submitted to a barb-whore." His jaw jutted out in affront.

She bristled as she recalled that it had been her question about where he'd bought the apparel that had prompted their estrangement a week ago.

"Don't go pike-stiff on me, Merry-Death," he advised. "I've had more than enough of your willful ways this past sennight. 'Tis time you shut your teeth and opened your ears to my story."

The crude clod! She squirmed, trying to break free.

"I will gag you, if necessary," he warned.

She turned her face away, but he took her chin in a vice-like grip, forcing her to meet his gaze.

"I love you, Merry-Death," he said, "but sometimes you make it sore hard. And know this, I'll not pursue you forever."

Biting her bottom lip, she tried to keep tears from welling in her eyes at his words. She wanted him to say he loved her.

"My time-travel reversal did not work," he started.

She speared him with a condescending glare. *Tell me something I don't already know.*

"In the beginning, I contemplated coming back to your keep, but I worried about putting you through the agony of repeated leave-takings. I would have had to try the time reversal, over and over. Then I saw you on the television screen. The news scribes questioned whether the project would be canceled because of the danger. That gave me further evidence that my return would jeopardize not only your well-being, but the Trondheim Venture."

"So, you went to London?" she scoffed, her upper lip curling with disdain.

"Nay, I went to Norway. Many weeks I searched my homeland, its libraries and museums. Finally, I found the answer. Ah, Merry-Death, 'twas wondrous news I discovered. The famine ended when I entered the time portal—the night of the Demon Moon."

Despite herself, Meredith was interested in Rolf's intriguing story.

"Can you see what that means, dearling? My return to the tenth century is no longer necessary."

Meredith's heart expanded at that significant disclosure. Still, there were so many puzzles. And forgiveness for his cruelty in pretending to be dead came hard for her. "Exactly when did you make that discovery?"

He hesitated and avoided direct eye contact, mumbling something under his breath.

"What did you say?"

"Three sennights ago," he admitted more loudly.

"Three weeks ago!"

"Now, Merry-Death, I still needed to know why I was sent through time, to another country . . . to you."

All these endless weeks I've suffered, and he stayed away because he needed answers. I'm going to kill him. "Did you find the answers?" she inquired with icy sweetness.

"Well, some of them. I went to Lindisfarne—Holy Island—to return the sacred relic."

Lindisfarne? He was sightseeing while I sat here crying my eyes out.

"There I met a monk. You'll not credit this, I warrant, but

the man claimed to be St. Aidan. In any case, the priest took the crucifix from me, and then directed me to go find my destiny."

"Destiny?" she sputtered. If she wasn't so angry, she'd laugh. Or cry.

Rolf released her shoulders and raked his fingers distractedly through his hair. She sat up with her legs still extended behind him on the sofa.

"Yea. At first, I didn't understand . . . till I saw a single rose blooming in the ruins."

The fine hairs stood out on Meredith's skin as she sensed what would come next.

"And I knew—" his eyes lifted to hold hers with bleak entreaty "—I knew that you were my destiny."

"Me?" she choked out, her defenses crumbling with each soft-spoken word. Oh, this Viking was a formidable warrior, even in the battle of emotions. She couldn't stop the tears from brimming over now, but she pushed his hand away when he attempted to brush them off her cheek. No way would she concede this fight yet. "If that's so, why did you go to London? I presume that's where you went after Lindisfarne."

He flinched at her sarcastic tone, and then nodded. "You said once that I'd be unable to live in your modern times, that I couldn't adapt. I needed to prove that I can make a life for myself here, with you. So, I went to Hair-rod's in London to purchase myself some business apparel. From there, I journeyed to Christie's. That's an establishment that auctions artifacts."

"I know what Christie's is," she snapped. Her fuzzy brain suddenly cleared. "Oh, no! You gave them the talisman belt."

"Yea, I did. And they assured me that it would bring a half million dollars, possibly more."

She rolled her eyes.

"Those funds, in addition to the three hundred thousand additional dollars I got from the dealer in Bangor, should be enough. The dealer had a strong craving for *a set* of arm rings." He smirked at her, obviously pleased with his business acumen.

She narrowed her eyes at him. "Enough funds for what?"

"Rosestead: A Viking Village," he said, beaming.

"What Viking village?" A stress headache kicked in behind her forehead, and she could barely comprehend all the information he was throwing at her.

"The one we're going to build together, dearling."

She snarled with frustration at his confusing answers. "You plan on building a village on my property?" *Over my dead body!*

"Nay, there is not enough room. That's why I needed money—to buy more land. Later, I will take you to view the property I am considering. 'Tis a beautiful spot, close to a narrow river leading to the ocean, about thirty miles from here."

"How much land?" she asked reluctantly. The man had not only been gallivanting all over Europe while she'd been salting the earth with her tears, but he'd been roaming Maine, as well. He must have a death wish.

"Oh, a hundred acres or so," he informed her, waving a hand airily.

"And why would you be needing so much land?" She braced herself for his reply, fearing the worst.

"The longhouses, farms, shops, shipbuilding wharves, schools. It would be a working village—entirely self-sufficient," he explained with boyish enthusiasm. "I'm thinking about manufacturing and selling fine sailing boats, along with textiles and soaps in the old style, perhaps Viking-style jewelry. . . . Do you think Jillian would come live in our community as the master jewelry maker? Herbs, swords, a mead brewery, and, of course, raising animals. Cows, horses, pigs, ducks, chickens . . . How do you feel about goats, Merry-Death?"

Yep, it was the worst. Her eyes were so wide she feared they might pop out. "G-g-goats?" she.sputtered.

"Now, sweetling, do not distress yourself. We don't need to have goats, if you do not favor them. In truth, they are smelly beasts. And contrary."

"Aaarrgh!"

"I knew you would be pleased, dearling," the blockhead said, leaning down to kiss her lightly on her gaping mouth. The fact that her lips tingled in no way mitigated her heightening anger. "You could assist me in managing this working village. Or else you can scribe that book you once said you yearned to relate about outrageous medieval women. I could help you, especially if you seek data on medieval women." He jiggled his eyebrows at her, undaunted when she didn't smile.

"You've been a real busy bee, haven't you, Rolf? Making all these plans . . . all on your own. But the big question is 'why'? Surely, all this isn't just to prove you can adapt. In fact, you'd be doing just the opposite, trying to establish a Viking community in modern times."

"Destiny . . . it's my destiny." He took her hands in his and spoke with heartfelt sincerity, his voice raspy with emotion. "Oh, don't you see, Merry-Death? I finally realized why I was sent to your time. There is no Viking culture today. By blending into all the societies of the world, we Norsemen lost the most important thing—our own identity. You referred to me once as The Last Viking. Well, that's just what I am. And it's my mission to teach future generations all the good things about my people and our way of life."

Meredith was about to tell him then that he wasn't The Last Viking, that his line would endure with the small child growing already in her womb. But her throat choked over with emotion as she fought for words.

Rolf stood and walked over to the patio doors, staring out at the ocean. "There is another reason I want to establish this village," he said softly. "In my travels, I saw so much poverty and despair. So many homeless people. Homeless children, even. Can you credit that, Merry-Death? There are children wandering your streets with no one to care for them. Do you not think it would be a good idea to bring those children here . . . at least, some of them? Do you not think they would benefit from living the simple Viking life?"

A soft sob escaped her lips. She unfolded herself from the couch and moved up beside him. "You're doing this for me, aren't you? So I can be surrounded with children?"

"For both of us, sweetling."

Geirolf was soul-weary from all he'd been through these past six sennights . . . and fearful. He'd tried his best to do the right thing for Merry-Death, but mayhap he should have consulted her first. 'Twas not the way of his people or men of his time, but modern men apparently shared decisions with their women. No doubt, he had much to learn yet on adapting.

Mayhap she would have preferred that he be a male profess-whore, like Jeffrey, or a race-car driver, or a cowboy— though he did not think he could jam his feet into those high-heeled boots. Truly, he had studied all the possibilities, and this had seemed his destiny. Had he been wrong? For a certainty, he cared not a whit for his destiny if he could not share it with Merry-Death.

He turned and took her by the upper arms, staring down at her. Her emerald eyes glistened with tears, but they gazed up at him with love.

Love? For the first time that evening, he felt a surge of hope in his heart. "I love you, Merry-Death. Can you forgive me? Will you share my destiny with me?"

She let out a little hiccoughing sob, and then blurted out, "You are an overbearing, arrogant, domineering man."

"Whate'er you say, dearling." Despite her insults, Geirolf could see the love glowing in her face and he was encouraged. *Hmmm. Her face is glowing. Well, no doubt 'tis with admiration for all those qualities she claims to loathe. Truly, women think they want a weak-sapped man, but what they really crave is a real man, like Tim Taylor, and me. But now is not the time to point that out. I wonder if I look meek enough.*

"You shouldn't have made all these decisions without consulting me first." She was still frowning at him, but her body leaned unconsciously closer to him, her breasts under her silken *shert* brushing against his chest.

"Whate'er you say, dearling." Were her breasts fuller? He didn't recall her being quite so buxom afore. Now that was a nice homecoming surprise. Did modern women's breasts grow? Or mayhap 'twas one of those Victory's Secret wondrous bra things. He restrained himself from putting a palm out to test his theory. *Slowly, slowly*, he cautioned himself, *let her set the pace for surrender. But, please, God, let it be soon.*

"I don't think I'll ever forgive you for pretending to be dead all that time."

"Whate'er you say, dearling." He did feel terrible about that. But, he swore, he would spend a lifetime making it up to her. And, no doubt, she would spend a lifetime punishing him in the nature of all women.

"I love you, Rolf," she said then, and looped her arms around his neck.

He let out a long sigh of relief, and blinked away the tears that stung his eyes. Despite his outward bravado, Geirolf had been scared to the bone.

Just before he pulled Merry-Death into his embrace, she

tilted her head saucily and informed him, "You're not The Last Viking, you know."

He didn't grasp her meaning, at first, till she took his palm and placed it over her flat stomach. When comprehension dawned, his heart lurched.

"We're going to have a baby, Rolf."

Merry-Death's words hit him like a battering ram, tilting his world off-center. He inhaled sharply to catch his breath. Finally, when he saw that she was serious, that she was waiting expectantly with trembling lips for his response, he choked out, blood roaring in his veins, "A baby?"

She nodded.

A tear slid out of Geirolf's eyes and ran down his cheek, but he could not care. He was holding his destiny in his hands. Both hands, actually. His one hand caressed Merry-Death's face, and the other was pressed against her belly.

"And one more thing. I do like goats," she informed him with a hysterical laugh. "They remind me of you. Stubborn."

"Whate'er you say, dearling," he whispered. And he meant it this time.

Later, after Geirolf showed her how randy this goat was, and stubbornly insisted on prolonging her pleasures, he grinned at her. "Do you know what I missed most whilst I was gone? Aside from you, of course." The whole time he talked he kept caressing her bare belly, still stunned by the wonder of her quickening with his seed. A miracle.

"Oreos," she retorted.

"Nay. Hilda got those for me," he remarked idly.

"Hilda!" she shrieked and punched him in the stomach.

"Ouch!" he exclaimed with mock injury. Then he chucked her under the chin. "Tsk-tsk, my suspicious wench. Hilda is eighty years old."

"Oh, well then," she sniffed, "what *did* you miss most?"

He stood and swaggered in all his nude glory over to the bottom of the steps.

Vikings were renowned for their nude glory, and Geirolf was not above using it to his advantage.

Then he turned and winked.

Geirolf knew that his wife loved it when he winked, though she would never admit it. He would wager she was tingling about now. As he was.

Crooking his finger at her with his usual Viking arrogance, he answered in a lazy drawl, "Drekking."

"Whate'er you say, dearling," Merry-Death said.

READER LETTER

*"One need not be a lord or prince's son to be a
Viking hero. But one must be a man of unbreakable
will. For the unbreakable will triumphs over the
blind injustice of all powerful Fate and makes
man its equal."*

—GWYN JONES, NORSE HISTORIAN,
author of *A History of the Vikings*

Dear Reader:

Gwyn Jones had the right of it. You gotta love a Viking.

Recently, on one of the on-line services, a well-known author of medieval novels asked, "What is it about Vikings? Why are people so fascinated by these brutish people? I just don't get it."

Well, that writer was deluged with responses from writers and readers alike.

Vikings were renowned for their good looks—long, well-groomed hair; tall, muscular bodies; and they were cleaner in their bodily habits than most men of that time. No one denies that they invigorated the races of those peoples they conquered, by force or seduction.

They were men of many contradictions. Brutal and merciless in battle, they could be gentle family men. The skaldic poetry of that time exemplified their sensitivity and creative souls.

Their greedy appetites and spendthrift ways were deplored by the Anglo-Saxon clerics who recorded their deeds. But maybe those greedy appetites were appreciated in the bed-chambers where so many women came to them willingly. And as for spendthrift, well, the Vikings were also generous to a fault.

Early historians described them as rapers and pillagers of innocent people, uncaring of morality or law. Whose morality and whose law? Much of the English legal system stems from the Vikings' reverence for law codes. In fact, the word law comes from their language. And many of them wor-shipped both Norse and Christian gods.

They were talented men, skilled in shipbuilding, sailing, weaponry, combat, trading, hunting, trapping, and storytell-ing. Love of adventure ran in their blood.

The story related in this book about King Olaf having a talent for throwing two spears simultaneously at his enemies is true. And legend says that some especially skilled Viking warriors could do just what I describe my hero doing: catch a spear thrown at them midair, flick it around in their fingers, and thrust it right back at the enemy.

There is a poignancy in these Vikings who no longer exist as a separate people and have no country of their own. Over several centuries, they melded into the various countries they explored and settled and, yes, ravaged. That's why, in a sense, I am presenting you with Rolf, The *Last* Viking.

In many ways, I thought of that 1984 movie *Starman*, featuring a young Jeff Bridges, when writing this book. An alien, not a time traveler or a Viking, he, too, appeared out of nowhere, and he left the heroine with a baby. That movie did not have my happily-ever-after, however.

And speaking of movie stars . . . I modeled my hero Rolf on Kevin Sorbo, as he played a tongue-in-cheek, gorgeous Hercules in that 1990s TV series. In fact, when Meredith first sees Rolf, she thinks he's Kevin Sorbo. Ironically, many Kevin Sorbo fans took this to heart when this book was first issued, and talked it up on their fan bulletin boards. (Hey, guys, he's baaack!)

And here's another irony. I was at Dragoncon, a huge conference for sci fi fans, and who should I run into but . . . yep, Kevin Sorbo. When I told him about my book, he laughed and signed a copy saying, "That's not me on the cover, but it should have been." Oh, yeah! See a photo of me with Kevin on my website. The boy does age well. <grin>

Let me add this disclaimer: The word Viking would not have been used in the tenth century, nor would certain geographical terms for countries, such as Norway. I elected to use them for the sake of my modern readers.

Ironically, no sooner did I mail this story off to my editor than I saw a segment on one of the morning network news shows. Apparently, a Viking ship was being assembled on Hermit Island in Maine, using blueprints modeled after a Viking longship only a few decades older than my tenth-century boat. The project—"VIKING VOYAGE 1000"—was the brainchild of historian W. Hodding Carter. It included the re-creation of Leif Ericsson's historic trans-Atlantic voyage from the southwestern coast of Greenland to L'Anse aux Meadow in Newfoundland, site of the only confirmed Viking settlement in North America. Though the journey had to be aborted due to rudder damage, it was successfully completed in the summer of 1998. For more information about this twentieth-century adventure, check http://www.Viking 1000.org/index. html on the Internet.

After reading my fictional story, you must see the romantic

coincidence in Carter having said of his project, "What started as a vision of one man became the dream of many, and touched the hearts and imaginations of people throughout Maine."

Life is truly more fantastic than fiction.

I have taken the artistic license of using Oxley College as the name for a nonexistent college in Maine; likewise the Silver Oak Zoo.

The Last Viking is the first of my contemporary time travels featuring the Ericsson family. Please look for the soon-to-be reissued sequels: *Truly, Madly Viking, The Very Virile Viking, Wet and Wild,* and *Hot and Heavy.*

Please let me know what you think of Vikings, in general, and my Viking, in particular.

Sandra Hill
P.O. Box 604
State College, PA 16804
shill733@aol.com
www.sandrahill.net

GLOSSARY

Adz—a cutting tool used for rough trimming.

Asgard—home of the gods, comparable to heaven.

Berserk/er—an ancient Norse warrior who fought in a frenzied rage during battle.

Braies—slim pants worn by men.

Concubine—a woman who cohabits with a man who is not her husband.

Danegeld—in medieval times, especially Britain, a tribute or tax paid to Vikings; in other words, you pay or we plunder.

Diadem—a crown or headband.

Drukkinn (various spellings)—drunk, in Old Norse.

Fjord—a narrow arm of the sea, often between high cliffs.

Futhark—the Old Norse runic alphabet.

Garderobe—latrine or privy.

Hedeby—market town where present-day Germany is located.

Heimskringla—saga of the Norse kings written by Snorri Sturlason, circa 1230 A.D.

Hordaland—Norway.

Jarl—high-ranking Norseman similar to an English earl or wealthy landowner; could also be a chieftain or minor king.

Jorvik—Viking-age York, known by the Saxons as Eoforwic.

Karl—social class, one step below a jarl.

Knarr—Viking merchant ship.

Hel—or Niflheim, a gloomy place of ice, snow and eternal darkness ruled by Hel, the gruesome Queen of the Dead.

Loki—blood brother of Odin, often called the trickster or jester god because of his mischief.

Manchet—a small flat circular loaf of unleavened bread popular in the Middle Ages.

Mimir—a god who watches over the fountain of all wisdom.

More danico—multiple wives.

Mjollnir—Thor's hammer.

Norselands—early term referring not just to Norway but all the Scandanavian countries as a whole.

Northumbria—one of the Anglo-Saxon kingdoms bordered by the English kingdoms to the south and in the north and northwest by the Scots, Cumbrians, and Strathclyde Welsh.

Odin—king of all the Viking gods.

Pennanular—a type of brooch, usually circular in shape with a long pin across the back for attachment to fabric.

Runes—letters of the Old Norse futhark alphabet.

Sagas—oral history of the Norse people, passed on from ancient history.

Sennight—seven days, one week.

Skald—poet or story teller.

Skyrr (or skyr)—soft cheese similar to cottage cheese.

Thor—god of war.

Thralls—slaves.

Tun—252 gallons, as in ale.

Valhalla—hall of the slain, Odin's magnificent hall in Asgard.

Valkyries—female warriors in the Afterlife who did Odin's will.

Yngling clan—oldest of the known Scandinavian dynasties.

Can't get enough of *USA Today* and
New York Times bestselling
author Sandra Hill?
Turn the page for glimpses of her amazing
books. From cowboys to Vikings, Navy
SEALs to Southern bad boys, every one
of Sandra's books has her unique blend of
passion, creativity, and unparalled wit.

Welcome to the World of Sandra Hill!

The Viking Takes a Knight

For John of Hawks' Lair, the unexpected appearance of a beautiful woman at his door is always welcome. Yet the arrival of this alluring Viking woman, Ingrith Sigrundottir—with her enchanting smile and inviting curves—is different . . . for she comes accompanied by a herd of unruly orphans. And Ingrith needs more than the legendary knight's hospitality; she needs protection. For among her charges is a small boy with a claim to the throne—a dangerous distinction when murderous King Edgar is out hunting for Viking blood.

A man of passion, John will keep them safe—but in exchange, he wants something very dear indeed: Ingrith's heart, to be taken with the very first meeting of their lips . . .

Viking in Love

⊗

*C*aedmon of Larkspur *was the most loathsome lout* Breanne had ever encountered. When she arrived at his castle with her sisters, they were greeted by an estate gone wild, while Caedmon laid abed after a night of ale. But Breanne must endure, as they are desperately in need of protection . . . and he is quite handsome.

After nine long months in the king's service, all Caedmon wanted was peace, not five Viking princesses running about his keep. And the fiery redhead who burst into his chamber was the worst of them all. He should kick her out, but he has a far better plan for Breanne of Stoneheim—one that will leave her a Viking in lust.

The Reluctant Viking

The self-motivation tape was supposed to help Ruby Jordan solve her problems, not create new ones. Instead, she was lulled into an era of hard-bodied warriors and fair maidens. But the world ten centuries in the past didn't prove to be all mead and mirth. Even as Ruby tried to update medieval times, she had to deal with a Norseman whose view of women was stuck in the Dark Ages. And what was worse, brawny Thork had her husband's face, habits, and desire to avoid Ruby. Determined not to lose the same man twice, Ruby planned a bold seduction that would conquer the reluctant Viking—and make him an eager captive of her love.

The Outlaw Viking

☙

As tall and striking as the Valkyries of legend, Dr. Rain Jordan was proud of her Norse ancestors despite their warlike ways. But she can't believe it when she finds herself on a nightmarish battle-field, forced to save the barbarian of her dreams.

He was a wild-eyed warrior whose deadly sword could slay a dozen Saxons with a single swing, yet Selik couldn't control the saucy wench from the future. If Selik wasn't careful, the stunning siren was sure to capture his heart and make a warrior of love out of **The Outlaw Viking**.

The Tarnished Lady

✵

*B*anished *from polite society, Lady Eadyth of Hawks'* Lair spent her days hidden under a voluminous veil, tending her bees. But when her lands are threatened, Lady Eadyth sought a husband to offer her the protection of his name.

Notorious for loving—and leaving—the most beautiful damsels in the land, Eirik of Ravenshire was England's most virile bachelor. Yet when the mysterious lady offered him a vow of chaste matrimony in exchange for revenge against his most hated enemy, Eirik couldn't refuse. But the lusty knight's plans went awry when he succumbed to the sweet sting of the tarnished lady's love.

The Bewitched Viking

❧

Even fierce Norse warriors have bad days. 'Twas enough to drive a sane Viking mad, the things Tykir Thorksson was forced to do—capturing a red-headed virago, putting up with the flock of sheep that follows her everywhere, chasing off her bumbling brothers. But what could a man expect from the sorceress who had put a kink in the King of Norway's most precious body part? If that wasn't bad enough, Tykir was beginning to realize he wasn't at all immune to the enchantment of brash red hair and freckles. Perhaps he could reverse the spell and hold her captive, not with his mighty sword, but with a Viking man's greatest magic: a wink and smile.

The Blue Viking

☙

For Rurik the Viking, life has not been worth living since he left Maire of the Moors. Oh, it's not that he misses her fiery red tresses or kissable lips. Nay, it's the embarrassing blue zigzag tattoo she put on his face after their one wild night of loving. For a fierce warrior who prides himself on his immense height, his expertise in bedsport, and his well-toned muscles, this blue streak is the last straw. In the end, he'll bring the witch to heel, or die trying. Mayhap he'll even beg her to wed . . . so long as she can promise he'll no longer be . . . **The Blue Viking**.

The Viking's Captive

(originally titled MY FAIR VIKING)

⊗

Tyra, Warrior Princess. She is too tall, too loud, too fierce to be a good catch. But her ailing father has decreed that her four younger sisters—delicate, mild-mannered, and beautiful—cannot be wed 'til Tyra consents to take a husband. And then a journey to save her father's life brings Tyra face to face with Adam the Healer. A god in human form, he's tall, muscled, perfectly proportioned. Too bad Adam refuses to fall in with her plans—so what's a lady to do but truss him up, toss him over her shoulder, and sail off into the sunset to live happily ever after.

A Tale of Two Vikings

❦

*T*oste and Vagn Ivarsson are identical Viking twins, about to face Valhalla together, following a tragic battle, or maybe something even more tragic: being separated for the first time in their thirty and one years. Alas, even the bravest Viking must eventually leave his best buddy behind and do battle with that most fearsome of all opponents—the love of his life. And what if that love was Helga the Homely, or Lady Esme, the world's oldest novice nun?

A Tale of Two Vikings will give you twice the tears, twice the sizzle, and twice the laughter . . . and make you wish for your very own Viking.

The Last Viking

⚛

He was six feet, four inches of pure, unadulterated male. He wore nothing but a leather tunic, and he was standing in Professor Meredith Foster's living room. The medieval historian told herself he was part of a practical joke, but with his wide gold belt, ancient language, and callused hands, the brawny stranger seemed so . . . authentic. And as he helped her fulfill her grandfather's dream of re-creating a Viking ship, he awakened her to dreams of her own. Until she wondered if the hand of fate had thrust her into the loving arms of . . . **The Last Viking**.

Truly, Madly Viking

❧

A *Viking named Joe? Jorund Ericsson is a tenth-*century Viking warrior who lands in a modern mental hospital. Maggie McBride is the lucky psychologist who gets to "treat" the gorgeous Norseman, whom she mistakenly calls Joe.

You've heard of *One Flew Over the Cuckoo's Nest.* But how about *A Viking Flew Over the Cuckoo's Nest*? The question is: Who's the cuckoo in this nest? And why is everyone laughing?

The Very Virile Viking

ॐ

Magnus Ericsson is a simple man. He loves the smell of fresh-turned dirt after springtime plowing. He loves the feel of a soft woman under him in the bed furs. He loves the heft of a good sword in his fighting arm.

But, Holy Thor, what he does not relish is the bothersome brood of children he's been saddled with. Or the mysterious happenstance that strands him in a strange new land—the kingdom of *Holly Wood*. Here is a place where the folks think he is an *act-whore* (whatever that is), and the woman of his dreams—a winemaker of all things—fails to accept that he is her soul mate . . . a man of exceptional talents, not to mention . . . **A Very Virile Viking.**

Wet & Wild

❦

*What do you get when you cross a Viking with a Navy SEAL? A warrior with the fierce instincts of the past and the rigorous training of America's most elite fighting corps? A totally buff hero-in-the-making who hasn't had a woman in roughly a thousand years? A dyed-in-the-wool romantic with a hopeless crush? Whatever you get, women everywhere can't wait to meet him, and his story is guaranteed to be . . . **Wet & Wild**.*

Hot & Heavy

⊕

In and out, that's the goal as Lt. Ian MacLean prepares for his special ops mission. He leads a team of highly trained Navy SEALs, the toughest, buffest fighting men in the world and he has nothing to lose. Madrene comes from a time a thousand years before he was born, and she has no idea she's landed in the future. After tying him up, the beautiful shrew gives him a tongue-lashing that makes a drill sergeant sound like a kindergarten teacher. Then she lets him know she has her own special way of dealing with over-confident males, and things get . . . **Hot & Heavy**.

Frankly, My Dear . . .

☙

*L*ost in the Bayou . . . *Selene had three great passions:* men, food, and *Gone with the Wind*. But the glamorous model always found herself starving— for both nourishment and affection. Weary of the petty world of high fashion, she headed to New Orleans for one last job before she began a new life. Little did she know that her new life would include a brand-new time—about 150 years ago! Selene can't get her fill of the food—or an alarmingly handsome man. Dark and brooding, James Baptiste was the only lover she gave a damn about. And with God as her witness, she vowed never to go without the man she loved again.

Sweeter Savage Love

⊛

The stroke of surprisingly gentle hands, the flash of *fathomless blue eyes, the scorch of white-hot* kisses . . . Once again, Dr. Harriet Ginoza was swept away into rapturous fantasy. The modern psychologist knew the object of her desire was all she should despise, yet time after time, she lost herself in visions of a dangerously handsome rogue straight out of a historical romance. Harriet never believed that her dream lover would cause her any trouble, but then a twist of fate cast her back to the Old South and she met him in the flesh. To her disappointment, Etienne Baptiste refused to fulfill any of her secret wishes. If Harriet had any hope of making her amorous dreams become passionate reality, she'd have to seduce this charmer with a sweeter savage love than she'd imagined possible . . . and savor every minute of it.

The Love Potion

✧

*F*ame *and fortune are surely only a swallow away*
when Dr. Sylvie Fontaine discovers a chemical
formula guaranteed to attract the opposite sex.
Though her own love life is purely hypothetical,
the shy chemist's professional future is assured
. . . as soon as she can find a human guinea pig.
But bad boy Lucien LeDeux—best known as the
Swamp Lawyer—is more than she can handle
even before he accidentally swallowed a love
potion disguised in a jelly bean. When the dust
settles, Luc and Sylvie have the answers to some
burning questions—can a man die of testoster-
one overload? Can a straight-laced female lose
every single one of her inhibitions?—and they
learn that old-fashioned romance is still the best
catalyst for love.

Love Me Tender

☙

Once *upon a time, in a magic kingdom, there* lived a handsome prince. Prince Charming, he was called by one and all. And to this land came a gentle princess. You could say she was Cinderella . . . Wall Street Cinderella. Okay, if you're going to be a stickler for accuracy, in this fairy tale the kingdom is Manhattan. But there's magic in the Big Apple, isn't there? And maybe he can be Prince Not-So-Charming at times, and "gentle" isn't the first word that comes to mind when thinking of this princess. But they're looking for happily ever after just the same—and they're going to get it.

Desperado

☙

*M*istaken *for a notorious bandit and his infamously* scandalous mistress, L.A. lawyer Rafe Santiago and Major Helen Prescott found themselves on the wrong side of the law. In a time and place where rules had no meaning, Helen found Rafe's hard, bronzed body strangely comforting, and his piercing blue eyes left her all too willing to share his bedroll. His teasing remarks made her feel all woman, and she was ready to throw caution to the wind if she could spend every night in the arms of her very own . . . **Desperado**.

Grab These Other
Dafina Novels
(trade paperback editions)